Tristopolis
Revenge

JOHN MEANEY

Nulapeiron Press

ISBN-13: 978-1-8381217-2-3

BOOKS BY JOHN MEANEY

Paul Reynolds series
On The Brink

Case books (Case & Kat)
Destructor Function
Strategy Pattern

Josh Cumberland series
Edge
Point

Donal Riordan (Tristopolis) series
Bone Song
Dark Blood (UK title) Black Blood (US title)
Two For Tristopolis (short stories)
Tristopolis Requiem
Tristopolis Howling
Tristopolis Revenge

Pilots universe
Absorption (Ragnarok 1)
Transmission (Ragnarok 2)
Resonance (Ragnarok 3)
Paradox (Nulapeiron 1)
Context (Nulapeiron 2)
Resolution (Nulapeiron 3)
To Hold Infinity

Standalone
The Whisper Of Disks (short story collection)
New Jerusalem

PRAISE FOR JOHN MEANEY

"A brilliant, inventive writer." *The Times*

"A spectacular writer. He makes SF seem all fresh and new again." Robert J. Sawyer, Hugo Award-winning author

"Cumberland leaps off the page, a trained killer whose anger and grief at his daughter's condition is brilliantly portrayed; the depiction of his simmering rage, barely held in check, and how he channels it, provides a masterclass in characterisation." *The Guardian*, reviewing Edge (Josh Cumberland book 1)

"What starts off as a simple missing persons enquiry develops into a full-blown coup against a fascist state... Set in a Britain extrapolated from today's violent streets, yet still highly recognisable, Edge is the first in what will hopefully be a long running series." *Total Sci-Fi*, reviewing Edge (Josh Cumberland book 1)

"Within five pages...I was completely hooked... the perfect blend of action and science fiction... I can only hope that there will be more." *The Eloquent Page*, reviewing Point (Josh Cumberland book 2)

"I absolutely don't want to live in the world [Meaney] has created. I didn't want to in Edge (the first book in the series) and I most certainly don't want to now. I do, however, want to read about it. It's relentless and gripping, with a brilliant balance between the personal and the political." *BiblioBuffet*, reviewing Point (Josh Cumberland book 2)

"Absorption is the best hard science fiction I've read this year, well written, exciting, mysterious, full of interesting characters and ideas..." *The Times*, reviewing Absorption (Ragnarok book 1)

"...the world building is phenomenal and the pace as chapters switch from time zones is just right, keeping the tension levels up. The female characters are particularly strong and literally jump off the page, particularly the WWII code breaker Gavriela. The novel is also steeped in historical accuracy and authenticity." *Terror-Tree.co.uk*, reviewing Transmission (Ragnarok book 2)

"Resonance is a book driven by big ambitions. Meaney has penned a story that aims to be epic beyond even the level of Dune or similarly famed series. Furthermore, the amount of research that has gone into the book adds a surprising degree of credibility..." *Starburst Magazine*, reviewing Resonance (Ragnarok book 3)

"Meaney's creepy death-haunted world lingers in the mind long after the book is closed... a smart and spooky read." *The Times*, reviewing Bone Song (Tristopolis book 1)

TRISTOPOLIS REVENGE

DEDICATION

To Ollie, Norah and Talia, who brighten up the world.

TRISTOPOLIS REVENGE

ONE

Donal prowled the empty boxing gym, while shadows flickered as a sign of his agitation: the flamesprites in their sconces were picking up his mood.

He paced everywhere except the corner where the presbytery door stood – the *former* presbytery door, now leading to the apartment he shared with Mel – as all around the irregular pentagon of its frame, white-blue runes were glimmering, growing incrementally brighter as the big moment neared.

Except the moment had been drawing near for over seven Death-damned hours, and *when*, for Thanatos' sake, was something going to happen?

He checked his watch, not for the time – which his mind automatically tracked – but for the visual reminder of when, exactly, he needed to plug in his zombie heart for recharging.

Only a narrow black sliver showed on the watch face, like the final remains of a pie, telling him what he already knew: barely three hours left, and he should have plugged in long before this, but he'd be damned if he was going to miss the big event.

Last week, when Sister Amber came along with Harald to drop off scarab-cream doughnuts and a bunch of glistening black inkblossoms for Mel, she'd privately murmured to Donal that the process might prove a long one.

"It'll be fine," Donal had told her. "I'm sure of it."

Fine as these things go, he'd meant, and Sister Amber had merely smiled and patted his arm, no doubt thinking him clueless, and accurately so.

How long could this stretch out?

The heavy canvas bags hung waiting, and Donal took half a step towards the nearest, intending to slam a few heavy hooks into the thing, just as a scream pierced the gym and the runes around the interior door flared white – only for a second – before settling back to a steady glow.

But brighter than before.

"I'm coming in," he muttered.

1

And managed two paces before Ingrid Johannsdóttir's voice sounded right inside his head: "Stay where you are, Donal. We've got this."

Witches. Almost as bad as mages.

"I heard that." Again inside his skull, by direct induction of the auditory nerves, or something.

Donal inhaled and let out a breath, as if he remained a redblood, still in the first, unresurrected phase of his existence.

Zombies are supposed to gain conscious control of their deep cognitive processes, previously automatic, and Donal had managed at times to shift around his mental architecture, or so it felt; but not recently. And definitely not tonight.

I've never been so nervous.

And helpless.

In that moment, a soft scrape of sound from the street outside drew ice along his spine, because the stone walls were thick, almost soundproof, with the windows high up and small, as befitted a former temple: robust as a castle from millennia past, deconsecrated and repurposed, with only the *Mel's Gym* sign outside to indicate that minor (though dangerous) eldritch beings from the compactified dimensions no longer made their home here or joined in the weekly worship.

It wasn't just that.

He felt an approaching presence, his back tingling as if the air had grown charged, though he remained unable to parse the exact cues that his sensory receptors were picking up.

Zombies don't need to breathe very much. It allowed him to hold statue-still, listening and watching for anything new among the shifting shadows of the mostly empty gym. The raised heptagon where the fighters sparred during training sessions looked skeletal against the flamesprites' dim, dancing orange light. Barbells and black iron clubs rested, like mediaeval weapons in some historic armoury, against one wall.

All felt motionless, besides the sprites.

No sounds from outside now. But Donal spread and lowered his shoulders, and adjusted his centre of gravity downwards, ready to burst into movement, because some quality in the air was changing; and even the flamesprites sensed it, as they stilled their dancing and dimmed their light, shrinking to small, steady flames in their sconces.

His Magnus in its shoulder holster hung from a hook inside the bedroom where Mel could reach it, if she were able to stagger a few paces (having stowed away her Draken pistol a week ago); but to use the weapon himself, Donal would need to sprint through the glimmering, rune-guarded threshold into the presbytery annexe, and that would cost time.

Leave that as Plan B, or maybe C. If anything bad happened, the witch, Ingrid Johannsdóttir, would sense the danger. She and her apprentice, currently helping in the bedroom, along with Mel herself, amounted to one Hades of a potential fighting force.

Donal preferred to shut down threats, imminent or already starting, as fast as possible. He stared at the far-end door, zeroing in on the carved bone handle a full second before it shifted, stopped, then began to turn.

With a bounce back to get a sprinter's start, for the myotatic reflex of redblood humans survives resurrection, Donal burst forward...

Oh, bleeding Hades.

... and stopped, as the door swung open to reveal the tall, regal-looking woman smiling there, her skin glistening scarlet, the exact hue of fresh warm blood, while the irises of her eyes formed polished orange heptagons that were capable of blazing brightly, like those flamesprites rising up from their sconces to dance a floating jig around the gym, celebrating her presence.

Donal stopped and grinned. "Hellah, sweetheart. I can't believe you're here."

"Klaudius is holding the fort." She stepped inside the gym proper, glanced up at the still-dancing flamesprites, and nodded acknowledgment. "Our friends are in a quiet mood."

Not the sprites: by *friends* she meant the eldritch denizens below the minus two hundred and seventy-third floor of Police HQ on Avenue of the Basilisks.

Mighty entities, vast and powerful and ultimately unknowable, as at home among the microscopic compactified dimensions of crawlspace – and whatever voids that lay beyond those regions – as much as in everyday, macroscopic reality.

They remained willing to obey the ancient treaty with the ordinary city dwellers for no good reason that Donal had ever heard or read about, except perhaps that the entities could rarely be bothered to stir from... whatever they did down there.

But *rarely* isn't *never*, and the Guardians' work was real. Hellah and her brother Klaudius worked in ways that no one else, except perhaps the most senior and smartest of mages, could imagine. The strain of knowing that one mistake could end Tristopolis – even the world – had to hang over them, constantly.

"Tell Klaudius I said hi." Donal added, meaning it: "He should come here and visit some time."

Then he spread his arms, and Hellah stepped forward, and they hugged – tightly, for their friendship had grown through the past seven months, yet carefully, because they could only ever be just that: friends, not lovers.

"I'll tell him." Hellah stepped back, her twin seven-sided irises growing briefly lambent. "He still shakes his head every time I remind him that you managed to knock him out... which I probably do too often. But I think he likes you, all the same."

3

"Thanatos. If he wants a rematch, forget it."

"Hardly. My brother can act weird, but he's never vindictive."

They both knew that a human, resurrected or otherwise, against a fully aware Guardian, was like a mammoth against an ant when it came to actual force. Somehow it made no difference at all to Donal and Hellah's friendship.

What Donal couldn't understand was why everyone else besides flamesprites – literally everyone, even his former TPD colleagues, experienced and hardbitten cops to a man, woman or wraith – grew terrified at the merest sight of Hellah. He tried not to dwell on it, because whenever he did, the sheer ingratitude and bigotry annoyed the Hades out of him.

Hellah was a good person, and he liked her.

That was enough for him.

And almost enough for Mel, who tried her best for Donal's sake, but could only hold her ground for a minute or three before retreating from Hellah's presence. Better than anyone else, but then, a lifetime of boxing training had moulded Mel into the tough woman that Donal loved.

She yelled now, did Mel, the sound piercing the gym from the closed presbytery door, and Hellah's eyes glowed in momentary sympathy.

"Almost here," she said.

"Yeah." Donal tried to breathe, but couldn't.

Good job it didn't matter any more, the breathing. He was in his resurrected phase, and things went differently these days.

Zombiehood usually implied sterility, so much so that Mel's news, seven months ago, had sent him in near panic to the reference sections of the Tristopolitan Central Library to learn about his own kind from books, which felt weird and ironic, even embarrassing, but not enough to stop him reading everything he could.

He studied until the sheer number of medical mishaps that could derail the process caused his head to swim and he finally closed the books and placed them carefully back on the shelves where he'd found them.

Resurrected folk formed a minority for sure, yet Donal's own ignorance felt troubling. For a tiny portion of resurrected men, it turned out – and for an even more minute fraction of resurrected women – reproductive biology was able to proceed pretty much on redblood lines, at least in the first few years of zombiehood.

He'd never known. Never really thought about it.

Then his thoughts snapped back to his surroundings.

What the Hades?

It started with a blue-grey wriggling on the floor, a shift of movement as if from an over-large worm, suddenly expanding into a single large tendril rearing up towards the arched ceiling, dominating the space of the gym.

Donal took two steps forward and slammed a kick into the rubbery mass, thrusting hard from the hip and bouncing back, a stagger-step to regain balance before launching himself forward once more, slamming a hard left leading punch, more thrust than jab, and the hardest right cross of his life, with a strong quarter twist of his fist smacking into slimy flesh.

All to no effect.

The tendril flicked, smashed into him and knocked him flying, tumbling; and yellowish spots flared in his vision as he rolled sideways across the floor and came up on one knee.

"I've got this, my friend." Hellah's orange eyes burst into flame: twin heptagons of fire. "Someone's being naughty tonight. *Bad* entity."

Then she spoke a word that caused reality to tremble, the stone walls to shake, and Donal's guts to feel liquefied... and the tendril to whip back down into solid floor and out of sight, in some tiny fraction of a second.

It was gone.

"And stay there," added Hellah, pointing at the floor.

Donal wiped his face – a gesture from his redblood days when he might have sweated during action – and rose to his feet.

"That's never happened before." He crossed to the spot where the tendril had ascended, lowered himself into a rock-bottom squat, and touched the fossilised floorboards with his fingertips. "Feels the same as always."

"It would." Hellah had turned to stare at the inner doorway. "The insertion into macroscopic dimensions began in clear air, maybe a hair's breadth above the actual floor surface."

Donal powered himself up to standing, following Hellah's gaze. Green ripples were chasing around the white-blue glowing runes surrounding the door.

"Good defences," added Hellah.

"Enough to protect them if you hadn't been here?"

"Perhaps. At a push. With a certain amount of luck."

"Thanatos."

"But I *am* here, Donal. Clearly."

"Yes..." He thought back to some of their earlier conversations, mostly at Police HQ, reappraising his memories. "When I told you about Mel... you didn't really seem surprised."

"Women have been producing babies for the whole of human history, with a tiny bit of help from their menfolk." A dimpling smile, while highlights glistened on her blood-red skin. "Clearly, or none of us would be here."

They'd never talked about Hellah's forebears, in terms of exact species or anything else, but that wasn't the point.

"She told me the news, um..." Donal thought back, flicking through memories in a way that belonged entirely to the resurrected phase of his existence. "Thirteen days after the party we had here, the one you came to."

A party that Hellah had spent mostly standing by herself, watching the proceedings with a soft smile and a gentle orange glow lighting up her eyes.

"And you must have told me that news," she said, "what, a week after that?"

"Yes," said Donal. "But when exactly did you find out? When I told you, or earlier?"

"About thirteen days before you did."

Meaning at the party.

Donal shook his head. "Bleeding Hades, sweetheart."

"I could have told you the moment I looked at Mel, the very first time, but I thought it might go better if you heard the news from her. Am I tactful, or what?"

He had to smile, though briefly. "You didn't just happen to drop by tonight."

"Of course not. We're friends."

There seemed to be a missing step in Hellah's logic, but when Donal glanced again at that spot on the floor, he realised he didn't care. "Thank you for coming. And for being smart enough and wise enough to pick the right time, precisely."

"You're welcome, Donal, and so is Mel. And the baby."

Baby. The word that he hardly dared hold in his thoughts, never mind an actual baby in imminent reality.

The runes were glowing brighter now.

Incandescent.

"It's time for you to go in." Hellah gave his shoulder the gentlest of pushes. "Go on."

"I don't—"

"Nothing will get past me. No threat, okay?"

Well of course nothing could. She was a Guardian, powerful and dangerous beyond imagining, and she was at the same time his ordinary friend. As for why she needed to stand guard – a tactical question – he had no way of telling.

Right now he didn't dare dismiss the offer.

A tendril burst from the floor. Here. In our home.

No good explanation presented itself.

The surrounding runes blinked as he took hold of the door handle, but no defences activated – they weren't supposed to, not against him, but momentary doubt had arisen all the same – so he twisted the handle and took a step inside.

They had their backs to him, Ingrid the witch and her apprentice, Ludmila-call-me-Ludka who normally looked too young to have left school, while tonight Donal didn't care how either of them looked but they were blocking his view of the bed and Mel and—

The crying began in that moment.

Almighty Thanatos.

A baby.

Yes, the awareness of imminent arrival had been a growing sensation in his zombie heart for an entire seven months, but this felt different because it was real. His son or daughter was finally here, thanks to his amazing Mel.

Ingrid was wrapping the red-faced, tiny squalling baby in some kind of dark-gold velvet shawl while Ludka moved to tuck bedclothes high up around Mel's waist – Mel, whose sweat-drenched face shone with radiant joy alongside an overwhelming fatigue, a kind of emotional superposition that Donal had never seen in his life before, in either phase.

There was an intravenous drip keeping Mel hydrated, a smell of disinfectant tinged with incense, and a circle of yellow painted runes on the floor surrounding the bed that looked old and well-worn, but hadn't been there eight hours earlier when the women had dismissed him from the room, in fact from the entire annexe apartment.

We have a baby.

Red-faced and bawling, which meant alive and healthy, an everyday occurrence for the world at large and utterly astounding in Donal and Mel's subjective universe.

He looked in Mel's eyes, sharing a level of love he hadn't imagined possible, and stepped – almost floated – to the bed, and reached down and placed his fingertips on the soft scalp of the still-mewling baby, opened his mouth to speak and realised he had no words.

Mel gave him a smile that told him everything, including her understanding of his reaction.

"His name is—" she started.

"NO!" Hellah's voice, filled with a dread, commanding tonality, came through clearly from the direction of the gym. "You will *not* enter here!"

Donal turned, eyes widening like a threatened cat's, a growl rising from deep inside him. A threat, to his lover and their newborn son?

Scarcely aware of Ingrid and Ludka drawing aside – Ingrid with one hand grasping an amulet that hung from sinew-cord draped around her throat, an amulet that was starting to glow amber – Donal pulled the Magnus from its hanging holster without really looking, and stalked through the doorway, looking for something to kill.

Daring to threaten us? Tonight, of all nights?

He wanted badly to destroy whatever – whoever – might have ventured inside his home uninvited, with malicious intent.

But the air had come alive with a floor-to-ceiling ring of fire, strong orange flames that circled like some rushing torrent, brightening to whitish yellow, while inside the ring, at its centre, some diminishing scaly form reached out with desperate talons in a final futile gesture as Hellah brought her hands together and the flames imploded to a white, incandescent fist-sized ball and snapped out of existence altogether.

The silent contrast was shocking.

Whether the would-be intruder had perished or simply been banished to the crawlspace dimensions or some void beyond, Donal couldn't tell; but either way, he felt even more thankful for Hellah's presence here.

"No sweat, buddy." Hellah's skin glistened as if covered in fresh blood, but that was normal and healthy for her. "Not even close to becoming a real problem."

"Maybe not for you. What the Hades was that thing?"

"Someone else being naughty. Mostly curious, but she was also rather hungry in a way that could have turned unpleasant. Better safe than sorry, eh?"

"If you say so. Thank you again. There's something weird going on, isn't there?"

"Donal, you've just become a dad. Go hold your son, and we'll hold our gabfest later, alright?"

"Right." He turned back in the direction of the presbytery apartment. "A dad. Me. Dear Thanatos, I have no idea how to do that."

Parental role models: the closest had been Sister Mary-Anne Styx in the orphanage, stern and disciplined but without the attendant cruelty employed by most of her colleagues in the Order. Then again, Coach O'Brien, when Donal started boxing aged ten and during the years that followed, had taught him an awful lot about what it meant to be a strong, courageous adult willing to fight for what was right, and never mind the odds.

"You'll be a great dad," Hellah told him. "Starting right now."

"Yeah." He breathed. "Yeah. I've got this."

Behind him, Hellah chuckled, hummed a snatch of some old tune, then said: "Yes, he's happy alright."

She wasn't talking to Donal, and the only other entities here were the flamesprites.

Almost no one ever talked to sprites, no one besides her: even Donal, always open to chatting and joking with wraiths and people whose skin was blue or scaled or mossy or even – in Illurium – chitinous, rarely said a word to his own flamesprites, except to acknowledge their feelings in states of occasional agitation, and nothing at all to sprites elsewhere.

He still had so much to learn about being the best he could be. How was he supposed to raise another human being all the way from soft helplessness to functioning, autonomous, responsible adulthood?

What were the steps, the procedures to follow?

Then he walked into the bedroom and realised that his doubts didn't matter. The reality of his son, crying there in Mel's arms, red-faced and tangible, meant his love and responsibilities were simply facts to act on, while nothing else could be allowed to hold him back.

He stood by the bed, pressed his palm against Mel's sweat-drenched cheek, and kissed her softly. "Well done, you."

"Yes."

"And hello, you." He kissed his son's warm forehead. "Welcome to the world."

So small, yet alive: a new human being had entered the universe.

Mel looked over at Ingrid, the witch. "Is he supposed to keep crying like this? He hasn't stopped…"

"I think it's fine." Ingrid paused as her apprentice Ludka made a sound in her throat. After a second, Ingrid glared at Ludka, formed a one-handed mudra gesture, turned back to Mel and the baby, and made some passes in the air that left behind faint glowing traces. "He's strong enough, at any rate."

Donal felt his face tighten.

Ludka thinks there's something wrong. And Ingrid doesn't want to say.

But Mel looked triumphant after a long, excruciating ordeal that no man was equipped even to imagine going through. She held the incredible baby, his and her actual son, murmuring words that did nothing to stop the crying.

Hellah entered the room, causing Ingrid and Ludka to retreat to opposite corners, as far from Hellah as they could manage without actually fleeing.

Her eyes stilled glowed a soft, gentle orange as she approached the bed, leaned over, and touched the baby's forehead with one fingertip.

The crying stopped, just like that.

"I'm always here to help." Hellah's eyes brightened for a second, then reduced to candle-flame gentleness. "Remember that."

Mel shook her head, tears springing up, and said: "I don't know how to thank you, but I don't want—"

"Hush," said Hellah. "It's far too early to know for sure."

Donal took half a step closer. "Know what? Something good, or something bad?"

"Just girl talk, dear Donal."

"Thanatos."

His brain didn't respond to stress quite the way it used to, and one of the differences was the way his peripheral vision continued to operate instead of shutting down, which was why he could clearly see Ingrid and Ludka's reactions to this so-called girl talk.

Ingrid's mouth tightened, while Ludka mostly looked confused, out of her depth and worried, and Donal couldn't blame her.

Still, even Ludka seemed to possess some level of understanding here that Donal himself had failed to reach.

Hellah turned to Ingrid, who blinked in obvious fear.

"Your brother, Mage Kelvin Johannsson," said Hellah. "Is he well? Recuperated enough for quantal messaging?"

Ingrid blinked again. "Um, yes…"

The last Donal had heard, Kelvin was out of full-time rehabituation but still undergoing painful therapy, determined to regain full health after risking his life to transport Donal and another mage, Lamis, through blocked microdimensional pathways in order to save the city.

Anyone of lesser strength or ability, said those in the know, would have perished without managing to transport anything at all.

"You or your apprentice," said Hellah, "will be here all the time for the next three days at least, correct? Until we make some longer-term arrangements, I mean."

"Er." Ingrid swallowed, and nodded. "That would be best."

"Ludmila." Hellah smiled at the girl. "I won't presume to call you Ludka. You're smart enough to operate a call amulet, I can tell."

Ludka nodded, looking far too scared to speak.

As Hellah turned back to Ingrid, the amulet that hung at Ingrid's throat flared the exact orange hue of Hellah's eyes, then dimmed back to its normal, polished amber appearance.

"Use that to make a call," said Hellah, "at any time, no matter the hour, and don't worry about false alarms. Better to overreact than fail, right? And if you need to be elsewhere, leave Ludmila here with the amulet fully enabled for her to use."

"My brother…" began Ingrid.

"I'll make sure Mage Kelvin is called at the same time I am, so he can pass the word among his colleagues."

Ingrid's mouth tightened once more, and she gave a small, sharp nod that looked determined as well as fearful.

"Donal." Hellah hugged him, as hard as before, and kissed his cheek and murmured: "You'll all be fine, okay?"

"Yeah. Just… Yeah."

Then Hellah turned and walked from the bedroom and out into the gym; and a second later, Donal could no longer sense her presence at all, though he'd heard no further footsteps or any opening and closing of the outer door.

But the warmth of her friendship remained, so that was fine.

Donal turned back to the birthing bed, about to say something good and triumphant and loving, but the words fled as his mouth opened and for all his zombie self-control there was nothing he could do but stand there and watch and try to process the reality before him.

This new, unexpected reality…

What?

… with blue light front and centre.

I don't understand.

For Mel's eyes were glowing a soft, sapphire blue… and so were the eyes of their newborn son, calm now, while gentle filaments of that same blue light joined those two pairs of eyes together, mother to son.

Chains of light in catenary curves, the shape of hanging clotheslines –

hyperbolic cosines, according to a stray fragment of memory, of Sister Mary-Anne Styx at the purpleboard in the orphanage school pointing at a yellow chalk equation and diagram and who the Hades cared about all that?

Shining blue light from his lover's eyes.

From his son's...

Quite often, when he kissed the side of Mel's throat, Donal kissed her earlobe also. He would have thought he could recall the exact shape of both ears, yet their appearance now was new: subtly pointed, just a little, scarcely noticeable at a casual glance.

Donal had always paid attention when he looked at her.

"I love you, Donal Riordan," she said, though the soft blue glow partly hid her moving lips. "And so does your baby son Finbar."

He let out a long breath, realised he couldn't speak with empty lungs, inhaled, then said the only thing that mattered. "I love you both. Dear Thanatos, I love you more than I can say."

Whatever was happening here, that was the truth.

Glowing eyes. Big deal.

In the corner of the room, young Ludka began to sniffle, while in the opposite corner, even Ingrid, that tough experienced witch, and no-nonsense widowed mother in her own right, dabbed at her eyes and said: "Kiss her, you fool."

So Donal did just that.

In the distance, the sound of sirens rose and fell, attending some emergency; but that was somewhere else. Here things were going to be fine.

They had to be.

TWO

The grey-skinned being, a winged daemonid approximately humanoid and twenty-one feet tall or thereabouts, was forced to crouch in the wide stone chamber, and keep his tough, rubbery wings almost fully curled up.

He had given up tugging at the polished, rune-inscribed platinum chains that bound him in place; but angry yellow ellipses swirled in the great obsidian globes of his eyes. Tiny drops of poisonous exudate continued to form along his three serrated horns.

Vanessa Frisch smiled, the kind of smile that made people shiver, even the smarmy politician types and business high-flyers with whom she dealt so often, to such lucrative effect.

This creature, her captive, might not perceive the nuances of human expression and body language, for he was purely monomodal in the everyday world, at the scale of mesoscopic dimensions. But even though he lacked a human or quasi-human aspect... he knew enough to fear her.

Even when Vanessa took her human form, as now.

Good enough.

A thin hex-field shimmered inside a nine-sided vertical framework formed of fresh, slender bones, mounted on a stalk-like, narrow pedestal made of resin drawn from living sprawl-trees in the swamps of distant Surinam – the trees were said to howl at each incision – mixed with dried human blood acquired close to home.

Daemonids could howl as well, of course.

Given the right amount of pain.

The construct looked like an oversized version of a child's toy for blowing bubbles, but the membrane in the loop wasn't soapy or even, strictly speaking, made of matter.

Hex was its own thing, though the seven core equations that described its properties bore a profound resemblance, under the right kind of symmetry transformation, to Malvolanto's equations of necromagnetism.

Vanessa liked tricky, advanced theories and symbolic manipulation. She also enjoyed the application of such esoteric knowledge, especially when that application produced exquisite pain in others.

I exist to improve the world through suffering.

She understood her mission, her place, and herself. How many people could say the same?

So many prey to devour, so few significant predators to vanquish.

Perhaps she needed to go up against some stronger enemies, or risk growing stale. Or perhaps, when her plans came to fruition and she ascended to a new level of power, a superior breed of enemy might seek her out of their own volition.

That would be lovely.

The daemonid captive shifted his great body, and glowered.

"We need to talk," she told him, and smiled knowingly once more.

The hex-field membrane began to pulse within the confines of its enclosing, nine-sided frame of slender bones.

Across those patterns, rainbow hues shimmered and danced.

The air around the construct grew hot and cold at the same time, rendering the air both heavy and ozone-sharp, like the heart of a thunder-cloud.

"Tell me," commanded Vanessa as the hex translated her words into the energy symbols of the captive daemonid's tongue, dripping with dreadful hunger, "the location of the new neuronal composite."

She and her captive shared some evolutionary lineage, sure enough; but then again, the same thing could be said of a standard human and a dung beetle. She needed significant hex processing to enable speech here.

The winged daemonid opened his fanged mouth, shifted in his platinum chains, and shook his horned head: an almost human gesture.

"Is it human twins, this entangled composite?" Vanessa pressed on. "You should hold no loyalty to humans. Plus I can keep you here and make you suffer for as long as I want… and I promise you, I intend to live an awfully long time."

The daemonid hunched his shoulders and lowered his chin and glowered: yellow ellipses, brighter than ever, shifted in the four-foot-wide black orbs of its eyes: a wordless promise of bloody, unstoppable vengeance should he ever break free of these chains.

Chance would be a fine thing.

"You have no choice," she told him, and smiled once more, and softened her voice in ways that the translation hex ought to be able to transmit. "Up to a point, a certain point, I will enjoy this game all the more, the longer it lasts. But it will end, eventually, and you will tell me what I want to know."

He opened his mouth, her captive, and emitted a cascade of overlapping hisses at multiple high frequencies, like the roar of surf in a stormy sea shifted an octave above its natural harmonics: the sound of a thousand radios tuned to static and turned up high.

Vanessa didn't need the hex to understand that part.

"Oh, dear. Such language," she said. "And, well… You can't say I didn't warn you."

She crooked one finger, made prominent by the ideogram-engraved polished gold of her elongated metal fingernail.

All of her nails bore such decorations, every symbol taken from a lost archaic tongue called Sunskril, whose writing system featured in the Umbral Codices of Delkor Xyniakothrotl, encapsulating the very knowledge that destroyed that civilisation.

She gestured, and the steel door ground open, revealing the corridor beyond, its walls painted in the varicoloured blood of thirteen sentient species, depicting scenes of ritual dismemberment and suicide beneath a disembodied eye in the sky.

Pretty colours, but she saw them so often, her enjoyment failed to stay fresh. Pity.

Two of her street soldiers were directing three purple-skinned, bulky golems, each with a single slot-shaped eye of featureless yellow, blocking Vanessa's view of the atrium that stood at the corridor's far end.

The golems were carrying a heavy, barbed framework of black iron and platinum, containing something transparent that shifted and glittered like living glass.

Razorfluid: malleable and viscous and simultaneously able to cut through virtually any kind of matter, and enjoy itself while doing so, for it was pretty much alive in some sensual yet mindless way.

One of Vanessa's more interesting discoveries.

She looked back at her grey-skinned daemonid captive. He pulled and snapped at his chains, even though he was smart enough to have learned already there could be no escape, not that way.

The dull ellipses in his eyes morphed from yellow to green, which Vanessa read as a kind of frustrated anger, still a long way from hopelessness.

"Good," she murmured, then frowned as the hex-field in the pedestal-mounted bones began to translate the word. It stopped as she waved the membrane into stillness.

She had hours more fun to come with her captive, maybe even days, before he would be willing to speak to her, to tell her what she needed to know, which was when the translation hex would really prove its worth.

Vanessa possessed some abilities in the so-called crawlspace dimensions, particularly in her other form; but she couldn't communicate with a full-on monomodal daemonid here in the everyday world, not without significant hex computation.

Which was ironic, given the nature of the information she needed to extract from her captive.

Once the torture frame was in place and beginning its work, there would be agonised howls along with the pheromones and fluids of suffering, which needed no translation hex for Vanessa to absorb and enjoy, bathing in her captive's pain, renewing and energising her own personal strength.

Confirming her superiority of purpose.

How fortunate that I enjoy my work.

And that no one, no outsider, could penetrate or catch any distant sense of what went on in this place, her most magnificent fortress-home: technically within the Greater Tristopolitan jurisdiction but actually situated deep below ground, beneath a nine-sided clearing in a forest with no name.

The corridor outside was one of many, radiating from the central atrium that the golems, having halted at the street soldiers' command, currently blocked from Vanessa's view.

Inversion Tower was a masterpiece: a seventeen-storey construction shaped like an impregnable tower but entirely buried. The man who had constructed it, or rather paid for it be constructed, had used a Zekorian architect and a Sklavic workforce, resulting in no publicity whatsoever.

For official purposes, Inversion Tower did not exist. Not often enough, Vanessa remembered to be thankful she'd stumbled across it.

The previous owner, utterly reclusive, had determined to live out his days here, rich but isolated from people, surrounded by books. He'd maintained his solitary existence until the day a younger Vanessa discovered the place.

She remembered the fear-thrill inside her, during the chase through forest land, on the run from a team of Mordanto combat mages she had crossed, back before she truly came into her power. On discovering Inversion Tower, she'd simply taken the place from the old man, and turned him into her servant until she grew weary of his ineptitude and ended him.

It's great to be me.

And it would feel even better once the prisoner told her everything he knew: enough to let her find the new resource that she sensed in the world.

A quantally entangled resource that she felt *almost* certain would prove perfect for quantal hex computation, to run specific calculations regarding particular thaumic field equations: a breakthrough that might prove as significant as the original invention of necrofusion reactors.

And at worst, a patentable technique for improving current reactors' efficiency by an order of magnitude.

More likely, she was going to gain everything she needed to raise her powers – both political strength and actual, tangible hex manipulation drawing on crawlspace-dimensional energy fields – to a new, unstoppable level.

I just need to find the Death-damned thing.

She couldn't pinpoint the twin clumps of entangled organic matter in everyday time and space.

To find their location or locations – she couldn't tell how far apart the two clumps of neuronal matter were right now, for entanglement remains independent of spacetime separation – she needed her daemonid captive's cooperation, his ability to detect crawlspace-dimensional field induction and map it to a corresponding place in the everyday world.

Unwilling cooperation always tasted best.

Beautiful torture.

Her three golems were waiting in the dark hall, the barbed framework held easily in their stubby hands. Waiting for her command.

Razorfluid rippled along that framework.

Such sweet, fragrant pain to come.

She gestured for the golems to enter the chamber, set down the torture frame, and ready it for use.

THREE

Donal was running through the catacombs for the first time in a couple of years, and with each easy footstep the old enjoyment renewed itself.

There had been a period when the used-up, discarded bones and skulls on their forgotten shelves, and the more intact remains within sealed sarcophagi (whose families had at some point paid for their loved ones' bones to escape the usual fate in the reactor piles) had changed.

Then, they had whispered to him, those bones, their words crawling into his mind and disturbing his sense of self at that time; but no longer.

It felt more like the old days now: quiet in contrast to the busy streets above, a place of dusty peace.

A good place to run undisturbed.

He hadn't even been sure of getting down here, for many of the entrances had in the past responded only to his police badge; but at Conklyn Dropwell, the street level gates had squeaked open before he even touched the dark-green ironwork, as if the same silent and never-seen wraith that operated the gates now was the same one he greeted so often as a youngster, even before he left Lower Danklyn to join the Army.

"It's good to be back," he'd said, touching the metal with his fingertips, before following the spiral steps downwards into gloom but not total darkness, due to spots and clumps of bioluminescent fungi in the damper places, on walls or ceiling or under foot.

The shadowed galleries beckoned him onward, or seemed to.

Simply running, for the joy of it.

I'm a father.

That one incredible thought dominated, drove him forward. He hadn't wanted to tear himself away from Mel and little Finbar, but Mel had insisted, and Ingrid the witch, after some kind of whispered consultation with Mel, had joined in and practically pushed him out of the door once he'd pulled on his tracksuit and tied the laces of his old battered running-shoes.

Fastened into his tracksuit jacket pocket with a safety pin, along with his wallet, was a clearly written shopping-list of baby items, most of which they already had; but Mel was worried about running out of those things, or so she said.

Mostly, he realised, she just wanted him to keep active, and knew he could pick up the shopping at the end of his run.

She'd tapped him on the nose and wagged a finger. "Seven weeks, I reckon, and I'll be exercising again myself. So you, dear Donal, better keep your fitness up as well."

"Yes, ma'am." A salute had been in order, so he'd given one, and grinned.

He'd already been filling in for Mel in the gym, teaching the kids in particular, his investigative case load having hit another lull, a quiet period that for now was very welcome.

There'd been a consulting gig with Broadaxe Insurance which turned out more lucrative than expected, when uncovering a simple arson fraud led to the recovery of some previously stolen artwork for which anxious, well-connected owners had put up a pretty decent reward.

There were other options, career-wise.

If the offer remained open, he could always go back to the Department, picking up where he'd left off as a detective lieutenant. It wasn't what he really wanted – at least, he didn't think it was – but securing the future had become important: more important than before.

Running easily seemed to loosen up his thoughts, as it always did.

Growing up as a cop's kid?

He had no idea whether that might prove good or bad for Finbar.

And if I remain a freelance PI?

Totally unpredictable as a long-term career. Some ex-cops made it work, some messed it up and slid downhill into poverty or even, through desperation and long-term exposure to professional wrongdoers, into criminal activity.

He'd once arrested a gang of counterfeiters filling up chitin-covered crates with dodgy florins in a nasty old warehouse at the worst end of the docks, and when Donal and his team had hauled them in a van to Shadwell precinct, the desk sergeant had immediately recognised the gang's foreman as a former colleague turned private investigator turned bankrupt turned lowlife.

There'd been some kind of private reunion in one of the cells that night, and Donal had never found out what happened, exactly; but the prisoner's face looked battered, purple with blood and bruising the next day, and walking upright looked painful.

And his chest obviously hurt when he sat in the hard-backed chair in the interrogation room.

But the prisoner didn't rat on the officers who worked him over, and the judge sent him to solitary instead of general population at Wailing Towers Penitentiary, so that was a happy ending... of sorts.

Three white lizards scuttled down a side tunnel at Donal's approach, but he was past the opening in a flash, continuing onwards, upping the pace a little because he felt like it.

There was some kind of movement far ahead: a glimmer of light, shifting and pulsing, then sliding to the left and out of sight.

Not my private playground, the catacombs.

Still, it was unusual for anyone else to be down here: small lizards were usually the largest creatures around, and you didn't see much of them.

No one had commissioned new sarcophagi in this part of the city for a long time, but perhaps some city workers were checking to see if the place could fit in a few more heavy duty tombs; or perhaps they were just architectural engineers making safety checks.

The catacombs had maintained their integrity for a thousand years, but that didn't mean they'd last forever, so someone had to examine them from time to time. It made sense.

Maybe.

Donal's holstered Magnus hung from a door-hook back at home. He really hoped the explanation for that presence up ahead was innocent.

I'm not a cop these days.

He no longer had a duty to investigate the slightest suspicious occurrence, and he did have an overwhelming obligation to look after his family above all else, which had to exclude stumbling into danger for no good reason.

Danger?

He sniffed the air while still running, and it caused the back of his neck to prickle in a way he knew how to interpret: the subliminal scent of stress, and not his own.

Dropping the speed a little allowed him to quieten his footfall, getting closer without giving himself away. He breathed in and out rapidly nine times over, increasing his adrenaline in a way that went back to his redblood days, still useful when heading into likely danger.

Slowing right down now, stopping his breathing in a purely blackblood zombie way, chin tucked and narrowing his eyes, taking cover behind a broken tomb that stood shoulder-high, bigger than most sarcophagi, not large enough to be called a mausoleum.

Three winged, fanged statues, squat and ugly as Hades, crouched upon its top.

Is that the sound of voices?

The rustling was possibly a natural sound – although there should be no shrubbery down here, there could be some kind of hanging fabric for some maintenance-related reason, and draughts could flow through the subterranean air with surprising strength at times – likewise the trickling might be flowing water, and those faint complex whispers could be something like the gabbling of gathered geese: natural sounds producing an auditory hallucination of human voices.

On the over-large sarcophagus, one of the stone figures turned its head, creaking, to look down at Donal.

That's different.

Gargoyles, underground.

Donal stared at the bulbous stone eyes, wanting to ask what it was doing down here instead of perching on a rooftop where it belonged, but knowing that if people were up to something nearby, perhaps in the next side-tunnel, they might well be close enough to hear him, even if he whispered.

The gargoyle raised a stubby finger to its stone lips.

Donal waited for a deliberate second, then nodded agreement. Gargoyles could be nasty, but he'd never known one to be anything but honest and driven by duty.

A clank, a thud, and the definite sound of a man swearing, and someone else hushing him. At the same time, a wraith slid out of the solid wall up ahead, turned back towards the sound for a moment and solidified further, just enough to shake itself in what looked like exasperation, before growing more transparent and insubstantial once more.

It drifted towards Donal and the gargoyles, and came to a sudden stop in mid-air.

So there could be no more hiding. It was the kind of thing that Donal himself might have done, in charge of some clandestine operation: assign a wraith (or several wraiths) to sentry duty, for they were the best kind of watcher you could hope for.

The wraith just hung there, billowing.

It had to be aware of Donal.

Here we go, then.

Still massively unsure of what was happening, Donal rose to standing and stared at the wraith, and tilted his head to the right, and raised an eyebrow: a silent question as to the wraith's intentions.

The gargoyles remained unmoving, no doubt hoping to be perceived as simple statues. Too bad Donal couldn't pull that trick.

The wraith seemed to wriggle in mid-air, then it curled around and whisked back down the tunnel, in the direction the voices had come from.

All three gargoyles opened their living stone wings and hissed.

"Sorry, guys," said Donal.

The nearest gargoyle turned and nodded to him, acknowledging his apology.

Then all three leapt from the top of the tomb into slow flight, wings creaking as they beat against the air, as Donal wondered for the thousandth time how such heavy – high density, really – stone creatures could fly at all.

Unlike any kind of bird he'd seen, gargoyles flew slowly, scarcely faster than walking speed, except when swooping from a height, at which point they became truly terrifying.

No chance of that down here.

Have I ruined their mission?

Not the way he normally thought of gargoyles – they were sentinels by trade, not mission-focussed operatives or soldiers or cops – but they'd been watching with a sense of purpose and now they were following up, and none of them had shown the slightest sign of anger towards Donal, even though he'd clearly blown their surveillance and whatever else they were up to.

I'm a father now, with responsibilities.

Which included being the kind of man that young Finbar should be able to look up to as the years went on; and while prudence was allowed and maybe encouraged, cowardice never could be.

So Donal smiled, recognising that as a zombie he was no better than a redblood: arguing with himself, shooting down his own objections, so he could do what he'd wanted to do all along.

Duty calls.

He broke into a slow jog, following the flying gargoyles.

FOUR

Commissioner Sandarov leaned back in his big, normally comfortable chair, pushed back a little from his desk, and shook his head, his concentration broken: too frequent an occurrence these days.

He was growing used to unhappiness, invariably signalled by this acid churning in his stomach, despite the excellence of the dinners he enjoyed at home and the packed lunches he brought to work, because Maisie excelled at cookery almost as much as deep mathematics.

As a professor at Windsigh College, she'd picked up principles of political manoeuvring from classic books on strategy in the main campus library – to survive the bitterest of infighting for the tiniest of stakes, she told him, which was par for the course in the rarefied world of academia.

"Everyone knows it's stupid, and no one knows another way to behave."

Her descriptions of faculty common room arguments – and verbal back-stabbing among the quadrangles and colonnades and professors' offices that they preferred to call studies – were often funny, sometimes delivered with sad smiles over the anguish her colleagues endured in such meaningless pursuits.

Meanwhile he was beginning to realise just how much he, as a Police Commissioner nearing the end of his second year of office, still had to learn about political manoeuvring, whether from books or from Maisie herself.

I need to get better at this.

He continued to overlook hints that he recognised too late, and to lack informants in the higher echelons of city and even federal political life, to possess so many blind spots when it came to persuasion behind the scenes, to privileged networks and secrets, all geared to the gaining and keeping of power and money and influence, which might or might not boil down to the same thing.

The skeleton clock at one side of his refurbished office ticked loudly and definitely, and when he looked at the crystals mounted in its eye sockets, they seemed to stare right back.

"Not my imagination," muttered Sandarov. "You tick a lot softer when everything's going okay."

The next three ticks were louder still, as if to say: *tsk-tsk-tsk*. After that, they quietened to normal volume.

"Alright. Point taken."

There was a knock on the door, dull and distant because of the thickness of the armour and maybe the saturation of hex that protected his office, necessary because of his duties and the documents he worked on here, but not because his own skin was precious in any way: it was the officers out on the streets who needed the real protection.

He often wished he could give them more.

"If that's Sergeant Yorak," he said, "then open up, please."

The big door hesitated, then its saw-tooth join grew visible and widened, and the heavy metal pulled open to reveal the blue-skinned sergeant standing there with his usual fussy expression.

"Sergeant, come in." Sandarov rose, walked around the desk, and waited.

"Er, yes, sir." Yorak held a green slimedog-hide folder against his chest as he came inside and stopped, holding himself dead still.

"No need to close," said Sandarov, gesturing to the door.

It was a private signal, and while the doorway remained open, the air within it began to shimmer with a powerful privacy hex that did more than deaden sound: anyone looking this way from the open-plan office outside would see near-static versions of Yorak and Sandarov whose expressions and lip movements were impossible to read.

"I've got the information on Alderman Turnstile and Alderwoman O'Reilly." Yorak offered the green folder. "It's not much, certainly no proof of collusion, but there is a so-called businesspersons' society they both belong to and attend pretty often, along with three members of Bloodfist Bank's executive board."

On the street, Sergeant Yorak had been a disaster, but this task had been a hunt through existing files and records, poring over piles of vellum: encyclopaedic amounts of analytical reading and interpretation, the kind of work Yorak seemed born to carry out.

Right now, though, he looked worried.

Sandarov took the folder from him. The cured hide felt rubbery, and was naturally thick, but he didn't think it contained more than six or seven sheets of vellum, if that. "You don't like me spying on political opponents, do you?"

"Er…"

"And you can speak openly."

Yorak glanced at the doorway, seemed to spot the hex, relaxed a little, and shook his head. "I had misgivings at first, sir, but I found a travel chit authorised by Accounting, I mean our own department, flying an unnamed but senior law enforcement officer in from Fortinium for an official consultation meeting with unnamed City Council members, the day before Bloodfist Bank's annual general meeting. The City Council being a major stockholder, you see, though it might just be coincidence."

That was the AGM where stockholders were told they'd receive triple the expected dividend for the past financial year, at a time when so many businesses had struggled. The *Tristopolitan Gazette* had stopped short of accusing the bank of widespread money-laundering... but only just.

BLOODFIST WINDFALL DIVIDEND SURPRISE

While the city economy gears up for rebuilding after last Sextober's unprecedented events and the upheavals of the previous Octember, it seems that Bloodfist Bank's shareholders are already reaping the benefits of an economic recovery that for the rest of us is only just beginning to happen. Perhaps their primary asset is an interestingly diverse client portfolio and platinum-level investors providing funds of intricate provenance...

Sandarov had wondered, as he read the article, at the journalist's sources and whether an investigation was warranted, but hadn't at the time associated it with the political manoeuvring that seemed to be targeting him and the way he ran the Tristopolis Police Department.

Yorak added, "Travelling first class and paid for by us, this person visiting from Fortinium, so it definitely had to be someone of senior rank."

"I presume that's unusual." When Sandarov had flown to Santo Lacrimoso for the Police Federation conference last year, his seat had been in second class and his name appeared on all the documentation.

"With the way it's taking me such a long time to work out who the visitor was, then yes, it smacks of obfuscation and indirection" – Yorak's blue skin darkened slightly – "and general clandestine skulduggery. Sir."

Yorak continued to look flushed, and no wonder: this outspoken delivery and literature-teacher vocabulary was a step up from his usual manner.

"Tell me," said Sandarov, placing the folder on his desktop and turning back to face Yorak. "I'll read everything, and thoroughly, but I want to know your thoughts."

"You're popular with the current City Hall administration and with most serving officers in the Department, sir." Yorak blew out a breath. "And nobody wants any more civil disruption or divisiveness or any of that, not after the last few years of turmoil, so your political enemies, yours and the mayor's, aren't going to move openly."

For the first time, Sandarov looked at Sergeant Yorak and imagined him wearing an academic's purple gown, and wondered whether he could arrange for Maisie to have a chat with Yorak, and form an opinion on his potential.

For a police commissioner, *popular* didn't mean lacking in enemies, and Sandarov knew that his views on propriety and discipline – and honest-to-Thanatos courtesy and manners in general, especially when dealing with the public – didn't sit well with every kind of officer. Any political moves against him could come from within the Department as easily as from outside.

"You're saying there's a conspiracy to turf me out of this office."

Yorak gave the tiniest of shrugs. "We're having a private conversation right now, Commissioner, that other people might call a conspiracy, or part of one."

"I know. When exactly does a private conversation, or a series of them, become a conspiracy? I've had enough Death-damned debates on that with the BA and her prosecutors."

The Borough Attorney was hardcore, having begun her career in the Ministry of Retribution, but she was adamant on the dividing line between idle speculation among friends and conspiracy to commit a genuine crime, and the principle at stake wasn't just the kind of thing that students argued about over beers: it had practical implications, from sending defendants to jail versus not even sending them for trial.

"I'd say she's one of your allies right now," said Yorak.

"Yes." Sandarov looked at him. "Given that you're not even invited to the relevant meetings, that's a pretty astute observation on your part."

"I try to keep my eyes open, sir."

The grandfather clock, standing opposite the skeleton clock, sounded a soft *bong*, but when Sandarov looked, it was seventeen minutes to the hour, too soon for the regular chime.

It meant his visitor was early, and on the way up.

"Thanks." Sandarov nodded to the clock, then looked at Yorak. "You're not the only perceptive one around here."

"Some kind of trouble?"

There was a gulf in rank between them, but Yorak's trustworthiness had been apparent pretty much from the moment Sandarov took office.

"I don't know, but I would appreciate a witness for the conversation I'm about to have."

"Um…"

"If you don't mind remaining standing for the whole thing, you can do so invisibly. Hidden, I mean."

A fabric-covered panel slid forwards, away from the wall, revealing an alcove big enough to contain a large person. For Sergeant Yorak, that would make it positively roomy.

"I can see and hear from inside?"

"Only if you get in quickly. But… it's a request, not an order."

"I'll do it." Yorak nodded, and stepped quickly into the alcove. "Sir."

The fabric panel pulled shut a full seven seconds before the privacy hex in the office doorway shimmered, wavered and fully evaporated. A shape moved across the opening.

And his mysterious visitor walked in, with her reddish-brown hair piled up and bound in gold wire, her white fur coat open and revealing a plush, ruby-coloured gown, as if she were attending the opera or a grand ball or some such lavish affair. Her fingernails were long and appeared to be of blank, polished gold.

"Mrs Frisch?" said Sandarov.

There was something disturbing about the curve of her smile, her dipped chin and half-lidded, knowing eyes.

"Commissioner. How wonderful to meet you."

She held out her hand, palm down, and Sandarov took hold and had to force himself to shake hands gently instead of simply kissing the back of her hand, as instinct had wanted him to do.

Her skin felt soft and electrifying.

Good job Maisie isn't here.

He blinked and steadied himself.

"Please take a seat." He held the back of his most comfortable visitor's chair in invitation. "Oh, let me take your coat first."

There was something beguiling about the movement of her shoulders as he helped her slip the coat off. He carried the coat across to the wall-mounted horned-lizard sculpture he used as a coat hook, noting a soft yellow flare in the sculpture's amber eyes – a warning of power here, as Sandarov had already guessed – before covering the sculpture as he hung the fur coat in place.

"You're very kind." Mrs Frisch looked very elegant as he settled her on the chair.

He went around the desk, placed his hands on the blotter to steady himself, and sat down in his work chair, aware of the authority it was supposed to lend him.

Mrs Frisch leaned forward, not so much revealing cleavage as hinting at its wonderful yet hidden existence. "And I hope you'll call me Vanessa, dear Commissioner, at least when you realise I'm on your side."

Sandarov forced himself to say: "Have we met before?"

"No, but I've followed your career as best as an outsider can manage." A knowing smile punctuated her silky words. "An outsider in some circles, an insider in others, maybe even among people who can help you consolidate your position and, who knows, *maybe* see you run for office in Fortinium."

"The police department there doesn't need my help."

"I was thinking of the Senate, Commissioner."

"Oh."

At that Police Federation conference in Santo Lacrimoso, Sandarov had presented an argument that no law enforcement jobs, especially senior positions, should be political in the sense of being voted into office, or directly appointed by a single politician. He had presented his case in the light of the Glian system, widely regarded as an exemplar for civilised countries across the globe.

There, on the other side of the Umbral Ocean, all police appointments – apart from one Parliamentary Cabinet Mage at the very top – came from within the profession, just like promotions in a large corporation: no external elections of any kind involved.

The system was opaque to outsiders, unaccountable in many ways, but immune to short-term thinking and crowd-pleasing initiatives that were all flash and no lasting substance: a very real problem throughout the Federation, in Sandarov's judgement.

"I'm aware that you don't think much of politicians." Her eyes looked dark, yet the actual colour was impossible to determine. "That's what makes you the kind of man I'd be delighted to support."

Her words seemed to waft through the air, carrying gossamer sheets of multiple meanings, subtleties that needed to be tasted and savoured, not brutishly grasped at.

Sandarov blinked, and realised the armoured door had not fully closed: the saw-tooth join remained visible, as if the office didn't want to seal itself up right now, not with Vanessa Frisch inside.

He returned his attention to her elegant face, and that beguiling smile grew in place once more.

"Tell me, dear Commissioner, what you would do with, say, three more years in office guaranteed free of internal trouble, with an increased city-wide budget for the Department and a free hand in allocating those funds."

Sandarov blinked. "Quite a lot."

"They say that the best way to improve an education system is to increase teachers' salaries. Perhaps that applies to police departments also. Would paying your officers more money be part of your agenda?"

"Long term, if I could get away with it, yes. For the lower ranks only, and for teaching staff at the Academy. While making it easier to get rid of existing serving officers who don't live up to TPD standards."

It was more than he had expected to say, and Mrs Frisch – Vanessa – curled her lips once more in that beguiling fashion he was beginning to expect from her.

"You'll be effectively raising the entry criteria for enrolling in the Department," she said. "Higher wages on offer mean more qualified candidates will apply."

"Up to a point. Anyone motivated too much by money is open to all kinds of manipulation." Sandarov leaned back in his chair. "It's all too easy to be blind to reality, when an unexpected offer comes your way. Don't you think, Mrs Frisch?"

"Well. Quite." Something like black ink seemed to pass across her eyes, just for a moment. "You do in fact live up to your billing, Commissioner Sandarov, which is a rare occurrence these days, and maybe always has been."

Whether that constituted approval or disapproval, Sandarov couldn't tell.

"In any case," continued Vanessa, "it's been illuminating and enjoyable, and thank you so much for taking the time to see me."

Suddenly she was standing, tall and regal in her ruby-coloured robe: an instantaneous transition from one position to another, no actual rising from the chair.

It was a show of power.

"I really am glad you came." Sandarov rose with deliberate slowness, and reached across the desk to shake hands. "Thank you, Mrs Frisch."

The handshake was more like an ephemeral touching of palms, but again the softness of her skin took Sandarov's breath away.

"No need to see me out."

Another instantaneous transition, and she was standing at the doorway with her white fur coat draped cape-like over her robe, and giving a last, amused glance at the room. Then she passed outside and was gone from sight.

Dear Thanatos.

When Sandarov could speak, he called to the door: "Close yourself, will you?"

After several seconds, it swung ponderously closed and thumped into place. Solid, reassuring, and possibly too late.

Was seeing her a mistake?

He sat down and stared into space, seeing nothing. After a while, he swivelled the chair to look out through the window: from this high up, the view was a cityscape of Tristopolitan towers beneath the ever-dark purple sky. His city: the city he served, not owned.

Last year his parents had gone abroad, travelling close to the Lightside, where such cities as existed faced a whitish world where it was brighter outdoors than inside, a reversal of normality so profound that it struck him as perverse, and never mind the fact that for half the globe's surface – though a minority of people – it formed everyday reality.

A muffled sound brought him back to the moment.

"Oh, Thanatos," he muttered. "Sorry, I forgot."

He placed one hand on the green rubbery folder on his desktop, and gestured with the other hand for the fabric-covered panel to pull open.

"Yorak," he added. "Are you okay?"

"Um, yes." Yorak blinked, several times. "What's happened, has your visitor cancelled?"

"Say what?"

"You just said you wanted me to watch and listen while you talked to someone. Are they not coming after all?"

It took Sandarov a moment. "Are you saying you don't remember her?"

"Remember who?" Yorak gave the beginnings of a smile, then stopped as he realised that Sandarov wasn't joking. "Er, have I missed it? Did I sleep through the whole thing, or something?"

"Definitely something," Sandarov told him. "Listen, I think you're alright, no harm done, but I want to be certain."

"Sir?"

"Get yourself down to the medics, tell them I've said you need a full work-up for possible hex infection and all the rest. Full anti-ensorcelment scan, to the level of something a senior-level mage might have tried to instantiate."

He had all the jargon. It didn't mean he understood the processes involved.

"Your visitor was a senior mage, sir?"

"I don't know what the Hades she was, Sergeant. I wish I did."

It had been so beguiling, that knowing smile, and so very soft and electrifying, the touch of her skin.

"Can I ask what she wanted? What happened?"

"You can ask, but I don't know." Sandarov stared at the heavy, closed protective door. "I really have no clue at all."

"Would you like me to investigate her, sir? What's her name?"

Sandarov shook his head. "Conspiracies be damned, this might not be a police matter at all, strictly speaking. And that means departmental resources aren't the right thing to use."

He meant ethically more than strategically, but the latter applied as well: getting Yorak to pore through archive files was as far as he was willing to go in allocating work resources to political matters, while going further would involve a greater risk of being found out as well as feeling dishonest.

"I don't think you should let it go, sir. If you don't mind my saying so."

"No, Yorak. I don't mind." He rubbed his chin for a moment. "I'm not rich, but we have two salaries coming in, and my wife and her parents are what you might call shrewd investors. I can pay for someone to look into this as a private matter."

Yorak nodded. "Excellent idea, if you could find someone trustworthy enough."

"Hmm... Could you make calls to two officers, both detectives, one of them a sergeant, possibly both. One's called Levison and the other is Sergeant Zarenski, Ruth Zarenski. Ask them to come and see me, separately."

He'd seen them briefly in action last Hextember: two detectives who didn't normally work together, interrogating the same person of interest, a Night Sister from St Jarl-the-Healer Hospital.

"I'll get right on it. Should I tell them what you want to talk to them about?"

It was the kind of thing you could achieve with a phone call, but better done in person, where you could check the body language and all the rest.

"I'm after a character reference. Tell them that much."

"Okay, sir."

Sandarov looked at Yorak, and decided he deserved an explanation.

"I've remembered pretty much by accident that both detectives used to work for the same detective lieutenant, but at different times. A cop turned PI who's worked some hard cases in the past, and did something with Mordanto and the feds that pretty much saved the city last Hextember."

"Oh. That."

Sandarov rubbed his chin again. "I don't just want someone who's effective. I want an honest investigator."

Yorak nodded. "I'll set up the meetings, sir."

"Thank you, Sergeant."

After Yorak had left, Sandarov got up and stood with his forehead against the cool glass of the armoured window, looking down at the long boulevard that was Avenue of the Basilisks, running right to left a long way below, where vehicles and pedestrians looked tiny compared to the vastness of the city all around.

My career doesn't matter much, not to the world, but those people do.

He turned back to his desk, and let out a long breath.

Time to get back to work.

FIVE

Donal followed the slow-flying gargoyles along the gloomy tunnel, moving at a jog and trying to keep his footsteps quiet, even though it might prove a waste of time.

The watch-wraith would have told the people up ahead about him and possibly about the three gargoyles – Donal wasn't sure whether the wraith had realised they weren't statues – and if this was some kind of crime in progress, then the criminals would assume that whoever the wraith had seen, that person was coming for them.

They might also assume that armed police were arriving in force, in which case this was exactly the wrong kind of encounter to be hurrying towards; but there was nothing else he could do.

He wished he had his Magnus. And his old badge. Or maybe carrying a police badge would turn him into a legitimate target as far as armed criminals were concerned. Firepower, though: he'd have welcomed that.

There was nothing there when he rounded the corner.

Blank stone wall, a dank dripping sound, and a simple dead end… except, where could the gargoyles have gone?

He touched the stonework and it *rippled*, his fingertips feeling wet, heavy fabric, like a sodden raincoat but bigger, far bigger. When he used both hands, he felt a water-soaked curtain, for all that his eyes were telling him about stone blocks forming a wall.

With the toe of his running-shoe, he felt for the bottom of the curtain, then lowered himself into a rock-bottom squat position, closed his eyes to remove the sensory dissonance, and grabbed hold of the heavy fabric at the bottom.

Then he came up, pushing his hands high as he rose – like lifting a bizarrely light barbell overhead – creating a way in, and opening his eyes as he took a single step forward, then another as he let the fabric go, and it fell in place behind him.

A gargoyle lay on its back, stubby taloned hands outstretched, face frozen in an ugly snarl, a dark nasty crack upon its chest. Donal touched its stone body and felt a tiny vibration, a distant whisper of life.

"Hang in there," Donal murmured rather than whispered: less likely to be heard by whoever was up ahead.

The tunnel continued with a lower ceiling here, and grew narrow because of some kind of buttress intruding from the right hand side – down here, it must form part of some building's foundations – and widened again maybe ten or eleven yards beyond that, as far as Donal could tell in the gloom.

A soft blue light began to glow there, beyond the foundation, and sudden voices rose, a woman called: "No!", and the flat thump of a silenced pistol sounded: fired once, then again, followed by a moment's silence and then a soft, mewling sound that might have been grief or physical suffering.

"When the bad guys got guns and you don't, that's the time to hunker down or skedaddle," an old training sergeant had told Donal and the other recruits in what felt like a distant epoch.

Good advice. Except when it isn't.

He moved forward, careful with his footsteps, listening and sniffing the air as well as focussing his visual attention forward, trying to decipher the ripple of shadows in the bluish light.

Into the narrower area, taking twelve careful steps forward and halting near the end of the foundation, face tightening at the sight of another fallen gargoyle, this one with a shattered wing: a triangular section had broken right off, and lay a yard away from the unmoving stone body.

My fault, for blowing their surveillance.

Donal crouched, right hand against the stonework, and tilted forward to peek around the corner. The blue light was shining downwards from a seven-foot-wide hole in the ceiling, which had to mean some kind of cellar that had been entered from below.

Perhaps the most sensible thing to do would be to sprint back for help and call in a full tac team, and he might have done just that if it weren't for the whimpering up above.

He crept forward until he was below the edge of the opening, his attention upwards, seeing an angled shaft of blue light and above it, made shadowy, a dome-shaped ceiling adorned with some kind of geometric pattern.

Not exactly your standard cellar design, but unless he had his geography all wrong, they had to be at least forty feet below ground, and more likely seventy: central Tristopolis was flat, and the catacombs ran pretty much horizontally, and if he'd paid more attention he might have known exactly which building he was under.

Not a bank vault.

Although you couldn't be sure, not in this city, and the lack of a hex-induced crawling sensation on his skin might mean professional thieves who knew how to disable high-grade security, rather than a simple absence of professional protection.

Squinting against the blue light, trying to make out details of that shadowed ceiling, he thought there might be a break in the pattern there, and after a moment, the tiniest of movements confirmed his thought.

It looked more like an absence than a presence, that dark shape in shadow, but it was small and clinging to the ceiling of the chamber above.

If Donal knew anything about gargoyles, it was waiting for the opportunity to drop and use its strength and neurotoxin venom to maximum effect: shock and awe with a vengeance.

Only one gargoyle left functional, but if the enemy didn't know it was up there, then one might be enough, with Donal's help.

In a way he could never have achieved as a redblood, Donal let his awareness flow from vision to hearing, not ignoring smell, but trying to create a three-dimensional model of the chamber overhead – and more precisely the people or entities within it.

He listened to the scrapes of shoes and the shifting of fabric with breathing, and the obvious sounds of agony from the person who had been shot, for that mewling was accompanied by awful undertones of liquid gurgling, most probably blood in the lungs.

Seven people, including the injured woman – he thought it was a woman, but wasn't sure – but not counting the gargoyle perched on the chamber ceiling and waiting to drop. The criminals' watch-wraith could be anywhere, might appear at any time, perhaps with companions.

Can't be helped.

Three individuals were close together, relatively close, about thirteen feet behind and above Donal's head, approximately opposite the point where the injured person lay, now reduced to quiet, intermittent whimpering.

Within Donal's field of vision, two men in black coveralls were working at something, as if dismantling heavy machinery, while another paced around, muttering something to himself.

Or talking to some distant witch or mage: you never really knew without checking, which meant the man on the move had to be the first target, in case he was able to summon help or act as a conduit for channelling hex or some such Thanatos-damned malarky.

Donal looked up and pointed in the direction of the moving man, tracking him with his finger, then aimed at the gargoyle, and back at the same man. Then he pointed to his own chest, followed by the trio above and behind him.

Even in the gloom, he could make out the baring of fangs, and imagined the first drops of venom already glistening at their tips, and found his own lips pulling back from his teeth in an atavistic grin coming from a kind of joy that was not amusement.

Life on the edge. Back on the brink, where he belonged.

Can't think about Mel and Finbar.

He held up his hand, thumb and fingers splayed, then curled his thumb, then his little finger – blackblood self-control – then the next, counting down.

On *one* he leapt forward for the spring-effect assistance, then vertically up, high enough to grab the edge of the hole above using both hands with upward momentum to spare, chin-up to muscle-up, back muscles then triceps, forcing himself up, his head rising above the level of the chamber floor.

He had to get fully inside before anything else could happen.

A grey shape dropped fast in his peripheral vision, struck a black-clad man in the back of the neck and dropped him, face-forward, while a long-barrelled pistol with silencer fell clear and clattered to the tiles.

Gargoyle venom acts fast.

Donal swung his right knee up, pumped with his arms and side-rolled onto the floor, onto all fours and into a sprinter's crouch, but the explosive shot that sounded wasn't a starter's pistol: it was meant to end his life.

One of the three men standing together. Too bad for the gunman that he had missed.

There was a choice to make: go for the silenced weapon on the floor or close the distance to his targets fast.

Movement and geometry for mortal stakes.

Go.

Donal sprang towards the gunman, peripherally noting the dark coveralls that all of them were wearing like a uniform: like a military enemy's uniform, and they'd already employed lethal force, so this was serious.

He went in low, driving his shoulder into the gunman's torso just above the hip, one hand hooking the calf, the other clamping the guy's hamstring, lifting and driving and smashing him backwards while torquing front to back, the enemy's head flipping back and down faster than his core.

"When you throw the enemy, drive your own head towards the spot where you want *them* to fall." That was the dictum from his close-quarter battle training that Donal had carried with him since.

He powered himself directly towards the bottom of the wall where it met the tiled floor, and that was where the back of the gunman's skull made impact with a flat crack of sound.

A broken neck for sure.

Almost for sure, but there was no time to check, not yet.

With his left hand Donal ripped the weapon from the man's failing grip but there was no time for proper deployment as the other two were almost on him, the one on the left swinging what looked like a butcher's blade dripping with glowing blue fluid.

Donal punched him in the throat with the back of the pistol, elbowed the other in the chest, driving forwards, clearing an inch in space, enough to whip a right uppercut under the chin, before slamming the side of his head against the jawbone, tilting to ensure he struck with the hard part of his skull – no one expects a lateral head-butt – and drove a right hook to the side of the neck.

He followed with a thrusting knee to the spleen and, as the big man folded forward, a downward hammering blow with the pistol, targeting the upper vertebrae.

Rules for the ring, and rules for the street: he'd always known the difference.

The man with the silver-blue butcher's blade was huge and less affected by that throat punch than Donal had hoped for. As the blade whipped down once more, Donal lunged backwards, unable to get inside the arc of the blow because the falling man was in the way and his own momentum was wrong.

Another cut that missed, then a dark shape whipped in from the side and the gargoyle was at the man's neck and the venom was scarcely necessary as fangs ripped open the neck and arterial blood spewed out like someone stamping on a ketchup bottle, hard and fast.

Nice.

Donal stamp-kicked the side of the big man's knee to help, and checked that the guy he'd first dropped hadn't moved: chin on chest, neck looking broken, unconscious if not dead; so okay.

Two more threats still active.

He swivelled away, switching the pistol to his right hand in a proper grip, not needing to check the safety because its previous owner had just fired the thing, almost certain there was a round in the chamber and more in the mag, but moving fast in case he was wrong.

There was something odd about the remaining two men and the machinery they were working on.

A big framework or cage of black metal with some steel-coloured sections and struts, a lot of pulsing blue light, and some kind of weird transparent rippling *stuff*, maybe a gel: the two men had continued to work on it even when Donal and the gargoyle launched into action against their colleagues.

Hard grey skin and opaque eyes like stones, but not sniper implants: these were something else.

One of the men turned to Donal while swinging a straight-arm backfist, a big, obvious movement that might have been laughable were it not for the hard strength implicit in their bodies, more like gargoyles or golems than standard human.

Donal ducked, and continued the movement sideways as the other man threw something, a glob of that motile gel, and Donal continued the motion, evading the attack, tripping over something – the floor had cracked because of the strange framework's weight, that was it – but going with it, dropping and shoulder-rolling on the diagonal, coming up on the outside of his second attacker, and slapping the palm-heel of his left hand into the side of the guy's head, like hitting a stone wall.

Donal drove backwards, a reverse lunge into a stable stance with the gun coming up in a two-handed grip, and he shouted: "Stop! Stop now."

Both men froze, like baleful statues.

Where the glob of gel had struck, partly on the leg of a fallen man and partly on tiled floor, it began to shift and wriggle. Acrid, yellow-grey smoke rose from the man's flesh as the gel ate it away, even as it began to dissolve a part of the floor.

The man who'd thrown the stuff wore gauntlets, and no wonder.

"Step away from that thing." Donal tilted his head towards the framework, but didn't gesture with the gun: the only reason ever to raise a weapon is to train it on a target. "Step sideways."

The two men looked at each other. Their lips were straight incisions in what looked like living stone, and their faces were hard-featured masks. The one with the gauntlets sported rust-red tattoos on cheeks and forehead; the other man's facial ink shone a pale fluorescent green.

"Do it," added Donal. "Now."

"Okay." The gloveless man raised his bare hands. "I do it."

His voice sounded guttural, the accent maybe Vostokian, maybe something else.

He was the one who moved first, exactly as Donal had commanded, while the other, the man with the gauntlets, jerked to the side and cartwheeled – or something like it – spinning sideways into the framework, towards the core of blue light which instantly blazed up and consumed him, or maybe transported him elsewhere: there was no way to tell when you dealt with strange energies.

It had an effect.

The big, solid-looking framework seemed to collapse in on itself as if disassembling, black and silver struts falling into the brilliant light until all of it was gone, followed by a final flaring pulse before everything winked out, leaving darkness.

Which was when the remaining man, the one with the green face tattoos, came for Donal.

Bad move.

Donal closed his eyes and pulled the trigger, shifted his front foot laterally a little and swivelled on it, his other foot arcing through forty-five degrees, tracking the movement he could hear even in the aftermath of shooting, and aimed a fraction ahead of the sound, and fired twice more.

Splinters of stone-like skin and actual bone struck his face, and he was glad he'd squeezed his eyes shut, because he'd been aiming for the centre of mass but the big man must have tried to come in low since one of the shots had blown apart his skull: Donal was almost sure of it.

He kept the gun trained on the fallen man, listening for further movement, hearing nothing.

Opening his eyes made no difference at first: the chamber remained dark. After a second, though, his eyes adapted as apparent darkness lightened into gloom, from tiny amounts of glowing fungus in the tunnel below the hole in the floor.

Something clicked, and lines of red light framed the dome ceiling, shining steadily for seven seconds – a part of Donal's mind kept track – before beginning to blink, and he assumed it was some kind of alarm system that was only now being allowed to operate.

The gargoyle, perched at human chest-height on the wall, still had one taloned hand pressed against a softly glowing button.

"Good work," said Donal.

A creaking nod from the gargoyle, but its expression remained grim, even for a creature that to human eyes seemed always to scowl; and no wonder: one of its companions, the one with the shattered wing down below, was almost certainly dead.

Donal hoped the other, with the chest wound, was clinging on, but it had looked bad.

The tiniest of sounds, less than a whimper, rose from a prostrate body at the far side of the chamber: the wounded woman, shot by one of the criminals, and dressed differently from them: a dark silk blouse – burgundy or dark grey: in the blinking red light, you couldn't tell the difference – and a darker skirt and stockings.

She probably worked here, wherever this place was, but during Donal's time with the TPD, more than one cop had been shot by a criminal looking like a civilian in trouble; so you had to remain careful but you absolutely had to help.

On the other hand: was a human's life worth more than a gargoyle's?

"Keep watch on her," said Donal. "I'm going to check on your friends."

The gargoyle's eyes, already bulbous, grew more so. Then it nodded.

Donal kept hold of the gun just in case, squatted next to the hole in the floor, and swung himself down through the gap one-handed, and dropped into a crouch.

Dead for certain, the gargoyle with the shattered wing.

I killed them all for you.

Vengeance, if not justice – the criminals died too easily for that – although the one who went into the glowing framework might have been transported elsewhere, to safety.

Unfinished business, then.

He went back to the gargoyle whose chest had been split, knelt down and felt for that tiny vibration of life, and eventually detected it, weaker now and almost gone.

"Help is coming," he said. "Your friend was able to trigger the alarms."

The words might not help, but they were all he had: that, and the simple fact of his presence, so that if the worst came to the worst, this brave, wounded gargoyle would have some kind of company in the final moments leading to oblivion.

Donal held the creature's hard, stubby-fingered hand of stone – a redblood would have found it cold – as he knelt there, waiting, hoping the medics would arrive in time.

There was nothing else he could do.

SIX

Senator Anna Fitzgerald stared at the dark-suited man in black shades, and fought down a fleeting urge to pee herself from nervousness, reminding herself it was the enemies of law and order, not her, who had everything to fear from federal spellbinders.

She and Federal Agent Bouchard were standing in her book-lined office in the Capitol where she normally felt secure, but not today.

For all her ordinary weaknesses and shortcomings, criminality and evil represented everything she stood against, and if the spellbinders' budget had been under her absolute control, she'd have tripled their allocation with a stroke of her stylus.

In theory, she and the feds were allies through and through.

Still, Bouchard radiated something inherently terrifying, an intensity and implacable composure that Anna read as merciless. Her nervous reaction felt justified.

"Last week, Senator, you met with Kristof Dahlberg" – Bouchard pronounced the name correctly: even though it ended with b-e-r-g, it was *dal-BARE-ee-eh*, not *DAHL-burg* – "and his colleague Eva Kaldini, for coffees in Café Clysm and again later on, for supper in Arena Stalix."

"I did meet with them." Anna let out a breath. "And over breakfast in a small deli near the Borough Attorney's office next morning, I shared my concerns with BA Bryce, regarding the previous evening's conversations."

"And she escalated those concerns," said Bouchard, "hence my presence here at unreasonably short notice."

"Zero notice." Anna felt the weakness in her twitching smile. "Which is obviously okay."

"Please relax, Senator. We are on the same side."

Picking up her subvocalised thoughts, or simply reading her expression and analysing her voice? Either way, Anna was surprised to feel a softening in her shoulder muscles, and an easing around her upper abdomen.

"That's right," added Bouchard. "Perhaps we should sit down?"

This time Anna's smile felt more natural to herself. She was supposed to be the hostess here, but the normal rules had evaporated, and she suddenly felt in the safest of hands, with a federal spellbinder right here in her office.

A schoolgirlish joy rose inside her, remembering the *Secret Binders* adventures she'd read as a kid; and she had a flash of inner vision: a fleeting fantasy of sending a handwritten letter back in time to her younger self, telling her it was going to be okay and that some of her most exciting dreams were going to come true.

More or less.

Two couches faced each other across a low coffee table carved a century before from a single fragment of a giant preserved human knuckle – a present from the Surinese embassy to one of her political forebears – and she gestured Federal Agent Bouchard towards the couch nearest the bookcases, and sat down on the other couch, facing Bouchard.

"Would you like some coffee?" she asked, knowing that her assistant, Fredo, was probably making a pot already.

"In a minute or three. If I may, I'd like your reading on what kind of people they are, Mr Dahlberg and Mrs Kaldini."

"They're interesting." Anna thought about it, remembering the way they had alternately cajoled and enticed her into setting up meetings for potential international business deals requiring federal approval.

They made good use of silent intervals also, not afraid to give her time to think.

"They're capable for sure," she went on. "And they'd done their homework, setting out all the steps for—"

"Please, just for now… Your impression of them as people, of their personalities."

"Hmm." Anna thought she understood: Bouchard was after the kind of details you couldn't get from written documents or summarised descriptions of negotiations.

"Eva's the quiet one," she went on, "but Kristof is more thoughtful all the same. Despite him being the better conversationalist, is what I think I mean."

She shook her head, deciding she wasn't making a very good job of this.

"If you were to ask me whether I trust them," she added, "then my summary answer is no. But I would trust Eva to do something in her own interest. I'm going to go with declaring her a narcissist, and I don't mean because of the way she dresses and presents herself."

"And Dahlberg?"

"Kristof…" Anna paused. "I'm using their first names because that was how we interacted at the time. Just so you understand. If I weren't trying to recreate the memory properly, I'd distance myself from them."

"I understand. That's why you went to the BA with your concerns."

"Exactly. So, Kristof is something of an intellectual, and he can quote all sorts of philosophers on why society is the way that it is, and the ways in which it could be different. Like quoting Dalkin on the polyphyletic origins of our various species of citizen."

"Okay," said Bouchard.

"Don't worry," Anna told him. "I had to look up 'polyphyletic' in the *Vebber's* myself. It means—"

"Multiple common ancestor species. I know."

"Well." Anna should have known better than to underestimate a federal spellbinder; but even for a fed, Bouchard was impressive. "Kristof claims to have beaten several chess grandmasters in private games."

She thought back for a second, and continued, "I didn't quite credit that at the time, but my uncle knows one of the people he mentioned, Owen Glencullen, and I got Uncle Sean to make a phone call. Totally true, it turns out."

"That's useful information. Go on, Senator."

"He's a sharp dresser, is Kristof, who doesn't actually care about clothes. Knelt down in a puddle of spilt wine to help a waiter who'd tripped without even thinking about it." A pause, replaying her words in her mind. "I mean it was Kristof who didn't think. Didn't hesitate."

She looked up diagonally, remembering, and added: "There's an odd mix of empathy and ruthlessness in his makeup, which I can't quite decipher."

On the opposite couch, Bouchard leaned back a fraction, and adjusted his shades on the bridge of his nose. "I see."

"I was quite taken with him in the moment, yes. But he's too focussed a strategist and tactician for me to trust, and in retrospect that's easy to see. At least it is, if you work in this place."

She gestured at the book-lined walls, but she meant the Capitol and the everyday machinations of the Senate. Bouchard nodded: of course he was smart enough to understand.

"Dahlberg remains a Sverian citizen," he said, "even though he spends most of every year in Fortinium, or at least in the Federation. Did he give any indication of applying for citizenship?"

Anna wondered if that changed things from the law enforcement angle.

A crime committed on Federation soil was surely a matter for Federation law regardless of where the suspect came from. Maybe the authorities here would need official Sverian assistance to impound documents or other evidence from Dahlberg Industries' head office in Ledzheim, on the far side of the Umbral Ocean; and citizenship might have an effect.

"We didn't talk about that kind of thing," she said. "No, it was all about business for Dahlberg Industries, their subsidiaries and associates, and a lot of detail on import and export tariffs, government subsidies here and in Sveria and its Greater Rohpa neighbours."

"Along with interesting discussions on philosophy and culture."

"Well, yes. Exactly. Partly that would be Kristof, and Eva as well, establishing rapport like any good negotiators. But it also has a great bearing on business, especially face to face meetings, more so than on legal systems and their local differences."

Bouchard tilted his head a little, and reflected spritelight slid across the lenses of his shades. "Could you give me an example, Senator?"

"The kind of thing you'd be expert at, Agent Bouchard. Let's see... I was in some Glian trade commission talks last year, and that moron Senator Galreedy – feel free to quote me: he knows what I think of him – put forward an outrageous suggestion that the Glian team made no comment on."

"Ah."

"Right. Galreedy thought he'd slipped in a sneaky extra clause, right in the middle of the agreement, without the Glians' caring... because he *thought* silence meant consent. Either that, or it meant they hadn't even noticed."

Bouchard smiled. "Whereas in fact the Glians thought it so stupid, it would have been embarrassing for Senator Galreedy if they brought it out into the open and pointed out his blunder. I'm guessing."

Anna smiled back, realising anew how completely her earlier nervousness had slipped away; and she wasn't bothered by the notion that Bouchard might have put her at ease deliberately, using psychological techniques so subtle that even she was blind to them.

"As I said," she told Bouchard. "You'd be expert at that kind of thing. And you've clearly worked with Glians, too."

"I spent a year at our embassy in Dinium. Cold and damp, with awful food, but great libraries and museums and ancient colleges." He gestured at the bookcases. "I think you'd have liked it there, Senator."

"Call me Anna."

"Call me Agent Bouchard." He grinned, and even with the shades across his eyes, the expression changed his demeanour completely. "I'm kidding. My first name's Jean-Marc, but everyone shortens it to Marc."

Anna realised he was most likely about the same age as her. For a senator, she was pretty young, while Jean-Marc – she liked the name in exactly that form – was obviously senior in his field, even though she didn't know his exact position in the Bureau.

Then Jean-Marc did something she really hadn't expected: he slipped off his anti-hex shades, revealing blue-grey eyes whose intensity made her shiver.

"Are you married, Jean-Marc?" she found herself saying.

It was one Hades of a leap in conversation, and it was hard to believe she'd made it.

He blinked. "I was. To a fellow agent."

"Oh. I just happen to know that most of your profession are married with children. Very settled." Anna twitched a smile. "Not the way they present you in pulp thrillers, fond though I am of them."

She had hundreds at home, always with one on the go, lying on her bedside table... in the bedroom where she slept alone, as always since her beloved Peter had died, seven years ago last month.

Jean-Marc looked at the volumes on her bookshelves here. "I guess those titles aren't quite appropriate for you to have here in the office."

"No. Not quite."

Anna had always — absolutely always — been the consummate professional, and never once stepped over the bounds into personal relationships, not even over convivial drinks at trade conventions or official late-night dinners at Kerridge's or the Cinque Saisons or, for that matter, the Glian embassy.

But now she added, "Did your wife die, Jean-Marc?"

She couldn't have said exactly how she knew, how she sensed an inner grief held steadily in place and mirroring her own.

"Five years ago, during a federal operation." Jean-Marc blew out a breath. "This wasn't how I expected our meeting to go."

"Me neither." Anna's eyes stung a little as she blinked. "Even though I was a little excited to spend time with one of my childhood heroes."

"I beg your pardon?"

"Did you ever read *Secret Binders* when you were a kid?"

Jean-Marc looked at her and laughed. "I had the entire series, at what must have been an impressionable age. Given where I ended up."

"A good influence, then."

"Probably. Look, er, Anna... You said you were quite taken with Dahlberg, then realised later how tactically oriented he was. How manipulative."

"That's right."

"But I came here to put you at your ease and persuade you to help..."

"I know."

"I'm trying to say" – Jean-Marc stared at the shades he was holding in his hand – "that maybe I'm no better than Kristof Dahlberg, since I'm doing exactly what he did, trying to get you do something."

"And are you acting that way now?"

"Er. Well." Jean-Marc gave a half-sad, half-surprised smile. "Not deliberately."

"So there's the difference, right there."

She meant it. However calculating he might have been earlier, Jean-Marc had shifted his mental state; and the resonance between them was real: natural, not deliberate.

"Okay." Jean-Marc nodded. "Okay."

"I read pulp thrillers, sure enough, but I've also read those books, nearly all of them." She gestured to the shelves. "I've been thinking of a return to academia, that or actual retirement, instead of running for office yet again. Maybe resigning before my term is up, in fact."

"I'm sure any university would be glad to... Er, what exactly are you saying, Anna?"

He understood that she wasn't just making conversation.

"Two things," said Anna, "and one is that it would be nice, if I'm leaving office, to go out with an exciting adventure. And if it's an adventure that I can't tell other people about, that makes it even better. More thrilling, you see."

"No." Jean-Marc shook his head.

"You came here to recruit me to help in some federal operation against Dahlberg Industries, didn't you? I'm volunteering, Jean-Marc."

"I don't want you to do it. It's why I came here, yes, but now... No."

"Am I less able than you expected? Not up to the task?"

Jean-Marc's blue-grey eyes were focussed entirely on her. "You're the most impressive person I've ever met."

"So then."

"I can't risk... You said there were two things, Anna."

"I did."

The second was a fragile thought, too risky to bring out in the open, to be framed in words that were spoken aloud; but if she remained in public life, it would be hard to form a lasting relationship with a federal spellbinder whose private life had to remain just that, hidden from public view.

"Oh," said Jean-Marc.

Federal spellbinders didn't have the power to read people's minds: Anna was almost sure of it. On the other hand, she seemed to have a good handle on what Jean-Marc was thinking right now, so perhaps it had nothing to do with profession or training.

Perhaps this was something simply human, something that occurred once in a person's life, if they were lucky.

A soft knock sounded, coming from the door.

"That'll be my assistant," said Anna.

"Right." Jean-Marc slipped his shades back on, becoming Federal Agent Bouchard once more: all business and professionalism.

"Come in," called Anna.

Fredo Braun, her assistant, entered with a silver tray in hand, including the best dragon-head coffee pot and a plate of Cicada Crunchies, which were Anna's favourite cookies of all time.

He placed the tray carefully down on the table between Anna and Jean-Marc, and reached for the pot.

"It's okay, Fredo," Anna told him. "I'll pour."

"Certainly. Thank you, Senator."

"Thank you."

She waited until Fredo had left and the door clicked shut, and smiled at Jean-Marc. "So tell me all about it."

He took off the shades once more. "You can probably guess at the outline."

"Get to know a bit more about them, Dahlberg and Kaldini and their senior staff, play along a little, arrange meetings at a place where you've got surveillance going, maybe carry or plant some eavesdropping device, something to do with quantally entangled hex, or along those lines."

"And you know there's mortal risk if you play this role, Anna."

"I don't think Dahlberg or Kaldini" – she was using their surnames now deliberately – "would try to harm a Federation senator, at least not without building up to it in obvious stages. Escalating threats, I mean. No sudden switch to violence, surely."

"It's not really you who'd be at risk," said Jean-Marc.

"Not me? Why not?"

"I mean, if they so much as hurt your feelings, I'll kill them all."

Anna let out a breath. "The way you say that... It ought to be scary."

"And is it?"

"Of course not." She smiled. "You already know me better than that."

"I guess I do." Jean-Marc leaned forward. "Let me pour the coffee."

He reached for the pot, and Anna touched the back of his hand.

"Make yourself at home," she said.

And wondered how in Thanatos' name she could be so lucky as to meet a man like this. As for helping him investigate Dahlberg Industries, that was going to be fun.

However it turned out.

SEVEN

"There was a wraith on guard as well," Donal remembered to say, "and it saw me out in the tunnel, and flew back in this direction, presumably to warn its colleagues. But I didn't see it again, when I actually climbed up here."

With proper lighting and the alarm switched off, the dome-shaped chamber was soft blue and dull gold with all sorts of ceiling paintings that Donal hadn't had time to look at properly.

Bellis shook his bald head. "That's not climbing. More like flying."

Donal looked at the hole in the floor. "Well I jumped, and pulled myself up."

He'd already explained this to a younger officer, who'd written everything in her notebook before disappearing upstairs into the building proper.

"More than I could've managed." Lieutenant Bellis patted his stomach: maybe the beginnings of a small paunch, maybe not. "I'm getting soft."

Donal had always thought that, physically speaking, Bellis was energetic more than truly athletic. Yet the one prolonged case they'd worked together, years ago, had also shown how sharp Bellis could be: intuitively perceptive and decisive under pressure.

It was a good combination, and Donal had thought at the time that Sergeant Bellis would go far, and here he was: already a lieutenant, and senior investigating officer on what might turn out to be a major crime, although it was far from clear right now.

"Scene-of-crime diviners are held up in a traffic jam," added Bellis. "Sewer burst on Crawlshade Drive, and some nervous idiot drove into a bus at the other end of the street, apparently, so the diviners' van is stuck in the middle of two holdups."

"And, what, they don't know how to walk?"

"Don't get me started. There's a bunch of them on board, so you'd think one could stay with the van while the others make their own way here, but apparently that's not procedure."

"Ah," said Donal. "Procedures. I remember them."

"Must be great, you being your own boss and all."

"Brilliant, when the money's coming in."

"Ah."

"Right." Donal looked down at his scuffed tracksuit. It hadn't torn during his escapade earlier, but it seemed a lot shabbier than when he'd put it on. "I don't need to be rich or anything, but stability might be nice."

"Stability? You?"

"I'm, er…" Donal felt a grin break through. "I just became a dad."

"What? Oh, congratulations." Bellis's handshake was pretty strong. "And that means, since we've already had a proper statement from you, taken down by one of my professional officers, you are now totally out of here."

"What are you getting at?"

"I mean, jog off back home and leave this mess to the people who are paid to sort it out, good buddy. That's me and, Thanatos help me, this rabble."

Bellis gestured at his junior officers, one of whom turned and stuck out her tongue for a second, before turning back to the prone body she'd been examining.

"They're obviously terrified of you and your authority," said Donal.

"I wish."

"Any news of the woman?"

The medics had already arrived and taken her away, along with the wounded gargoyle from the tunnel below. The dead gargoyle remained in place, and would stay there undisturbed until the SOC diviners could do their thing.

"Not yet. Are you sure you heard two shots, Donal?"

The unknown woman had appeared to have sustained a single wound to the body, just above the liver: no major external bleeding, considering, but no way of telling what damage had been done inside.

Her business clothing had suggested a staff member of some kind, but although Bellis's people had come down via the main building above, he'd yet to share any information about the woman's identity with Donal, which was fine with him.

Standard operating procedure: officers ask questions, and witnesses answer, not the other way around.

One of the junior officers, a pale red-headed guy with nictitating membranes that flicked across his otherwise standard-human eyes with metronomic regularity, gestured towards one wall where a stack of huge sacking-wrapped rectangles – probably large paintings – rested at an angle.

"Sorry, sir. Should've said, as soon as you came back down." He meant when Bellis returned, just a few minutes ago, from talking to other civilians up in the main building. "A single round went part-way through that stack," he added. "We're leaving it for the diviners to check before we dig it out."

"You're right," said Bellis. "You should've told me. For punishment, that's either nineteen lashes with my razor-whip, or you buy scarab cream doughnuts all round this afternoon."

"Tough choice, sir." The young guy grinned.

"Hmm." Bellis took hold of Donal's upper arm and led him away to one side.

"You're not really my type." Donal looked down at the offending hand.

"Sorry." Bellis let go. "Is there anything you want to tell me off the record?"

"Say what? No. I didn't miss out a thing."

"You charged up here and did serious damage to a professional crew, all because you heard something suspicious while you were jogging in the catacombs?"

"The gargoyles," said Donal. "Don't forget about the gargoyles. I kind of followed their lead."

"The one who helped you is upstairs and frantic to get back to its ledge near the top of this tower."

"So why don't you let it go?"

"I'm waiting for someone who knows how to communicate with the things, and there's not many witches like that around. And even fewer who want to work with us, for some reason."

"Because you don't treat the gargoyles with enough respect, maybe?"

"But they're only…" Bellis stopped. "I've just proved your point, haven't I?"

"Looks that way."

"Hades, I hate it when that happens." Bellis turned to the young detective with the nictitating-membrane eyes. "Joel, nip up and tell them to release the gargoyle under my authority. Straight away."

"Got it." Joel rose and headed for the ladder-like stairway that had been lowered into place from the level above. "And I'm going to congratulate it for a brave job well done, while I'm at it."

Donal smiled. "Good man."

"Oh, don't encourage him," said Bellis. "Ah, Hades. Joel, tell the gargoyle the whole team recognises its courageous actions, and well done."

"Sir."

Donal and Bellis watched Joel climb up and disappear from sight.

"When your witch arrives," said Donal, "she'll find the right gargoyle soon enough. It'll be at its designated post, not wandering around."

"Yeah, got it." Bellis rubbed his face. "Makes you wonder why it and its two friends were down here at all, doesn't it?"

"You might start by working out which way they entered the catacombs."

"And I should be able to ask the building watch-wraiths, but according to my initial questioning, none of them sensed that anything was wrong."

"Ensorcelment of wraiths?" said Donal.

"Oh, boy. I've never come across that before. Is that a real thing?"

"Beats me, officer. I'm just a simple civilian."

"Bleeding Hades, Donal."

"Maybe the wraith I saw was part of the building's complement, working with the intruders' gang."

"This is going to be a painful one. Although" – Bellis gave a thoughtful sideways tilt of the head – "an inside job would explain a few things."

"What sort of things?"

"The things we TPD detectives work on without telling the unwashed mass of ordinary plebs, except when we absolutely need to. Unless you're thinking of signing back up?"

"Well..."

"Seriously, Donal, I reckon they'd love to have you back. And Commissioner Sandarov's parents are, well, they're just like you, old buddy."

Donal stared at him. "They're my kind, you mean?"

"Not like that. I mean yes, they're resurrected. But you already know there are bigoted morons in the Department. I'm just saying, with Sandarov in charge, the morons have to watch their step, that's all. So you'd be fine."

Wonderful.

There had been zombies and freewraiths serving in the TPD for as long as Donal could remember, and when he'd volunteered to work for Commander Laura Steele, he hadn't given her status a moment's thought.

It was her zombie heart beating inside his chest right now, put there a matter of minutes after her head had been blown apart and Donal suffered a mortal chest wound and would otherwise have died for real.

Still, when he joined Laura's team, he hadn't been naïve enough to think that everyone would be blind to her resurrected status in the same way that he was. And later, there'd been the Unity Party's attempt to disenfranchise all non-standard humans completely, which might have succeeded if things had played out differently.

Was Bellis trying to be helpful, the way he was talking now, or just revealing his own, unrecognised bigotry?

Forget it.

You could second-guess other people's thoughts forever and simply make yourself miserable; or you could just get on with life. Or unlife. Whatever.

Donal looked up at the rising stairway-come-ladder and failed to discern any meaningful details in the shadowed room overhead. There was no clue at all as to the building's identity or purpose, apart from the fact that down here, the domed chamber was pretty fancy for a basement, and it was used for storing old objects that might include large paintings.

"Can you do me a favour?" he said. "Can you time one-and-a-half minutes exactly?"

"Er... Okay, I'll play." Bellis extracted an honest-to-goodness pocket watch and flipped back its dragon-engraved lid. "From... now."

Donal turned his back to Bellis, and hummed the unofficial anthem of the military's Death Brigades, a stirring old marching tune, originally instrumental, later embellished with nine encouraging verses and a chorus that started: "Straighten up and kill 'em hard/Smashing their bones into shards," which rhymed well enough for the kinds of soldier the Brigades recruited.

At the exact required moment, Donal stopped and said: "Now."

"That's... impressive," said Bellis. "You timed a minute and a half in your head while butchering a tune. You counted musical beats, did you?"

"Nothing so smart. Part of my brain is able to count seconds, minutes, hours, you name it, while I do something else entirely."

Bellis snapped his watch shut one-handed, and rubbed his face with the other hand. "Great party trick. I've got a case to work, Donal. So the thing is..."

"I'm pretty good at doing the same kind of thing spatially. I didn't keep track while I was running, but I can revisit the memory in my head. And for sure, when I retrace my steps, I'll be able to check my accuracy."

Bellis shook his head.

"So I think," continued Donal, "that we're underneath Dredgeway Avenue here. Maybe the third tower along from Twistover Pits, where the sunken pedestrian plaza is. Where Bloodbath Johnnie used to have his newsstand, after he finally got out of the joint. How am I doing?"

Another shake of the head from Bellis, but this time he was smiling. "I give in. If I don't tell you where we are, you'll just look it up in a city directory or, what, go up to Dredgeway and take a look directly?"

"You've always been a smart cookie, Lieutenant."

"And how about my judgement? Smart problem solving and wise decision making aren't quite the same thing."

Donal raised an eyebrow, wondering what he was getting at. "I always rated you highly on both counts."

"Good. So here's my judgement, right now. You should go home and kiss your wife and baby. Son or daughter? Or one of each, or neither? Some other combination?"

"A son, called Finbar. His mother and I aren't actually married."

"Tsk, tsk. But you are together?"

Donal felt his expression soften. "We're a couple, and we're in it for the long haul."

"So..."

"So." Donal looked up at the stair-ladder one last time, then nodded to

Bellis. "Thanks for all the advice, explicit and between the lines. If we do get married, Mel and me, then you're invited to the wedding."

It wasn't a new thought – marriage – but this was the first time he'd said anything aloud to a third party.

"Good," said Bellis. "And about staying away from my investigation?"

"I wouldn't dream of treading on your toes, Lieutenant."

"Is that a promise that you're going to stay away?"

Donal raised his watch. "Is that the time already?"

Bellis sighed. "I know what kind of watch that is, and exactly what the display signifies. Looks as if you've got three days, almost, before you need to recharge your heart."

"Just talking to you has energised me, old friend."

"Oh, for pity's sake. We've got your work and home addresses, right? In case we need to get in touch."

"We live in Mel's workplace. Mel's Gym, it's called. And I'm Riordan Investigations ULC, work-wise. I've a telephone in the office, just installed and with an actual honest-to-Thanatos answering service."

For domestic purposes and boxing gym business, he and Mel relied on the call box at the end of the street. He added, "Both business addresses are in the city directory. In case you and your professional team lose your notes."

"Alright. Good." Bellis held out his hand. "Congratulate this Mel for me."

"I will."

They shook.

"She must be a tough woman."

"Because she puts up with me?" said Donal.

"Well, sure. But Mel's Gym trains boxers, right?"

"You've heard of it?" Donal knew that Bellis lived in West Xalix – a long way from Lower Danklyn – unless he'd recently moved.

"Locker room gossip, the good kind." Bellis patted his stomach, the same way as earlier. "I'm trying to keep trim with lots of cardio in the HQ gym."

"Good for you."

"Take it easy, Donal. You're okay going back the way you came?"

"Sure."

"Just don't mess up my crime scene on the way out."

Donal grinned, tried to think up a smart reply, and gave up. Instead, he walked backwards to the hole, keeping his attention on Bellis and the way Bellis's eyes widened in horror, his mouth beginning to open in warning.

A yard before the reaching the edge, Donal jumped backwards – he'd kept track, by sense of hearing, of movements down below, so he knew that no one had dragged any kind of obstacle into place – and dropped through the hole.

He landed in a crouch, and said: "Sorry. It's only me."

"Hades!" A uniformed officer jumped.

"Show off," came Bellis's voice from above.

The dead gargoyle's body remained in place. Boards, the same kind painters used when decorating, had been set in position like three-inch-high bridges across sections of floor, in this case to preserve possible forensic traces.

Bellis's team were good.

"As you were," said Donal.

The uniformed officer put her hands on her hips and shook her head, but said nothing.

Donal turned away. The heavy curtain, the one imbued with some kind of hex camouflage to look like solid wall from the other side, had been tied back with rope. The way out to the catacombs was clear.

Ideally, the tunnels should be sealed off for half a mile in each direction, pending forensic analysis. Still, any SOC diviner worth their salt would be able to discount minor movements that post-dated the crime, especially if someone told them what went on.

"I'll let the diviners know you went that way," said the officer.

"Huh. You read my mind."

"The lieutenant's always been a stickler for detail, even before he transferred to the ECU." A twitching half smile. "And he says he learned everything about working crime scenes from you, sir."

Donal glanced up at the hole he'd dropped through. "You're kidding."

"No, sir."

"Huh. Well... Good luck."

"You too, Lieutenant."

There was no point in correcting her, and besides, *ex*-Lieutenant didn't exactly roll off the tongue.

Maybe if Donal had still been with the Department, he'd have known that Bellis was now in the Esoteric Crimes Unit, because the mention of the ECU was news to him. You could miss the gossip even though it sort of went with office politics, and politics was one thing Donal felt glad to have left behind.

Time to get out of here. He walked the length of the low boards and through the gap where the curtain was tied back, careful not to touch anything, then out into the tunnel, where he continued walking, eyes already adjusted to the gloom.

He reached the over-large sarcophagus where the three gargoyles had been perched before, paused for a second without breathing, and decided there was nothing more for him to see here.

After a few yards, he upped his pace to a steady jog. Sometimes, when he felt like it, his endurance runs lasted an arbitrarily long time; but Mel wouldn't expect him to be gone for hours and hours today: even she would at some point grow worried.

He accelerated to a decent running speed.

Feels like I'm running away.

But from a case that wasn't his, that no one had hired him to work on.

No. There's Finbar, and there's Mel.

Running towards home was a different proposition: something good, not shameful.

All the while, as he continued to run, legs pumping and bent arms swinging easily as his footfalls echoed back from the tunnel of the dead, he told himself that he would not even consider returning to Dredgeway Avenue to investigate this whole thing further.

Not thinking about that.

Definitely not thinking about continuing the investigation by himself…

Alright, I give in.

So long as he remembered to keep his priorities straight, nothing should go wrong.

EIGHT

Vanessa liked Fortinium. Staring out through the small aeroplane window at her left shoulder, she smiled at the great grey buildings below: low and powerful-looking fortresses that spoke of strength and defensive power, so different from the rearing confidence, even arrogance, of dark Tristopolitan towers.

When it came to political power, those ancient government complexes – along with the surrounding greater city, an expanse of low buildings, five storeys tall at most, even lower in the suburbs – formed the obvious heart of the Federation.

It's good to be back.

While none of the great corporate empires kept their head offices here, many commercial deals at extraordinary levels of importance began with subtle hints and scarcely spoken promises down there, in the rarefied clubs and restaurants and committee rooms that graced this city.

Contracts for building federal highways or public universities, not to mention military deals: they grew from conversations beneath those very rooftops she was staring at.

"We'll be landing soon," announced a steward from the front of the plane, projecting his voice above the propellors' whine. "Please make sure your seat belt is fastened securely."

Vanessa was flying in disguise, pretty much. Her tweed skirt-suit was expensive enough, for those who knew how to judge a garment, but not extraordinarily so. Her fingernails were scarlet, a hard conjured veneer covering the gold beneath.

The lighting changed as the aeroplane banked, revealing a distorted, reflected Vanessa in the window. Her small feathered hat, worn at just the right angle, struck the kind of jaunty note she was aiming for: like an ambitious journalist or upmarket boutique owner, smart and feisty at the same time.

It was a good look, though so much less than the real Vanessa Frisch, who already possessed more power than any of the fools on board here could imagine.

She smiled at her reflection, as if sharing a secret.

There's no such thing as having too much power.

That was obvious, though she remained glad that so few people understood as much, or took the steps needed to gain that power: money and political influence as much as hands-on hex manipulation.

Prey everywhere, and I'm the predator among them.

Or predatrix, for in her view gender mattered.

Final descent.

Vanessa's hand went to the amulet worn underneath her linen blouse, checking its state. She felt its soft warmth indicating readiness, not expecting to need it on landing, but prepared just in case.

She'd flown long-haul flights with security witches on board and managed to obfuscate their hex perception and generally cloud their minds, every single time; and this shorter flight, from Brody Airport Tempelgard, featured no security measures to speak of.

But she also knew better than to lower her guard.

Touchdown.

The seat bounced beneath her, the vibration going up into her diaphragm, causing her to catch her breath; and then the plane was whining along the runway, and slowing as the brakes kicked in.

"Aleph Airways would like to welcome you to—"

The man in the seat to her right leaned closer. "Is this your first time in Fortinium, miss?"

He'd slept lightly throughout the flight because Vanessa had willed it; but she'd brought him out of it for landing.

"I'm here quite often for funerals," she told him. "People die so easily, don't you think?"

"Er... Quite. Yes." He swallowed and turned his attention to the folded newspaper on his lap, and kept it there while the aeroplane came to a halt.

Everyone dutifully waited for the wraith-powered steps to roll into place outside, the hatch to clunk open, and the steward to announce they could leave their seats.

"Be careful of the overhead lockers as we disengage the necromagnetic locks... now." The steward smiled as if he'd performed a great trick.

Then he backed up to clear the aisle for the first passengers heading for the exit.

Vanessa waited, not caring to be part of the scrum – the man who'd sat next to her fumbled his belt free, jerked down a small overnight bag and briefcase with shaking hands, and stumbled into the exiting mêlée, needing to get away from her – and she waited with a soft smile, breathing lightly.

Finally, just a few stragglers remained, and she could exit comfortably.

Once outside the hatch, she paused on the top step, took in a breath of cold air, and looked around. Flamewraiths constrained by wrought filigree tubes spelled out DARKSWORD AIRPORT across the main terminal roof.

The low buildings and wide airfield emphasised the dark dome of the sky, closer to indigo than purple, yet streaked with permanent dark clouds: just a bit different from Tristopolis.

Sometimes a predatrix needs to change her hunting ground.

The Fortinium taxis were uniformly dark maroon, the colour of blood spilled in shadow, and it pleased her to ride in one like an ordinary pleb instead of hiring a limo and driver in advance.

The seat upholstery smelled clean and the driver sensed the need for silence, so Vanessa relaxed to the extent that decorum and good posture allowed.

She kept an almost idle watch through the windows: travelling past meadows of black grass at first, then wooded stretches with black iron trees, and soon enough a suburb on the outskirts of the city proper.

Here the houses shone darkly beneath the streetlamps: two- and three-storey structures clad in deep-grey chitinous material with ink-like mottling, front yards with tidy black lawns or knuckle-bone gravel gardens that were raked to perfection.

"Pull over at the next corner," she told the driver.

He nodded, entirely subdued, and obeyed her command.

Vanessa smiled, undid the twisted-serpent clasp of her purse, extracted seventeen florins, and reached over the partition with the coins. The driver turned as much as he could manage in his seat, and nodded his thanks as she dropped the coins onto his cupped palm.

At no point did the driver try to look at her face, and she hadn't even needed to lay a compulsion upon him, hence the generous tip. Reasonably generous: not truly memorable.

He won't really forget me, though.

Amnesia could be forced on anyone, easily enough; but today she saw no need for it.

This visit was low-key, without servants to open vehicle doors for her, or perform any of the duties she normally required.

Enjoying the minutiae of behaving like a pleb, she kept track of her own actions as she pressed the carved-bone handle down, pushed the door open, swivelled with her knees together – the decorum automatic – and slid out of the taxi to a standing position, then turned and closed the door.

It clunked softly, as if afraid to make a noise.

For the count of seven, she waited, wondering whether the driver would take the opportunity to slam into first gear and floor the accelerator, but no: he was far too smart, it seemed, to offend her in that way.

She nodded, turned away, and paid only superficial attention as the taxi started up and edged its way around the corner, upped the speed just a little from the sound of it, and soon enough diminished with distance and became lost to her awareness, dismissed and forgotten.

The house she needed was seventh along, on this side of the street, and there was no one to see her walking steadily to the bone-gravel front yard and pausing there, examining the dark, polished-chitin house while listening and feeling for any odd vibrations on the air.

Nothing.

No entities focussed specifically on her, though some of the neighbouring houses possessed passive hex defences and other security measures, including one detached property with a small guard-wraith in the front yard and a second wraith out back.

Everything as it should be for a neighbourhood like this.

From the sidewalk, she stared and gestured, causing the front door to click open and swing inwards: not so much an invitation as surrender, acknowledging Vanessa's ability to overwhelm the house defences with ease.

Good enough to hold off a SWAT team for a while.

Federal spellbinders would be another matter, but if the situation degraded far enough for the feds to stick their nasty noses in, then Vanessa would already have abandoned her entire Fortinium network or – more likely – killed every one of them herself before getting clear.

"Success can't always be guaranteed," Grandfather Skalix used to tell her in between beatings, "but when the alternative to failure is excruciating death, your chances improve dramatically."

That terrible old man had known what he was talking about.

She walked inside the house – her body thrumming with defensive hex that warmed the feminine core of her – enjoying her own existence in a way that most people lost as they grew out of teenage years, into sorry adulthood.

The possibility of betrayal loomed right now, perhaps requiring lethal force to fight her way clear of: one more small excitement in the ongoing adventure of her life.

The hallway stood bare, except for a skeleton clock not too dissimilar from the one in Commissioner Sandarov's office in Tristopolis.

This morning will decide the Commissioner's fate.

Sandarov's resistance to normal private persuasion formed a minor temptation – minor because she felt confident in her ability to overwhelm his objections, one way or another – but if better tactical alternatives existed, she would take them.

She entered the lounge, a dimly lit room, larger than expected, its walls coated in grey fabric that looked expensive and smelled of anti-acoustic hex

– the kind that could deaden screams quite nicely – while the floor was carpeted in some form of thick black fur.

Floating glowglobes held captive flamesprites inside, writhing to produce interesting patterns of dancing light.

The houseowners, a bland couple, stood at the back wall with their hands clasped in front of them like the servants they were, saying nothing, simply waiting to obey any commands that Vanessa might utter.

For the moment, she dismissed them from her thoughts.

The man rising from the kimodo-hide couch was another matter. His hair was slicked back and flattened with oil or hair tonic, his pale jowls were shaved clean and redolent with expensive aftershave, and his silk cravat was pinned in place with a tiny obsidian skull of a kind that Vanessa had seen before.

Its pseudo-fossilised eyes were real, and within lay a tiny, shrivelled brain, shrunk to less than a hundredth of its size in life.

A very particular kind of trophy.

I wonder which of his enemies that is.

That tiny brain remained active, powered by the living man's hex, filled with tiny thoughts that Vanessa could almost sense: an inchoate mess, dominated by suffering.

"You have good taste in personal effects." Vanessa held out her hand, palm down. "Nice to meet you again, Mayor."

"Please call me Abraham." The man took her hand – half handshake, half a sketched attempt to kiss the back of it – and released it. "I'm delighted by this chance for a tête à tête, Mrs Frisch."

"You may call me Vanessa." She smiled. "In fact, I insist on it."

And though she went by the married title, there was no Mr Frisch, and never had been.

"Thank you." Abraham Mirakov's smile flicked on and off, a little too abruptly.

It was a good sign. Not even Mirakov, perhaps the most corrupt mayor in the history of Cargotho – a windswept northern city with the kind of history that newspapers called "troubled" – ought to feel relaxed and safe in Vanessa's presence.

She sat in an armchair and waved Mirakov back to the couch.

Then she turned and looked at the couple by the rear wall. "I don't need anything. You're dismissed."

They bowed their heads, swallowed, and exited the room without a word, closing the door quietly.

Mirakov sat back, crossed his legs, and adjusted the heavy fabric of his suit trousers, centring the crease on his over-large thigh.

His appetites are the way to control him.

Fear was such a useful tool, it would be easy for Vanessa to employ it for every single purpose; but flexibility remained important.

"I expect you're wondering why I called this meeting," said Mirakov, and raised an eyebrow.

At that, Vanessa did something highly unusual for her: she tipped back her head and laughed with delight. "Thank you, Abraham. You've made my week. Maybe even my entire year."

Because of course, not a single shred of doubt existed as to who had actually decided this meeting should occur. It was a nice way for a man with his own inherent power to acknowledge Vanessa's superiority.

"We're going to get on," she added.

Between her armchair and Abraham's couch – she had decided to think of him by his first name – faint glimmers popped and sparkled in the air at her silent command.

They strengthened and grew, elongating and joining up to form a filigree cage of gold and green energy: light and fire throwing off sparks in all directions.

From within that cage came a mewling sound, the kind of suffering that always warmed Vanessa, while Abraham's half-lidded eyes and subtle licking of his lips indicated similar desires: similar but less controllable.

More like insatiable hunger than Vanessa's own exquisite sensibilities.

Useful to know.

"I can't see the creature," said Abraham. "Will we be able to?"

He seemed to understand that the daemonid's location was a distant one. Abraham might even have guessed that Vanessa was holding the daemonid captive in Tristopolis, or thereabouts.

"For now, we can only hear the thing." Vanessa gave a momentary smile, acknowledging Abraham's desire for more. "It's enough. I can direct its energies into the mesoscopic dimensions without opening a true breach in our reality."

That was close enough to the truth for tactical purposes. Redirecting her captive's energies was easier, not harder, this way; but there was no need for Abraham to know that.

"Senators have ferocious security." Abraham shrugged inside his heavy suit jacket. "I understand you know that, Vanessa. I'm just acknowledging the risks you're taking."

"That *we* are taking, surely."

"Of course." A pause. "Have you ever met Senator Fitzgerald in person?"

"I have not. Is she as smart as they say?"

"Well, I believe so. I haven't actually talked to her myself, but I was having dinner in the Cinque Saisons with some associates when the senator met up with Kristof Dahlberg and his, well, partner. Or whatever she is."

After a second, he added: "Fitzgerald didn't look like someone overwhelmed by Dahlberg's money or desperate for his support. "

"You mean Dahlberg as in Dahlberg Industries?"

"Exactly."

"Hmm." Vanessa stared into the gold-green cage of fire and light, not really seeing it. "If they're after the same thing we are, life just grew more complicated."

"The appropriation committee is meeting in nine days. I've been able to find out that much."

"Not the location?"

"Not yet," said Abraham. "I've an asset in the bureaucracy, a frustrated middle manager who doesn't understand her own inadequacies. In any area of her life."

That implied a deliberate seduction by some young man employed by Abraham – probably a young man, though weaknesses varied and all could be catered for – and Vanessa nodded, not needing to hear details.

"And she's definitely in the loop for the final arrangements, this asset?"

Abraham nodded. "Definitely."

He didn't show any desire to elaborate, and after a moment Vanessa decided to trust in his confidence and competence.

"If the vote goes in Dahlberg's favour," she said, "then I'm afraid the gentleman might meet an accident."

Abraham raised a slick eyebrow. "The authorities might be suspicious if something odd just happens to occur right when his industrial-scale projects – pilot projects, yes, but big ones – get the go-ahead."

"Indeed," said Vanessa.

He was right, and it gave her an idea: Dahlberg's demise, should it prove necessary, needn't be subtle at all. Something spectacular would do the trick nicely, while her own bid for the contracts, if she went ahead with those particular plans, lay months in the future.

If the police suspected corporate rivals, well, good... Right now, she wasn't one of them.

Not yet.

"I'm going to say something," said Abraham, "but I'm not fishing for details, or any response at all. I just want you to understand my thinking."

"Alright. Go ahead."

"In your position" – Abraham closed his eyes, slowly and deliberately, and kept them that way – "I'd want more than one contact on the committee, just in case."

Vanessa allowed no expression to show on her face, despite Abraham's closed eyes. For one thing, the shrunken-head pin on Abraham's cravat still faced her, and Abraham might be capable of interrogating the small head's memory afterwards.

Those tiny pseudo-fossilised eyes might still be able to see, after a fashion.

Tactically, Abraham was correct in his assessment: observing Senator

Anna Fitzgerald was key to Vanessa's plans, but Vanessa hadn't actually attempted to suborn the woman, not yet.

But she did have another committee member under her control.

After a second, she said: "Fair enough. Open your eyes, my friend."

Abraham did so, and gave a tiny nod. "And the great thing is, I'm still alive."

Vanessa laughed, just a little. "You are, and I'm glad of it."

For one thing, when the time came to build experimental reactor piles that made use of crawlspace-dimensional phenomena in addition to the usual techniques, the probability of catastrophic detonations was non-negligible, no matter what the risk assessment reports would say.

She wanted the main, phase-two installations near Tristopolis, but not the risky early ones. Building those initial installations in Cargotho – a considerable distance from both Inversion Tower, her home outside Tristopolis, and Fortinium as the capital of the political system she wanted to make use of, not destroy – would be a smart move.

The glowing cage between her and Abraham fell silent. Her daemonid captive at the far end of the link – a link maintained by tapping the daemonid's own energies – no longer mewled with pain or growled in anger.

"Problem?" said Abraham.

"No." Vanessa could sense distant resonances that had nothing to do with sound, and they felt diminished but steady: her captive remained alive. "In human terms, you could say our prisoner just passed out. Nothing worse than that."

Abraham took in a deep breath, his nostrils dilating as if pulling in a scent; and perhaps he could, at that, sense some of the captive's suffering.

Vanessa's opinion of Abraham's abilities increased another notch.

He's gluttonous for pain, but could he be the one?

Planning for the really long term included arrangements for succession, and a daughter of her own was on the cards for next year or the year after, and a certain male input was required, though any kind of partnership or actual marriage remained a low-probability feature of that future.

Low probability, but greater than zero.

Vanessa spread her hands wide, then brought them slowly together, causing the gold-and-green framework of light to reduce in size to match. At the end, she slammed her palms together, and the framework winked out.

At the far end of the terminated link, her captive would be able to recuperate while unconscious. Enough to survive the next round of interrogation, at least.

She looked at the rear door of the room here, and the glowglobes' light grew more agitated as the captive sprites writhed harder.

"Your picture has been in the papers from time to time." Vanessa spoke without looking at Abraham. "There's a possibility that our caretaker couple will have recognised you."

"Is that a problem? They didn't look like people able to prevent an amnesia conjuration."

"Agreed. My people have used this safe house a few times, though it's my first visit here in person. It might prove useful to keep it for future use."

"The house," said Abraham, "but maybe not the staff?"

"One has to be careful to manage morale within one's organisation, but individuals on the fringes tend to lack resources and connections."

Abraham licked his lips. "You mean the caretakers, the man and the woman out back, are potentially disposable?"

"They are." Vanessa thought carefully as she made the suggestion. "A shared experience, Abraham. A private pleasure for two friends – two extremely close friends – to share."

After sucking in a breath and exhaling, Abraham swallowed and did something few men were capable of: he looked her straight in the eyes as he answered, "It would be my privilege and my honour, Vanessa."

"Good." She allowed intimacy and satisfaction to surface in her tone and expression.

"And disposal afterwards? Just thinking about the practicalities."

Vanessa stared at the spot where the cage of light and fire had been, and caused a single golden spark to appear and disappear, just that and nothing more. For now.

"My prisoner will be famished when he wakes up." She gave a smile that would have caused most men to shudder. "He won't be too fussy regarding what I send his way to eat."

The link could be used to transport matter, more easily done when keeping that matter alive had ceased to be a consideration.

"Ideal." Abraham's smile mirrored hers. "Quite perfect."

There would be blood spatters and perhaps some ruined furniture, but nothing beyond her power to remove with some concentrated hex and deliberate focus.

Vanessa turned to the door at the rear of the lounge, raised a finger, and sent a summoning hex, designed to manifest as words inside the couple's brains, as if murmured in their ears.

Come to me, both of you.

Kimodo hide squeaked as Abraham shifted on the couch, anticipating the pleasures to come, licking his lips once more.

This was going to be intense.

NINE

When Donal asked Mel about her family and her childhood in Illurium, she told him that her childhood was a happy one. "Really. My mom died the month after I left school, and Pop went a year later out of grief, but they gave me all the love and support I needed to reach adulthood, so I can't complain."

They'd talked a little about her background before, but this was the first time Donal had framed the discussion in terms of happiness.

Mel was sitting up in bed with Finbar, happily fed, sleeping in her arms, while Donal sat on top of the covers beside them, his shoes off, and legs stretched out. "Any witchy or mage stuff in the family tree?"

He touched Finbar's tiny nose with total gentleness.

"Not my parents." Mel smiled with a gentle radiance. "They were brilliant, and Mom's side of the family were great. Standard human all the way back, as far as anybody knew, but they wouldn't have cared either way."

"And your dad?"

"Pop left home when he was fourteen and never talked about it much, about any of his background, except to say that Mom and her folks saved him. But there were hints…"

The soft blue light linking Mel's eyes to baby Finbar's, even though Finbar's eyes were shut – so fragile-looking, a newborn's skin – shone dimly once more: a phenomenon that seemed to come and go at random.

"Ingrid says that this" – Mel waved her hand through the twin streamers of blue light without affecting them – "will fade with time, probably in the next few weeks. A handful of months at most."

"And has she explained what it's all about?"

"Come off it, Donal. You know she hasn't."

"Yeah." He raised an eyebrow to show he wasn't serious. "I could always tie Witch Ingrid Johannsdóttir to a chair and interrogate her the old-fashioned way."

"Uh-huh. Sure you could, if she let you. Thing is, I've always known that I was a little different. But only a little bit."

Careful not to disturb the baby, Donal shifted around until he was on hands and knees atop the bed, then kissed Mel's pug nose, very carefully, followed by each of her still-pointed ears in turn.

"Not different enough for it show," he murmured. "Not before now. Even with a close examination."

"And you should know, dear."

"I certainly should."

Mel sighed and leaned back deeper into the pillows supporting her. "It's not serious, whatever our little thing here" – she gestured at the blue streamers of light as they faded out, gone for now – "is all about."

Donal looked at her, while in his mind's eye a tendril rose up from the gym floor once more, and some other strange being shrank away in a trap of floating fire produced by Hellah, the most fierce person he had ever met.

"Not serious." He echoed Mel's words but not her tone. "Right."

"We'd have a cartload of mages here if it was something significant. They'd have me and Finbar in the maternity wing of Mordanto, don't you think?"

"Does Mordanto *have* a maternity wing?"

"Hades, Donal, I don't know. You're the Tristopolitan born and bred. I'm just saying."

"Well, okay."

The door to the bedroom was shut, but the too-young-looking Ludka was sitting outside, reading one of Donal's old paperbacks – she seemed to have taken a liking to the *Humans* series – temporarily in possession of Ingrid's amulet, the one that could summon both Hellah and Mage Kelvin or his friends if needed.

Ludka was a young apprentice but able to call on powerful forces for help. If Donal thought about it tactically, the implication was a low probability of further danger, although any danger that did occur was likely to be major, hence the amulet for calling in serious reinforcements.

All of this in Hellah's estimation, while Ingrid clearly concurred. The Guardian and the witch in total agreement.

Wonderful.

"You don't like being dependent on others," said Mel. "That's all."

"Thanatos' blood."

"Language." Mel shifted Finbar a little in her arms. "He's at an impressionable age."

"Me too." Donal kissed her on the mouth, then baby Finbar on the forehead.

"Ha. Maybe Daddy should go and get some work done."

"Maybe I should."

There was nothing in his case load. The events below Dredgeway Avenue cried out for investigation, and he was definitely going to poke his nose in later, but there was that little matter of being paid for his time.

That wasn't going to happen on the Dredgeway thing.

"Go on. We'll be fine here."

"I'll send Ludka in to keep you company."

"We don't need... Sure. Whatever keeps you happy."

"Right." He kissed her again, then slid off the bed.

He pulled on his shoes, tied them with double knots as always, did up his tie and straightened it, grabbed his suit jacket from the back of a chair and his shoulder-holster harness and Magnus from their hook.

"See you in a bit, Daddy." Mel moved sleeping Finbar's tiny hand up and down as if waving see-you-later.

"You too."

He went out, smiled at Ludka while scarcely seeing her, and strode into the gym proper, where he could drape his jacket over one of the ropes of the boxing heptagon, allowing him to slip on his gun rig and check the feel of it, shrugging it into perfect position.

The bedroom door clicked shut as Ludka took up guard inside, taking her duties seriously.

Good enough.

Donal pulled on his jacket, fastened one button, and looked around. It was empty, and as clean as it ever got, since he'd swept the floor earlier.

The youngest boxers would come in later, then the adults. The latter could look after themselves, and three of them had volunteered to turn up early and coach the kids, and generally watch out for them. It felt like the start of a community, but that wasn't where Donal's professional talents lay.

"Right." He checked in his pocket, and decided that he had enough change for the callbox. "Let's get to work."

Outside, the street was dark as always, deserted as usual. He checked the environment, taking extra care, sensing nothing untoward. No sign of danger; not even a hint of subliminal twitchiness.

Does parenthood cause paranoia?

He supposed it did, in a way. His upbringing in the orphanage hadn't provided much in the way of relevant guidance, but so what? He would just have to figure it out, one step at a time.

Reaching the callbox, he pulled the door open and checked inside, but he sensed no hex traps or urine smells – you never knew – or anything remotely untoward. Maintaining full alertness might prove tiring, but for the time being, hyper vigilance was the name of the game.

He plucked the handset from its cradle, shovelled coins into the slot, and spun the cogs to the number of his answering service.

"Riordan Investigations," came the matronly voice. "How can we help you today?"

"Riordan here."

"One moment." The line hummed. Verification hex could take a few seconds. "You have only message, sir."

"Come on, Deirdre. You really can call me Donal."

"I'm not sure that's proper."

"Well Hades, Deirdre. Maybe I'm not proper."

A wheezy chuckle sounded. "You're a cheeky young man, is what I think."

Donal grinned. Maybe there was a protocol that governed how clients were supposed to speak to their answering-service person, but no one ever taught it at the orphanage.

"I'm from Lower Danklyn," he said. "Maybe I should've told you that before."

"Well, I don't suppose you can help it." Some of the refinement dropped away from Deirdre's voice. "I'm a Deeper girl myself, way back in the day."

"Never."

"You can take the girl out of the neighbourhood…"

Danklyn Depths was the next neighbourhood along, if you were headed east.

"So when did you…" Beeps sounded. "Sorry."

Donal shovelled in more coins.

"You're in a callbox." Deirdre's voice grew brisker. "Let me give you the message."

"Alright then."

"The gentleman – and I'd say he *is* a gentleman, Donal – didn't want to leave his name, but did say you'd recognise him if you met in a public place."

"Because he's famous, or because I know him personally?"

"I have absolutely no idea. He suggested meeting at a Fat'n'Sugar, and the thought of doughnuts made it hard for me to concentrate, but I managed to take a note of the address all the same."

Donal had never met Deirdre in person, but he could picture someone fond of cakes and chocolates and the like. "Okay…"

"It's 1701 Scaleway Drag, corner of Scaleway and Mawmouth."

"I don't think I've ever been in that one," said Donal.

"I expect it's the same as all the rest."

"Probably. No mention of what this guy – sorry, gentleman – wanted to talk about?"

"He kind of implied it was for a job. He wanted to sound you out for something, is what he actually said."

"Well, okay. That's good."

"We're here to help, sir."

Donal grinned. The *we* referred to Deirdre and no one else: hers was a one-person business, the same as his.

"Thank you very much, ma'am."

"Take it easy, Donal."

"You too, Deeper Girl."

He tapped the cradle to break the connection, smiled and replaced the handset.

A paying job, with luck.

Plus a chance to buy some doughnuts for Mel, and maybe for Deirdre too, if this Fat'n'Sugar delivered. Some did, some didn't.

Time to focus on business.

The Dredgeway Avenue affair would have to wait.

TEN

Scaleway Drag hovered between griminess and thriving commercialism, a mix of discount furniture stores and upmarket antique shops, of greasy-spoon diners and well-appointed Surinese restaurants. Bookstores catering to the literati rubbed shoulders with pokey specialist shops where the customers left with books and magazines carefully wrapped in plain wormskin bags so the titles wouldn't show.

Standing on the busy sidewalk and scanning the passers-by, Donal felt right at home. Perhaps that wasn't a good thing, but never mind.

I can read and I can fight.

What more could a Danklyn boy hope for?

But this was a time for watching, not thinking…

A municipal scanbat slid past overhead, a grey shadow against the deep purple sky, moving in silence.

Staring up at the scanbat, Donal almost missed the arrival of a purple taxi on the far side of the road, diagonally opposite the Fat'n'Sugar where he was supposed to meet his prospective client. Donal had turned up early and checked out the interior of the doughnut shop: nothing to worry about.

He'd bought a take-out cup of coffee, more from old redblood-days habit than any particular need for caffeine, and sipped from it now. The dregs, barely lukewarm by this time, tasted surprisingly weak.

"Bleeding Hades," he said aloud, causing a passing grey-haired lady to glance at him, hitch her wicker shopping-basket – it was ringed with woven good-luck runes – and shake her head without breaking step.

Across the street, the taxi's passenger had disembarked, and was smoothing down his overcoat and checking the briefcase in his left hand. He turned to cross the road as the taxi moved off.

But Donal had already recognised him, even before he fully showed his face.

Why would Commissioner Sandarov want to meet me in private?

Donal moved into a shoe shop doorway for cover, listening out for anyone exiting from the shop behind him, while keeping his visual attention on the Commissioner across the way.

Commissioner Sandarov waited like any other dutiful citizen for the traffic lights to turn red and the crossing-signal sprites to burn blue before making his way to this side of the street, glancing to left and right – Donal shifted out of sight just in time – and entering the Fat'n'Sugar.

The old Commissioner, Vilnar, had never forgotten his street-cop roots and skills. People spoke highly of this Sandarov – people whom Donal trusted – but situational awareness didn't seem to be his strength.

Donal scanned the environment once more, not just for movement at street level, but for the glint of reflected streetlights on binocular lenses behind an upper-storey window, or the faint translucence of an insubstantial wraith moving through walls.

Nothing.

He could rule out a mobile team following Sandarov, unless they used a whole bunch of coordinated radio cars as well as tags on foot, but static surveillance remained a possibility: Sandarov might have already stepped into a setup, even though the Fat'n'Sugar had seemed okay when Donal went in earlier.

This bore the hallmarks of subterfuge: an off-the-books meeting between the serving police commissioner and an ex-cop investigator, which implied a task that needed to be carried out in secret.

Is Sandarov as honest as they say he is?

Donal sniffed in sooty air, and exhaled.

Let's find out.

He moved out of the doorway, discarded his cup in a bin attached to a streetlamp, and headed for the Fat'n'Sugar entranceway.

The chitin-topped counter ran along the left-hand wall. Sandarov had taken a table near the back right-hand corner of the place, with a drink-in cup already on the tabletop. His expression looked tight, perhaps because he wasn't used to the bustle of a Fat'n'Sugar.

"Three black coffees and five termite-jelly doughnuts to go as usual, dearie?" came from the large scaley woman behind the counter. Her apron practically fluoresced, a hideous shade of green that any Fat'n'Sugar regular would recognise immediately.

A small wizened man, almost drowning in an over-large overcoat, moved to the head of the queue. "Same as always, Betty. How's your sciatica?"

"About the same as yours, I shouldn't wonder."

Maybe it wasn't the environment making Sandarov tense. He must be feeling the weight of two years in office as Commissioner, and Thanatos-knew-how-many more to come. Sitting behind a desk all day sounded like ease and luxury to a junior officer out on the beat, but Donal had interacted with Commissioner Vilnar enough to pick up on the stress and difficulties involved.

It didn't take long for Donal to reach the head of the queue. "Two scarab creams and a small black coffee, please."

He slid a nine-sided third-florin across the counter, received two farthings in change – you could say what you liked about Fat'n'Sugar, but at least they were cheap – and carried his serviette-wrapped doughnuts and coffee across to Sandarov's table, and sat down.

Donal pushed one of the doughnuts over to Sandarov. "They're good. Try it."

"Maisie will kill me for eating it." Sandarov picked up the doughnut and bit in. Cream squidged out but didn't drop.

"Your wife? Perhaps you shouldn't tell her, then."

"There's confidential stuff from work that I'm not able to talk about. Doughnuts aren't exactly in that category."

Donal nodded, took a sip of coffee – a lot hotter than the one he'd discarded outside – and made a quick judgement: so far, he liked the man.

"You're looking for me to carry out an investigation for you?"

Sandarov gestured with the doughnut, then laid it down, careful to keep it on the serviette, although the tabletop was pretty clean by the standards of your average Fat'n'Sugar. "Commissioner Vilnar rated you highly."

"More than he ever said to me." Although Donal had heard the same thing, also at second hand, from Mage Lamis: a sort-of friend he hadn't seen for months.

"From what I knew of Vilnar, he wouldn't." Sandarov's mouth twitched, not quite smiling. "The entries in his old office journals are pretty eloquent, some of them. I found them after I asked some serving officers about you."

"Ones who've never met me, I hope."

Sandarov shook his head, dismissing that line of conversation. "I need a seasoned investigator who understands how the world works, and the more politically savvy, the better."

"I don't like to turn down business, but I'm no politician."

"But you're honest and if things get tough, you'll deal with them."

Donal raised an eyebrow, an even more deliberate act than in his redblood days. "Interesting that you mention honesty. Why me, when you've so many people you can assign the job to? Why work off the books?"

The clamour of the Fat'n'Sugar rose even higher, but Donal held back from explicitly pointing out that Sandarov was the police commissioner: the words might drop into a random silent moment, and there was no need for that.

"Because I don't want to spend the Department's money on work that safeguards my career and achieves nothing else, when there's so much actual policing to be done."

"Oh," said Donal. "I hadn't thought of that."

"So how do you charge, weekly or daily? And what's your rate?"

Donal told him.

"Okay." Sandarov nodded twice. "I'll write you out a cheque for the first nine days."

He started to reach inside his overcoat, but Donal raised a hand.

"You haven't actually said what the job is. And I haven't actually said yes."

"Oh, right. Hades." Sandarov leaned back, and the stress lines on his face evaporated for the moment. His mouth twitched again. "That minor detail."

"So…"

"So someone in the Department arranged for an unnamed senior officer to fly in from Fortinium, and to meet with City Hall officials who invested municipal funds, sizeable funds, in Bloodfist Bank. And Bloodfist has a reputation for handing out kickbacks in such circumstances."

"You think they want to oust you from office, these officials? Replace you with someone they control?"

"I do," said Sandarov. "And I also received a visit from a rather scary lady called Mrs Vanessa Frisch, who more than hinted that she could help me hang onto my job. No, more than that: advance it to a point where I could run for Senate."

Donal lowered his voice to a mutter, just enough for Sandarov to hear, and no one else. "And you want to become a senator?"

"No, I do not. And when I rejected the Frisch woman's offer, she gave the impression of… Well, not of giving up, but deciding on some other course of action."

"So she might be involved with the City Hall people, or she might not. Is that what you're saying?"

"It's not much of a starting point, but I've made some notes of details." It was like a mage's trick: the envelope that Sandarov drew from inside his overcoat looked too large to have fitted in an inner pocket. But it was simply good tailoring, nothing spooky. "Here you are."

He slid the envelope across the table, and Donal laid his hand on it.

"Sounds okay," said Donal. "Anything else I need to know?"

It occurred to him that Sandarov hadn't even glanced at his briefcase, which would have been the obvious place to carry sensitive paper, therefore the first thing a thief might target. Perhaps Sandarov's security awareness wasn't all that shoddy after all.

The briefcase served as a pretty decent decoy.

"Whether this is one, well, conspiracy, or two separate ones, either way it seems like people want me out of here." Sandarov wasn't referring to the Fat'nSugar. "I'm trying to work out if that's because of any particular initiative I've started, rather than my overall approach. So far, I can't figure it."

"So, it's a question of whose interests you're working against," said Donal.

At the start of an investigation, sometimes you held a scattering of random facts and nothing more; other times you could see a way in. But it wasn't always the right way.

"Well, maybe. If it was only business as normal, I wouldn't worry so much. But weird things have happened over the last few years, and I'm feeling a kind of general twitchiness."

Donal kept silent. He understood the importance of intuition.

And the serving police commissioner had access to all sorts of classified archives and the like. He'd be able to compare current happenings with previous decades in ways not open to the general public, and perhaps not even dedicated scholars.

"The City Council members," said Donal after a moment. "You know which ones, specifically?"

Sandarov glanced down at the envelope. "Some of them, I think. I've made a note of what I know and what I'm guessing, next to each name."

"That's good. You said something about flights being arranged by people inside the Department?"

"I've someone who can follow a paper trail and navigate bureaucracy. I don't want to use him more than I have already. Not unless it's necessary."

"Because of trust?" said Donal.

"I trust him, alright. But the city pays his salary, and mine. I'd prefer to use him further only if there's actual criminality involved."

"And Internal Security?"

"Same answer. Office politics are business as usual, not criminal activity. Unless I've got really strong grounds for suspecting that someone's crossed the line, I don't want the ISD on their case."

"Okay. Good." Donal took a bite of his scarab cream doughnut, his first food in four days. "Mm."

Sandarov was looking thoughtful. "You're not quite what I expected, Mr Riordan."

"I'm taller than I look."

"You remind me of a parish priest I knew, way back."

Donal put down the doughnut. "You have got to be kidding me."

"Nothing ever fazed him. I once saw him face down a mob of drunken strangers intending to beat the Hades out of some innocents. All on the basis of mistaken identity, though the details only came out later."

"Well, okay." That didn't sound so bad.

"Empathic and spiritual, but tough," said Sandarov. "Seeing him stand up to danger that way was one of the things that made me become a cop after graduating."

Not graduating from an orphanage school: that was for sure.

At the rear of the shop, behind the counter, a door cracked open.

Here we go.

"Do me a favour," said Donal. "When I say drop, drop to the floor and stay there."

A civilian might have said *what?* But Sandarov just gave a silent nod.

Only a vertical slit of darkness showed in the doorway. Donal inhaled, exhaled, and kept his lungs empty.

Watching.

Then a gun barrel poked through the opening and Donal flowed out of his seat and threw himself sideways onto the countertop, rolled across and dropped, hooking his left hand over the gunman's forearm and pulling close to his body as he descended, reached under and across with his right hand and ripped the weapon free…

"Ow!"

…even as the boyish features and stature and weakness of muscle became obvious, and the barrel that Donal grasped felt like painted wood, while the entire weapon weighed so little it could only be a toy, no matter how realistic the colouring.

The "gunman" was just a boy, wearing a dark striped t-shirt and baggy shorts.

"Hades," said Donal. "Sorry, kid."

Something hit him on the back of the head. When he turned, the large lady in the near-fluorescent apron had her hand raised, ready to smack him another good one.

"No," he said.

The woman dropped her scaley hand. "You didn't need to hurt my nephew."

Donal looked at the boy. "Just playing, were you?"

The boy nodded, rubbing his hand, though the damage wouldn't be severe, not with such a loose grip on a lightweight toy. A real handgun might leave broken fingers if you levered it away just right.

"You might want to paint the gun a different colour, or wrap some bright tape around it, especially the barrel." He handed the toy to the woman. "Something that makes it obvious there isn't any threat."

He looked across the counter, and what he saw impressed him.

"Not bad," he added.

Sandarov hadn't dived for the floor, but instead leapt to put himself between the threat and a shocked woman with two children sitting at the next table. If there'd been firing, he'd have taken the bullets in his unprotected chest.

"Sorry, mister," said the boy next to Donal.

"No harm done, kid." Donal squatted to his level, undid his jacket, and tapped his Magnus in its shoulder holster, causing the boy's eyes to widen.

"Wow."

"Practising with them can be fun, but the real things are serious."

No need to be too explicit.

"Okay."

That was when he noticed the bruising on the boy's left cheek, and a larger faded patch on his leg. Donal rose slowly and swivelled to look at the counterwoman once more.

Not me, she mouthed.

Donal's mouth tightened, and he nodded.

"I don't suppose," he said, "that you live in Lower Danklyn."

The woman frowned. "Close enough."

"Alright." Donal turned back to the boy. "What's your name, kid? I'm Donal."

"Rupert, sir."

Not a name anyone should inflict on a kid, not if they lived close to Lower Danklyn.

"You like sports, Rupert?"

Rupert shook his head.

"He reads," said his aunt, the counterwoman. "A lot. All the time."

"A fellow bookworm. Me too."

Donal held out his fist, and after a second, Rupert formed a sort of fist of his own, and they bumped knuckles.

When Donal looked in Rupert's eyes, the kid looked back with a clear, intelligent gaze. Donal nodded, then straightened up and reached inside his jacket for a business card, turned it upside down on the countertop, and pulled out his fountain pen.

"I'm Donal Riordan," he told the aunt. "The printed stuff on the other side of the card, that's my actual business, but *this* place is run by my... well, my much better half."

He unscrewed the pen and wrote *Mel's Boxing Gym*, just to make it clear what kind of place it was – the official name being simply Mel's Gym – along with the address. Then he pocketed the pen and waved the card gently until the ink had pretty much dried, and placed it near the woman.

"If you take Rupert along any evening," he said, "someone will show him the ropes, literally, plus the punch bags and everything else."

"My name's Betty, and I think maybe you mean well, but we can't afford anything like that."

"Not a concern," said Donal. "Really."

Nobody paid a penny to train, if they or their family weren't earning enough. Betty looked at him for a long hard moment, then gave a strong nod.

"Just do me one favour," she said.

"Sure."

"Use the hatch to go join your friend, instead of rolling all over my nice clean counter."

"I can manage that," he told her.

Sandarov was already seated back at their original table, with his cheque book in front of him and a mother-of-pearl fountain pen in his hand. It looked classier than Donal's pen by far.

What mattered was that Donal had a case to work on. Purpose and obligation: what more could a man want?

"I'm glad you came in today," said Betty, wiping her hands on her sickly green apron.

"Me too," said Donal.

And he meant it.

ELEVEN

Senator Anna Fitzgerald had zero sense of walking into a trap.

Maybe it was the plushness of the limousine that Dahlberg Industries had provided to fetch her here, and the politeness of the valet who'd opened the door for her, and the impressive marble steps and floating flamewraiths – not sprites, but actual wraiths manifesting fire, exceedingly rare – leading up to a classical building reminiscent of a Greater Rohpan palace.

Or maybe, she reflected as she took her time ascending the steps, it was the small understated brooch pinned to her lapel – and the sure knowledge that Jean-Marc, meaning Federal Agent Bouchard, could use the brooch's amber heart as a conduit, allowing him to see and hear what she did – that gave her comfort as she walked up the steps.

More practically, she felt glad she was wearing sensible heels.

"Welcome to the Holdex Club, Senator."

A white-gloved butler led her to one of the club's drawing-rooms, where Kristof Dahlberg and Eva Kaldini were waiting for her, sitting in wing-backed armchairs formed from the stuffed, transmogrified corpses of giant Surinese bats (or Zurinese if you'd undergone an old-fashioned classical education, which Anna had, but partly rebelled against).

In either case, the bats were the kind that fed on mountain bears, therefore huge. Three such bat-form armchairs ringed the low table, one chair clearly meant for Anna.

Dahlberg rose from his chair to shake Anna's hand, while the Kaldini woman remained seated to offer her hand in turn, which Anna shook also.

All very correct and business-like. Whether that also meant above board, well, that was something Anna – and Jean-Marc, watching and listening from a black government-issue Coronet saloon parked around the block – intended to find out.

Dahlberg suggested a gin and tonic before eating, and gestured to the glasses already on the table. He and Kaldini were drinking something clear with bubbles, but Anna suspected an absence of alcohol, because this was a time for keeping heads clear and eyes sharp.

"I'll have a mineral water, thanks," she said, taking her place on the old but comfortable armchair.

The butler gestured to a maid, who dipped her knee in a quarter-curtsy and headed for a bar. Dahlberg gestured with his forefinger, not pointing anywhere in particular, and the butler took it as a signal, bowing from the neck before heading back out.

"Formality and subservience." Anna perched straight-backed on the armchair and looked directly at Dahlberg. "Twin cages of abstraction that shield us from the real-world consequences of our processes and manoeuvrings, obscuring the simple *qualia* of goodness-as-instinctive-perception."

Dahlberg smiled. "Quoting Lord Storer-Martin this early in the day? But then, we all need philosophy to keep our heads straight, especially in confusing times."

Eva Kaldini's mouth twitched, perhaps in appreciation of someone who could play Dahlberg at his own intellectual game.

"I like smart fantasy myself," she said, "when I need to forget the world, or even make sense of it. I don't suppose either of you has read *Humans: the Resurgence?*"

Dahlberg sighed, an apparently natural reaction – so much of their previous interactions had felt rehearsed – and for the first time, Anna felt some real warmth for both of them.

The maid appeared with Anna's drink on a silver tray bordered with a twisted Ouroboros shape – reflecting the club's insignia, and its historic link to the original Society of Bone Artificers that give rise to the modern Energy Authority on which the whole Federation depended.

With another quarter-curtsy after putting down the drink, the maid backed off and departed without a sound. Anna watched her go.

That nameless maid was a real person, with ancestors and a future and a personal universe no less important than anyone else's. To depersonalise her – or anyone – was a fast way to lose your soul.

Anna focussed on Dahlberg.

"I'm thinking of retiring." She said it without thought, acting on instinct more than logic. "Not immediately, but I wanted you both to know that I might not wait until the end of my term before leaving office."

Too bad the link with Jean-Marc went only one way. Had he sucked in a breath and felt his heart beat faster when she said those words?

She really hoped so.

Or maybe he'd crossed his fingers and made the Sign of the Axe, praying that she wasn't about to screw up his investigation before it got started.

"Does that mean," said Kaldini, "that you want a last big win to make your mark before you go?"

She'd pitched the middle part of that question – *you want a last big win* – as a subtle command, which caused Anna to smile in appreciation, for they were all professional persuaders here, all three of them.

Although Jean-Marc, alias Federal Agent Bouchard on the other end of the quantal link to Anna's brooch, was surely more proficient than any of them, even Dahlberg.

"I hadn't really thought about it," Anna told Kaldini. "Not that way. I was hoping to celebrate my modest accomplishments so far, not add to them."

It was important not to seem too malleable or desperate. And that felt easy, because it was true.

I'd walk away right now, if it wasn't for Jean-Marc.

She wasn't foolish. She and Jean-Marc had only just met, and there were distinct stages to any sane relationship, an ascending ladder of trust along with increasing intimacy; but on the other hand, they weren't exactly youngsters: time felt too precious to waste.

"You're on the appropriation committee for portal-reactor research." Dahlberg just came out with it, as though he too had been mulling on the value of ever-diminishing time.

"And we're going to be considering all our options," answered Anna, "when it comes to allocating federal funds to contractors, especially for R&D with low prospects for any return at all."

"But a heads-up on the contents of your Requests For Tender" – Kaldini leaned forward in her chair – "would be in everybody's interests."

"You think we're going to produce multiple RFTs? How so?" Anna tried to sound blunt rather than furious, but there was no way Kaldini should even suspect that much.

They've got their hooks into someone else already.

Maybe not a committee member; but if not, then someone's aide or assistant: still beyond the bounds of acceptable behaviour.

"We know the field," said Dahlberg. "Certainly our research mages are among the best. They assure us that there are multiple avenues of approach to adding portals to reactor piles. New approaches, suggested by deep analysis of last year's events."

From everything Anna had read – summaries by experts being the best she could manage – the crawlspace dimensions had produced resonances in the ordinary world that hinted of effects that might exist and *might* be made use of in energy production.

Anna didn't know much about the deep theories formulated by mages, but she knew her history well enough: where civilian engineering went, military applications followed. Or led the way.

Dahlberg added, "Our folk also reckon that, whichever experts the federal government has talked to, they'll have formed the same conclusion."

"That hardly rules out an umbrella project doled out across many contractors." Anna shrugged, then sipped from her mineral water. "Either way, it's early stages."

Dahlberg and Kaldini tried not to look at each other, or at least that was the way Anna read their body language. She had the feeling that they knew better, that they understood exactly how far along the deliberations were.

"Surely an umbrella *programme*, comprising multiple projects, is the most likely outcome for the committee's recommendations." Dahlberg sounded relaxed once more, and his eyes twinkled in a way that Anna read as genuine.

He's enjoying this.

It was a game he felt at home with, clearly.

"Federal law enforcement," said Kaldini, "referred to the thing that manifested in Tristopolis seven months ago as the Void Threat. It's quite an evocative term."

"Indeed. I'm no expert," said Anna, "but from what I've read, no new fundamental principles were involved." She looked around, hoping there might be some device like an elevator or one of those rising trays in a shaft connected to a basement kitchen – dumb waiter, that was it – or any other artefact that might be powered by an indentured wraith.

She saw nothing to point at as an example, but continued anyway: "No different in principle from any wraith rotating part of its body mass out of the crawlspace dimensions."

"Engineering can produce new, fundamental understanding," said Dahlberg. "It's not always a case of theory first and application afterwards. Nothing so neat. The whole field of thaumadynamics evolved from existing hex transfer techniques. Practical processes."

"So I believe," said Anna, and stopped there, giving Dahlberg nothing to grab onto.

"If we can reach one of these voids and really tap into its energy…" Kaldini left the words dangling.

Anna tilted her head. "What kind of energy, and why would that be possible? How can that be easier than, say, travelling to the planet Oberon, or even some distant star in our macroscopic dimensions? Speaking of fantasies, and meaning no disrespect."

Kaldini's cheeks grew pink.

But Dahlberg's smile looked gentle. "Because the Void Threat came here all by itself. There must be some kind of navigable connection, or it could never have reached our world."

"You have a point," Anna told him. "But 'energy' is a pretty woolly term in everyday conversation, to such an extent that mages and witches smirk when you use it wrongly. You must have noticed, if you've actually been talking to your researchers."

She meant that none of this weirdness – talk of resonances and all the rest – implied the definite existence of useful energy sources; and she was pretty sure that Dahlberg understood that much.

"Our researchers are far too polite to make fun of us." Dahlberg still sounded gentle, certainly unfazed. "But I've had a reasonably technical education myself, so I know exactly what you're getting at."

"And you still think there's something in this new-source-of-energy idea? Even when the equations are supposed be insoluble?"

An article in the *Fortinium Times* had used the word "intractable", which Anna took to mean the same thing.

"I do," said Dahlberg. "Don't you?"

Anna shook her head.

It was a shame that her connection to Jean-Marc, via the brooch, went only one way. She couldn't tell which possible response made more tactical sense – in terms of drawing out Dahlberg and Kaldini to the point where their suggestions actually broke federal or perhaps international law – so she settled for speaking the literal truth as she saw it.

"I really don't think so," she said. "Not that part of it."

"So your reticence is natural." Dahlberg lowered his chin in a way that might indicate respect or a fighter protecting his vulnerable throat. "If this is a defence matter, then be assured that we know how to cordon off intellectual property among our companies."

So Dahlberg *had* thought of the implications for arms manufacturing.

Well, of course he had.

"We can ensure," said Kaldini, spelling it out, "that any knowledge which ought to remain in the Federation does so."

"I understand," said Anna.

They'd talked about it in committee, the notion of weapons research, but the overall tone had felt dismissive, and Anna wondered if her own thoughts had been swept along by the current of the group, for if Dahlberg Industries were making a pitch from this angle, they had to be taking it seriously.

Kaldini said: "We have no knowledge of your military assessment reports, but we do have analysts of our own, and of course we've existing contracts with the Rohpan Alliance premier research agency."

Anna said nothing.

Maybe it's beyond my pay grade.

But if not hers, then whose? Whatever she did, she would remain a tiny part of some huge enterprise far greater than any of the individuals involved, even stand-out business leaders like Kristof Dahlberg or the most senior members of government.

"If you're thinking of leaving government," said Dahlberg, "then I presume you'd not be averse to some corporate appointments? Directorships that need not take much of your time, unless you genuinely want to get more involved."

"Tell me more." Anna hoped that Jean-Marc was seeing and hearing everything.

Kaldini looked about to speak, but Dahlberg answered first: "Details later, in the light of your news about your career intentions."

Anna nodded, aware that Jean-Marc needed far more specific evidence than this.

"But you'll need to set up a schedule," she said, "so that the offer is in place before I vote. Maybe we can meet—"

"You misunderstand." Dahlberg's voice was pitched low and steady, an exemplar of sincerity. "My offer is not contingent on the way you vote when the tenders come in, or on whether you're able to provide any hints in advance regarding the RFTs. I mean before the tenders go out."

"It isn't?"

"Senator Fitzgerald, I mean it. Your expertise would be invaluable. The reason I'd like to nail down specifics regarding directorships in advance would be to guarantee just that: so you *don't* have to wait to find out. It's not, absolutely *not* a question of your getting more if you vote in our favour."

"Still, there's an expectation of goodwill," said Anna. "Such an offer would predispose me to find in your favour."

"True enough, but that's as far as I – as we, Dahlberg Industries – are prepared to go in terms of lobbying. I have my own boundaries, Senator, and so do the companies I head."

Anna let out a long breath, and shifted back in the tall bat-chair, and deliberately relaxed, just a little. "My career plans aren't definite. I might simply retire, cleanly and without obligations to anyone."

"You don't look young enough for that, if you don't mind my saying so." Dahlberg gave a genuine-looking smile. "But when my time comes, I too will simply step away from everything."

But Kaldini shook her head. "I doubt it. There'll be some cause you need to throw your energies into."

They seemed to have moved beyond the expected script, at least in Anna's view. She wondered what Jean-Marc was making of all this.

That was the moment when it happened.

What?

Red exploded everywhere from Dahlberg's chest.

No...

His shredded head and shoulders flew up and back as the percussive wave of gore-laden air smacked against Anna and the bat-winged chair that mostly protected her, but Eva Kaldini was hit straight on with a glistening mess that knocked her backwards into unconsciousness or worse.

Anna could only sit as if paralysed, as if time had stopped, wondering if she'd caught a glimpse of final awareness in Dahlberg's eyes, in the head and shredded shoulders and arms blasted upwards right in front of her...

No...

Unable to breathe, she wondered if she too were dead or in the process of dying.

And she remained that way even as, some untold number of moments later, a dark-suited man wearing hex-protective shades lifted her from the chair, his arms so strong and steady, and she could only marvel at the twin tracks of silent tears running from beneath those shades, before the world began to move and the effort of continuing awareness felt way too hard and so she closed her eyes and allowed it all to fade away.

Release.

Wondering if she would ever wake again.

Jean-Marc...

Whatever would happen, would happen.

No more effort needed.

Or available.

TWELVE

Vanessa prowled among the black sculptures in her gallery, loving the sensual shapes, the touches of gold in the eyes of living statues, the tortured twisting of motile paintings and the figures trapped inside, all the while anticipating her new acquisition, the latest treasure to unwrap.

Inside herself, she felt a dull, comfortable ache: the somewhat corpulent, wet-lipped Abraham had proven a surprisingly robust lover, goaded and excited by the blood and final screams of the otherwise insignificant servants whose names Vanessa had already forgotten.

Further pleasure would come, she felt sure, when she read the evening newspapers, the cheaper ones featuring what she hoped would be lurid descriptions of Kristof Dahlberg's spectacular death in one of Fortinium's older and more respectable dining clubs.

While tomorrow's respectable broadsheets might focus on the effect upon Dahlberg Industries, perhaps with speculation on the unknown killer's motives. In the absence of forensic evidence, the police would be clueless – literally so, and with luck, metaphorically also.

An obvious suspect might be Dahlberg's closest corporate rival for the federal contracts, but Vanessa had stopped short of planting hints in that direction: anything too obvious, and the misdirection would misfire.

She was hoping for a profusion of confusion: wild competing theories among the informed industry watchers, and no hint of a scoop from police insiders, because their sources had nothing to give.

Give it several months, factoring in the certain delay in the funding committee's deliberations while the homicide investigation got under way, and the path would be clear for her to step in – via corporate proxies – and make her own winning bid.

We'll see what we'll see.

The police investigation wouldn't matter, given her resources and the cutouts she'd employed; but she daren't hurry up the contract bidding process. For now, she needed to focus on unlocking the crawlspace resonances via hex computation that only someone of her particular background could have devised.

That didn't rule out moments of pleasure in between stints of long, hard work. The whole point of her efforts was to bring a kind of fierce joy into her life.

Here, her gallery comprised a series of nine chambers strung together in a nonagon, deep below ground.

Soft indigo and crimson light emanated from floating spiky 3-D polyhedra in which tortured sprites writhed and glowed the colours of pain. It was a place of quiet yet immense suffering, and its ambience delighted Vanessa every time she walked inside.

She always left feeling fresh and renewed.

And the exhibits, her collectibles: sculptures or flattened paintings, frozen while living or slowly changing within the confines of a rune-encrusted frame glowing blackly with hex; or lifeless but formed from the bones and preserved organs of her enemies and prey.

The purple-red webs of arteries and dyed tendons were perhaps her favourites, including the seven-foot-high so-called nightmare-catchers: a fanciful name, not literally true. Yet in their own way, those constructs dreamed, and not of pleasant things.

A discreet clearing of a throat, and a soft male voice saying: "They're ready to unveil, ma'am."

Ashes swirled in the entrance to the next chamber, like a dust-devil approximating the shape of a man.

"Very good."

Vanessa snapped her fingers and the ashes rotated faster, expanding and fading, and were gone.

Someone who'd displeased her once through inattention to her obvious needs: that's who she thought the once-person had been. A clumsy waiter at a tea house, perhaps? She could no longer remember the details, so perhaps it was time to let him go, to release him from service and into death.

But she was too busy to train a replacement, so never mind.

She walked past a petrified family group encased in viscous acid. Their slowly dissolving bodies had turned a delicate shade of greenish grey, resembling coral; and on another day she might have stopped to enjoy her artwork's progress, but she wanted to see the unveiling before returning to the world of work.

No rest for the ambitious.

Time to inspect the sculpture that her team had stolen from one of the grandest towers on Dredgeway Avenue, in a carefully planned operation that should have gone off without a hitch, leaving only one person dead: the insider who helped them get inside.

I don't like mistakes.

If the insider remained alive, that wouldn't be so bad: nothing the woman could say would lead the police here. Losing some of the team during the operation, though: that was something else.

But first, the treasure itself.

In the next chamber, seven of Vanessa's servants, all dressed in matching grey jackets, stood ready to undrape the large abstract sculpture that her acquisition team had taken. Dark sheets covered the construct, specially treated so as not to snag anything while being removed.

The entire veiled shape possessed the width and approximate depth of a grand piano, while standing twice as tall.

Off to one side stood one of the acquisition team members. Bulky with muscle, petrimorph skin, and grim-looking facial tattoos the colour of rust. A blunt tool, this man, but useful.

His name was Larexo, and his dark jumpsuit was torn and scuffed; and he was the only member of the team to have returned from the other end of the portal once they ran into trouble.

She would want his report, but first the sculpture.

"Show me," commanded Vanessa.

The seven servants coordinated their actions, slipping off the dark sheets smoothly, revealing the grey, knobbly curves of twisted bone and the dull black threads that webbed the gaps within the sculpted framework.

One of her servants blinked wetly. It didn't look impressive at all, this sculpture, and the servants were perceptive enough to sense Vanessa's immediate reaction. They feared for their lives, which was a good thing, but the moment of their judgement was yet to come.

Amused, she said: "You need to plug the thing in, don't you know."

The chief servant's mouth made a silent O, while three of the others scurried around the back of the sculpture, searching for the power cable.

"Found it," said one, holding up a five-pin plug from which a black lead trailed.

"The wall socket over there," said another, pointing. "That's nearest."

It took a moment, once plugged in, for the sculpture to come to life.

Though delayed, the change when it happened was fast: from the first hint of humming to the bones thrumming with power, while the black threads of nerves shifted from dullness to glistening beauty: that part took an instant.

Vanessa could feel the power of necromagnets concealed within the lumpy knots of bone that made the large curves of the framework look interesting and organic more than artificial.

The interference patterns laid down within the bones during life – a part of her reckoned it took seventeen skeletons to make up this framework, and in these matters she was rarely wrong – reacted wonderfully to the nerve impulses induced among the shining black threads, treated and enhanced to an even higher standard than the telephone company managed when creating its major exchanges and trunk lines.

You could play great arpeggios of suffering and longing and even twisted pleasure with such a sculpture-come-instrument, or you could allow it simply to play itself, creating musical agony from random drifts and interactions arising, fundamentally, from the probabilistic quantal realm itself.

"It's magnificent," she said, and all seven servants sighed in unison.

She gazed at the sculpture, drank in its dark suffering, and felt transported, scarcely aware of her servants slipping silently away, understanding her needs in this moment.

That sensitivity made them valuable, less likely to require killing, although you never knew: every now and then you just needed a clean sweep in your life, and blood would always remain the finest cleanser.

Now, for a timeless time in a boundless subjective space, she touched the very nature of being and existence in those dark chords of suffering, the dissonance of peace and the resonance of struggle, all cloaked with the lovely timbre and passion of death itself.

Vanessa sighed, shuddered, and brought herself back to the moment.

Then she turned away from the sculpture, and remembered she was not alone.

One person had remained when the other servants left, though he'd kept his distance and remained very still: Larexo, sole survivor of whatever went wrong during the acquisition of the masterpiece behind her.

The rust-red tattoos on his face looked too identifiable for Vanessa's taste. On the other hand, removing or disguising the tattoos with makeup would make him unrecognisable to anyone who normally saw him like this.

"Tell me," she said.

"There were gargoyles…" began Larexo.

Vanessa stared at him, and his tattooed face froze into ordinary lifeless stone – literally lifeless, just for a moment, long enough to serve as punishment and threat – before regaining the power of movement once more.

"You were supposed to be careful," she said, "precisely because gargoyles might sense the music when you started to physically move the thing."

At least they'd managed to push the sculpture through the portal before the violence had started. Larexo had been able to follow the sculpture, incongruously cartwheeling his way to safety in the moment of the portal's collapse.

Only he, besides the team members who'd come through earlier or remained on this side throughout the operation, had survived.

"The woman," said Larexo. "The one who let us inside the defences. She started to argue with us, like she was maybe changing her mind, or just afraid. I think she'd done something earlier to make the gargoyles suspicious."

It was feasible.

"How many gargoyles were there?"

"Er, three, ma'am. But" – Larexo sped up his words, obviously aware that Vanessa could kill him with a gesture – "there was someone else, and he was worse."

Vanessa lowered the hand that she'd started to raise. "Someone else?"

"An armed zombie, er, resurrected man, like. Came in from the tunnels, the way we brought in the gate." He meant the framework that enabled the portal to exist at that end. "This guy had a firearm and he knew how to fight."

"Building security?"

"Not in uniform. Looked like... like he was jogging."

"In the *catacombs*? And carrying a firearm?"

"Um... Actually, he snatched Petro's pistol. Before that it was all hand-to-hand. What we called gutter fighting in the Army. But ma'am, he was *fast*."

Vanessa frowned, and Larexo swallowed.

"I don't like this," she said.

Thefts, her thefts, were supposed to be silent, quiet affairs, with the owners finding out only later – often much later – that some prized possession no longer hung or stood where it should. Some operations didn't go to plan in every detail, but they'd never left dead bodies behind before.

Not of their own people, and not even the bodies of insiders who needed to be silenced. Killing them was fine, but the protocol was for the team to take any bodies with them, and deploy trace-wiping hex as they left.

"All of your comrades are definitely dead?" she added. "The others caught up in this confrontation, that is."

Not counting the ones who'd come through to here, to another chamber in Inversion Tower, before the violence began.

"Yes, ma'am."

"Good." She gestured.

Larexo toppled forward as if hinged at the feet and smashed face-first into the floor. Chips of stone flew off, but he was no longer alive to care.

Death that fast was a mercy.

Call it a reward for hard work and courage in the past.

Behind her, the sculpture, a most marvellous acquisition, tempted her with its finely crafted music of pain; but her pleasures could not be so sweet were the moments not made rare by the pressure of work, by the ongoing struggle to become the person she was meant to be.

I don't like the idea of some random stranger stumbling into my operation.

Perhaps she'd been wrong to abandon that blindly upright police commissioner in her mission to expand her power behind the scenes of local city government. An intelligence source able to provide her with details of this intruder would have been useful right now.

"Get rid of this thing," she called out, knowing that some of her servants would hear, and understand that she meant the corpse formerly known as Larexo.

Weak-minded criminals were sometimes caught when they returned to the scene of the crime. Simply staying away from the whole thing was often all you needed to do in order to remain unsuspected; but that also meant remaining in the dark regarding the investigation's progress.

"Double check the framework segments that came through," she added, again confident that servants would hear although none were in sight. "Count them all, and do it three times to make certain. I need to know that every piece came back through the portal as it collapsed."

The chances of a segment not making it through were remote, extremely so; but forensic diviners were highly trained and the only sure way to frustrate them was to leave nothing behind.

Larexo's dead comrades remained, but there would be nothing in or on those bodies to link them to one Vanessa Frisch, the city's richest and most beautiful and surely smartest mover and shaker behind the scenes.

Time I talked to my favourite prisoner again.

That tri-horned daemonid had needed time to recover from the last questioning, for Vanessa had taken him close to death, but his natural robustness meant that so long as he didn't die, he could come back quite quickly from a state of brokenness and suffering that would destroy a human being.

On her long golden fingernails, the ancient Sunskril runes copied from the Umbral Codices began to glow black and pulse like a beating zombie heart, and reality itself seemed to wobble around her in a haze.

I will find the quantally entangled clumps.

Such things came about so very rarely. It might be years before a resource of such quality appeared again. And entanglement was tricky: it could be broken, decohered by reacting to ordinary physical surroundings, so very easily.

Which means I need to keep the pressure on.

She swept out of the gallery and along obsidian corridors where servants ducked back out of sight into side corridors and alcoves as she passed, because they could read the signs and probably sense the pre-storm charging of the air itself, and knew she could flick them out of existence if they distracted her, killing them without even bothering to taste their pain as they expired.

Down the final ramp, and gesturing the great shielded doors to open like lupine jaws, fluorescing with hex, the open space crackling with energy that would burn an ordinary person to cinders, but not her.

She enjoyed the lightning across her skin as she strode through the membrane-like inner shield and stopped before her prisoner.

He raised his ugly, three-horned head and stared at her with eyes grown older by millennia in the few days of his captivity. They held a kind of sick knowledge, a realisation that his kind were not as automatically powerful here in the ordinary world as they blindly assumed.

Twin green nonagons, nine-sided irises of faint emerald light, showed in those daemonid eyes, just for an instant.

"Time for another little chat." Vanessa smiled in a way that might have been pleasant in other contexts, while the amusement in her voice was genuine.

Yellow spots fluoresced, replacing the green flickers in the great black orbs of her captive's eyes.

Good.

Fear was always useful.

As well as tasting addictively sweet.

The runes on her fingernails pulsed harder than ever.

THIRTEEN

Donal had been hoping for more of a challenge.

Perhaps a stay-at-home Mrs Smythe might have proven difficult to interview, or perhaps the premises might have been empty – Councillor Smythe was working right now in City Hall, or should be – but with ferocious hex defences in place around the actual apartment, maybe with building security wraiths flitting through the corridors non-stop.

Smythe was the first name on Sandarov's list, therefore the logical place to begin investigating.

So, the building: Niflhame Towers looked expensive enough, but so far the building appeared less secure than your average downtown business hotel.

In the event, Donal had come in via the rear service entrance. Someone had propped the iron door open with a length of twisted mammoth bone that once served as a standard lamp but looked broken now; and people in work clothes were going in and out, with no security awareness to speak of.

He'd walked straight through with a clipboard in hand and set expression on his face, ignoring the carpenters and cleaning staff he'd passed, and taken the stairs rather than allow a wraith to carry him up in an elevator shaft, and reached the nineteenth floor and Smythe's apartment at just the right time: a maid with orange spikey skin was in the process of leaving.

She let herself out without even glancing in Donal's direction, closed the apartment door with a click, and pushed her small trolley of cleaning gear ahead of her to the next apartment down, where she knocked, announced herself and waited for a count of seven, then let herself in with a master key.

So it was that kind of building: run like an upmarket hotel but containing plush apartments, not standalone guest rooms. Housekeeping provided. Very posh. Flamesprites flickered in their sconces along the corridor, but Donal didn't expect any of them to worry about him.

He waited long enough for the maid to get busy inside the other apartment, drew out his lockpicks, knelt down at Smythe's door and got to work.

The door clicked open, and he pushed it a few inches, stopped and listened, and softly sniffed the air. The maid had gone overboard with strong beetlewax polish in the hallway, but there was nothing untoward besides: call it a ninety-seven percent certainty that the apartment was empty.

Donal slipped inside.

A framed blue-and-white photograph on the wall, with the bride in a dark flowing gown, indicated there was a Mrs Smythe, or had been. The couple looked happy, but the picture wasn't new.

It seemed a strange place to hang a wedding photo, so close to the front door, but what did he know?

Donal turned and closed the door as quietly as possible. There was a hushed, deadened quality to the air in the short hallway, and he felt certain the acoustic insulation was excellent: if you lived here, you wouldn't hear the neighbours in any direction, including up or down.

"Building inspection," he called out quietly.

There was a name for what he was doing right now, and every cop knew it: breaking and entering. He had a private investigator's licence and all, so he wasn't doing it on a whim, but it felt a lot different from barging in with a warrant.

In some ways it felt liberating, as he walked into the lounge, looking everywhere, appreciating the art deco ambience and dark bronze fireplace and table sculptures and long kimodo-hide couches, two of them facing each other across a slab of quartz, all milky swirls of violet and grey, that served as a coffee table.

Just a little too upmarket for someone in Councillor Smythe's position.

Without a background check it was impossible to be certain – the guy might come from wealth, after all – but Donal had heard rumours about Bloodfist Bank and backhanders to officials during his time in the Department, even though financial crimes of that type were far outside his remit, handled by specialist officers with soft hands and bookish features and, in Donal's limited experience, no sense of humour whatsoever.

He could have done with a team of those guys right now, but it was just him on his own, so where to start?

Filing-cabinet, maybe a safe. The first would be okay, but safe-cracking needed its own kind of specialists. Leaving the lounge, he checked the kitchen – spotless, which maybe meant Smythe could afford to eat in restaurants all the time, a suspicion strengthened by the near-empty pantry shelves – and all three bedrooms in turn. The last one had been turned into a home office.

There were two small filing-cabinets, identical in black, both locked. Neither was a challenge when you carried a handy pocket set of burglar's tools, and after slipping both locks, Donal flipped through the hanging drawers, prioritising his search, planning to go through everything if he had time.

Sitting at the desk, he read through several folders, and after a while pulled out his own notebook and began to jot down times and dates and – verbatim, but in shorthand – Councillor Smythe's descriptions of meetings and transactions.

Some of the participants, identified by initials, were identified elsewhere in filed letters that revealed their full names and even featured their signatures.

It was intricate but wouldn't have been exciting in ordinary surroundings. Illegally inside a city councillor's apartment, however, Donal was able to keep his focus, and soon enough a pattern began to emerge.

On the 17th of every month, a payment went into an account held by a Xalesian offshore bank whose name Donal couldn't pronounce, and whose existence didn't feature on Councillor Smythe's income tax returns despite the generous interest earned, according to the statements.

The payments had begun shortly after Smythe's first meetings with "AH", who in one diary note appeared next to the letters "BB" ringed with ink and followed by an exclamation mark.

So far Donal hadn't found any evidence of Smythe moving against Commissioner Sandarov, but there was a particular annotation regarding one of Smythe's off-site meetings with some fellow councillors – again identified only by initials, but with the information provided by Sandarov, it wasn't hard to figure out who was who, although "AH" remained a mystery.

This entry included the words *new policing priorities* highlighted in an ink-drawn box with shading, along with a smiling sketched skull that actually bore signs of personality.

Maybe Smythe was a frustrated would-be artist. Perhaps a career drawing the funnies for the city rags would have satisfied him, and kept him away from criminal wrongdoing. Too bad it worked out differently.

White-collar crimes could get you a cell in Wailing Towers just like the physically rougher kind that Donal mostly worked with, at least when he'd been with the Department.

He heard a click.

Donal rose without a sound from the chair, checked his jacket was open and hanging straight with his shoulder-holstered Magnus easy to reach, but kept his hands empty as he walked back to the lounge. Hiding might have been an option, if embarrassing, but life feels simpler when you approach things directly.

"Hello, Councillor," he said.

Smythe was fleshier than in his wedding photo, though entirely recognisable. The woman with her blouse already half off looked nothing like the bride in the picture, because she wasn't the same woman. She also looked one Hades of a lot younger than Smythe, maybe young enough to be an intern at City Hall.

Except there was something hardened and cynical in her eyes when she looked at Donal, which hinted at this being a sordid transaction rather than actual romance: perhaps this was her actual line of business.

"And hello to you," he added, addressing her. "Not Mrs Smythe, I presume."

"Now look here." Smythe drew himself up in a way that only emphasised the soft convex look of his stomach and the jowls around his chin.

Donal did just that: looked Smythe straight in the eyes.

Smythe's skin went sweaty and blotchy all at once.

"Maybe I should wait in the bedroom, honey." The young woman's voice, addressed to Smythe, held a kind of knowing amusement, as if she'd been party to many embarrassing situations in her life, and at least knew how to get some money out of them.

"No, you should—I don't know." Smythe wiped at the sweat on his face, looked at her then Donal. "What do you want? How much?"

"What's your name?" Donal asked the young woman.

"Melody," she said. "Melody de Sonance."

"Cute." It was clearly a work name. He wondered if her customers ever got the joke, or were too confused with lust to notice. "Go to the bedroom and close the door. If you don't make a fuss, I'll go easy on your boyfriend."

She smirked at the word *boyfriend*, then gave a collegial wink and headed into the bedroom. The door clicked softly shut.

"So, Councillor. How is your lady wife?"

It was a good guess in terms of targeting weakness. Smythe swallowed and managed to say, "You, er, you need to leave her out of this. *Please.*"

"Sit down." Donal pointed at a couch. "There."

"Okay…" Smythe obeyed.

Donal remained standing. Partly it was tactical advantage, but Smythe was hardly a physical threat. What Donal needed was to keep the man off balance psychologically and get him habituated to obeying orders.

"Take your tie off."

"Why, er… Okay." With fat, fumbling fingers, Smythe managed to undo the knot.

"Give it to me, Alwyn." From reading the bank statements and all the rest, Donal knew Smythe's full name was Alwyn Arkady Smythe the Third, but suspected the "Third" part was a social climber's affectation, not a sign of actual old money.

Smythe, with a shaking hand, offered the necktie to Donal, who took it, pretended to examine it with a sneer, and tossed it onto the quartz-block coffee table.

The tie could be used for binding wrists or ankles, but its main use was to further diminish Smythe's confidence and self esteem.

"You can call it bullying if you like," a grey-haired detective had told a younger Donal and his classmates back at the Academy. "But you keep them off balance and you pound at them verbally – at least – because in the end it's about keeping your honest citizens safe. And if your suspect is innocent, well never mind. They'll get over it."

Questioning suspects had become second nature, but it didn't always feel good afterwards. No one had mentioned that part at the Academy, not as far as Donal remembered.

"Do you party on the 17th of every month when the Bloodfist cash comes in?" asked Donal. "Or just take advantage whenever the missus is away?"

"It's not like…" Smythe's voice trailed off, as he began to realise how much Donal knew already.

Donal shifted his jacket so Smythe could see the holstered Magnus.

"Tell me everything," he said.

So after a coughing start, and in dribs and drabs punctuated by moments of sweating panic and breathless swallowing, and the occasional prompt from Donal, Councillor Alywn Arkady Smythe the Third did exactly that.

While Donal memorised every single word.

Before Donal left, he tapped on the door to the biggest bedroom and said: "Are you okay in there, Melody?"

"Sure, big guy. You coming in?"

"I wouldn't want to spoil things for your boyfriend."

"Sure." The door muffled the overtones, but there might have been a touch of genuine regret in there. Maybe.

In the lounge, Smythe was sitting with his head bowed forward and his hands clasped between his fleshy thighs. He was guilty of accepting bribes – one-off payments plus an actual monthly retainer – and awarding contracts to crooked third parties and, yes, of manoeuvring against Commissioner Sandarov in the hopes of getting a more tractable figure into office; but his primary problem was weakness.

The discarded necktie remained on the coffee table. Tying Smythe up had not been necessary. His own guilt had trapped him.

"You're a grown man," Donal told him. "But it's not too late to change."

Smythe looked up and blinked. "Excuse me?"

"If this ends up in court, you'll have to take your punishment. In which case, just do it."

"I don't… You mean it might *not* go to court?"

"Just remember you're guilty, and there will be people in authority who know exactly what you've done. But the easiest way to change yourself is to begin with the physical, and stick with it. Every day."

With the Lower Danklyn kids, this approach worked just fine. Maybe Smythe was too far gone to hear the message, but for some reason Donal felt he had to try.

"Push-ups, from your knees if you have to. Air squats, meaning freehand knee bends, and a rowing motion while holding your knees bent and hanging off the kitchen counter to work the pulling muscles."

Maybe he'd spent too much time coaching in the gym. Or maybe Smythe was in exactly the right kind of emotional state to grow angry at himself and wrench his life around.

"Then jumping-jacks or jogging on the spot, for pure fitness. A little bit of stretching – you'll work it out – and you're done. Cold showers are great when you're used to them, too."

"I've never… It's weird," said Smythe, "but I believe you."

"Good."

"What about…?" His gaze drifted towards the closed bedroom door.

Donal mostly held back the grin that wanted to surface.

"That," he said, "I'll let you figure out all by yourself."

There was also the matter of Melody's messed-up life, but that wasn't something Donal could change in an instant.

So he retrieved his clipboard and notebook from Smythe's office, left the apartment, letting himself out quietly, strode down the corridor, and decided to exit via an elevator shaft instead of the stairs.

The wraith who carried him down manifested a clearly female persona, and she was chatty enough to remind him of Aggie, or more accurately her former identity of Gertie, back in Police HQ on Avenue of the Basilisks.

How're you doing today?

"Alright." He wondered if she was about to ask which apartment he'd been visiting.

Nice to deal with someone who isn't all stressed out.

Donal smiled as they drifted downwards in the shaft at an easy pace.

"I don't know," he told her. "But I think I might have done a little good in the world today."

That is good.

"I might be wrong, mind."

They stopped, hovering at the threshold of the ground-floor lobby.

Maybe the attempt is its own reward.

Donal smiled. "Maybe it is. You're a good person, you know."

They bobbed in mid-air, as if the wraith were curtsying while holding Donal aloft.

Why, thank you. Have a great day.

"You too."

He got out and left through the lobby, clipboard in hand and notebook in pocket, hoping a great day was actually on the cards. He ignored the concierge's raised eyebrow and unspoken question as he reached the exit and stepped out onto the sidewalk.

The faintest of quicksilver rains had begun to fall, and pedestrians were walking a little more smartly than usual, but in this part of town most people had had their shots, so a little bit of quicksilver would do no harm.

An outdoor elevator shaft rising to an elevated Pneumetro station stood two blocks away to the right. To the left, although you could see no real sign of it from here, lay the series of city block-sized bowls sunk in the ground that was Twistover Pits, where the surface roads made crossed infinity symbols to navigate their way around.

Directly ahead, on the far side of the street, stood a coffee shop called Gandolfo's, not a name that Donal recognised, therefore not a chain. He was a zombie with almost total control over mental and physical processes considered autonomic among the redblood population; but for all that, he was still a human being.

Maybe a little triple espresso, a small reward to himself, would help to ease him through the rest of the day.

He crossed over and went inside.

FOURTEEN

Gandolfo's was an upmarket joint, and if Donal hadn't been a self-controlled zombie, he might have winced at the prices written up on the wall in golden script. Maybe the curlicued characters were actually gold leaf, given how much the coffee cost.

On the other hand, this was downtown where the rents and rates and insurance must be through the roof. They were on the ground floor of a twenty-seven-storey tower, though you couldn't get through to the lobby and elevator shafts from here: from the normal residents' viewpoint, Gandolfo's was tucked away at the side.

There was a window table free, so that was where Donal sat to sip at his triple espresso. It tasted dark and bitter, superior to Fat'n'Sugar's offerings for sure. If only he'd brought a book with him to read, he could have whiled away an hour or more quite easily.

Batchelor thinking. If he really had time to spare, he'd have gone back home to Mel and baby Finbar.

He pulled out his notebook and fountain pen, made a rapid shorthand list of the things that Smythe had confessed, and put notebook and pen away. It would help his memory, but for the most part it filled in details of the misdoings he'd already written down when he examined Smythe's files.

Things like the name of the banker that Smythe had been dealing with: the source of his bribe money.

Fourteen minutes after Donal sat down – by automatic mental reckoning – he saw a purple taxi pull up outside Niflhame Towers, and a frowning Melody tip-tapping her way through the quicksilver rain on stiletto heels, and climbing into the back of the cab.

She wasn't angry or annoyed or afraid, so Donal figured she'd been paid whatever sum she'd agreed with Smythe. Maybe she'd already had the money in her purse when Donal surprised them in the apartment lounge:

experienced professional girls get the cash as soon as possible.

Maybe, in the time since Donal had left, there'd been time for a quickie with Councillor Smythe; but Melody's expression suggested otherwise.

And maybe I've missed a clue.

Downtown traffic could jam up at random times, but right now the streets were pretty clear and Melody's taxi had already moved off by the time it occurred to Donal that perhaps she was part of it, the network of influence and corruption he was starting to investigate.

Maybe she'd been specifically pointed at Smythe by someone who wanted to compromise a city councillor.

Smythe would be able to provide details of how he met Melody, so there was still a possible lead to follow; but there were other names on Sandarov's list to investigate, a higher priority, and Smythe had already filled in a lot of the missing pieces concerning them.

Donal took his time finishing his espresso, then headed out, still with clipboard in hand, in the direction of Twistover Pits. He might have used the clipboard as a rain hat, but the fall of quicksilver had eased to almost nothing, so he continued bare-headed.

It took him seven minutes to reach the Pits, but three times longer to navigate the tangle of curved subterranean road tunnels, most of which featured railed sidewalks raised higher than the cars, where being a zombie helped a lot: no need to breathe in the sooty stink of exhausts.

After climbing the pedestrian ramp to Dredgeway Avenue, he paused to take in his surroundings, the geometry of the street's dark towering buildings which would have merged into the dark purple sky were it not for the myriad yellow lit windows. He looked for signs of police or criminal activity; but there were none.

The third tower along looked just like all the others, with nothing to indicate the violence that had occurred in its cellars the day before.

And maybe every building held dark secrets, but that was a cynical thought and Donal wasn't in that kind of mood today. He headed for the tower he'd known all along he was going to visit, without any actual plan for how to proceed once inside.

The first surprise was the scanwraith that passed through him as he was entering via the revolving doors. It was a neat setup: if the wraith raised the alert quickly enough, someone could lock the turning doors in place before the suspect visitor reached the lobby.

As it was, Donal passed through but immediately spotted two uniformed doormen heading in his direction, while behind his desk, a concierge had leaned over to take hold of something that might even be a shotgun. All three were broad-shouldered and hard-faced, though one of the "doormen" was actually a woman. A doorperson.

Her face was the palest grey-blue – just a shade away from pure porcelain white – that Donal had ever seen.

Someone like me.

Resurrected, but not originally standard human, not quite. Highly unusual.

"Hi," he said. "I'm Donal Riordan. I'm a licensed investigator, and I've a concealed-carry permit for the weapon."

"If you would care to remove your jacket and then your harness at the concierge's desk, sir, we can then discuss who you want to see."

"And keep the weapon holstered throughout?"

"Exactly, sir."

Donal nodded. "Good procedure."

The scanwraith hadn't just moved fast: it had alerted its colleagues to the exact manner in which Donal was carrying the Magnus.

Very carefully, he did as the doorperson had asked: walked to the desk, put his clipboard down, slipped out of his jacket, folded it and placed it on top of the clipboard, and wriggled out of his harness which he offered to the concierge, the Magnus dangling in its holster.

Then he showed his licence to the zombie doorperson and said: "I was in the basement yesterday."

The redblood concierge and doorman gave identical tough frowns, but the doorperson raised her eyebrow and spoke mildly: "You're the one who helped the gargoyles."

"I did what I could. It was my fault they got exposed down in the tunnel in the first place."

"Still." She looked at her colleagues and gave a nod. "He's okay."

The other two looked only half-convinced, but the doorman returned to his station all the same. The concierge told Donal: "If you're going inside, we'll need to keep the weapon until you leave."

Donal slipped his jacket back on but left the clipboard on the desk. "Sure. Knock yourself out."

A twitch of a smile from the doorperson. "My name's Karlasdóttir. I heard you used to be with the TPD."

Someone had been chatty. Maybe Lieutenant Bellis, maybe the young officer with the red nictitating-membrane eyes. Joel.

"Yeah. You?" He knew she'd been through something a lot tougher than greeting business folk and tradespeople.

"I was an MP back in the day."

There was something in her voice that made Donal ask: "Which regiment would that be, exactly?"

"The 666th. An enforcement platoon."

They were speaking quietly, and something in the lobby air prevented voices from carrying. The concierge was out of hearing range, depositing Donal's firearm and clipboard in a secure cupboard.

"Your colleagues know what that is?" asked Donal.

"Probably not," she said.

Donal wanted to ask how come she ended up here, working a job like this; but maybe she could ask the same of him. Not that he'd ever served in a Death Brigade.

"The Department's not asked for my help," he said. "It's just that I was there on the scene yesterday and I'm, what, professionally curious."

"And you just happened to be in the neighbourhood today. Again."

"I actually was on a job," said Donal, "but I kind of shifted my priorities around a bit, otherwise I'd have been halfway across the city today."

The home addresses on Sandarov's list were widely scattered, nearly all in well-off neighbourhoods. Two even lived near Lieutenant Bellis; Donal had briefly considered starting with them.

"I can't let you down in the basement alone, Mr Riordan."

"No, I don't suppose you can, Miss Karlasdóttir."

"And I can't leave my post right now, but I can send an escort with you."

"That... would be great."

"Maybe." The faintest of smiles once more. "You're not a nervous man, are you?"

"I wasn't until you asked that question."

"So long as you don't try to filch anything down there, you'll be fine. Give me a moment while I square things with my colleagues."

"Sure. And... thank you."

She nodded, and went back to the desk to talk to the concierge. Whatever his initial objection was, it caused Karlasdóttir to lower her voice and say something that made the blood drain from the concierge's face, after which he picked up a brass telephone, spun only three of the six cogs – an internal extension – and spoke a few words before hanging up.

Karlasdóttir tipped her forehead in salute to Donal, then went back to stand by the doorman.

Donal waited.

Ninety seconds later, three figures came drifting along the wide internal corridor, a richly-appointed set-up with dark-green metal and bronze forming walls and ceiling and square-edged pillars, set off by a floor of some polished blue mineral with sparkling silver highlights.

The ragged grey shapes looked out of place, moving this way without quite touching the ground.

Donal glanced in Karlasdóttir's direction, but she wasn't meeting his gaze, though the corner of her mouth had turned up.

"You've got to be kidding me," he said.

With security like this, he'd have felt confident leaving valuables down in the building's basement, assuming he actually owned any.

The trio drifted closer.

Where the three figures' eyes should have been, the void looked out. Their presence chilled even Donal's zombie bones. They weren't wraiths and they weren't even ghouls.

Ghasts.

Right here in downtown Tristopolis.

"I'll behave myself," he told them.

And meant every word.

Ringed in by his escort – two ghasts in front and one following – Donal passed elevator shafts where wraiths would normally be waiting, but not today: not with ghasts nearby.

At the rear, doors slammed open to reveal a darkened stairwell, with steps spiralling down into near-complete darkness, for the sprites that should have lit the well were high overhead, not daring to come lower.

Donal could make out empty sconces on the walls all the way down, where the sprites would normally be stationed.

"I can see well enough to use the stairs," he said.

None of the ghasts replied; nor had he expected any words from them. It was said that even the softest of their moans could cause a heart to stop. Maybe even the kind that pumped black zombie blood.

That didn't make the silence any less eerie as they descended, the ghasts never touching the stone steps, keeping a constant distance from Donal while he kept his pace steady. With a human escort he might have played games, altering the rhythm of his steps to keep them off balance; but this was a time for moving carefully with no surprises.

When they reached the bottom of the stairwell, Donal realised he had no idea how much time had elapsed in the descent. That was perhaps the most disconcerting feature of the situation so far.

Another set of doors slammed open as if afraid the ghasts might touch them if they moved too slowly.

A short unlit corridor, almost totally black, led to already open doors and into a large space, big enough to be a ballroom, lit by firesprites up at the ceiling corners, again ignoring the sconces where they would normally be stationed.

Donal and his escort passed through an archway to another space, this with a domed ceiling, again hard to see because of cowering sprites scarcely able to raise a glimmer, but you could just about tell the ceiling would be blue in normal light.

It looked familiar, and the sheet of glistening black material in the centre of the floor, weighed down by metal barrels at the edges, was clearly covering the hole that led down to the level of the catacombs.

The three ghasts drifted towards a wall then stopped and hung there, billowing coldly, void eyes trained on Donal.

Bleeding Thanatos.

He forced himself to work.

Donal spent two-thirds of an hour going over the place. To check the floor opening, he carefully told the ghasts of his intentions to shift one of the barrels and take a peek beneath the protective sheet, but not to leave this cellar: just hang his head over the edge.

In the absence of a reply from the watching ghasts, he'd taken his time to do what he'd said, leaning over the opening once he'd pulled back the edge of the sheet, and peering down into the room where early yesterday he'd held the hand of a wounded gargoyle and waited for the medics to arrive.

Satisfied, he replaced the sheet and moved around the cellar, checking the stored artworks and an antique piece of machinery, carefully polished and wrapped, that seemed to be a printing press. He supposed it was valuable to someone.

A sound from the archway froze him, before he recognised the woman standing there, although she was dressed in ordinary clothes now. Reasonably ordinary: few women wore baggy trousers beneath short tunic jackets, but on her they worked.

"Miss Karlasdóttir," said Donal. "Going off shift?"

"Something like that."

"Or maybe you're not just a doorperson."

A shrug of wide shoulders. "You never know."

"Are you head of security here? Or brought in to troubleshoot?"

"I travel around a lot." She glanced in the direction of the ghasts. "Not necessarily alone."

"So they brought you in after the break-in."

"Break-in and murder. Not what management expects in this place."

"No," said Donal. "It's always so much worse when violence strikes downtown. Not like the poor areas, with the unwashed working classes. With them, what else does one expect?"

Karlasdóttir raised that eyebrow again. "I'm here to do a job. You think I was raised in a place like this?"

The ghasts had drifted fractionally closer.

"I'm pretty certain you weren't." Donal gestured towards the black covering over the hole in the floor. "Did the scene-of-crime diviners tell you what happened?"

"I had a summary briefing. What do you know?"

Donal pointed to one corner of the cellar. "There was a kind of portal there. Mage kind of thing, although for some reason, I'm not entirely sure it was a mage doing it this time. Shining the same shade of blue, though."

"You've transited through a mage portal?"

Most people would have no idea what such a thing looked like.

"Not as a matter of habit, but yeah. This one was supported by some kind of framework, which kind of dismantled itself and disappeared into the portal as the whole thing collapsed." He considered adding a remark about disappearing orifices, then dismissed the thought.

Karlasdóttir was looking at him steadily. "So you saw that much yesterday. Learned anything new today?"

There was no reason to hold back what little he'd deduced. "That framework, I'm guessing they couldn't sneak it inside through the front doors, or even some kind of service entrance. They dug in from the catacombs. If you look carefully, you can see the floor was excavated from underneath."

"Okay." Her tone didn't reveal whether she'd known that already.

"The woman who was shot, I'm guessing she was the insider who let at least one crew member in through the front door. You can see there were hex defences on the walls down there" – again he gestured at the covered hole – "which had to be disabled from the inside. Professional. And they didn't hesitate to escalate from robbery to homicide."

Legally, that applied only to killing the woman, not the gargoyle. Donal had a feeling Karlasdóttir wouldn't make that distinction, any more than he did himself.

"Quantal bilocation portals created by some kind of framework or apparatus," she said. "That can't be usual."

"Mages use their own central nervous systems, or something. Neural configurations in their brain controlling an external energy source." Donal shrugged, just a little. "I've been reading up."

"A scholar and a detective."

Maybe this was getting too personal. "And father to a newborn son. I can't let whatever happened here take up too much of my time."

"Too bad." Her tone was cool enough to be ambiguous. Perhaps she was only thinking of the job, after all.

Donal looked around the room once more. "I'm not sure I've learned anything else. Except that whatever was stolen was a pretty large and heavy object, stored over there." He pointed. "And it's left a weird kind of resonance in the floor. The kind of thing you get around reactors."

Each reactor pile contained the bones of a thousand dead, stacked inside a resonance cavity where standing waves of necroflux, modulated by diffraction patterns laid down in the bones during life, replayed and amplified fragmented thoughts and memories of all those individuals as one chaotic, howling mess.

Most living people didn't even want to think about it.

"So you've been inside at least one Energy Authority installation," said Karlasdóttir. "And travelled through mage portals. And you read."

"Yeah..."

"And forgive me, because this is really personal, but... Did you mean you've become an actual biological father?"

She was a fellow zombie. Donal had mentioned fatherhood almost casually, as a redblood might; but for their kind, that was anything but an everyday occurrence.

"It came as a surprise," he said. "But yeah, that's what I meant. How long have you…?"

He tapped his chest over his heart.

"Nine years, almost," said Karlasdóttir. "I didn't think pregnancy was even possible."

"The chances fall off over time." Donal gave a carefully calibrated smile in which the sadness was deliberate. "I read up on that too, and pretty thoroughly. Motherhood is more likely than fatherhood, which is maybe a surprise. Nine years for you would be like two or three years for me. Same chances. Slim ones."

"In the Brigades, they don't tell you these things."

So she was resurrected while still serving.

"No one told me, either," said Donal. "For me it happened in Fortinium, on a case." Meaning his resurrection.

This conversation was a long way from what he'd expected to encounter revisiting yesterday's crime scene. Perhaps a similar thought had occurred to Karlasdóttir, because she took a deliberate step back from Donal, and glanced towards the ghasts, who'd drifted closer.

Now they stopped and hung in place, rippling as if in the softest of breezes, though the air felt dead in here.

"You've been very helpful," she said.

"Yeah, so have you."

"Alright, then."

"Mm." Donal didn't know what to say next.

"We've got to go." From her gesture, the *we* included the ghasts, but excluded Donal. "Take it easy, Mr Riordan."

"Take care, Miss Karlasdóttir."

He'd thought that he wasn't supposed to be left alone down here, but said nothing as Karlasdóttir left the way she'd come in, trailed by the trio of ghasts, leaving the place feeling empty and somehow diminished.

Had he learned anything meaningful? It didn't seem so, not logically, yet it felt like some kind of progress.

The thing that was stolen.

Before, he'd known nothing about the object. Perhaps that was the difference, the one thing he'd learned, but it seemed minor.

Maybe he could take one last look at the spot where it had been stored, whatever it was. He went back over, crouched down, and placed his fingertips against the ancient stone floor. There was some kind of resonance for sure, a remnant, a distant hum he could sense in his bones; but no more than that.

If he ever came across the object, whatever it was, he might recognise its signature. Right now, though, this wasn't helping.

He stood up once more and turned around in a widdershins direction, making a full circle, because something here was odd but he couldn't work out what it was.

What the Hades am I missing?

Nothing came to his attention. Nothing at all.

Remember everything.

Another full circle, anti-widdershins this time, scanning everything, letting it all sink in so he could think about it later, knowing it would probably prove fruitless.

"Alright," he said to no one at all. "Alright."

Time to head back out.

FIFTEEN

Vanessa was neither a mage nor a witch, not in any orthodox fashion. A hybrid of both would be a more accurate designation; but some aspects of her deepest being belonged to a very different category.

She wondered how many people in Tristopolis even knew what a bimodal daemonid was.

It helped to keep acquaintances off balance, that uncertainty about her nature combined with her aura of power, not to mention the abilities she could manifest. Mostly, she enjoyed the taste of everyone's confusion, spicing up the fragrance and texture of their fear.

Getting her daemonid captive to finally, finally give up the location of the quantally entangled organic sources: the daemonid's agony had been as beautiful and delicious as the precious information itself. Perhaps that was why she'd allowed him to cling onto life when the questioning was done.

Gourmet or gourmand of pain: she could be either, depending on circumstance and whim.

"I am a connoisseuse of suffering," she'd told her twin brother thirteen years earlier, three days before she killed him.

Before she allowed him to die, chained in his daemonid aspect inside a room much like this one: walled in plain black, with a heavy door of brushed steel fully saturated with defensive hex. Imprisoning hex, not that her current prisoner, newly arrived, possessed any kind of power at all.

No daemonid, not this one.

The man in front of her was plainly terrified, a scaley man with blocky features, holding his cap against his chest, trying to be respectful while wanting to turn and run, but intuitively aware she could strike him down with a gesture.

"Who are you?" she said. "What is your job?"

"I'm K-Katurah." Another swallow. "Kapeltin Katurah. I drive a taxi, that's all."

Vanessa looked at the three stone-faced men, her scouting team, standing behind the prisoner, standing to half-attention with hands clasped behind their backs.

One of them cleared his throat. "He dropped off someone at the target location, ma'am. Not a normal fare. He hugged the kid before the kid went inside."

People with scaled skin rarely blushed or paled, but this Katurah fellow pretty much blanched.

"Your son," guessed Vanessa.

The prisoner's lips tightened. She could take that as a yes, or close enough: a son or nephew or whatever.

"He won't be harmed," continued Vanessa, "if you answer all my questions. Neither will you. Fail me, though, and you get to watch me at work on the boy, and a young one can take days to die. It's really very pretty."

A wet blink from frightened eyes. Katurah looked frozen in place, shocked into paralysis like the trapped prey he was.

Too easy, really.

But this was about practicality, not the joy of challenge. She looked again at the stone-faced men, her street soldiers, inviting them to speak.

"A boxing gym, ma'am," said the same one as before. "Where he dropped off the kid. Trying to toughen him up, maybe."

Using an ordinary city map, Vanessa had already decided the location lay within Lower Danklyn: hardly the most upmarket neighbourhood in Tristopolis. She supposed a boxing gym was the kind of thing one found there, in the slums.

Vanessa had her own ideas regarding toughness and cruelty, but no desire to discuss them with subordinates. "Is this place permanently open? Is someone there all the time?"

Katurah blinked. "Um... No. There are kids' hours, and adults training at different times. They stay open till twenty-one o'clock, but not every day."

Vanessa could sense the subtle lessening of his fear, as if they were discussing harmless matters. If it helped him to talk, she would allow that misunderstanding to continue, just for now.

"And during the sleep hours?" she asked. "There's security on site, is there? Some other kind of staff?"

Katurah shook his head. "It's just a gym, is all."

"Really." The entangled source – both parts of the source in close physical proximity – had remained unmoving since she first sensed its appearance; and her daemonid captive, under the final barrage of torture, had eventually concurred with her perceptions.

Too bad she hadn't possessed the acuity to pinpoint the entangled source the moment it made an appearance.

The new prisoner, Katurah, said: "Um, it's in a kind of old temple, is the gym. Decarcerated, they said."

"You mean deconsecrated."

"Uh, yeah."

Maybe that was it. Maybe some composite denizen of the crawlspace dimensions, not necessarily of wraithkind – something that enjoyed worshipping with or being worshipped by a human congregation – had remained hidden in the building, rotated out of the macroscopic dimensions but recently starting to re-emerge and manifest its power.

A composite composed of a quantally entangled pair? Such symbiotic entities were very, very rare and exceedingly dangerous.

The people using the building now should thank her for what she was about to do, assuming they survived the process.

"What have you forgotten to tell me?"

Scaled humans typically don't sweat, but some form of exudate was glistening between the scales of Katurah's face. "N-Nothing."

"Tell me. Now."

"It's just a gym. A gym. Harmless."

Vanessa gestured.

I don't have time for this.

Katurah's corpse dropped like a pile of loose sticks. Black light rippled along the runes inscribed in Vanessa's golden fingernails.

"Dispose of it," she told her street soldiers. "I've got no use for this one's bones."

"Yes, ma'am."

"Afterwards, get your people ready to move on this gym location. Three teams of seven, and I'll brief you in the lower staging chamber, one hundred minutes from now."

"A portal transition, ma'am?"

"Not necessary." And risky: it could decohere the quantal entanglement, which would render the whole exercise pointless.

"You'll use trucks," she continued, "but obliterate the traces some miles after initial egress." She knew how to use her street soldiers' jargon. "You've a trace-wipe and solo egress setup near Cataclysm Chasm, as I recall."

"Yes, ma'am. The man in question is here on duty, and fully fit."

"Good."

Her people were well organised, enough for her to trust that every disposable car or truck would be just that: wiped of all identification. Residue resonance might remain, especially from the roof amulets that would disrupt the perceptions of any municipal scanbat that might pass overheard... but nothing that a witch or diviner might tie to a specific place or individual.

The approach would be low key and stealthy; the exit would be fast and furious, using speed to reach the trace-wipe location. And in between: shock and awe.

Sometimes she wished she'd been born a simple soldier herself.

But I've seen so much more than them.

The price had been agonising… and worth it.

"Good," she said, no longer looking at the lifeless lump on the floor, scarcely even aware of her three street soldiers getting into motion to obey her command.

Her mind was filled with something else.

Fiery mental constructs grew in her trained imagination: intricate topological models mapped to eleven physical dimensions, hypergeometric transitions determined by complex hex matrices. An architecture of power, of executing thought and energy.

No one besides a fellow adept could comprehend the heady wonder of such brilliance. No mundane possessed the power to visualise such complexity: to them it would be "just" hex manipulation, as if it were no more difficult than pushing a broom or adding up a column of numbers.

Yet modelling reality in this congruent way, a way that enabled actual manipulation of spacetime and energy, was "the greatest pinnacle of intellect and civilisation the world has ever seen" according to a recent essay by Kristof Dahlberg in the *Fortinium Post*.

It was a pity, but that kind of insightfulness was precisely why she'd needed to kill him. Companionship with someone at her own level could never be possible for someone like her.

The best she'd ever managed was decent enemies to fight.

Today, even that isn't likely.

And once she had the energy source in her possession, her ascension to a higher level still would be impossible to stop. Maybe all her worthy enemies had already perished. Maybe she would face better ones, when she ascended to new levels of personal as well as political power.

It wasn't just about new energy sources, made accessible by solving hex equations no one had been able to tackle before now. Similar, massively parallel calculations should unlock the remaining techniques of the Umbral Codices, giving her all the powers of the Delkor Xyniakothrotl, whose kingdom had lasted centuries in the southern jungle.

And never mind the manner of that culture's ending.

Forget the unworthiness of enemies. Either way, I win.

She left the room slowly, preparing for the coming confrontation, her heart beating nicely at the thought of it. Because this time, she suddenly decided, she'd be going into action alongside her street soldiers, or at least right behind them.

This was too important to entrust to others.

SIXTEEN

The next time Anna woke up, two tawny, vertically slitted eyes in a pretty female face were staring at her. The eyes widened, and the woman withdrew a little, but patted the back of Anna's hand.

"I'm Night Sister Katrina," she said. "Do you remember where you are, Senator?"

"Hospital…" One of the best in Fortinium, but saying that would be too much effort.

She'd come sort of awake before. Maybe more than once? It was hard to make sense of anything.

Except that Jean-Marc Bouchard had brought her here, and held her hand for what must have been a very long time.

"Right," said Sister Katrina. "And you're going to be fine. The doctors are really pleased."

Beneath Anna's head, the pillow felt soft and comfortable, too comfortable to move from. But she could speak. "Jean-Marc. Is he…?"

"Your boyfriend had to go." Sister Katrina's face dimpled. "A mature, handsome federal spellbinder, yet. He didn't move an inch until you woke up the first time, and even then he stayed for hours afterwards."

It seemed like too much effort for Anna to say that she and Jean-Marc had only just met. That the attraction was immediate and mutual and they were both of them old enough to skip over much of the initial stages of courtship – such an old-fashioned word, yet entirely appropriate – but you couldn't really call them boyfriend and girlfriend, not yet.

"What's… What's wrong with me?"

Kristof Dahlberg had exploded in front of Anna. The enormity of that seemed to have numbed her to her own body's feelings.

"Technically, Senator, it's called level four thaumatic trauma – level one is the worst – plus physical concussion from the shock wave. No whiplash

110

on the neck or damage to the eyes, which was lucky. Any complications would've shown up by now, so you're in the clear in that regard."

Anna swallowed drily, and Katrina responded – Anna decided to think of her by name, not title – by holding a cup of amber liquid to her lips. The stuff was sweet and tasted wonderful.

"Oh," said Anna as Katrina withdrew the cup. "Thank you."

"You'll be progressing in leaps and bounds from here. You want me to raise the bed a little?"

"I can sit up by myself, I think."

"Probably, but let's take it step by step, shall we?"

"You're quite bossy for someone less than half my age," said Anna, but her voice was mild and she followed the words with a smile.

"I'm supposed to be. Comes with the job." Katrina cranked a lever, and gears moved noisily but the angling of the bed was smooth enough. "How's that?"

"Better," said Anna. "Thank you."

She was in a private room, something she wouldn't normally take for granted, but right now her energy levels remained too low for political or social philosophy. The place felt secure, and she felt glad.

An opened book lay face down on the visitor's armchair, the title obscured by a face cloth, the one Jean-Marc had used to wipe sweat from her forehead: she remembered that now. And she wondered what he'd been reading, but with luck the real significance was this: he intended to come back, and take up where he'd left off.

And not just with the book.

She sighed, and decided she sounded just like a schoolgirl.

And didn't mind at all.

"I think I should ask you for tips, Senator," said Katrina, stepping back and crossing her arms. "See if I can get one for my own."

"What do you mean? And call me Anna, please."

"I mean you're safe as houses in here. Safer, because houses don't normally have a team of federal spellbinders guarding the corridors in all directions. Including" – she pointed at the ceiling and floor in turn – "the next floor up and the one beneath."

"Oh."

"I think Federal Agent Bouchard is pretty senior, which makes sense. The good-looking one near my nursing station is a lot younger, though. My age, I think. If you don't mind me saying so."

"Hardly." Anna shook her head, letting the pillow take most of the weight. "You're a young professional woman with your own career. You can live life on your own terms."

"I know," said Katrina. "And my terms are, I want a spellbinder in my life, and the one I've got my eye on looks terrific."

Aches rippled through Anna's chest when she giggled, but it felt good all the same. It felt as if life was continuing, where before she hadn't been sure.

"Then you go for it, sister."

Katrina nodded, smiling.

Maybe it was just chatting for the purpose of cheering Anna up, helping a patient to mend by improving her state of mind. Anna thought it was partly that, but not entirely.

"When he takes off his shades," she told Katrina, "that's when you know it's becoming personal."

"Ah. Good tip."

No spellbinder would remove their shades while on security duty, presumably, so Katrina needed to talk to her would-be beau after a changeover, assuming they needed to work in shifts.

Or maybe federal spellbinders could remain on guard for days on end without rest: you heard so many whispers about their capabilities, it was impossible to know what was true, what might be exaggeration, and what fell short of astounding reality.

Anna smiled and closed her eyes. A Night Sister like Katrina was more than capable of managing her romantic life. No need to worry on her behalf.

I'm going to be okay.

She felt herself drifting off.

What's that?

A kind of faint whistling that might have been her sinuses or something far off: it was so faint she couldn't tell. Her eyes snapped open, in time to see Katrina straighten up and her ears flatten slightly.

"I can hear something," said Anna. "What is it?"

Katrina shook her head. "You're not supposed to. Most people can't hear that frequency."

"Is there a problem?"

"It means we need to get ready. By *we* I mean the hospital."

Anna's feeling of peace was beginning to evaporate. "Ready for what?"

"It's a Level Orange Major Incident Alert."

"Here in the hospital?" Anna thought about the spellbinders on guard in every surrounding corridor.

"No, out in the city." Katrina's lips thinned. "Orange means an unknown number of potential casualties. It might be just a handful, maybe just one person."

Anna supposed a Night Sister wasn't supposed to be forthcoming with the details; but Anna's own status as a Federation Senator most likely made a difference.

"One or two casualties," said Anna, "doesn't sound like a major incident."

Katrina swallowed.

"That part," she said, "The *major* part... It means the risk might spread.

It means whatever's been reported, if it goes to Level Red, we're talking major loss of life."

So much for keeping the patient relaxed and calm. Anna began to wish she hadn't asked. "So what happens next?"

"You stay here," said Katrina. "We'll keep looking after you."

"You and your handsome fed?"

"Yeah." Katrina managed a smile. "Me and him. I was hoping if we'd see some action together, it would be after we both got off duty. Maybe I'm a bad girl."

She looked at the door.

"Do you need to go?" asked Anna.

"Only if you're going to be okay."

There was a call stone inscribed with white runes on the small bedside table. Anna reached for it slowly, took hold, and placed her hand on her stomach, resting with the stone lightly in her grasp.

"I'll squeeze if I need something," she said. "Go save some lives. Except you have to promise me one thing."

"What's that?"

"You let me know how it works out with you and you-know-who."

Katrina shook her head while smiling. "Sure thing, if you promise to do the same regarding your guy."

"Deal, sister."

"Okay, then. See you later, Anna."

"Later, Katrina."

But the smile was fading from Katrina's face as she exited and closed the door behind her, because she was a professional and the things she dealt with day to day lay beyond Anna's true understanding. That was pretty obvious.

Anna lay back and closed her eyes.

Too bad the universe doesn't listen to prayers.

All she could do was hope that Jean-Marc and Katrina and all of their colleagues were going to survive okay.

It mattered.

So very, very much.

Please let them be safe.

SEVENTEEN

Donal wanted to go home – to see Mel and baby Finbar and get in some hard rounds on the heavy bag – but work was work and Commissioner Sandarov was his one and only current paying client.

When Councillor Smythe had spilled what he knew about other city council members on the take, the name that kept cropping up was one Arrhennius Hawke: the "AH" from Smythe's diary entries.

Hawke was a banker of some kind, and his home address was in the city directory – Donal rang up Deirdre at the answering service, and she looked it up for him ("Anything for the young man who sends me doughnuts!") – and Donal wanted to take a peek at Hawke, as soon as possible.

A scouting mission, nothing more.

Donal held no preconceptions regarding bankers in general, but it bothered him – for some reason – that this Hawke, associated with Bloodfist Bank in particular and involved in bribing politicians, shared a first name with the late Commissioner Vilnar: the only Arrhennius that Donal had ever met, as far as he knew.

He felt unease as he travelled in a half-empty Hypoway capsule in the translucent tunnels over the gloomy Quagmire Chirality district with its black-roofed markets and slaughterhouses, past the oddly shining snake-shapes of the Argentile Arcs canal system, and the shadowed tenements of Sabre Depths and Deadbrook Sliver.

Two line changes and a final three miles via Pneumetro, and he was into a much plusher district by far. Donal came up from the Keening Broadway terminus via an escalator – he patted the rail and thanked the wraith, and didn't mind the lack of reply – and stepped onto a surprisingly clean sidewalk beneath the illuminated P sign.

A pair of scanbats travelled side by side overhead, which wasn't something you saw every day. Whether that was significant, Donal had no way of knowing.

At street level, both men and women were dressed in overcoats against the chill: dark greys and browns for the men, nearly all with belts and wide lapels, and subdued dark-green or deep-blue check patterns for the women, all of them looking newish or recently dry-cleaned.

Donal thought his own suit might just about pass muster, so long as he remained outdoors where the light was dim. Then again, he wasn't taking up residence here, and wasn't sure he'd want to, even if he could afford it.

In front of him stretched a row of dark-windowed shops lit by discreet firesprites inside golden lanterns. One exception was narrow and candle-lit, with shelves stacked with magazines and newspapers and candies: a newsagent, who might perhaps stock what Donal needed.

He went inside, nodded to the mossy-skinned, flat-capped man behind the counter, and scanned the magazine shelves until he saw a section of booklets, including the local volume of the Tristopolis Alpha-to-Omega. In his own office, he kept a full set of the street maps – bought second-hand from Peat's Bookstore, eleven years old but accurate enough for most navigation around the city – but they were too many to carry around everywhere.

Donal picked up the map book, turned to the page that showed Keening Broadway Station – it was easy to find – then used the index to look up Sawtooth Crescent, the street where Arrhennius Hawke lived.

He memorised the route and put the map book back on the shelf. When he turned, he saw the soft amber glower of the shopkeeper's eyes. The big guy's mossy green skin had darkened.

"Relax," said Donal. "I'm going to buy something."

There was an entire half shelf devoted to magazines for mothers of babies and toddlers. Donal ran his gaze over the titles, wondering which of them might catch Mel's interest, and ended up shaking his head. He looked over at the sports section, and saw the latest issue of *Fighting Heptagon*, and made up his mind.

He carried the fight mag and a bar of Midnight Scarab – purple chocolate was Mel's favourite, when she wanted a sweet treat – over to the counter.

The shopkeeper's expression had softened. "Boxing fan, huh?"

"It's not for me," said Donal. "It's for my wife."

It took a good five seconds for the shopkeeper to close his mouth and deal with the purchase.

Donal was smiling, still carrying the sight of the shopkeeper's expression in his memory, minutes after he'd exited the shop and turned in the direction of his destination.

Soon enough he was strolling along deserted residential streets, individual homes with spacious front yards, some fronted by shoulder-high stone walls, others by ornate railings you could see through. Semi-feral sprites hummed and danced along the black-leafed branches of silver screech trees, the sidewalks looked even cleaner than the ones back at the shops, and the air itself felt cool and calm and peaceful.

Maybe it would be good to live here, after all.

But it wasn't a serious thought, just a passing fancy.

I was rich, for a short while.

That money hadn't really been his, at least he hadn't felt it was; and it was gone now, so never mind. Perhaps the very thought of bankers was twisting his idea of money…

Silver letters glowed on a black iron sign.

SAWTOOTH CRESCENT.

Where with luck he might catch Arrhennius Hawke off guard.

With his fight mag rolled up into a cylinder in his left hand – if nothing else, he could use it as a weapon: you could crack a cheekbone or destroy an eye by stabbing with it, hard – Donal walked up a knucklebone-gravel driveway straight to a rune-inscribed front door that looked to be one solid sheet of black iron.

The gates had been hanging open. No wraiths lifted up from the ground at his approach. Nor did sprites move behind the curtains: no lights shone at all inside the house.

Some people were careless in their approach to security, but a banker? Especially a crooked one…

Deciding to continue with the direct approach, Donal took hold of the shrunken-pterosaur-skull knocker and rapped it hard, three times.

No sense of any reaction from the house or anyone or anything inside.

Doesn't feel right.

Unbuttoning his jacket, Donal took a few steps back along the scrunching gravel, tilting his head back to check the upper windows, the eaves above them and the roof itself.

Nothing.

No signs of anything weird, but an absence of reassuring life, of normal functioning in the house. Donal held himself still as only a zombie might, listening and feeling for odd resonances, sensing nothing at all.

On the right-hand side, a tall black iron door guarded an outdoor passageway leading presumably to the rear. Donal went over to it and pressed the handle down. The door swung open right away.

Definitely not right.

Dark walls formed the passageway, inscribed with black runes that should have glimmered or in some other way reacted as Donal moved softly along the passage; but again nothing occurred. He came out onto a heptagram-inlaid patio in a backyard dominated by carefully raked indigo gravel formed of fossilised rat skulls, where a dark fountain should have been splashing scented ink into a pool, but instead stood still.

The rear-door lock had been smashed open. Someone had pushed the door back into place, or almost, but a jagged hole larger than Donal's head formed one Hades of a giveaway: they hadn't bothered to leave a concealment hex, assuming they possessed that capability.

Which was likely, given the nature of the house they'd targeted. Everything hinted at formerly powerful defences successfully breached and broken. Professional intruders had killed the house.

And that didn't bode well for any human or other sentients who might have been inside at the time.

Donal drew the Magnus right-handed, and with his left hand used the rolled-up fight mag to push open the broken door. It squeaked, punctuating the silence, followed by nothing at all.

As softly as he could, Donal entered the kitchen and immediately smelled blood and the other bodily fluids that accompany sudden death. A maid lay sprawled, face down, in the hallway beyond the kitchen, beneath the tail end of a long streak along the wall: it looked as if one massive impact had done for her.

He stepped near and squatted down. The maid's head was partly flattened and the angle of the neck ruled out checking for breathing or a heartbeat. A living human with her own personal universe – family and friends and neighbours and enemies and millions of remembered moments – was gone, leaving behind only this thing: forensic evidence for now, and soon enough reactor fuel like everybody else.

There was a telephone on a stand at the far end of the hallway, near the front door, but it was too soon to make the call. It didn't feel like it, but the intruders might just possibly remain in the house: unless Donal checked, he couldn't be sure.

And if he wasn't alone, just picking up the phone would make him another target, and Mel wouldn't get her copy of *Fighting Heptagon*, not to mention Finbar growing up without a father.

There was a lounge, and through an arched doorway, a second such room, somewhat larger. Maybe Arrhennius Hawke called one of them his drawing-room. Either way, both rooms looked pristine as Donal passed through them, shelves and figurines spotless, the rugs freshly cleaned, all evidence that the maid had been a conscientious worker.

Time to check upstairs.

Donal went up carefully, Magnus at the ready, reaching a landing where he stopped, looking both ways along the upstairs hallway, noting the bookcases filled with volumes that weren't just for show: even without stopping to look properly, he could see bent spines on paperbacks and the general well-thumbed appearance of the hardcovers.

Not all bad guys are stupid.

The first two bedrooms he checked were empty of people and as well-kept as the rooms downstairs. But the third one smelled like the hallway where the maid had fallen, and when Donal peered inside, the splayed figure with the split-open head, still wearing an expensive-looking business suit, looked as if it once had been the same man posing in the blue-and-white photographs in frames on the wall.

Those photos showed him with people whose expressions said they expected to be recognised. Donal knew two: a former city mayor from the pre-Dancy years, and a notorious rabble-rousing speaker for the now-banned Unity Party.

Donal stared at the corpse of Arrhennius Hawke, wondering if he ought to feel sympathy. For Hawke to be murdered in his own home was a bad thing, yet the likelihood was he had brought it on himself... and on the maid downstairs, who probably knew nothing of her employer's true business deals. She was the one to mourn.

There were other rooms in the house to check, so Donal roused himself and did just that: looked in every one in turn, before returning to the ground floor and looking inside the shed and extra-large garage, finally certain that no intruders remained.

Time had been lost, but Hawke and the maid had most likely been dead long enough that a few minutes delay in making the call wouldn't affect the hunt for the killer or – more likely – the killing team responsible.

So now he had to phone it in.

In the front hallway he picked up the handset, thought about dialling sixes-and-nines the way any good civilian should, then reverted to former professional habit and instead spun the cogs to the direct Despatch number at Avenue of the Basilisks.

"I'm Donal Riordan, licensed investigator," he said, when the humming cleared from the line but before the despatcher could say a word. "I've a double homicide to report, in a private residence in Keening."

"Yes, sir," came a woman's voice. "Could you tell me the— Oh. Wait on the line, please."

This time only silence, not even a whisper of sprites.

After five seconds, a man's clipped voice came on the line. "Is that Lieutenant Riordan?"

"Former lieutenant, but yeah. Why do you—"

"Sir, are you in immediate danger?"

"What? No, I've come across a crime scene, homicide, but the killers aren't here."

"Please hold." A muffled scrape then low murmurs, as if the guy had his hand over the mouthpiece at his end. Another scrape, then: "Hello? Sir, if you wait a few moments, we're going to connect you to a radio car."

"What? Okay, I'm holding."

He was talking to a line filled with hissing. While he waited, he checked back along the hallway – the maid looked no less dead than before – and up the empty stairs and all around, seeing nothing new.

A crackle, then: "Donal? Bellis here."

"Hey, Lieutenant. You've got Hawke's number on your notify list, have you?" It was the only logical reason for Despatch patching him through.

"What?"

"I wasn't working on your Dredgeway Avenue case, but here I am talking to you anyway. So is there a Bloodfist Bank connection? I'm calling from Hawke's home," added Donal, "and it doesn't take a genius to—"

"Donal, stop. I'm calling from Hel Ave, around the corner from your gym. Your home. It's *your* name on the notify list."

The world seemed to stop.

"My…?"

"There's been an incident. I'm afraid… Your wife and child are gone, Donal."

A roaring filled his awareness, extinguishing all thought.

That's not…

Bellis's voice was a distant thing, devoid of meaning. "Donal? You still there?"

…possible.

Everything froze.

EIGHTEEN

Numb, as if surrounded by a cotton-wool cocoon insulating him from reality, Donal moved in slow motion: opening the front door from the inside, exiting the death house, walking the length of the gravel drive to the sidewalk and stopping there, arms dangling at his sides, the fight mag still in his left hand, the bar of Midnight Scarab chocolate still in his jacket side pocket: small stupid presents for Mel who meant everything to him, while the thought of something happening to baby Finbar was...

Simply too much to hold in his mind.

I...

The thought failed to complete itself.

He waited, like some statue or maybe a golem, scarcely functional. Only his trusty zombie heart continued to beat like a metronome, forcing his existence to continue.

Your wife and child are gone.

Bellis's words, forgetting that Donal and Mel weren't married, but that didn't matter.

Mel. Finbar.

Black light strobed at the end of the street, but the cruiser's flashers switched off as it turned into the crescent, slowed, and pulled to a halt by Donal.

Two uniforms sat inside, up front. The one in the passenger seat cracked her door open, but the movement roused Donal and he moved faster than she could: he yanked the rear door open, slid inside and pulled the door shut.

"I'm Riordan."

"Yes, sir." The passenger-side cop checked that she'd closed her own door. "We'll get you there at best speed."

She looked at her partner, who was already getting the car into motion, and he nodded as he accelerated into a tight U-turn and flipped the black-light flashers back on and drove hard to the end of the crescent, keeping to the middle of the road, checking the cross-street at the end and using a minimum-geodesic arc to cut across lanes and into the main road.

The driver had tactical training and experience – it showed – and at any other time Donal might have delivered a compliment, but right now he had nothing to say.

They drove fast, three times through crossroads where other cruisers with black-light strobes were holding back the traffic, and once even using a sidewalk – carefully – to bypass a block of jammed-up cars, but still the journey took too long, because there were too many miles to cover and this was, in the end, Tristopolis, not some empty backwater.

Donal's heart did its work while his thoughts looped in endless iteration without ever fully forming, trapped inside a sickening miasma of fear and loss.

Mel...

He was tactically trained himself, but some situations defied any attempt to grasp them.

Finbar...

None of this was possible.

When the cruiser stopped before the police barricade that stretched across the entire width of Helway Avenue, Donal felt paralysed despite the sight of Lieutenant Bellis climbing out of an unmarked saloon across the street.

He didn't want to get out and talk to Bellis, because if he stayed in here, in the back seat, perhaps nothing would have happened and he could wake from this nightmare and go home to, to...

"Sir?" The cop in the passenger seat had turned around, and her eyes looked sad and knowing.

"Thank you." Donal blinked and nodded towards the driver. "Thank you both."

He climbed out of the cruiser, feeling as numb as ever.

Time to snap out of it.

His thoughts cleared, though the part of him that processed emotion felt empty. Discontinued, decommissioned. Non-functional.

Automaton-like, he walked up to Bellis and stopped.

"Why are you here, Bellis?"

"Um, look Donal, something happened and the neighbours called it in and we came straight—"

"No, I mean why are you *here*?" Donal pointed at the nearest corner building. "My home is around there, half way down the side street. Why are you stationed out of sight with the main road blocked to traffic?"

And pedestrians. The sidewalks were clear for hundreds of yards in all directions.

"I'm holding off on sending in a tac team." Bellis rubbed his face. "Your house, I mean the gym... We can't get close right now because of the Guardian who's in there. She's throwing off dangerous amounts of energy, and it's not just that I'm afraid to send our people in. The way she's acting, she might bring half the surrounding buildings down."

Donal couldn't believe this. "Hellah's in there?"

"Yeah, her. We still don't know how she got here or why she's—"

"Hellah's my friend. I'm going in."

Bellis stared at Donal, then shook himself. "You've no idea how dangerous a Guardian can get."

"I kind of do. And I'd go in even if I thought she might harm me, which she won't."

"Hades. I don't know..." Bellis rubbed his face again. "Alright."

He turned to a group of officers at the barricade and called out: "Make an opening. One person going through."

Several of the officers exchanged glances, but pulled two reinforced-bone barriers apart to create a gap, then stood aside. None of them looked happy.

Bellis started to raise a hand towards Donal, then let it fall. "Good luck."

Donal managed the most microscopic of nods, then strode to the corner and around it, onto his street, which now lay deserted but felt alive with the bursts of light from the old temple windows, as if varicoloured explosions in random sequence were lighting up the inside of the boxing gym.

Hellah.

He already knew what he was going to find: a raging Guardian, a towering fury unable to vent her anger because the persons or entities responsible were gone and the only one left to target was herself. Whatever had happened to Mel and Finbar, Hellah was *not* the cause. That much, he understood immediately.

The rest, not so much.

Mel and Finbar are gone.

That's what Bellis had said.

He forced himself to walk on, even as the air grew increasingly electrified around him, as if lightning might discharge at any moment, lethal and uncaring.

Doesn't matter.

The *Mel's Gym* sign danced with blue electricity. The doors of the former temple were rattling hard, as if hammered by a cyclone from inside, which for all Donal knew might be literally true. All the while, explosions of crimson and fiery green and orange and blue continued to light up the street from inside the old, tall windows.

The old worshippers ought to see this.

It was a stray and stupid random thought, the kind of nonsense a redblood brain might throw up in the middle of a crisis.

I need to be better than this.

Miniature lightning played around his hand, especially his fingers, as he reached for the door handle; and the moment he took hold, everything brightened into whiteness and just for a second he felt absolutely certain that this was death and everything else was over forever.

Then he was stepping inside and the winds were dying down, a firestorm collapsing into a human-like figure, though not before he'd seen her as something else: twelve feet tall and raging, horns curling back from her forehead above eyes of living fire. She shrank in that moment, back to her normal self: a woman with skin the exact hue of freshly exposed blood, orange heptagons of flame forming the irises of her eyes.

"Thanatos, Donal. I'm so sorry."

"Hellah."

"Come here."

They met half way and she enveloped him in a hug, tight and hard enough to hurt a weaker being.

Grey stinging fluid obscured his vision and he squeezed his eyelids shut because he wasn't used to this, hadn't even known he was capable of producing such a thing.

Zombie tears.

Hellah squeezed him even harder, then released him.

"What happened?" he asked.

"I'm still… I haven't fully found out yet." Hellah's eyes blazed fire. "My rage got the better of me, but it should have worked, what I did. I flung out energy along the crawlspace dimensions, along the trails that must have been followed, I mean all the possible trails, but there's not a Death-damned trace of their passing."

Donal understood, pretty much. Like firing his Magnus down every alleyway a fleeing killer might have taken… But was *killer* the right word here?

He looked around the gym, seeing the equipment and the raised heptagon that remained intact, and he realised that for all her rage, Hellah's outpouring of deadly energies had not been entirely uncontrolled: she could indeed have brought the building down along with half the neighbourhood, but she'd kept some kind of discipline all along.

Three small figures were lying on the floor to one side: kids, around twelve years old, here for a boxing lesson. They were dressed in school uniforms, identical cheap black blazers, which meant they hadn't even changed into their training kit when the… incident… occurred.

"They're okay," said Hellah. "I'm keeping them in light trance until the investigators get here."

Donal looked into her fiery orange eyes. "The investigators are hiding half a mile away, peeing themselves at the thought of coming any closer."

"Ah. Sorry."

He realised he was still holding the rolled-up copy of *Fighting Heptagon*. Neither he nor Hellah had been thinking fully rationally. "Thank you for being here. Did Ingrid call you with the amulet?"

He tossed the magazine through the ropes onto the actual heptagon floor. It slapped the surface and lay there like an accusation.

"No." Hellah's mouth tightened as she shook her head. "It was young Ludmila who was here – Ludka – and she never had time to trigger the callback hex. She's on the floor, behind the boxing ring. Heptagon."

They rounded the heptagon together. Ludka was on her side, eyelids fluttering, moaning a little as she started to come round. The amulet at her throat looked blackened: amber coated with soot.

"It's still functional." Hellah could obviously tell what Donal was looking at. "I never expected a danger coming so fast that she wouldn't be able to call me."

Crouched down by Ludka, Donal looked around. "Is anyone else here?"

Hellah shook her head again. "No one, and I'd know."

There was light for Donal to see by, even though the incandescence from spillover energies while Hellah raged was gone now. When he looked up, he could see the flamesprites at the apex of the high ceiling, gathered together in a single group as if for comfort.

"It's okay," he called up. "It's gone now, whatever it was."

Ludka was beginning to rouse herself. If the first thing she saw on waking was just Hellah, her trauma would most likely intensify. Donal stayed squatting in front of Ludka, even though he would have liked to go outside and call for Bellis and his team.

Hellah's blood-red hand squeezed Donal's shoulder. "I'll let the others know they can come inside."

"Okay." He patted her hand. "Thank you."

She went to the side door, the one that led to the street, and looked out, took a few paces more, and waved to someone, then pointed back this way, in Donal's direction.

And came back inside the building, knowing the cops would be scared of her either way, but less so – perhaps – while she was out of sight.

Donal understood her thinking as much as she understood his.

Mel...

Trying to shut out visions of what might be happening to her.

Finbar...

To her and the baby, but he needed to concentrate, to focus on finding out what exactly happened, and following the trail.

"D-Donal?" Ludka's voice sounded shaky and weak and empty all at once.

He needed to follow the trail and kill whoever was responsible.

"Donal, I'm... I'm sorry." Ludka began to cry.

Kill them hard.
Stone dead.

NINETEEN

They'd made Ludka comfortable, sitting her up against the base of the heptagon and giving her some coal-weed tonic sweetened with heart-wasp nectar to drink. A female detective, the same one who'd been with Bellis at Dredgeway Avenue, was crouched down next to Ludka, using both hands to hold one of Ludka's, radiating calm and sympathy.

For Donal to stay patient was taking a massive, almost overwhelming effort, for all his supposedly implacable self control that came with his status as a zombie.

Lieutenant Bellis came inside, but before he could come over, a uniformed officer entered and called him back, saying a call had come in from HQ. Bellis nodded and went back out.

He'd probably already decided that there was little to be gained from talking to Ludka or the three schoolkids; but he was also thorough, so he'd be questioning them all the same: Donal felt certain.

"I'm... sorry." Ludka swallowed, and started to cry again. "There were so many of them, all running in, shouting. Dressed in black."

"Suits and ties?" said Donal.

"Coveralls. Boiler suits. And they all had... guns."

"And they broke in through the doors? Side or back?"

"Both. Most of them ran straight to the, to the..." She pointed, hand shaking, at the doorway that led to the annexe. To the bedroom where Mel and Finbar should have been safe.

But where silver runes should have glowed around the archway, only scorch marks remained, all of them misshapen. Every rune had been obliterated.

Not just thugs, then.

Acting like soldiers, and able to penetrate the defensive hex on both the outer and – surprisingly – the inner doors.

"There was a woman," added Ludka. "She looked at me, and I couldn't move my hand or anything." The tears came harder. "I just couldn't."

Donal wanted to tell her that it was okay, that she'd done her best, but he couldn't make the words come out.

Hellah spoke from across the room, keeping her distance so as not to terrify Ludka even more. "Can you describe the woman for us?"

"Her eyes were..." Ludka stopped.

As did her breathing.

"Thanatos." Donal's fingers were at her throat, checking for a pulse in the carotid artery.

A single beat, then nothing. Eyes staring at nothingness, unblinking.

"Oh, that's not right." Hellah came over and crouched down beside Donal, all her attention on Ludka. "She's in a Basilisk Trance."

Hellah pushed Ludka's eyelids shut, to protect the eyes from drying out.

"Bleeding Hades." Donal knew such things could last for years or decades or until the trance-trapped person simply died. "Triggered by a *memory*?"

"By my stupid question. But she said the woman simply looked at her, and that didn't sound as if there been any kind of delayed spell induction going on. If I thought the woman had actually talked to Ludka, I'd have been more careful in what I asked."

"Not your fault." Donal tried to give the reassurance he'd been unable to provide for Ludka, though it probably didn't help much.

"Amnesia regarding a verbal induction is common, but... No." Those twin fiery heptagons focussed on Donal. "I think my supposition was correct. I don't think this woman, whoever she was, took the time to install an event-triggered hex via the normal voice route."

"I'm not sure I understand." An understatement.

"I think she implanted this directly in Ludka's brain just by making visual contact, which is fast. We're talking fractions of a second. And that implies a level of power and expertise that's really not what I'd..." Hellah's voice trailed off.

"What are you thinking?"

Hellah's blood-red skin glistened. "It's not just that this woman, whoever she is, is powerful. Her capabilities are *different*, as well as strong. I can't think of a single witch or mage who'd leave resonances like this, or work this way."

For all his zombie sensory acuity, Donal was no longer sensing anything, no electricity on the air. The phenomena that he had sensed earlier were probably all Hellah's doing: by-products of her rage.

"And we have no detailed description," he said. "No visual description, the kind Bellis or I might be able to work with."

"No. What I need to do is—"

"But that tells us something." Donal touched Hellah's arm. "Sorry, I didn't mean to interrupt you."

"No problem. What does it tell us? Tell you?"

"That there's something about this woman's appearance that's striking, perhaps. Something that could be used to identify her."

Hellah shook her head. "Or the trance is just a way to prevent Ludka from drawing a portrait. She is an apprentice witch, remember. She could have given us realistic sketches from multiple angles, using a memory representation pattern to guide her hand while she drew."

"Oh," said Donal.

Catching the gist of Hellah's response, without knowing exactly what the Hades a "representation pattern" might be.

He stood up, turning around full circle, trying to take it all in without emotion. The previous automatic quality to his thoughts and actions was melting away, but he needed to stay in a rational, problem-solving mode because Mel and Finbar's lives might depend on—

Stay calm.

Focus was everything.

Two of Bellis's detectives were talking to the schoolkids, who were coming round. Physically, they looked fine. With luck, they'd lost consciousness before witnessing any aggressive moves. Except that wouldn't be lucky for the investigation, because Bellis's people and Donal himself needed all the information they could get.

A trio of pale-looking women appeared at the nearer entrance, all wearing indigo jumpsuits with the SOC initials embroidered over the hearts. One of the women stared with the bulbous eyes of a Bone Listener, while the other two looked standard human.

All three scene-of-crime diviners walked to the centre of the gym, stopped, and began to tremble.

"No..." said one of them.

"We must," said another.

They turned their backs to each other but shuffled backwards, inwards, moving closer until they touched, forming an outward-facing triangle, and then they linked hands. Their breathing synchronised, and when one of them swallowed, they all did.

Donal had never seen diviners act this way before. They usually just ran their hands or shiver-wood instruments close to objects or simply stared and sensed traces of whatever had happened.

But now their breathing was quickening, and they gripped each other's hands harder, knuckles whitening, faces growing lined with obvious pain.

The detectives and uniformed officers stared at the three women. Only Hellah looked calm, moving around the periphery of the gym, paying little attention to anyone, examining the walls, sometimes running her fingertips along the stonework.

This used to be a temple.

The thought just rose by itself. Donal wasn't sure of the relevance.

One of the scene-of-crime diviners cried out, and they released their hold on each other's hands and stumbled apart, breaking formation.

The nearest one looked straight at Donal. "You were close to the rupture, but not like the others." She waved towards the three schoolkids, then Ludka, but her attention remained on Donal "You witnessed it, but not today. Your exposure was yesterday, maybe the day before."

Bellis had re-entered the gym at some point. Donal hadn't noticed, which wasn't right. Something about the diviners' presence was causing him to feel disoriented: just a touch dizzy, but in a way he hadn't experienced since his redblood days.

So much wasn't right, in what should have been the safety of his family home, during what ought to be a time of joy.

The diviners turned to Bellis and bowed, which was not how they normally behaved towards investigating officers. Donal had never seen such a thing... although there had always been an oddly respectful relationship between diviners and Sergeant Bellis as was, back in the day.

Not to mention a distinct rapport with witches.

"Dredgeway Avenue," said Bellis. "Donal witnessed the murder and robbery, the one with the odd portal-enabled getaway."

"Not a portal," said one of the diviners. "Not a *normal* portal."

"Something different," said another.

"A rupture," said the third. "In the mesoscopic interface."

From the far end of the gym, Hellah joined in: "In the bridge from the compactified to the macroscopic dimensions."

Donal looked at Bellis. "Do you have any idea what they're talking about?"

But it was the young female detective, still crouched near the schoolkids, who offered up an explanation. "The portal you saw, Mr Riordan, wasn't actually a portal at all. It had a similar purpose... but it wasn't mage-built."

"What was it, then?" asked Donal.

"Something else." The detective shook her head. "I'm not being funny. I was talking to the other diviners this morning, the ones who attended the Dredgeway Avenue location. They're still trying to work out what the Hades it actually was."

Bellis said: "Martina knows what she's talking about."

Endorsing the younger detective.

Hellah walked over, causing even the diviners to shrink away, and placed her hand on Donal's forehead, held it there for three seconds, and took it away. "Tell me about it, Donal. What happened in Dredgeway Avenue?"

It took thirteen minutes to outline everything that happened, while the diviners looked interested – from afar: clearly not keen on proximity to Hellah – and Donal finally stopped, expecting Hellah to ask clarifying questions on the portal or rupture or whatever it was, but what she actually said came as a surprise.

"So this was the first time you'd run the catacombs for years, and you just happened to stumble onto this weird phenomenon. Do you think that was a simple coincidence, my friend?"

"I... Of course it was."

"Really?"

"I just decided to..." He stopped.

"Whenever someone says *just* in that way, it means they haven't thought about the details beyond that point. It means they *just* accepted some notion without diving beneath the surface."

"But Dredgeway Avenue is miles away. Miles from here, and miles from the entrance I used to go down to the catacombs."

There was no way, surely, he could have sensed anything at all from such a distance.

Bellis said: "The intruders carried some kind of framework along the catacombs for some considerable distance. Maybe that broadcast... something. Or left traces. Which entrance did you use to go down?"

"Conklyn Dropwell."

Bellis turned to the young detective and asked her: "Is that anywhere near the route the intruders took?"

"Close enough, maybe." She looked at the diviners. "I've got the full info from the other team back at HQ, if you three could help me with the analysis."

The diviners nodded, out of synch now, like normal people... if there was such a thing.

Donal was still trying to make sense of what Hellah and the others were saying. Could he really have detected some kind of resonance subconsciously, below the threshold of conscious awareness, despite his blackblood nature?

And a resonance induced in the catacomb walls by the passing of the disassembled framework, not even in its functional, working state...

"Why me?" he said.

Bellis shrugged. "These things never make sense. You just have to wait, and I promise we'll do everything to—"

"No," said Hellah, and everyone jerked back. "Donal means, why was he sensitive to that particular resonance?"

Donal looked at her. She understood him.

And then he got it.

"Is it Mel?" he asked. "Or is it Finbar?"

"It's sort of both. And maybe a little about you yourself." The flames forming Hellah's heptagonal irises softened to a gentle warmth. "Mel has some interesting ancestry mixed in there, but some of that was just potential before the baby arrived. A little epigenetic morphosis going on."

"So they give off the same kind of resonance harmonics as that portal thing, then." Donal shook his head. "Rupture. Whatever."

"Pretty much," said Hellah. "At least in spirit. The details are complicated, but that's the essence. It's related to the way Mel and Finbar are... linked."

"And that's why you've been so worried about their safety. Being on call even though we had a witch here at all times, and hex protection up the Death-damned wazoo. Because you sensed their... difference."

It was hard to focus on the conversation when images of Mel and baby Finbar were roiling in his mind.

"That's why," said Hellah. "That's exactly why."

Donal let out a long, long breath.

"How do we track them?" he said. "How do we get them back?"

Drops of blood were forming in Hellah's eyes. It was how she cried. Donal had never seen her weep before, but he knew it all the same.

"I don't know," she said. "I just don't know."

That word *just* again. Even Hellah, a Guardian, could not figure out the details. The necessary details, for finding Mel and Finbar.

They're not dead.

Hellah came close and grasped Donal's shoulders. "Are you sure? Do you feel positive about that?"

Donal hadn't realised he'd spoken aloud. Perhaps he hadn't.

"I feel they're alive," he said. "I *feel* it."

He put his fist over his metronomic zombie heart.

"Then we'll start with that," said Hellah.

And for the first time since hearing the dread news from Bellis over the phone, the tiniest spark of hope began to glimmer inside Donal.

Whatever it takes.

Hella nodded, her eyes blazing almost yellow now.

"Whatever it takes," she said.

They were going to do this.

TWENTY

A smart young man with cropped hair, the usual black suit and dark tie and wraparound shades, was standing guard *inside* Anna's private room.

There had been a kind of subdued commotion in the corridor outside, shortly after Sister Katrina's exit, and about a minute later this clean-cut federal spellbinder had stepped inside and said: "Just a precaution, Senator. We don't know exactly what the situation is just yet."

Anna lifted her head from the pillows, glad that Katrina had cranked the bed up to a near sitting position. "Any news of Jean-Marc? I mean Agent Bouchard."

There might have been a twitch of a smile at the corner of the young agent's mouth. "We know he's safe, ma'am. He's running two teams of agents on the ground."

"Thank Thanatos."

"Ma'am, I need to ask… Have any more memories surfaced? Of what happened before Dahlberg died?"

Exploded, you mean.

But Anna shook her head. "A single fragment of conversation. Philosophy. I quoted Lord Storer-Martin at Dahlberg, and he recognised it. But… I can't even remember what we ate. Or *if* we ate."

"I understand, ma'am. I'll just stand here quietly, if that's okay. You can pretend I'm not here."

"Of course," Anna told him.

The young federal spellbinder raised his chin as if scanning the horizon or trying to catch a scent. He remained that way, his expression calm and capable-looking; and Anna settled back against the pillows and released her breath, feeling the softening of her shoulders.

I'm safe.

A reassuring realisation sank deep inside her.

Jean-Marc is making sure of it.

So little time spent in his presence so far, yet her certainty was absolute. As a career politician, she'd made tactical compromises often, strategic compromises on occasion, and moral compromises maybe two or three times in total, and never without anguish, never for purely personal gain.

But however early in her relationship with Jean-Marc this present time might be, she felt with her entire inner being that she was right about him. Even if tragedy struck or Jean-Marc changed his mind so they didn't end up together for the rest of their lives, what she felt for him, the place he had carved in her heart, would not and could not change.

She'd never felt so certain of anything.

After a while, Anna returned to reading her book, an old novel – not a thriller, but historical fiction – that one of Sister Katrina's colleagues had fetched from the hospital patients' library after asking what kind of thing Anna liked to read. It took her away from the present day and into a distant past of knights errant and courtliness and a few ferocious women.

Much of it was fanciful rather than accurate, but even so, it rendered enough detail to have her wondering whether she herself, had she lived in such times and been born into the right class – a most questionable assumption, of course – would have spent all her days embroidering and reading, rather than trying to make a difference in the world.

Maybe she'd done enough, by now, in her actual life. All that striving and professional accomplishment. The thought of retirement, of living quietly by herself, had never really enticed her; but with the right person to spend her days with...

A soft knock, and the door opened, revealing Sister Katrina standing there. The federal spellbinder had already altered his expression minutely then stepped to one side, making room, which Anna read as his having received some kind of communication from his colleagues outside.

Maybe Jean-Marc could at some point explain how that worked, if she asked him nicely.

The agent said: "I can leave you alone with the Senator, Sister, if you need me to stand outside."

"No, we're good." Katrina smiled at him.

With the wraparound shades it was hard to be sure, but the clean-cut agent's attention seemed to be all on Katrina, though his lips remained straight, unsmiling.

He's the one Katrina's got her eye on.

Anna tried to hold back her own smile.

"Er..." Katrina turned to her. "No casualties out in the city after all, apart from some walking wounded. There's a whole bunch of them, but no fatalities or anything. The incident didn't go really bad at all."

"Well that's good news."

"Just some weird kind of hexplosion or something. The feds are still on site, looking into it." She looked at the agent. "Calling you *feds* isn't rude, is it?"

"It might be," he answered. It sounded as if he was teasing.

Anna held back the desire to make some smart remark.

Let the two of them get on with it.

She relaxed and tuned out Katrina and the agent's conversation. If all hospital stays turned out like this, you'd almost *want* to be admitted as an emergency, taking a welcome break from everyday life.

"—Holdex Club, apparently," Katrina was saying.

"So I heard," said the agent.

Anna snapped her attention back to the moment. "Excuse me? What was that about the Holdex Club?"

Katrina blinked. "Er, that was where it happened. The hexplosion or whatever it was. Knocked down over twenty people and destroyed a bunch of furniture. Cracked a ceiling or something."

Anna looked from her to the agent, or rather to the federal spellbinder's wraparound shades, and said: "I was in the Holdex Club when Kristof Dahlberg got killed. *That* hexplosion, or whatever… That's why I'm here in this blasted bed right now."

"Thanatos." Katrina was addressing the agent. "She's right. I mean, of course she's right. She was there. But I read about it, too."

"Give me a moment," said the agent.

For the next few seconds, his throat and mouth moved as if he were speaking without opening his lips, and though there was no sound, Anna thought that he was doing exactly that: sharing this observation with his colleagues standing guard outside.

Then he stopped and said: "I don't think the threat level has increased, Senator, where you're concerned. I think someone was making sure that no trace evidence remained. But we're going to act as if there is a threat, just in case."

"Thank you, Agent." Anna paused, then: "Can I ask what your name is?"

"Surely, ma'am. I'm Dexter. Saul Dexter."

"While it's just us, I'd be happy for you to call me Anna. And, Saul, this is Katrina here."

Katrina's vertically slitted eyes widened, then she realised Agent Dexter was holding out his hand to shake, so she responded. Their handshake lasted longer than most.

"Um." Katrina was still looking at Agent Dexter. At Saul. "I need to get back to the Night Sisters' station. It's at the end of the corridor, then turn left."

"Got it," said Saul. "I'll check in with you when my shift ends, at eighteen o'clock. If that's okay?"

"Of course it is."

After a moment, Katrina opened the door and stepped out into the corridor, and looked back towards Anna.

Thank you, she mouthed.

And allowed the door to softly click shut.

Anna smiled.

Good job, if I say so myself.

But the warmth inside her faded, just a little, as Agent Saul Dexter, Federal Spellbinder, regained his previous posture, an at-ease stance with hands folded together in front of him, at the level of his centre of gravity, looking totally calm and relaxed, not even remotely pressured.

And yet Anna sensed he could explode into action at a millisecond's notice, physical and kinetic or via hex arcana, at a level of reality only mages and perhaps some witches understood, and with a degree of violence that none of them could ever manage, no matter how hard they tried, because federal spellbinders formed a breed apart.

So yes, it made her feel safe, so very safe, to have Agent Dexter here.

But the Holdex Club.

She wondered when Jean-Marc would return, and tell her what was happening.

Or failing the latter, simply when he might come back, just so she could enjoy his presence, for the novel on her lap no longer enticed her.

On the other hand, perhaps she could help, even from her bed. She had so many contacts, after all.

"Saul? Do you think there's any way someone can run a phone in here?"

"Senator? Is there family or someone you need to talk to?"

"No, but I've contacts with varying amounts of information on Dahlberg Industries. We work in committees, you know."

"Ah."

"And you can listen in on every conversation. In fact, I'd feel happier if you did."

"In that case, Senator, I'll see what I can do."

An hour later, and she thought she might have something.

"You're sure?" she said into the handset.

The main apparatus stood on a hospital trolley next to her bed, and a long cord trailed out through the cracked-open door to the corridor beyond. Besides Saul Dexter standing right here, Anna could glimpse another federal spellbinder outside.

Jean-Marc wasn't taking any chances with her safety. It was a rather wonderful thought.

"How long have we worked together?" Even over a phone line, her old sort-of friend from the Senate press corps could sound sarcastic, exasperated and amused all at once. "Of course I'm not sure. But I'm *nearly* sure, and that should be good enough for you."

"Come on, Mikio," said Anna. "Bloodfist Bank, really?"

"You come on. Tristopolis is the ideal place for setting up new energy facilities, especially if there's any chance of them blowing up. You want something like that in *your* back yard?"

"Hmm. Okay. Can you call me back if you learn anything more?" Anna covered the mouthpiece. "Could you ask someone what extension number the nurses' station is?"

They'd have to take away this trolley phone thing: she needed a permanent number for Mikio to ring back on.

"It's 9-2-3," said Agent Saul Dexter. "I just happened to notice."

"Mm," said Anna, then relayed the number to Mikio, who promised to call if anything new cropped up.

They hung up at the same time.

"Bloodfist Bank, Senator? A Tristopolitan connection?"

"Maybe. Someone's been manoeuvring behind the scenes, setting up exactly the right kind of people and committees to make a bid for the new projects. But my friend doesn't think it's anything to do with Dahlberg."

Saul's head jerked up.

"What is it?" said Anna.

But Saul was holding still, his wraparound shades rendering his expression unreadable. After a moment, he nodded – to absolutely no one there – then breathed out and relaxed, and turned towards Anna.

"Something odd is happening," he said. "I shouldn't mention it to a civilian, begging your pardon, but it's happening – or did happen – in Tristopolis."

"That could really be a coincidence," said Anna.

"Yes, it could…"

Anna looked at the phone on the trolley. "Am I able to reach Jean-Marc, I mean Federal Agent Bouchard, on that thing?"

Reflected highlights slid across the shades as Saul shook his head. "Sorry, no."

"I think he should hear about—"

Saul held up one hand. "Senator. Anne. I can talk to him right now, it's just that there won't be a telephone involved."

"Ah."

"I'll speak aloud, so you can check I haven't missed anything. Is there anything specific I need to mention?"

Anna's mouth twitched. She couldn't help it.

"Tell him I miss him," she said.

Saul shook his head, but he was smiling.

"I'm going to get in trouble," he said. "But what the Hades… Agent Bouchard, sir. I'm vocalising as I communicate because the Senator needs to listen in."

Anna swallowed, half spooked and half thrilled by the way Saul could talk to Jean-Marc without a telephone in hand.

"Yes, sir," added Saul. "It's speculative, but the current alert in Tristopolis might have some distant bearing on the Dahlberg case."

Anna listened as he relayed everything she'd told him, and filled in details when prompted, trying to recall the exact words Mikio had said.

"No, sir," concluded Saul. "Nothing else except that, er… Senator Fitzgerald misses you. With respect, sir."

Then his demeanour changed: he relaxed and wiped his face, which Anna took to mean that the connection had ended.

"I don't suppose he had any kind of reply for me?" she said.

"Actually…"

"Yes?"

Saul took a deep breath, then blew her a kiss.

"Oh," said Anna. "Oh."

"Right."

Anna felt a blush warming her cheeks.

Saul cleared his throat.

And then they laughed, together.

TWENTY-ONE

Vanessa knew better than to allow herself to become engorged with triumph, to relax and celebrate her most definite victory, real and important though it was.

She had the woman and baby prisoner.

A mother and newborn child.

Not what she'd expected, but on the other hand, the emergence of quantally entangled composites was massively unusual and unpredictable: she should have tried to keep an open mind.

The pair were incarcerated in the most secure cell ever, in the second-lowest level of Inversion Tower: a cell even better shielded than the one that held her tri-horned daemonid captive, the entity that for all its strength had eventually yielded to suffering and torture, and yielded the location of the human – or nearly human – mother and son.

But self congratulation and reward would have to wait, because law enforcement might still prove a nuisance, particularly if those Death-damned federal spellbinders became involved, so every little detail needed to be dealt with.

In practice that meant this: standing in the middle of a dark, cold forest, surrounded by blackiron trees which smelled of recent ghoul activity, though it would be asking too much for any bloodghouls to show themselves right now.

Even the stupidest of them would know better, the second they tasted the scent of Vanessa's power on the cold, cold wind that permeated this part of Dreadcore Forest.

I want to be at home, drinking in delicious suffering.

A mother and newborn child. The possibilities were endless, provided she was careful not to damage their inherent properties, the ones destined to prove useful, though not to mother or baby: only to Vanessa herself.

"Ma'am?" It was one of her street soldiers, nameless as far she was concerned.

When she looked at him, the runes on her golden fingernails began to glow, a sign that he knew how to read: he stepped back, swallowing, eyes widening. Beneath the always-dark sky in this dense blackiron-tree forest, his expression was hard to read visually; but even an ordinary human without Vanessa's sensibilities could have tasted the man's fear in that moment.

I'm so hungry for it.

But she made herself simply say: "Any sign of the trucks?"

She'd left the main convoy, using her limo to transport the woman and child to Inversion Tower, and returned now to conceal the final forensic traces of her convoy.

If the street soldier assigned to detonate an obliteration blast had done his work correctly, then the main trail – comprising hex resonance and chemical traces: effectively the soldiers' and vehicles' scent – would have come to an end inside Tristopolis itself.

But eyewitness evidence might still point investigators in the direction of this forest, so the vehicles themselves were going to have to disappear, just in case. Her limo and saloon cars had protection that meant no mage or diviner could possibly follow their trail to Inversion Tower; but the trucks weren't quite at that level.

"Headlights, ma'am, about three miles away. We think it's them."

Vanessa nodded. The road in question meandered, taking anything but a straight route through the difficult forest, but there were a couple of stretches that her people were able to see from the nearest observation post.

Soon enough, she sensed the vehicles in a way that made her nostrils dilate, which was not at all lady-like but most definitely useful. By the time she heard their engines, she was already prepared for what she was going to find.

A minute later and the trucks were bumping their way off-road, guided by flamesprite lanterns held up by the people she'd brought with her: not counting the golems, there were seventeen of them, almost as capable as the lead team, who remained back at her reinforced underground home of Inversion Tower, debriefing and decompressing, celebrating a successful operation.

This spot, here, lay fifty-seven leagues from the nameless clearing above Inversion Tower, and Vanessa would have preferred to do this even further away, but timing was important, particularly given the burnt para-scent she was picking up from the trucks, all three of them.

Large and black, like furniture removal vans but entirely unmarked, they rattled and bumped their way carefully along the prepared trail, all the way to the edge of a still lake where nothing lived, not even a clan of ghouls or a colony of lizards: nothing at all.

The trucks pulled up side by side, facing the dark water, engines continuing to rumble until Vanessa nodded a command and one of her men waved his flamesprite lantern up and down three times, and the drivers switched their engines off.

Getting rid of trace evidence was a part of her normal routine, while the resonance on the air that only she could taste meant that this time, her precautions would really prove their worth. Had already done so, in fact.

"I want to see inside the trucks," she said.

Two people climbed down from each vehicle: a driver and a street soldier literally riding shotgun.

All six worked in near-synchrony to unlock the rear doors of all three trucks and pulled them open. Two of the interiors smelled faintly of burnt toast, and showed charcoal streaks across the inner surfaces, while the third had borne the brunt of the phenomenon: its side and roof were distorted into frozen ripples, and to someone like Vanessa the ozone-and-smoke scent, redolent of serious blowback, cut through the forest's fresh air. It pretty much stank.

Vanessa controlled herself, allowing no expression to show, not even a wrinkling of her nose. Let her people think of her as a stone-faced bitch. Despite all the things they'd seen her do, they didn't know the half of it.

It wasn't a witch who did this.

Nor was it a mage's doing, this energy blast that could have wreaked so much more damage than it actually did. Thank Thanatos. Vanessa could easily have left the rupture spillovers to heal in their time, to seal up at a natural pace, but she hadn't.

"Cousin Hellah," she said. "Not you, surely."

It was impossible to avoid leaving some rips and tears in the fabric of macroscopic reality, when you wielded rupture hex the way that she did: just transporting the segments of the framework apparatus was enough to leave traces.

But she'd worked shrewdly and tactically, deliberately squeezing shut as best she could every trail and pathway through the compactified dimensions of space and time. And never mind the ferocious concentration such tidy-up tasks required: she was capable, and the payback was worth all the trouble.

Such precautions made it even less likely that someone would be able to backtrack her movements, or the movements of her portal framework apparatus. But this was different.

What she hadn't expected was that someone might go beyond trying to sniff out the trail and actually blast lethal levels of energy along the geodesics.

Another bimodal daemonid.

It was a dangerous thought. She'd already created a subtle form of mayhem inside crawlspace to get the entities below Avenue of the Basilisks mildly agitated: enough to keep the Guardians busy, but not enough to threaten the actual city… probably.

It had been a preventative measure. And surely it wasn't one of them who'd turned up at the kidnap location and tried to fire energies along the trail to find out where Vanessa and her team had gone.

But if not Hellah or even Klaudius, then who?

Someone like me.

One of her own kind, or at least related. And one of her cousins, one of the two Guardians, might well have sensed the entangled composite – the mother and baby, quantally entangled, although destined to decohere unless someone like Vanessa did something about it – but they shouldn't have been taking an active interest.

Not given the duties they were sworn to perform.

But they didn't get me, whoever they were.

No damage to her, no injuries to any of her people, and above all, no way to follow the trail back to her. A forking trail through eleven spacetime dimensions, and three ends of the trail comprised the trucks right here.

"Everyone stand back," she warned.

Purple fire blazed inside all three trucks simultaneously. It billowed and writhed and flared in intricate patterns, and by the time it finally died away, all specific forensic traces had been totally wiped clean.

No one could track them now.

She turned, ready to give the command, but one of her men had already called her golems out of the heavy transports parked behind a particularly thick copse of blackiron trees. Nine huge figures stumped towards her, then stopped.

Awaiting her command.

"Take these trucks," she said. "Three of you to each vehicle. Lift them up and carry them to the centre of that lake." She pointed to the flat, still surface. "Place the trucks on the bottom and leave them there. Return to this spot."

The last part might be unnecessary, but golems functioned best with everything spelt out step by step, using simple explicit declarations.

She watched as they did her bidding: lifting the big trucks, walking with steady steps and unblinking yellow eyes into the dark, still lake; and when the waters closed over their heads, it was no big deal.

By that time only the top third of each truck remained visible, and that visible portion diminished soon enough as they moved further towards the centre of the lake. A few seconds later, the roof of each truck barely showed against the dark, viscous water. Moments after that, they sank beneath the surface and were gone from sight.

Let the authorities try to track her now. Every trace was obliterated.

After a while in the water, the trucks would no longer retain the final resonance, that of the cleansing act itself. A resonance that from the surface was already undetectable.

Nothing remained: nothing that could lead them to her.

After three minutes, nine convex bumps broke the water's surface, the golems' heads, and all nine golems came ponderously, implacably out of the water and stopped on the clay ground, and stood like statues as water sluiced off their bodies and diminished to dripping.

"Return to your transports and climb aboard," she told them.

They did as she commanded. At the same time, needing no explicit instructions, seven of her soldiers used the edges of entrenching tools to churn up then loosely level off the ground where the golems had walked, obscuring the evidence of immensely heavy footprints.

No need for hex, which might leave its own traces. Sometimes the primitive approach worked best.

She watched as the clean-up continued, not in any hurry to get going, sure in the knowledge that back in a cell near the lowest level of Inversion Tower, a captive mother with her baby son must be growing more frantic by the second, while every extra minute and hour spent in that intensifying state must push her closer and closer to the edge, to breaking point.

To where Vanessa could bend the woman to her will without having to destroy or damage her: to the point where mother and child became the most useful of tools.

In the distance, a wolf howled, not in challenge but in agony: the death-sounds of an animal trapped by bloodghouls, desperate to escape but knowing these had to be the final seconds of life.

And then it was gone, causing Vanessa to smile.

Hunters and hunted.

Always the way.

And she knew which one she was, and always would be.

"Come to me," she said. "Come now."

The runes came to life on her golden fingernails, and her hands formed claws, as for a second her daemonid and human arms coexisted in superposition, and she reached through the compactified dimensions in a manner no mage or witch could ever conceive of, and she felt her questing energy sink in its hooks a split second before the eldritch howl sounded from afar.

Not far. No distance at all.

Grinning, she hauled her prey towards her, dragging its mass along the crawlspace dimensions, enjoying the tug of its struggle, knowing it could never be a match for her. They both knew it, but her prey did not give up.

Its death would taste all the sweeter.

Her soldiers finished their work and hurried aboard their own transports just as she pulled her prey out of the compactified dimensions and fully into the human-sized world. It hung there, torn and rippling, no longer the harbinger of fear, but the victim.

It had a name, this wounded bloodghoul – Vanessa could sense that much – and she had the power to rip that knowledge out of its mind, but she didn't see the point. Bloodghouls are feared because they feed on any creature they get hold of, for their hunger is never truly satisfied.

But Vanessa was the apex predator here.

The bloodghoul screamed in ways beyond sound as she clenched and twisted her hands and caused the bloodghoul's form to tear apart, rending it into smaller and smaller delicious fragments, bringing the most exquisitely agonising form of death its kind could ever face.

"I recognise the taste," she said, though little of the bloodghoul's consciousness remained to understand her words. "I've taken some of your relatives before, haven't I?"

And she smiled as it screamed for the final time, before its remains wafted like airborne rags on an updraught, growing ever more translucent as their energies flowed into Vanessa; and then the bloodghoul, or what was left of it, evaporated from existence.

Was gone.

"How lovely," said Vanessa. "What a nice, unexpected snack."

She was solidly her human, gorgeous self once more.

Time to see my interesting prisoners.

Wet black grass slid and whispered across her shoes as she strode towards the trees where her car was hidden. It felt good to be moving.

Pressing forward, always.

TWENTY-TWO

Donal felt only despair, because nothing that Hellah was trying seemed to work. She prowled around the gym, over and over, even after the scene-of-crime diviners and all the cops had left, and all without result.

At times, Donal went to the bedroom where the bedclothes lay strewn in all directions and tried to make sense of what he saw, and of the roiling in his guts, the inchoate images tumbling around in his mind; but none of it was helping.

His earlier determination had sunk in a pool of helpless self-mockery. There was nowhere to start, no clue to analyse, no scent – real or metaphorical – to sniff out.

No Death-damned trail to follow.

I'm useless like this.

It was just him and Hellah now inside the building.

Grey-faced paramedics had taken poor Ludka out on a stretcher, destined for a long-term-care ward at St Jarl's. Uniformed officers had taken the schoolkids to reunite with their parents. The diviners had departed; likewise the detectives, unless they were working outside on the street: Donal hadn't looked out, so he didn't know.

But why a snatch?

Never mind the overwhelming force that had been employed, including but not limited to a highly professional quasi-military strike team. The means were important, but exactly what end, what objective, did the team's leader or employer have in mind?

A rich woman with a newborn child might conceivably get snatched for ransom, though Donal had never heard of such a thing: professional made men had qualms when it came to children, as did their bosses. Cops laughed at the notion of a criminal code of honour; but still, everyone recognised constraints and limits: there were some things a professional would not do.

Rich adults, alright: they were potential victims. But Donal and Mel possessed so little, no liquid assets to speak of; so it was all about the hex-and-mage stuff, exactly as Hellah had feared.

He walked back out to the centre of the gym and said to Hellah: "We need to bring in Mordanto or the feds."

Most likely, Bellis was already making calls from his desk back in HQ, or maybe just from a radio car parked on Hel Ave. When even your scene-of-crime diviners were acting twitchy, that was when the big guns were called for.

Mel. Finbar.

Sweet Thanatos, how was he supposed to find them when he didn't know where to start?

Stop.

He calmed himself. Despair and panic were counterproductive, and he was a blackblood, a zombie capable of self-control. For Mel and Finbar's sake, he had to maintain focus.

Stay disciplined.

If they were to have any chance at all, he would have to keep control.

Who do I know?

Among mages: there was Lamis, perhaps the most likely to want to help as a solo effort, but persona non grata to a large extent among his fellow mages; possibly Mage Kelvin, a rising star with some authority within Mordanto, who'd proven willing in the past but had suffered greatly the last time they'd worked together, and perhaps was still attempting to recover.

Donal hadn't talked to him for a good while.

And finally, the last on this very short list was Professor Helena Steele, who'd apparently rescinded her previous resignation and resumed the mantle of heading up Mordanto.

Had Donal's previous lover, Laura Steele, managed to survive, then Helena Steele might conceivably have become Donal's mother-in-law; but as things turned out, it was Laura's zombie heart beating inside Donal's chest right now, and Laura was gone forever.

Helena Steele had resented and despised him for a long time, and perhaps her feelings had mellowed, but not hugely.

Among the federal spellbinders, the only local agent Donal knew was Agent Chambers, and he wasn't even sure that she remained in Tristopolis.

I have to do something.

Then Hellah gave a small cry, and all his attention snapped back to the external world, centred on her.

"What is it?" he said.

"Something's happening." The fires in her eyes turned yellow once more: never a good sign. "Back beneath HQ. Klaudius can't manage on his own."

"Oh, Thanatos."

She was going to have to go. If the great entities that lived below the minus two hundred and seventy-third level of One, Avenue of the Basilisks broke loose, then the whole of Tristopolis would be at risk.

"Donal, I'm—"

"Go. You have to."

"Klaudius tried to hold them back solo, for as long as he could."

"Of course he did."

"I—"

"Go now."

Hellah bowed her head. "I'll be back, my friend."

Orange fire enveloped her, and she was gone.

So that's how you travel.

He wondered how it worked. He might be a layperson when it came to hex manipulation, but from what he'd been reading, the colours that blazed when certain transitions or reactions took place held some significance, indicating the specific energies involved.

"Necromagnetic wavicles," he said aloud. "Energy given by frequency times the von Arkon coefficient."

How that rote memory might help, he had no idea.

The so-called rupture that he'd witnessed beneath Dredgeway Avenue had shone the same sapphire blue as a mage-constructed portal, while Hellah employed some other technique to travel, and all he really knew was that the stuff he'd read in library books had been nothing like complete.

He walked to the small cash box on the table by the heptagon, thought about Mel's fingers touching it the last time she'd sat in on a training session and coached from a chair, her belly huge with Finbar, their unborn son just two days away from making his appearance in the world.

Focus.

Opening the box, he found enough coins for several phone calls, even long distance. More than enough to fill a pocket: he might as well just take the cash box with him.

He went out, cash box in hand, via the double doors at what would have been the furthest end from the altar, back when this was an actual temple. A uniformed officer, no one Donal knew, was standing guard.

"I'm just making some calls." Donal gestured towards the phone booth on the corner.

"Sure." The officer nodded her head. "Sir... We'll get them back, I'm sure of it."

Donal nodded back, unable to say thanks.

As he walked to the phone box, he glanced back, checking that there was another officer stationed at the side entrance beneath the *Mel's Gym* sign, and an entire team at the end of the road. This whole street remained cordoned off, by the look of it.

SOC diviners didn't get very far.

You didn't release a crime scene until you'd gathered all the evidence available. Bellis knew his stuff, and might not even have allowed Donal to remain inside the gym had Hellah not been there. Either the diviners were going to return, or the feds were on the way.

But he couldn't just hang around and wait.

Inside the phone box, he propped the cash box on the beetle-chitin shelf and extracted five-edged farthing coins, shovelled them in and spun the cogs to sevens-and-nines, the number that was also the title of a radio drama serial he used to listen to years ago, with the other kids back at the orphanage: 777-999.

A voice answered almost straight away. "Federal Spellbinders Agency. How may we—"

And silence.

"Hullo?"

But the line was dead: not even the hum of sprites.

Flat silence.

He replaced the handset, picked it up and tried again. Nothing.

Can't be just the feds affected.

So he tried the obvious, sixes and nines to report an emergency, and the line remained dead.

Wonderful. Probably it was just the phone cable in this street, affected by everything that happened earlier.

Or something that was happening now?

He walked back out onto the street, cash box in hand, looking both ways, seeing nothing untoward. Overhead, nothing moved against the deep-purple sky: no passenger aircraft high up, no scanbats on surveillance, no federal pteracopters or black winged ambulances.

That was usual, yet for some reason it didn't feel right.

The air felt deader than it ought to.

It's not the world.

Yet it had to be: the dead phone formed proof. Still, the feeling just grew stronger.

It's me.

He felt disconnected from everything, from reality itself.

Zombies don't experience shock. It's not in the job description. Except it wasn't actually a job and the documentation of the blackblood experience seemed to be missing an awful lot, when push came to shove.

A bloodghoul was moving along the street.

A ghoul. Here.

"That's not possible." His hand moved towards his shoulder holster, then stopped, because even if he'd loaded the Magnus with hex-piercing rounds – he hadn't – they wouldn't help against a ghoul.

It was coming closer, and the uniformed officer standing guard below the *Mel's Gym* sign showed no signs of seeing the damned thing that was headed her way.

"Officer! Run!" His shout sounded flat in the strange air, but with luck it was loud enough. He beckoned. "Run this way!"

She looked startled, recognised Donal, and made the sensible decision.

To sprint, as hard as she could.

"Come on!"

He moved sideways, to the centre of the street, gesturing at her to hurry. The other officer, at the end double doors, started to move also, but Donal waved him back.

"Stay out of sight," Donal called out. "Circle round back, find the others."

"What is it?"

"Ghoul." The word sounded weird and flat: something was wrong with the air for sure. "Bloodghoul on the loose."

The officer swore, and for a split second Donal thought he was going to argue, believing that a bloodghoul could not possibly appear in an ordinary neighbourhood with no warning; but then the officer's disbelief snapped out of existence, and he bolted.

Good.

But the female officer was in the ghoul's sight, and she was running hard this way, ever closer, while the ghoul simply drifted above the dark tarmac without any apparent effort, billowing slightly and appearing to be moving slowly while actually gaining on the officer no matter how hard she pushed; and she couldn't maintain this pace for long.

Five seconds, and she would be level with Donal.

Come on.

The bloodghoul was diagonally behind her, following a parallel course this way, the distance between it and the officer diminishing with every beat of Donal's zombie heart.

Four seconds.

Keep running.

A redblood human can sprint for ten to twenty seconds before the body has to shift to the second of its three energy systems, and while the second system is also anaerobic, it's not as efficient as the first; and by the time the third, aerobic system kicked in the officer would be dead because—

Three seconds.

—the bloodghoul was showing zero signs of slowing down and the two terms that the TPD used to describe bloodghouls officially were *merciless* and *always hungry* and nothing about this particular ghoul suggested any different.

Two.

Less than a second to go but the officer wasn't going to reach Donal's position in that final timeslice so the only way to shorten the remaining distance was for Donal to spring forwards, directly towards the bloodghoul, so that was what he did.

The cashbox went spinning as he jettisoned the thing but he never heard it hit the ground.

Zero, because he'd altered the timeline, cutting it down to nothing, knowing that he had to.

Mel. Finbar.

Contact.

With a ghoul.

After Donal died, the Department would do everything, absolutely everything in its power to find and rescue his family because he might have left the ranks but in some sense he remained one of their own; and they would honour that.

That thought offered a fragment of comfort.

The world was gone – distant, translucent – with no external sounds because it was all around him, the bloodghoul, its spectral body totally enveloping him, encasing him; and he should have remembered that a bloodghoul's prey rarely dies instantly.

That would be too easy.

They like to take their time to feed, do bloodghouls, as if the suffering enhances the flavour as they strip the enveloped body to bones and nervous system alone, sucking in all flesh, all organs save the brain and its connections, which they leave until the end when even the bones are gone, all but the final delicacy: just eyeballs (whose retinas form extensions of the visual cortex) and the fine black tracery of exposed nerves and the diminishing lump of sweet structured fat that forms the human brain, sucked at like a lollipop until it grows tiny and is gone and finally, replete, the ghoul becomes free to move on.

To look for its next morsel because: always hungry.

But…

I'm still alive.

Which clearly was impossible, but his thoughts continued to operate, and when he looked down, his hands, his entire body remained intact though encased in the ghoul's translucent form.

Not possible.

The ground wavered, dropping away though not by much: call it thirteen inches, give or take, though the rippled appearance of the world as seen from within a ghoul lent a measure of uncertainty.

It hasn't even begun to eat me.

But it wasn't ejecting him – rejecting him – either. Were bloodghouls less keen on absorbing blackblood flesh than the usual redblood kind?

Or did some like to carry the food within them for a while before beginning to digest their living prey? Perhaps he should have been reading up about bloodghouls instead of borrowing books about mages and his own Death-damned kind.

I don't understand.

Perhaps the strangest thing of all was his lack of desire to struggle. It didn't seem to gel with all the stories of creatures, human or otherwise, screaming as bloodghouls ate them: no notion of the ghouls anaesthetising their prey. No reason for Donal to remain physically quiescent as the road began to slide past underneath.

I'm travelling inside a ghoul, and I just don't seem to care.

Perhaps because he'd already accepted death, releasing all his previous concerns. Some part of him remained frantic over the fate of Mel and Finbar; but the rest of his mind had transitioned to a kind of peculiar conscious calm.

Or maybe it's happening for a reason.

Which made no sense at all, and outside his spectral, moving prison the world remained as before, including the officer he'd believed he was sacrificing himself to save: she was standing off to one side and even through the distortion he could read the horror on her face.

It's Hellah's doing.

It had to be.

Maybe there was another explanation, but he couldn't think of one. No witch or mage he'd ever heard or read about worked with bloodghouls in any capacity.

Iceghouls, their slightly more tractable brethren, could be used to guard premises, like the ones who flitted through Möbius Park around City Hall; but even they were rumoured to be hard to control, to occasionally snatch and devour innocent passers-by beyond the park walls, during the quiet hours when no one was around to see.

But Hellah was a Guardian, an almost unknown quantity as far as the world at large was concerned: her talents and abilities lay along axes of power that no one really discussed. Whatever it took to keep the entities below the HQ tower at bay: ordinary people just didn't want to know.

The world continued to slide past.

Something…

A faint violet line, visible only because of the colour showing while the rest of reality appeared washed out and tending towards monochrome. A thread of light that lay along or perhaps just above the roadway, and as the road curved slowly to the right, so did that trace of violet – and so did the bloodghoul's trajectory as it carried Donal along.

Still physically intact. His skin had not begun to dissolve. His eyes, he hoped, were working just fine: the distortion was caused by refraction and absorption within the ghoul's form – he had to believe this – and not by digestive processes starting work on his eyeballs.

And still he felt no desire even to wriggle just a bit: the more quiescent he remained, the more likely it was that the bloodghoul would simply carry him onwards and forget its normal purpose in life: to satisfy its endless, ravening hunger.

The journey continued.

At some point, he – they – crossed a junction with a major road, Coldwell Way, and he could see the barricades and officers holding people and traffic back, while a pale distorted face among them looked like Bellis but might not have been: the scene had already slipped away and Donal dared not attempt to turn his head while trapped inside the ghoul.

If it changed state and reverted to normal bloodghoul behaviour, he was done for, in the most agonising fashion possible.

For the ghoul to keep on carrying him like this required energy, yet by the time they had travelled a mile it showed no sign of slowing down. If anything, their journey had grown smoother and the buildings – more obviously when they crossed road junctions – were slipping by faster than before.

No wonder the Death-damned things, these bloodghouls, were described as always hungry. A wraith could slip most of her or his or its mass out of the macroscopic dimensions, but this ghoul was operating primarily in normal space, and if its current behaviour was anything like its normal mode of being, then its energy needs were high: the laws of thaumadynamics remain implacable, always and everywhere.

He wondered how soon it would need to feed, this bloodghoul; and when it did, whether it would utilise the obvious food source: the bedraggled, scared zombie already wrapped up inside its spectral self.

At least the cops were keeping ordinary citizens out of harm's way.

Have they worked out where we're headed?

Unknown.

Most likely they had roving patrols set up and were shutting down roads with minutes or seconds to spare, which meant sooner or later a mistake would grow in likelihood until someone got it wrong and this hellish ghoul floated straight into a crowd of people and there was no telling what would happen next.

Still floating onwards.

The violet trace they were following, he and the ghoul, slipped in and out of sight because its glow was growing subtly fainter, maybe due to the passage of time and nothing more.

He wondered if at some point the trace would evaporate to invisibility so that not even a bloodghoul could track the thing, at which time the hunt, if that's what this was, would come to an obvious end, because the one thing that Donal felt sure of was this: any interruption of the bloodghoul's current motion – he assumed it was acting under compulsion – and normal behaviour would be resumed and he would be done for.

We're following Mel and Finbar's trail.

They had to be. It was the only explanation that made any kind of sense: backtracking along some form of spoor left perhaps not by Mel or Finbar themselves, but by the specific hex used in their capture.

What if I'm wrong?

There were easier ways to die than being eaten by a bloodghoul, but he'd rather face that than lose his partner and their newborn son.

Mel, my love.

He could only hang on, thankful that he didn't need to breathe, and hope that the trail lasted long enough for the bloodghoul to follow it to the end.

Finbar, my boy.

For now, he had to do the hardest thing of all.

Nothing.

While the bloodghoul drifted forwards, carrying him along.

TWENTY-THREE

It was Sergeant Yorak knocking at the open door again. Sandarov looked up from the files on his desk that had long blurred into a morass of meaningless bureaucracy inside his mind, and blinked several times, trying to focus on the sergeant's pale blue features.

He looked so young, and Sandarov recognised that thought for what it was: his own middle age beginning to manifest. And with the way his eyes were acting up, sooner or later he was going to need reading glasses, just like his father.

Although Pop had reacquired twenty-twenty vision after resurrection, one of the perks that helped to counterbalance the inevitable losses that came with zombiehood...

"Commissioner?"

"Um, yes, Sergeant. What is it?"

"The disturbance in Lower Danklyn. We've more reports coming in from Lieutenant Bellis and his team."

"Show me."

"Evelyn is still transcribing, sir, but I think they've almost finished."

"Okay, I'll be right out."

Yorak had good instincts. He'd recognised that Sandarov wouldn't want to wait for a pile of vellum to arrive on his desk when he could easily start reading as Evelyn worked.

Sandarov retrieved his jacket from the back of his chair and followed Yorak out, shrugging the jacket on and fastening one button and adjusting his cuffs. It wasn't that he needed to be dressed formally: this just gave him the option of heading straight out elsewhere without returning to his desk if there was some kind of action he might take beyond picking up a phone and making a call.

Seniority came with a great deal of frustration, at least for him.

Evelyn possessed two main torsos plus a smaller central body with a central head approximately half the size of the other two.

They possessed a dozen major tendrils linking said bodies like fat cables, along with many minor filaments, and their skin was mottled orange, and they possessed five hands between them – the central torso with a single arm in front – which meant they could operate a customised scribacus, with five hand-cages to capture the finger movements, at blinding speed.

That wasn't why Evelyn worked a desk job, however. The reason for that was that three of their legs were prosthetics, following a nasty hexplosion during a raid on one of Sally the Claw's warehouses, back in the day.

They'd been offered a medical discharge on full pension, but begged to stay on in some capacity. And their worth to the Department went far beyond their scribing ability; but right now that was all that Sandarov could focus on.

Only their rightmost head wore a telephone headset linked directly to the signals desk in Despatch, but clearly what one head heard was available to all three, for all five hands were at work, the enclosing brass filigree cages squeaking and clacking like crazy.

Slender levers caused the nibs to shift across the scrolling vellum, rendering lines of cursive purple ink at a speed that no one using a simple fountain pen could dream of attaining.

This scribacus was state of the art, with a Guillotine blade that snipped across at preordained intervals, neatly cutting the continuous vellum roll into standard-sized pages for binding or filing.

Yorak started to head around the back of the apparatus, but Sandarov motioned him back and did it himself: squeezing between the outer brass framework and the back of Sergeant Selvyn's desk, currently covered in document boxes as Selvyn tidied up in preparation for leaving this section and taking up a plainclothes post in Robbery-Haunting.

Not all careers went from street to desk: some lucky souls got to make a transition in the opposite direction.

Sandarov had to bend down awkwardly to pick the newly cut vellum pages out of the tray, but he managed not to get his tie caught in the apparatus, and to back his way out without any embarrassing accidents, so that was alright.

But what he read was anything but okay.

His chest felt cold, and for a second his eyes blurred in a way that had nothing to do with age or eyesight. "The locus was Donal Riordan's home. This boxing gym."

He'd already picked up on the seriousness of the manifestation and the nature of the crime; but the link to Riordan was new information. And the fact that the kidnap victims were Riordan's family…

"Yes, sir," said Yorak.

Evelyn said nothing, all three faces rapt in concentration as their hands continued to shift at almost frightening speed inside the scribacus apparatus.

"Bleeding Hades." Sandarov couldn't imagine what kind of state Riordan was in right now.

Even Evelyn blinked and glanced in Sandarov's direction with their leftmost head, before resuming their focus on their work.

Sandarov never swore, even mildly; or so people thought. But this was something else.

As far as Sandarov knew, he was Donal Riordan's one and only current client, which meant that whatever had occurred, there was at least some possibility that it was linked to Riordan's investigation of the City Hall officials on the list that he, Sandarov, had provided.

I'm going to have to get involved directly.

And come clean about his hiring of Riordan.

Except that should disqualify me from getting hands-on at all.

This was bad. He'd tried to do the right thing, but somewhere, somehow, he must have messed up.

"Sir?" It was a plainclothes officer, Detective Pirnie, one of Selvyn's new R-H colleagues, who'd been loitering nearby, eager to get the transfer completed. "Your phone was ringing, and I answered it."

He pointed back to the open armoured door, which revealed enough of the office interior to show the handset lying on the desktop.

"It's Federal Agent Bouchard," added Pirnie, "and I happen to know who he is, because of last year. He's the deputy bureau chief for the Agency in Fortinium."

Pirnie had spent time on secondment to the FPD, and his information was always accurate.

"Thanks." Sandarov headed inside, lay the vellum pages down on the blotting-paper pad atop the desk, and picked up the phone. "Sandarov here."

"Commissioner, you know who I am."

Had the man heard Sandarov's conversation with Pirnie via the phone handset in here? Every time you thought you'd guessed the limits of federal spellbinders' abilities, along came something new to cause another rethink.

"Can I confirm," added Bouchard, "that you experienced a major hex incident in the Lower Danklyn district at 13:39 today?"

"That sounds right. Hang on." Sandarov used a fingertip to slide the vellum pages apart so he could check the details. "That's exactly correct."

"Thank you. Can you give me the street address?"

"Sure." Sandarov recited the details, then added: "It's a deconsecrated temple operating as a boxing gym. Trading name is Mel's Gym, operated by one Imelda Carson, known as Mel, whose business partner and common-law husband is Donal Riordan."

He took a breath, then went on: "He's a licensed private investigator and former detective lieutenant with this department. Miss Carson is missing, along with her newborn baby. A boy. Taken by a strong-arm team demonstrating military or quasi-military discipline, during the incident."

There was a short pause, perhaps because Bouchard was consolidating this information with what he already knew, perhaps because Sandarov's willingness to share details was surprising.

"I don't believe in inter-agency competition," added Sandarov. "Cooperation is the way to get things done."

"Indeed." There were overtones in Bouchard's voice, indecipherable to Sandarov. "Commissioner, I'm looking at a Tristopolis PD incident report from two days ago, at a building on Dredgeway Avenue. The forensic analysis shows hex frequencies consistent with today's event."

Sandarov felt his eyes narrow. Something odd was going on, and when he glanced around, he realised that the pendulum of his skeleton clock was holding still instead of swinging.

Either the clock was picking up on something that Federal Agent Bouchard was up to at the other end of the line – it was sensitive that way – or else Bouchard was doing something to Sandarov's mind and perceptions.

Or maybe to the flow of time itself.

With federal spellbinders, you could never know for sure.

"There's nothing to worry about, Commissioner," continued Bouchard, his voice smooth and resonant in the earpiece. "However, I note the inclusion of a witness statement from one Donal Riordan, investigator, in the same file."

"I... didn't know that."

As the police commissioner, Sandarov knew – of course – about a major investigation being run by Lieutenant Bellis; but Sandarov had decided not to interfere, and had read only the summary sheets, which contained no witness names: nor would he expect them to.

Bellis had also picked up responsibility for the Mel's Gym incident; but most detectives, most of the time, worked two or three cases in parallel as a matter of course: that was how every police detective team operated, in Tristopolis or anywhere else.

There had been no reason to assume or suspect a connection between the two cases.

"I've only just started to read today's report," continued Sandarov. "I don't even have all the pages yet."

"Okay." Again there was something in Bouchard's voice coming from the earpiece that Sandarov couldn't decipher. "I need to inform you that at 13:39 today precisely, a similar but smaller hexplosion occurred in an establishment called the Holdex Club, here in Fortinium."

"Er... I see."

"Call it an outlying tributary of the same event. Or a resonance, but that's a less accurate description."

"Okay..."

"The Holdex Club was recently the scene of an assassination, that of an industrialist called Kristof Dahlberg."

"Sweet Thanatos." The second time he'd sworn today. He'd read about Dahlberg, of course, in the business section of the *Gazette* as well as the front-page news.

After a moment, he added: "And the hex analysis? Are we talking about another link, Agent Bouchard?"

"Very astute, Commissioner. We are talking about exactly that."

Sandarov rubbed his forehead, trying to understand the connections here, wishing he didn't have so many things to deal with. "I'll need to think about this. How can I get back in touch with you?"

Bouchard recited a number, then: "I'd like to know more about this Donal Riordan, Commissioner. Tell me."

There was an odd quality to the air, something like being submerged under water, and the office walls and ceiling and floor all seemed to recede at the same time even though nothing was moving; and the thing was, every TPD officer went through trance-shield training and Sandarov more than most, taking all of the extra electives that the Academy offered, but none of that meant anything because this was a federal spellbinder on the other end of the line, and the fact that Bouchard wasn't present in the room made zero difference.

Sandarov was a police commissioner, and not just any commissioner: this was Tristopolis, after all. But Bouchard was a fed, a deputy bureau chief, and when it came down to it, Sandarov had no defences against him: none at all.

"Tell me." It sounded like the voice of Thanatos.

As if the universe itself were compelling Sandarov to speak.

"I... hired him. To work for... me. Personal... job."

Sweat was trickling down Sandarov's forehead, but he felt no impulse to wipe it away: the sensation was neutral information, nothing more.

"Politicians, moving... against me. Didn't want to... use... Department resources. My career... I'm here to... serve. Don't even like... the politics."

Something pale-blue at the edge of his vision. Sergeant Yorak, moving in excruciatingly slow motion.

"What did you task Riordan with?"

Yorak appeared to slow even further, to freeze into stillness.

"Investigate... names. Councillors Tanaka, Shaik, Smythe... Mathur, Robbins, Sweeney. Assistant staff: O'Flaherty, Schwaber... Duquesne. Patel."

Sandarov felt as if he were descending deeper and deeper into some invisible well. Though he remained in place, his office and ordinary reality seemed to recede from him, to grow ever more distant.

"Which of these people did he investigate so far?"

"Don't... know."

"Do you consider Mr Riordan trustworthy?"

"One. Hundred... percent."

"And is he honest?"

"Hundred. Percent." A distant thought: he'd always considered honesty and trustworthiness to go hand in hand; but perhaps you could have one without the other.

"Authorise Sergeant Yorak to retrieve Riordan's file, ring my number, and read every detail aloud to me."

"Yes..."

Of course Federal Agent Bouchard would know Yorak's name. It was entirely natural.

"Commissioner Sandarov, thank you for your cooperation. I hope you will feel free and motivated to answer my call should I ring you again."

"Yes. Of—"

The line went silent.

"—course."

And the world flicked back to its usual clarity with Yorak leaning his head around the doorway and asking: "Anything I can do, sir?"

"Huh. Give me a minute."

Yorak nodded.

As Yorak started to withdraw, Sandarov called him back. "Sergeant? Fetch Donal Riordan's personnel file from ER. You'll have authorisation by the time you get there."

"Sir." He nodded and departed.

A phone call to Entity Resources would take a fraction of the time of a visit to the archives, at least when the person making the call held the rank of police commissioner.

Sandarov would probably need to fill in some kind of form, but Yorak should be able to take the form back here for him to sign, acknowledging receipt of the dossier on Riordan.

Ah, the workings of bureaucracy.

The odd thing, Sandarov decided, as he looked around his office where the skeleton clock and grandfather clock were swinging their pendulums once more at normal speed, was the absence of any resentment inside him – any that he could detect – about the way that Federal Agent Bouchard had been able to control him – in a psychological sense – without even being present in the room.

It was surely an impressive skill, but it prompted a second thought, one that Sandarov had never had before: he wondered exactly what price a person had to pay in order to gain such abilities.

I think I'm glad I'm not a fed.

He picked up his desk phone, spun the cogs to the extension for ER, and waited for someone to pick up.

Yorak returned with the dossier two-thirds of an hour later, knocking diffidently at the threshold of Sandarov's office, and stepping inside when Sandarov called him in.

"Fast work, Sergeant." Sandarov knew how long it sometimes took down there, not to mention the psychological barriers most officers had to penetrate in order to step inside the ER domain. "I've a number written down for you."

He held up a slip of vellum.

Yorak came over and was about to place the dossier on the desktop when Sandarov stopped him. "Take the number and the file back to your own desk, ring that number and talk to Federal Agent Bouchard. He'll want you to read the file aloud to him."

"Um, yes, sir."

"You'll be fine, Sergeant. Is there a form for me to sign?"

"Er, I tucked it in here, in the folder…"

"It's alright. I'll sign it when you've made the call."

"Sir…"

"Go now."

Yorak swallowed, then turned and began to exit, dossier and slip of vellum in hand, more slowly than he'd entered.

At the doorway he paused.

Sandarov prepared himself to repeat the order, this time with a blunt authoritarian emphasis that he rarely needed to resort to. Yorak wasn't usually a problem, but then again, no one – almost certainly – had ever asked him to talk to a federal spellbinder before.

"Sir…" Yorak sounded diffident. "I could hear your conversation with, um, Federal Agent Bouchard. It was kind of speeded up, or I was moving slower, or something… But I learned to listen to triple-speed record disks when I was transcribing Academy training documents last year."

Of course he had. Yorak was one of a kind.

Sandarov smiled at him. "I'm not embarrassed, Sergeant. I was under a compulsion to speak, as I'm sure you realised, but considering who I was taking to, I've no problem with that. Really."

The purpose of the call had been legitimate and purposeful and surely justified. Riordan's wife and child were missing, hex of some unusual and highly powerful kind was somehow involved, and there were links to other serious crimes in Fortinium.

Sandarov and the Department needed all the help they could get.

"No, sir. I heard the names, of course."

"The people whose names you dug up for me, Sergeant. Was there a problem in the way you did your research?"

"Oh, no." Yorak blinked. "Some of what I found was tentative, but I told you that. I meant, maybe there was another name you should've mentioned."

"I missed a name from your list?"

Sandarov was sure he'd told Agent Bouchard absolutely everything.

Yorak shook his head. "Not from the list, sir. I meant that rather frightening woman who came to see you."

"Woman? Frightening?"

A smile started to form on Yorak's blue lips, then faded as he realised that Sandarov wasn't joking. "Er, Mrs Frisch, sir."

"Who?"

"Vanessa Frisch? Golden fingernails, red dress, fur coat…"

Sandarov wondered if Yorak was experiencing some kind of breakdown. Perhaps it had been unfair to rely so much on the man, to heap so many tasks on him. "Honestly, Sergeant. I don't think…"

His voice just trailed off. He felt it happening all by itself. It was the oddest of feelings.

Almost relaxing.

Sort of.

"Sir…" Yorak's eyelids lowered half way, like a child fighting off sleep at the approach of bedtime. "I don't…"

Deep, restful silence filled the office.

So calm.

A necessary rest.

Been working too…

Everything slowing down.

…hard.

Peace descended.

TWENTY-FOUR

Mel knew she was a fighter, literally as well as metaphorically, and giving birth had been a rite of bleeding passage – quite literally, by all the Valladin gods that she didn't believe in – involving so many hours of pain and effort and pain again.

After all that she couldn't wait to heal up and get back to hard training sessions in the gym, because given what it took to bring Finbar into the world, everything else was going to feel easy from now on.

If she could only get them out of here, this prison, and back to normal life.

Oh, my baby.

She'd just finished feeding him, and should have felt so content, but not in this cold, hard dangerous place.

The room was of pale blue stone and felt both clean and squalid at the same time: scrubbed with disinfectant and jellyfish bleach – the ozone scent still lingered – but the toilet was a carved stone block integral with floor and wall, and the sink was a recess off to one side in the same wall.

As for the bed, it consisted of another raised block that reminded her of the old altar stored outdoors in their backyard, the one that had needed pulleys and hoists and a large flat-bed trolley to shift out of the building's interior so the place could finally start to look like a gym instead of an abandoned temple.

Hiring a golem would have been quicker, but getting it through the double doors would have been problematic, maybe impossible, and as for access to the yard…

Finbar shifted, and she curled her body to a different position, fitting his altered position exactly, keeping him safe and secure, protecting her most precious boy. So tiny, so small, so fragile.

Daydreaming about home isn't going to help.

She wished…

No. Wishing wasn't going to do any good, or at least not yet. Paying attention to everything around her, every little detail, and only then letting her mind wander, allowing it to explore patterns and possibilities in the workspace of her imagination, to find some unexpected way out of this place: that was what she needed to do.

Hard, hard, hard.

Doesn't matter. Move.

She rose to her feet, stifling the yelp that wanted to come out as her strained internal muscles signalled that they didn't want to move, not yet; but that didn't matter: she wasn't giving them a choice.

Details…

Checking the lines of the stonework, noting the odd runes that looked like nothing she'd ever seen back in Silvex City or when she travelled to the Shaded North for fights or for work. She'd earned decent money from some of her bouts but never applied the word "work" to boxing: it was something else, a calling that lived inside her.

No one understands me, besides Donal.

And one of Donal's favourite words was "focus": exactly what she needed right now.

She'd been a crew chief for one of Silvex City's toughest shady operators, a big-time outfit that spread to levels of corruption among the high and mighty as well as the grimiest projects in the lowest Planes; and while most of her work had been legitimate transport and distribution, the individuals that she'd bossed had been hardened men, women and entities, all of them comfortable with violence.

And part of the reason she got on so well with them was that she always stood up for her teams, and never escalated discipline problems to higher echelons – problems that grew rarer and rarer the longer she worked there – but dealt with them herself: fast and hard, but always fair, and never vindictive afterwards.

If you discounted the fact that she'd just given birth and was cradling her fragile newborn baby in her arms – *if* you discounted that – then she'd been in worse trouble than this before.

Maybe.

So… Details, details. Details.

Nothing to work with in the cell, not that she could see.

So look again.

She commenced a second circuit of the place.

Hiding places: exactly one, behind the block that formed the bed, so that was no go. Correction: she could stow Finbar next to the toilet block – *no* – and out of sight from the doorway which might also protect him from any violence – *it might be the only way* – if she fought whichever of her captors came inside, which sooner or later they presumably would do.

Solid walls. The runes were just marks inscribed in pale-blue stone, nothing more. The sink recess included a stubby tap which she might be able to take apart, given enough time.

If she needed a metal tool, it might be worth the effort; but when it came to makeshift weapons, she had a platinum rule: if you can't do damage with your fists, then you can't hit hard enough to hurt regardless of what you're holding.

And you sure as Hades aren't capable of reacting at speed, which is often what violence is all about.

Accuracy and attitude first, my girl. Strength and speed come second.

Uncle Micky's words. Not a real uncle, but the mentor who'd dragged her through the awful teenage years and taught her how to become her true self: a debt she could never pay back but didn't have to, because that was the purpose of the gym that bore his name: to pay the debt forwards.

If only one of the kids who passed through the doors not only learned to handle life but also taught another generation in years to come, then all would be well.

Which won't happen unless we get out of here.

So hard to keep her focus: hard but necessary.

She hadn't found anything in her search of the cell, so she did the only thing she could think of: she began again.

Halfway through the search, footsteps and a scrape of sound froze her for some tiny fraction of a second; then in one motion she circled past the block that formed the bed, deposited sleeping Finbar on its surface, and was at the metal door, crouching and ready.

All this, before the person outside could even start to turn the handle, never mind stepping inside.

But that didn't happen.

Instead, a jagged sawtooth split appeared, running left to right across a section of the door at about waist height – at what would have been Mel's waist had she been standing upright instead of preparing for combat – and drew apart vertically like some form of mechanical mouth.

And perhaps that explained the zigzag shape: so it could slam shut on a prisoner's arm if they tried to reach outside.

A long strip of metal, with a food tray on top, slid inside. The guard pushing it in was standing a long way back. Even if she could trick him by slamming the strip back towards him, she didn't see how it would help: at best he might stagger back a little, unless she managed a lucky liver shot.

Even then, it wouldn't do any good. If the guard had any kind of professional sense – which hadn't been lacking from these people so far – he wouldn't even be carrying keys on his person, not for cell doors: he'd be relying on colleagues to do the opening and closing while keeping their distance from the prisoners.

Or are we the only prisoners, me and Finbar?

The setup was prison-like, but she had no reason to assume it was actually a jail.

"What's this?" she said.

"I believe it's called nourishment."

He sounded snooty, maybe fake posh, maybe the real thing: Mel's ears weren't completely attuned to Federation accents, not yet. Either way, the tone wasn't what she'd expected.

"And I'm supposed to trust armed kidnappers to provide wholesome food and drink with nothing harmful added. Right." Trying to match the guard's tone, but subtly.

"I wouldn't, in your shoes." It didn't quite sound like sympathy. "But you're a nursing mother, so at some point you'll have to take the chance."

"At some point."

Any drug or poison she imbibed would end up inside Finbar too, almost certainly, and if this toffee-nosed bastard was halfway as smart as he sounded, then he'd be well aware of that.

Calm down.

This was her first proper interaction with any of her captors. Tactics and strategy, not emotional gratification, were what she needed now.

"There's a timescale, of course," said the guard, "and it's up to you to decide what it is. You might hope for a rescue in some given number of hours from when the team took you, but whatever that number of hours is, you'll find that afterwards, your knight on a white steed is yet to show."

Mel wondered if this idiot understood the implications of his own words. If no one was coming, then escape was entirely her responsibility.

"And at that point," continued the guard, "if not before, you'll know that you need to eat and drink for the sake of your baby's survival. What's its name, by the way?"

The lack of gender in the question was the deciding factor: these people knew nothing about Finbar, nothing at all. Sympathy was absent: they didn't care in the slightest.

"You don't see us as people, do you?" she said. "What do you care about names?"

"Just trying to be civilised. Are you going to take the tray I'm offering?"

She looked at it. Two covered plates, one large and one small, and a beaker of carved bone with a lid on top. No way to tell what was inside, although faint enticing scents wafted from one of the plates.

"Take it away," she said.

Knowing it might be the wrong decision.

"The tray is staying inside your cell. If I pull this strip back hard, the tray just falls and you're the one with the mess on your floor."

He'd shifted the strip sideways, so that the tray would in fact catch the side of the fanged opening if the strip withdrew.

"Sod off."

"Well" – he jerked the strip back – "if you insist."

The jaw-like opening slammed shut, metal fangs clanging together while the tray did as the guard said: it toppled and fell, but not to the floor, because Mel's reactions were faster than that.

She caught it, kept it level, and lowered it into place on the flagstones.

And kept the covers over the dishes, knowing that the guard was right: at some point she would have to give in for the sake of nourishment, and that time might come before another tray showed up, so she'd better hang onto this one.

Then she changed her mind, but only in part, and squatted down next to the tray.

Slowly, she lifted the two lids. Both were malleable metal. She placed them on the floor, and examined the plates on the tray. They were ordinary china, one with lumpy tubers and a greasy kimodo burger on top, the other some kind of rice pudding laced with what might have been beetleberry jam.

No cutlery, of course: she was supposed to eat with her fingers.

She tipped the rice pudding onto the burger, scraped the remnants off with her finger, and replaced the lid on the main-course plate. Then she spun and flung the pudding plate hard so it smashed into the wall and scattered fragments like a ricochet.

Three of the pieces lay there on the floor like teeth extracted from a razordog: triangular and sharp. Another piece looked large and irregular; the rest were too small to be useful: shards to be ignored.

Good. It's a start.

Finbar should have started awake and begun to cry at the sudden noise as the plate shattered, but when she checked, Mel found him lying quietly where she'd left him on top of the bed block, although his eyes were open now.

"Good boy."

Before she could reach out to touch him, a change in the air became apparent: a form of localised stillness, and then the faintest, subtlest of visible shifts. Gradually, she became aware of the blueness that began at baby Finbar's eyes and ended at hers, or the other way round... or both.

My wonderful, wonderful boy.

She picked him up, and cradled him, and knew she would do anything at all to keep him safe.

And turned to stare at the door of their cell.

Wondering when it would open again, and who would be there when it did.

I'll be ready.

For Finbar's sake, she'd have to be.

TWENTY-FIVE

Not many cities include a feature like Cataclysm Chasm, but then, not many cities stretch as wide and far as Tristopolis. Nor do they usually include so many hundred-foot-high human (or quasi-human) skulls to act as monuments to forgotten giants of the past while serving mundane purposes in the present.

The skulls that Donal saw most often were the multi-level highway-and-flyover road junctions of the Orb-Sinister and Orb-Dexter freeways; but there were others scattered across his city, and the dark, ichor-streaked and battered-looking Trepan Tower was one of them.

To Donal, the word *tower* didn't suggest a skull shape, but someone important had named the edifice a long time ago, so that was that.

Riddled with small black openings in addition to the great empty orbs where perhaps giant eyeballs once nestled, it stood there as forbidding as ever. It might have been that huge in life. But perhaps the skulls had been ordinary-sized, belonging to normal humans – not giants – and mages of some kind had magnified them after death, maybe after the flesh had rotted away.

Scholars had been arguing for centuries. No one knew for sure.

Even though the world appeared distorted by the semi-transparent bloodghoul that enveloped him, Donal knew where he was. He could visualise Trepan Tower's location on a mental map of the city.

The great skull lay at an angle, some twenty degrees off vertical, nestled inside the thirteen-mile long giant trench of the well-named Cataclysm Chasm, whose inky depths looked murkier than ever.

At least as seen from inside a bloodghoul as it hung in place at the edge, above the broken end of the roadway. The road surface terminated abruptly, like so many other streets on either side of the Chasm.

People still attempted to build bridges from time to time, more from

166

speculative gambling than genuine optimism, and the projects always ended the same way: only jagged fragments remaining at either side of the Chasm.

From inside the hovering bloodghoul, even with his zombie's visual acuity, Donal could barely make out shifts of movement within the Chasm's darkness, and no definite shapes at all.

Then again, he might not have fared much better even if he'd been free of the ghoul.

Some of the beings that flitted endlessly down there bore some kind of relationship to ghouls or wraiths or both, but no one — as far as Donal knew: there might be mages in Mordanto who studied this place in secret — had ever identified them for sure.

Things happened to people who descended into the Chasm.

Most didn't come back. End of story. Those who did return were altered, and there were specialist teams in the TPD to take those individuals into custody in hex-armoured transports and remove them to distant, fortified complexes outside the city limits, where those once-human beings could live out their lives without harming others.

Was the bloodghoul contemplating all this, as it hung here in place, overlooking Cataclysm Chasm? Donal couldn't tell.

Why have we stopped?

The ongoing inner panic regarding Mel and Finbar and whatever was happening to them was starting to rise inside him, and it took every ounce of zombie self-control to quieten the feeling. He needed to watch and hold himself ready to act when the moment came.

What he would have to do, and when he would have to do it, he had no idea. That was precisely why he needed to stay alert: the opportunity might flare up at any instant.

Blackness strobing against darkness.

It took you long enough.

Donal couldn't turn his head — or didn't want to try and force his head to turn, for fear of breaking the bloodghoul's trance, if that's what was truly happening — but he could tell from the flickers of black against the walls of the shabby tenements on either side of the road — tenements that ended abruptly, like everything else, at the Chasm's edge — that Bellis's squad cars had managed to catch up.

After failing to anticipate the bloodghoul's last unexpected shift in direction: they'd fallen rapidly behind at that point.

Perhaps Bellis had deduced the same thing that Donal had: that the bloodghoul was somehow tracking, at Hellah's command, the fading spoor that might, if they moved fast enough, lead them all the way to wherever Mel and Finbar were right now.

Or at least to the people who'd taken them.

That would be a start.

Small dark airborne shapes were exiting the myriad openings in the giant skull of Trepan Tower. Vulturebats and viper falcons nested there, living among altered humans who remained within the Chasm, working at unknown tasks.

Why the Hades have we stopped?

In front, barely visible, a violet thread of light was glimmering, directed straight ahead of him, suspended in the air like a tightrope for him to walk along. The trail, he hoped, that led to Mel and Finbar.

It spanned the Cataclysm Chasm, or seemed to.

Donal couldn't be certain, because the thread looked so faint. Perhaps it finally petered out somewhere before the far side. And perhaps that was why the bloodghoul was just hanging here in place with Donal inside: the ghoul could sense the spoor was coming to an end.

We need to move, all the same.

But even as Donal thought that, a phalanx of dark airborne shapes shot along the central axis of the Chasm, moving from right to left across his vision. A third of a second later, and they were gone.

Possibly the fastest creatures he'd ever seen, and he didn't even know what they were.

Even in my own city.

So much to learn, so much to do, but the priority was Mel and Finbar and from now on it always would be, so why the *Hades* was this Death-damned ghoul just hanging in place and—

Movement.

Darkness, sliding underneath him.

Oh, Thanatos.

He was moving again, slowly. Airborne. Out above the dark abyss.

Over the Chasm depths, now it was safe enough for a bloodghoul to float across. The idea that a bloodghoul might feel fear or even logical hesitation seemed entirely new.

This ain't right.

Donal was a simple Lower Danklyn boy at heart, and here he was, suspended, slowly moving above the dark depths of Cataclysm Chasm, held up by a bloodghoul who should have dissolved him into nothingness by now.

Strictly speaking, he'd been airborne since the moment that the bloodghoul enveloped him. But their journey had involved floating only inches above the ground: this was something else.

They were almost above the centre of the Chasm when the bloodghoul slowed right down, and everything in Donal's vision trembled and the pressure of the ghoul against his skin grew colder and tighter. As far as he could tell, the bloodghoul was shivering.

From fear? From hunger?

Perhaps an urge to dive down and feast upon the Chasm's denizens, now the strange moving shapes had passed on, was growing stronger and stronger in the bloodghoul's mind. Donal knew it *had* a mind, even if he couldn't communicate with the Death-damned thing.

At exactly that moment, the bloodghoul shifted into motion once more, sliding onward while the dark abyss remained beneath.

Can you read my mind, ghoul?

No answer of any kind.

The motion continued, and maybe that was all that mattered. Except of course that Donal was on his own now, because even without turning his head, he knew damned well that Bellis and his people were stuck on the terminated road behind him.

And there were no bridges that Bellis could use. At best, he could crank up a radio and ask Despatch for another team to pick up the traces at the far side of the Chasm, because the most he could manage otherwise was to drive to one end of the Chasm – one end or the other – and make his way around it.

The nearer end was five miles or more away, and much of the terrain there was derelict and haunted. Bellis might make better time going the opposite way, perhaps a sixteen-mile round trip just to reach the road that Donal was floating towards.

Which was drawing closer now.

Just seconds away.

Keep going, ghoul.

The violet thread still hung in front of them, and perhaps it was drawing the bloodghoul onwards. Steadily, the broken edge of the next roadway drew closer and then, with no drama, they were floating above tarmac once more, Donal and the ghoul that held him up.

Well, that was easy.

Perhaps the bloodghoul was speeding up, just a little.

Good.

They had a trail to follow, and time mattered in so many ways.

Every street they glided along stood empty. Someone had sent the TPD here in advance and told everyone to stay inside and lock their doors. It was the obvious explanation.

Maybe they'd used scanbats equipped with voice broadcast to relay the message. The technique had been used in Fortinium, successfully. Viktor, one of Donal's former colleagues, had told him of plans to test the same procedure here.

Perhaps it should have felt reassuring, the emptiness.

I don't like this.

The lack of people in ordinary streets signalled danger, and maybe Donal – or else the bloodghoul pressing against his skin and distorting his view of the world around him – was actually the problem; but it didn't feel that way.

After thirteen minutes this side of the Chasm, having left the dark place behind – as always, a part of Donal's mind kept track of time – the bloodghoul began to slow. At first Donal thought that the spoor must be fading, but although it glimmered thinly, it didn't look any weaker now than it had a few minutes earlier, before crossing the Chasm.

As the ghoul slowed further, the reason became clear.

A man's figure, standing straight and tall in the centre of the otherwise deserted road, directly in their path.

Black suit, pale shirt, dark tie, along with the final giveaway.

Wraparound shades.

Now what?

Shivering, the ghoul drifted to a halt and simply hung there, while Donal felt unable to react, not knowing what to think. The violet trace that led to Mel and Finbar or at least whoever took them: that was all that mattered, and up until now the ghoul had seemed to know that.

But even bloodghouls are afraid of federal spellbinders.

The fed raised one hand.

The ghoul, with Donal inside, shivered to a halt and hung in place.

For Thanatos' sake.

And the air around the federal spellbinder began to glow, a shade of emerald green light that Donal had only seen once before, because the few people that get to see a fed in action tend to retain no memory of what they saw. The innocent people, that is.

Bad guys rarely save the encounter.

And what am I, in this guy's eyes?

Scent of ozone, even here, trapped inside the bloodghoul.

Iciness and pressure against his skin.

The fed's features looked like stone. His aura intensified, green and brighter by the second.

I don't—

A flash of nova brightness, if novas can burn green.

And darkness.

TWENTY-SIX

Vanessa loved jigsaw puzzles. And perhaps it was fate, the tapestry of spacetime geodesics woven by the Norns to create reality beyond considerations of past and present and future, that caused her to reflect in this particular moment on how long it had been since she'd worked on a puzzle.

This thought occurred just as the limo in which she was riding rounded a curve in the forest road and revealed a lone saloon car, stationary at a skewed angle, stuck on a bank that was thick with black grass and gnarly bushes, one of which the car seemed to have struck.

The front wing looked crumpled. A rear wheel looked skewed: perhaps a faulty axle had caused the accident. Or perhaps it was part of the result.

"Slow down," she commanded. "And stop."

"Ma'am." The limo driver, one of her soldiers clad in black, obeyed straight away.

A woman was standing next to the car, arms wrapped around herself, and she looked as if she'd been shivering there for a while. At the sight of the truck, however, she came to life, giving an ungainly wave and taking two steps forward, enough to reveal a limp that Vanessa guessed was recent.

No one else in the car – no one human, or nearly human – or waiting in the trees. Vanessa didn't need to get out of the truck and look: she knew it.

Vanessa didn't need to open her door either. One of her street soldiers, who'd been riding in a covered jeep right behind, had already climbed out and jogged forward to take up position outside the limo, waiting for the nod.

Which she gave.

The soldier turned the handle and stepped back as he opened the door, knowing better than to offer a hand. She enjoyed the trappings of power, but drew the line at courtesies that might suggest a weakness of any kind.

She stepped onto the grass and gestured, freezing the woman in place.

And walked closer.

Yes, you can see me, can't you?

Vanessa could not have described, not properly, the hint in those eyes that spoke of awareness retained even while the body stayed locked in place, because this form of paralysis was the ideal.

The woman's glands and heart would be functioning still, which meant the flesh remained warm and nourished with blood even as fear softened and sweetened the mix.

It was the feelings, not the flesh, that Vanessa savoured now. That fortuitous memory of puzzles told her what to do, and it had to be done within minutes. But those minutes tasted wonderful.

I've only just eaten a ghoul.

Vanessa closed her eyes, absorbing and appreciating the paralysed woman's suffering, the shock and fear adding a burst of flavour to the quite delicious melange of sensations.

But you're a fine one.

A part of Vanessa's awareness, even with her eyes shut, tracked the location of her convoy. Every vehicle had stopped, and every street soldier remained inside, other than the one who'd opened her truck door for her.

And then it was time.

She opened her eyes and waved both hands downwards to effect the transformation. The woman locked into a different kind of stillness, all the liquids in her cells undergoing a transition to viscous hardness, effectively solid in the same way as glass, but rubbery to the feel.

"Fetch a tarpaulin." Vanessa spoke without taking her gaze off the transformed woman.

Strictly speaking, the woman wasn't quite dead, because at this stage the process remained theoretically reversible. But that would spoil Vanessa's creative pleasure, so it wasn't going to happen.

The soldier returned with a colleague, and between them they were carrying a slick-looking groundsheet wrapped up into a nine-foot-long cylinder.

"Spread it out," said Vanessa. "And lay that thing on it."

Neither soldier needed to question what she meant by *thing*. They undid the ties and unrolled the groundsheet on lumpy tussocks of black grass, then tilted the transformed, solid woman and lowered her onto the groundsheet.

One of them murmured an observation, and they both stepped back, saving Vanessa the necessity of ordering them to do just that.

All around, the dark forest felt stiller than ever, as if she'd frozen everything and not just one hapless piece of prey who'd been stumbling through life utterly clueless and finally paid the price.

The purple sky seemed darker than ever.

Okay. Let's make it a good one.

Vanessa closed her eyes again, visualising a fractal spreading of invisible two-dimensional rippled sheets and meandering one-dimensional threads, a translucent organic vision that remained when she half-opened her eyes and gestured to control the floating image.

Causing it to float down upon the woman, and then to sink inside her, leaving a moiré pattern across her skin and clothes, which by now had combined to produce one solid whole: call it a sculpture, of sorts.

Now.

Vanessa smiled as the vision flared, every thread and sheet neatly shearing through whatever matter it found itself inside.

Cutting the three-dimensional shape of the transmogrified woman into exactly three thousand, three hundred and thirty-three irregular pieces, all of them small.

"Good," she said aloud.

Knowing it had gone well even before the shape lost its integrity and collapsed as the pieces slid apart, spilling out to form a multi-coloured pile of puzzle pieces, mostly grey or red, which at some point Vanessa would glue back together just for fun, to pass the time.

Puzzles enthralled her, and always had.

If this one turned out well, the refashioned puzzle-sculpture might look interesting enough to join her art collection in the part of the gallery set aside for her own works. If not, she'd most likely consign the thing to the basement storage floor in Inversion Tower, where so many other relics of mayhem had been laid to rest.

The mayhem always tasted delicious, but not all of the results were worth appreciating afterwards.

"Wrap it up," she added. "And stow it in one of the vehicles."

"Ma'am."

She returned to her limo, waved back the soldier who half-stepped forward to help, climbed inside and pulled the door shut herself.

The runes on her golden fingernails were glowing a soft, creamy hue. It was a sight to make her smile.

Good luck, and a good omen.

A precious titbit falling into her metaphorical lap, like an appetiser before the main course: the captive woman and baby waiting for her to deal with back at Inversion Tower.

Soon Vanessa would be undergoing a transition of her own. To a level of power no one would be able to stand against.

And then what?

First the City Council in Tristopolis, followed by their counterparts in Fortinium, wealth upon wealth as her energy production plants grew in size and importance, and soon enough the greatest single power behind the entire Federation would be her.

Just her.

Beautiful.

And when she twisted everything to chaos and collapse, the energies she would feed on then would be sublime.

But first she needed to survive the short term. As her driver headed for Inversion Tower and the escort vehicles stayed close, Vanessa sank deep inside herself until the Sunskril runes on her golden fingernails were blazing white, building up to a crescendo.

A tidal blast of energy through the crawlspace dimensions should put paid to any mage or witch or even federal spellbinder who might be trying to track her now. It wasn't a step she'd expected to take, but it was a rehearsed contingency plan.

"Pull over when I tell you," she told the driver. "And get out of the car because there's going to be a bright light in here."

"Yes, ma'am."

The voice of experience, knowing what a nova-burst of spillover energy looked like and the damage it could do.

An extra bit of assurance, just in case.

No harm in making certain of the win.

TWENTY-SEVEN

Waking up was painful. Donal's eyes seemed to hurt as he opened them to a squint, and his forehead felt like a lump of pain. Youthful hangovers were a thing of the past, but this was like returning to redblood weakness all over again.

The fed hadn't gone anywhere. Donal himself was still standing in the middle of the deserted street – deserted apart from him and the man in front of him – which felt weird in itself: to have blacked out completely without toppling to the tarmac.

I'm alive.

It was an important point. One Hades of an important point.

Wraparound shades, dark tie and suit, the usual appearance of a fed. Grey hair, maybe fifty years old, and lean like a distance runner.

No one could fake being a federal spellbinder, because it involved so much more than clothing or even demeanour. At deep subliminal levels, below even a resurrected person's consciousness, some kind of hex-related phenomenon – call it an aura – caused a reaction in the core nerves and guts of every onlooker whenever a fed appeared.

An unmistakable reaction.

"I'm... not. Dead." Donal's voice came out as a croak.

"My name is Federal Agent Bouchard. I needed to scan you, in a very particular way. It wasn't an attack."

Of course it wasn't, or Donal wouldn't be here any more. He still didn't understand how he could have lost consciousness, even for some tiny fraction of a second, without all his muscles giving way and causing him to fall.

He still felt light-headed, and without truly thinking about it, he placed his right foot back behind him, and lowered himself to a split-squat or genuflection position, his right knee touching the rough tarmac. It felt hard through the fabric of his trousers. All around, the entire road glistened as if in the aftermath of aqua rain, though it had been weeks since anything other than quicksilver had fallen from the skies.

The street was deserted, apart from Agent Bouchard and Donal himself, but there was something else odd as well. Something he couldn't quite work out, although – it was strange how he felt sure of this – it was also something that should have been obvious.

What did he do to me?

Still kneeling, Donal bent forward and pressed the palm of his hand against the road surface, feeling its rough hardness. Dry, not damp. The sheen was something else, some weird after-effect: the aftermath of a burst of hex from the fed.

But that wasn't the key thing here, was it?

"Give it a moment," said Bouchard. "It will all come back to you."

Donal stayed there, kneeling in place with one hand against the ground, knowing that Bouchard was right. His vision was clearing, the pain in his eyeballs had gone, and the sensation in his forehead was melting away.

Clarity returned, just like that.

"I was inside a bloodghoul." Donal rose with total control to standing, and stared straight into Bouchard's shades. "You killed it?"

His voice was hard with threat, and never mind that this was a fed, because it was the ghoul that had made the violet spoor visible: the trail he needed to follow if he were to find Mel and Finbar.

"Nothing so mundane," said Bouchard. "And the result of what I did turned to be more interesting than I predicted."

The words made no sense.

"What are you talking about?"

Bouchard took two steps to one side, and pointed straight along the road, although his body seemed flicker, just for an instant. "What do you see, Mr Riordan?"

"I…" It was the violet trace, still glowing.

"Tell me."

"A… trail. To my partner and son. Or the bastards who took them."

There was another possibility, of course: that the trail led nowhere, or petered out far too soon, so no one could extrapolate as far as the endpoint.

But Donal had nothing else, so he had to believe in this.

"Good." Bouchard's expression remained unreadable.

He seemed to be waiting for something.

Thanatos. I'm slow today.

How could Donal be seeing the violet trace when *he was no longer inside the bloodghoul?* That was the difference, the massive change he'd been blind to as he came back to consciousness with all the pain and brain fog that had now dispersed.

He turned his hands up and examined them.

"I'm back to normal." He looked up at Bouchard. "But where did the bloodghoul go? Did you kill it?"

Ghouls were generally considered unkillable, but Bouchard was a federal spellbinder, and that changed everything.

"You said that you see a trail."

"I do. Glowing, but not bright."

"No human can see such things, not even when they're resurrected."

Donal breathed right out, and his lungs remained empty of air while he considered Bouchard's words. Then he breathed in enough to speak.

"I'm human and always have been," he told Bouchard. "But I'm not going to argue because my family's in danger, and if you want to help that's great, but I'm moving now."

And he did just that, shifting from standing to a running pace with a suddenness no redblood could match. Running shoes and a tracksuit would have been better than business shoes and a suit and tie, but none of that mattered.

The shoulder holster harness felt just tight enough. The weight of the Magnus bounced and jostled a little as Donal ran, but not enough to put him off his stride, and for sure the weapon felt secure.

His pace was moderate, as running paces go.

It took Bouchard eleven seconds to catch up, sprinting then slowing to match Donal's speed, running easily enough. The fed might be older, but he looked as if he could maintain this pace for hours.

"I can go a bit faster." Bouchard's conversational tone was proof of his words.

"The trace... It's changed direction several times. If I run past a shift, I'm not sure I could find it again."

He felt almost certain of this: that if he shifted off the path too far, the glow would no longer manifest at all, not as far his perceptions were concerned. It wasn't literally a beam of light, and he couldn't expect it to behave like one.

If he lost the trail, he might never find it again. And that was terrifying.

"Okay," said Bouchard.

Then Donal noticed something peculiar, which for a resurrected detective was slow going, because he should have realised straight away. Bouchard's footfalls were silent, and not just that...

His feet weren't quite making contact with the ground in the way they should. The angle and motion weren't right.

Feds.

You never really knew where you were with them.

"But I'm pretty sure," said Donal, "that no matter what speed I accelerate to, you'll be able to match me. Because you're not really here, are you?"

A smile creased Bouchard's lean features. "I'm running on the spot in my office in Fortinium. I can stop if you like."

At that, he took up a normal standing position as if at rest, while continuing to float alongside Donal at exactly Donal's running speed.

"Holomantic projection," added Bouchard. "The same way mages do it."

"I might have known." Donal upped his pace a little, partly from spite, partly because he thought he could manage it without losing the trail even if it suddenly changed direction.

"You're working for Commissioner Sandarov," said Bouchard.

It was an unexpected shift in the conversation, so perhaps this was more of an interrogation. Donal wouldn't let it faze him. "Not right now. This is urgent, Agent Bouchard."

"I'm aware, and I *will* help, any way I can."

"Appreciated."

Still running along deserted streets. Just how far ahead had TPD cleared the area?

Or was something else frightening the citizens enough to drive them all indoors?

"Active bloodghoul warning," said Bouchard, as if he understood Donal's thoughts. "A thirteen-strong formation of scanbats equipped with loudspeakers went through the area broadcasting a shelter-in-place warning. FPD trialled the technique a while back, and it worked pretty well."

"I know." Donal kept his new pace steady. In his redblood days, at this speed, there would have been pauses in his sentences due to the effort level.

Bouchard simply floated alongside.

It was a trick Donal had never seen before. Bouchard had said it was the same thing a mage might do, but Donal wondered how many mages could in fact manage a projection whose location remained in motion, smoothly and without a blip.

"So you're not aware," said Bouchard, "of any connection between your work investigating City Council officials and the abduction of your family. Or any connection with a homicide on Dredgeway Avenue."

"The diviners said something about a resonance being the same, or something. That's all I know."

His eyes remained on the violet trace, now subtly dimmer than before.

It has to stay there long enough.

If the trail vanished…

"When I talked to Commissioner Sandarov," said Bouchard, "he gave me names. Tanaka, Shaik, Smythe, Mathur, Robbins, Sweeney, O'Flaherty, Schwaber, Duquesne, Patel. Six councillors, four assistants."

This was a fed who might help rescue Mel and Finbar, even if his physical self remained far away in Fortinium. Donal couldn't just tell him to get lost.

"My work is confidential unless my client tells me otherwise, Agent

Bouchard. But I don't know why anyone on the City Council would want to snatch Mel and Finbar."

"To stop your investigation?"

Donal slowed a fraction because of the dimming of the violet thread. Up ahead, a lone figure started to step out of a front door, turned this way, then ducked back inside and slammed the door shut.

Just an ordinary citizen.

"This is too heavy duty," said Donal. "Overkill for warning me off, if that's what you're thinking of. And besides, there was reason to suspect some kind of mage- or witch-type interest in my son. I think the snatch is something else."

Except for the link with Dredgeway: the nature of the translocation hex that differed from mage-standard portals. But that wasn't anything to do with the politicos moving against Sandarov, was it?

"Go on." Bouchard was still matching Donal's pace exactly.

"One of the Guardians at Avenue of the Basilisks is a friend. Actually, they both are, but Hellah more than Klaudius. You know about the Guardians, right?"

Bouchard shifted so he was diagonally ahead of Donal, facing him, floating backwards to maintain this new separation.

"Tell me more."

Of course Bouchard would be aware of the Guardians. But a normal person, if they possessed such knowledge, would have expressed surprise that Donal had even met one of the Guardians, never mind befriending them both.

"Hellah was worried." Donal tried to keep his analysis objective. "She sensed something about Finbar even during the pregnancy. I don't know what, exactly. But we had a witch in place to guard the gym, I mean our home, twenty-five hours a day, every day."

He described the creatures that had manifested shortly after Finbar's birth, and how easily Hellah had despatched them both.

"That's unusual," said Bouchard. "Did any other phenomena occur? Anything else you wouldn't expect to encounter?"

Donal could have told him about the sapphire blue light linking Mel and Finbar's eyes from time to time, but so far the information flow was entirely one-way, and that would have to change.

"Is there a time limit to this conversation?" Again, he subtly slowed his running pace, as the violet trace faded by another tiny increment. "Or can you keep this holomantic projection thing going forever?"

"I can keep it going," said Bouchard, "for as long as I need, so long as I don't get distracted."

There was a cross street up ahead, still with everything deserted, but Donal couldn't make out the thread of violet beyond it. Perhaps it went left or right and would grow clearer as he neared the junction.

"Can you help me follow the trail if it grows too faint for me to see?"

"I don't think so," said Bouchard. "Not remotely. I can't do everything from here that I could manage in person."

Wonderful.

The amazing thing, of course, was that a federal spellbinder could project an image in this fashion at all; but the idea that he might have been able to help more if he'd been closer... That felt frustrating.

"Can you get some local agents to help me?"

Something tightened in Bouchard's expression. "Perhaps. There are some odd effects in the compactified dimensions right now, something like a storm tide at sea. If I break contact with you, re-establishing this projection might prove a little challenging."

"Hades, Bouchard. I thought you feds could manage anything."

Not the way a normal, sane person would ever talk to a federal spellbinder, but Bouchard simply twitched the corner of his mouth.

"We do our best. A better risk management approach, I think, would be for me to keep in touch with you like this for as long as possible. When and if you reach the end of the trail – or if it looks like you're travelling a long way from the Tristopolitan bureau – I'll take the decision whether to help you remotely or break off and call the locals for help."

It sounded like a definite tactical decision. Not asking whether Donal agreed.

But I don't have the information he does.

There was no way an ordinary man, resurrected or redblood, could know enough about a fed's capabilities to offer a better suggestion regarding tactics or strategy or anything else.

Donal continued to run.

How long can I keep this up?

He'd always been a runner, and zombiehood had provided him with an extension of every physical ability so long as he worked at it: the true gain had been in work capacity, and the extent to which doing the work provoked a beneficial adaptation.

A zombie who didn't exercise could degenerate to a shambling level that would kill a redblood, yet still persist. Blackblood athleticism didn't come for free. It was more that an enhanced work ethic applied to exercise – *if* the zombie in question actually did the work – produced greater gains than before. That was all.

But I don't know how far the trail is going to stretch.

Bouchard might be capable of keeping the holomantic projection going as long as necessary – *might* be: clearly there were limitations on even a fed's capabilities – and it could be Donal whose energies gave out first.

But he had to reach Mel. Reach Finbar.

180

I need to.

His footsteps echoed more clearly here. Something about the natural acoustics of the empty street.

Up ahead – he could see it well enough now – the violet trace made a smoothed-off ninety degree turn to the left. So he still had a trail to follow.

So long as he could carry on running.

Time to turn left.

There were cars up ahead, and some kind of moving glows. Patrol officers, gesturing at the vehicles, halting them and leading the drivers out to shelter in commercial buildings on either side of the street.

The violet trail seemed to continue straight on, beyond the gathered stationary vehicles.

"Bouchard?"

"Yes?"

"I couldn't see the trail before. Not until the bloodghoul took me."

Bouchard still floated alongside without apparent effort, whatever the reality of the projection process might be. "That would be normal, wouldn't it?"

Not exactly an explanation.

Five seconds passed while Donal continued to run, trying to interpret the undertones and implications of Bouchard's words. And failing.

Finally, Donal said, "Do you know how it is that I can make out the trail now?"

"Yes."

Donal wasn't going to put up with this. "So tell me, damn you."

"Bloodghouls are sensitive to the form of hex radiation emitted by para-portal frameworks."

"That just means they can see the trail." Big words, simple meaning.

"Exactly."

Another five paces. "You're not telling me anything new, are you?"

"Actually, I am."

Seven more paces while Donal considered the words. "No. I still don't get it."

"It's still the bloodghoul who can see the trail, not you. In effect."

This time, Donal couldn't help it. His pace broke, and he jogged to a near halt, not daring to stop totally.

"What the Hades are you talking about, Bouchard?"

The fed's projection had drifted on. Bouchard hung in place as Donal jogged forward to reach him, then matched Donal's new, slower pace.

"When you started to follow the trail, Donal, you were inside the bloodghoul."

You used a person's first name when they were a suspect you wanted to intimidate, but Donal didn't care. He just wanted information. And besides, he didn't know Bouchard's first name, so he couldn't reflect the same technique back at the man.

"That's right," said Donal.

Nine paces this time, before Bouchard spoke again.

"So now the ghoul is inside you," he said. "Call it a role reversal. You've pretty much absorbed its body."

"I've done *what?*"

"You—" Bouchard raised his hand, and for an instant, surprise crossed his face.

Then he winked out of existence.

The fed was gone.

I've absorbed a…

That thought was too ridiculous to complete.

His pace slowed, broke.

And he came to a halt, with Bouchard's words replaying in his mind.

The ghoul is inside you.

It took twenty-nine seconds according to his innate time sense, but he finally shook his head to break the state of immobility, and twisted his shoulders back and forth, using physical movement to dissipate the psychological paralysis.

A ghoul, inside me.

He needed to keep running.

And yet: not just any kind of ghoul.

A bloodghoul.

He had no idea how that might be possible. How much of that was the federal spellbinder's doing? Bouchard hadn't intended the effect – or at least, that was what he'd said – but was it still because of what he'd done?

Or was it something that any ghoul could do if they chose to?

And some other thing broke Bouchard's holomantic projection hex.

He was sure of it: the surprised look on Bouchard's face in the fraction of a second before the holomantic projection disappeared.

Side effects of whatever the unknown enemy was up to? Bouchard had talked about a storm-tide in the compactified dimensions, and Donal remembered another time when some phenomenon in those dimensions prevented mages from using portals in the normal way.

Or was it some kind of deliberate attack, specifically targeted, to prevent Bouchard from helping Donal?

That would make this trail important.

Not a false trail, but the real thing.

It still hung in place above the road, faint and violet.

"Alright, then," he said aloud.

His job was simple.

Get running.

He shifted into motion once more, again transitioning from stillness to full-on running in far less than time than a redblood could manage. He kept it going for thirteen paces, then upped the speed a little.

I can keep going.

It didn't matter how far the trail stretched: he would follow it until the end.

I'm coming for you.

For Mel and Finbar, or for the faceless enemy who'd taken them: either way worked, because he wasn't just going to rescue his family. This was more.

The enemy was going to pay.

TWENTY-EIGHT

Vanessa saw something of herself in the hardbitten, cynical young woman who faced her.

There were tawdry things in Stephanie di Granno's past, not to mention her current working life, but a certain ambition and ruthlessness formed a spine in her personality that Vanessa recognised as belonging to a lesser but kindred soul.

The young woman – Stephanie di Granno according to her current legal documents, Melody de Sonance to her lustful clients, and something else entirely to the parents who'd thrown her out on the streets nine years ago – sat on the black couch with her legs crossed in a faux lady-like manner, and looked around the elegant room, and gave a tiny nod.

From someone else, Vanessa might have considered that sign of approval to be an insult, depending on her mood, because she sure as Hades didn't need anyone to validate her choice of furnishings; but sometimes it was better to observe social niceties, even with obvious underlings.

And in this case, it seemed likely that Stephanie wished she could be more like Vanessa, which was really rather pleasing.

Vanessa said, "Tell me about Councillor Alwyn Arkady Smythe the Third, and explain how it is that I smell death upon your hands. *His* death, I think."

She was sitting in her throne-like business chair carved of mammoth bone and decorated with runes whose origin few scholars would recognise, and whose meaning would baffle most witches or mages.

Normally she'd have been positioned behind her rather ornate desk, but for this meeting, she'd commanded her servants to place the chair directly opposite the couch.

Her dress was a deathberry-coloured gown from House Shervorne, a present to herself acquired during her trip to Fortinium. It felt both comfortable and glamorous, just as she deserved.

Stephanie cleared her throat. "The councillor and I met up at Shazzy's Bar like usual, and normally we need a hotel room, but his wife's away at the moment, so we went back to his place in Niflhame Towers. Except" – she paused to think about it – "I guess she's his widow now, right?"

"Go on."

"There was a detective there, already inside. Came out of Alwyn's home office and confronted him. I went into the bedroom to wait and listen. I reckoned the flick, the detective, would chuck me out otherwise."

Vanessa nodded. Stephanie could read people, especially men, so her analysis of the situation had most likely been accurate.

"It helped that I already had my blouse off," continued Stephanie. "Or almost off. So anyway, from the bedroom, I could hear most of what they were on about, and the flick must've read all Alwyn's documents, because he had a load of the details already."

"Which helped convince Smythe to spill the rest, no doubt."

"Yeah, exactly. Plus the detective was kinda hard-looking. Good shoulders and like a lean face, could be charming, kind of thing. But with that edge to him, like a potential, you know?"

"Okay." Vanessa had been going to ask about the detective afterwards, but Stephanie's thoughts had sidetracked, so it might be easier to follow this path first. "What else can you say about him?"

"Well, suit and tie, decent enough but ordinary, like. Probably earns a lot less than I do, right?"

Vanessa said nothing.

"And he's a zombie," added Stephanie. "There's a lot of cops in this city, but that maybe narrows it down a bit. Very human, though. Not like some of them."

By which Vanessa assumed she meant zombies, not cops. "Tell me more about the *potential* you sensed in him."

It was an interesting word choice, and worth following up.

There was the other important point, of the man being resurrected, but jumping to premature conclusions could prove disastrous.

"So he was nice-looking. Like, I wouldn't chuck him out of my bed, and wouldn't charge him for it neither. Probably. Well, maybe." She twisted her mouth in a half smile with only the faintest hint of sadness. "But you could tell he's a fighter. Everything about him, all the little signs that add up, you know?"

Vanessa did. "A fighter. And a killer?"

Stephanie didn't need long to think about that. "Yeah. I reckon so."

A dangerous zombie. And just such a man, dressed in running gear and unarmed, had attacked Vanessa's people in the Dredgeway Avenue job, albeit with gargoyles as allies. Somewhat improbable allies, when you thought about it.

"And he's with the TPD?" asked Vanessa. "Or some other agency?"

"I… I don't think he actually said. He had Alwyn so intimidated, I'm not even sure he showed a badge. Might have, because I was in the bedroom with the door shut so I couldn't see, only hear."

"Too bad," said Vanessa. "But you did the right thing. So what happened next?"

She wondered if Stephanie understood the seriousness of that question, and the consequences of confessing to doing something stupid.

Like killing a valuable asset on the City Council, for a start. Vanessa had gone to some trouble – not a huge amount, but enough – to recruit him in the first place, after pointing Bloodfist Bank in his direction.

Stephanie said, "One of the names that Alwyn spilled was Arrhennius Hawke, and I know who he is, because he's another of my regulars, although a bit of a strange one. Actually, more than a bit. But anyway… Apparently Alwyn had written the initials *AH* in his notes, and the flick wanted to know who he was."

Vanessa decided that Stephanie *was* going to survive this meeting, almost certainly. If that idiot Smythe had been keeping actual written notes *and* he'd revealed Hawke's identity without even being tortured, he'd also deserved whatever Stephanie had done to him.

"Thing is…" Stephanie hesitated, then: "When I saw the notes later, after I killed Alwyn, he'd used initials to identify most of them. At least in the diary. I didn't have time to take everything, so I dumped the letters in the housekeeper's trash bag, on the trolley. It was a stomach bag, the kind that digests stuff, you know?"

Not a foolproof way to get rid of evidence, but sufficient if no one thought to investigate. Stephanie had made a good decision under trying circumstances.

"That was good thinking," said Vanessa. "Initials are bad enough, even if his contacts weren't featured in those letters. Terminating Alwyn was the right choice."

"Thank you." Stephanie let out a long, somewhat shaky breath.

So she *had* understood the consequences of getting it wrong, here and now. Good for her.

Stephanie added, "But the detective knew a bunch of names already. Er, Tanaka and O'Flaherty and, um, Patil. Or maybe Patel. I couldn't catch the other names, because they moved around a bit in the lounge, so what they said wasn't always clear. Even with my ear against the bedroom door."

Vanessa felt her mouth tighten. This was worse than she'd anticipated.

"Might have mentioned someone called Duquesne," added Stephanie, "though I couldn't swear to that one."

Two of those four names belonged to people that Stephanie should not have heard of at all, not the way Vanessa had compartmentalised her security;

but by her actions, Stephanie had increased her worth, so that part was okay.

In fact, O'Flaherty wouldn't have been known to Smythe at all, which meant the zombie detective had acquired that name – at least that particular name – beforehand.

Someone had been investigating the City Council staff that Vanessa controlled, and that wasn't good at all.

Probably Sandarov. Had to be, really.

Well, if the commissioner had initiated such an investigation, with luck Vanessa's asynchronous hex trigger listeners had dealt with that. And she knew for a fact that her hex had been triggered.

Earlier, she'd received the twin tingling bursts of signal pulse that indicated both Commissioner Sandarov and his flunky sergeant had thought and said key words that triggered the waiting hex function she'd embedded deep inside their brains, when she'd visited TPD Headquarters.

Both the commissioner and his sergeant were trapped in Basilisk Trance, and neither could possibly form any kind of problem from now on.

Of necessity, there'd been a timeout spell first, a countdown that had needed to elapse before the second hex function even started to listen out for trigger words: words that would imply Sandarov and his sergeant were going to make moves against her.

Once triggered, the hex invoked the Basilisk Trance in an instance.

The timeout beforehand had involved a calculated risk, allowing Sandarov a grace period in which he'd been able to think and talk about her and the City Council political situation.

But she'd needed to give Sandarov time to consider her suggestion, to accept her offer and come on board with her.

If he'd done so in time, she'd have removed the embedded listener hex, and replaced it with something similar but subtler and more detailed, as she did with all of her most strategically placed assets.

Never mind. She'd dealt with worse disappointments.

"I'll handle all these people, the councillors and assistants," she said now, bringing Stephanie deeper into her plans. "I intend to protect most of them if I can, but I'm concerned about Hawke in particular. Give me a moment."

"Er…" Stephanie had blanched.

"What is it?"

"I kind of assumed… Ma'am, I had no way to just pick up a phone and call you, see."

This was true. Stephanie was here because Vanessa had summoned her, on learning of Smythe's death through a contact among the first responders, via a chain of intermediaries linked to Vanessa's street soldiers.

More precisely, Vanessa had sent some of her people to bring Stephanie here to Inversion Tower, using one of the anonymous vans from her small fleet of vehicles.

And Stephanie would have made the journey unconscious, experiencing revival once she was inside the windowless building. No way for her to know where she was in relation to the world outside.

"But I knew," continued Stephanie, "that if the cops got to Arrhennius, he'd spill everything he knew, even faster than Alwyn, and the cops would most likely cut a deal, wouldn't they?"

That last part was almost certainly correct. If the TPD or some other agency were investigating Bloodfist Bank – yet again – and this time they found someone to put real pressure on, they'd most certainly offer a plea bargain in order to bring down a network of conspirators, if not the entire bank.

"I made a call to someone I know…"

"Arrhennius Hawke is dead?"

Stephanie's face tightened as she nodded. "I rang up and got confirmation before I came here."

She had taken an initiative that would result in her own death if Vanessa disapproved, and she clearly knew it.

"So you made a phone call regarding Arrhennius Hawke," said Vanessa. "After you'd killed Alwyn Smythe yourself."

"Yes, ma'am."

"How did you do it? Deal with Smythe, I mean."

"I went out into the lounge, made him lie on his back on the rug. He usually liked it when I took charge, so he sort of obeyed by habit, then he said he'd changed his mind and tried to push me off, but it was too late."

Stephanie's eyes defocussed for a second.

She continued, "I straddled him like usual, except this time my legs were scissored around his liver and kidneys and all, and I squeezed hard enough for it to hurt. Like, to the point where he couldn't really think any more."

Vanessa supressed the urge to lick her lips, but she did allow a small smile to grow on her lips. She was beginning to enjoy this story.

"So I reached to the coffee table," continued Stephanie, "to where his necktie was just lying, like, ready for me to use. And I looped it around his neck with my hands like this" – she crossed her wrists – "then just leaned forward to put my bosom into his face and tighten the garotte, and it didn't take long at all for his breathing to stop."

"But you kept the strangle in place for a while, just to make sure."

"I did, yes. I counted to nine hundred before I got off of him. Still checked for a pulse, but it was long gone."

"And you did well." Vanessa felt her smile broaden. "I'm actually quite proud of you."

A faint pinkness arose on Stephanie's cheeks. It had probably been a long time since anyone had made her blush.

"There are a couple of things I'd like to follow up on," added Vanessa.

"Just one thing for now, though. The person you called to deal with Arrhennius Hawke. Are we talking about a professional?"

"Won't have left any traces, ma'am. Ex-military, elite forces, experienced in what they call covert removals."

That sounded more like kidnapping than assassination, but whatever the terminology, Stephanie's judgement appeared to be rock solid. And she'd definitely said that Arrhennius Hawke was dead.

"And I didn't make the call until after I left Niflhame Towers," added Stephanie. "Just in case the cops check Alwyn's phone records."

"Good." Vanessa nodded. "I'll refund you. Whatever amount you paid, that doesn't matter."

Since Hawke had been Councillor Smythe's only direct contact with Bloodfist Bank, and since Stephanie had despatched Smythe herself, the links that might have led eventually to Vanessa had been severed.

"Er… She did it for free, ma'am." Stephanie gave a half smile, but her eyes looked old and empty, just for a moment. "My friend… Well, not actually a friend. But her younger sister disappeared. Years ago, like. Taken by someone a bit like Arrhennius, you see."

Stephanie blinked a couple of times, and added: "She never found the ones responsible, so she takes down anyone who acts that way. When she discovers them."

"A vigilante, then."

Stephanie nodded. "Helped me out of a tight situation once, when a client got out of control, kind of thing. How we met."

Vanessa understood. Stephanie moved in a sordid world, but sordid didn't necessarily mean simple. She was really rather interesting.

And ruthless. She'd made a phone call to eliminate a regular client as soon as it became expedient. While presumably keeping quiet about the fact that she'd known about that client's proclivities for a while, most likely a considerable length of time.

"I have so much going on," said Vanessa, "that I'm afraid I can't ask you to join me for dinner this evening."

"Oh." Stephanie's mouth remained partly open.

"But I should be free tomorrow. Can you memorise a phone number?"

"Um, sure."

Vanessa recited one of the numbers for Inversion Tower. "The ring tone will sound unusual, because of my anti-sprite measures, but otherwise it's all normal. Ring at seventeen o'clock tomorrow, just to confirm. Someone will pick you up shortly afterwards. Dinner itself will be two hours after that."

Stephanie blinked, three times. "Thank you. Thank you, very much."

Again, Vanessa smiled. "And you are very welcome. I look forward to seeing you again."

There was no need for direct wording. Stephanie understood the dismissal. She nodded, uncrossed her legs and rose with elegance from the couch.

She crossed to the door with pretty good deportment – Vanessa's judgement was rather exacting in such matters – where she rested one hand on the carved-bone door handle, nodded once more, and went out.

And closed the door with the faintest of clicks.

"Well, that was nice." Vanessa addressed the empty room. "Really quite promising."

Leaning back against her throne-like business chair, she allowed herself to sink deep inside a restful trance.

Perhaps twenty-something minutes later, a tap sounded on the door, bringing Vanessa smoothly back to normal consciousness.

"Yes?" she called. "Enter."

It was one her senior servants who entered, his expression business-like as always. As with all of her long-surviving staff and street soldiers.

"The interrogation framework, ma'am." He cleared his throat slightly. "I believe the reconfiguration is complete, as far as we can test it ourselves."

"That's good enough," said Vanessa. "Have you moved it to a chamber near the woman's cell?"

"Yes, ma'am. We were able to cleanse the remains from Room 7 and shift the framework into there, so it's just along the corridor from the Carson woman's cell."

"Good enough. And the baby survives?"

"So far, ma'am. It looks healthy enough, though I'm not qualified to judge such things."

"Don't worry. I won't hold *you* accountable." The stress was faint, but the message would be clear.

Larexo from the Dredgeway Avenue team had already paid the price for sloppy work. She hoped to avoid terminating any more of her soldiers or servants for a while.

There was a fine line between enforcing discipline and dampening morale to a point where not even fear could make people useful.

"Plug the framework in," she said. "And while it's warming up, I think a pot of helebore tea and some gecko finger biscuits would be in order. Bring the tray in here."

"Ma'am." The servant touched his forehead and went out.

Vanessa settled back in her mammoth-bone chair.

Promising. Very promising.

A smart young woman rising in her entourage, that Stephanie, with enough promise to maybe last for years. She might even learn to control that decisiveness enough to remain the right side of the line: the line that, if crossed, meant instant death at best, and a prolonged, agonising journey to the end at worst.

All that, plus the captive woman and baby whose power would unlock the barriers that held Vanessa back from a significant breakthrough, one which would allow her to reach through all eleven spacetime dimensions at will, utilising a form of archaic hex that no one had seen for centuries.

Reinforcing necroflux with crawlspace energy resonances was only a part of what she planned, though that scheme by itself might make her the richest business person in the Federation.

But she wanted to reach levels not seen since the Delkor Xyniakothrotl culture had enjoyed its heyday: a time and place of bloody sacrifice and beings of great power stalking across and ruling the land. Such ancient glories!

And she would be the greatest of the new powers.

Maybe I'll even let you join me, my cousins.

It would be nice to enjoy company that was *almost* as powerful as her. For the moment, her cousins, the so-called Guardians who used their powers for little personal gain in the service of their inferiors, remained too strong to face as enemies, even as individuals. Certainly the two of them together held a vast amount of power.

But soon enough, she would be the strongest.

She opened her mind to the compactified dimensions colloquially known as crawlspace, while the Sunskril runes blazed white on her polished golden fingernails, and she allowed herself a smile, feeling the rivers of energy like continuous lightning that were continuing to pour towards a particular location below Avenue of the Basilisks.

Energies that prodded and annoyed, rousing the great, eldritch entities that normally rested there, getting them worked up, but not too much.

Not enough to destroy the city. Well, enough to do just that if there'd been no one to hold them back, but that's what her cousins were for.

And the reason she was doing this.

"Dear Hellah. Sweet Klaudius. Nice to see you keeping busy."

More than that: even from here, an hour's travel by normal means from Avenue of the Basilisks, she could sense waves of exhaustion tinging the flavour of the barriers that her cousins, the two Guardians, were fighting to keep in place. It was a worthy battle.

And it was keeping them out of her hair.

Do you even suspect my part in this?

Most likely not. The last time they'd bumped horns, Vanessa and her cousins, she'd possessed nowhere near her current level of power.

Smiling, she shut down her perceptions of the compactified dimensions.

Good.

A tap on the door.

"Yes?" she said.

"Your tea and biscuits, ma'am."

"Place them on the dragonclaw table. I'll pour the tea myself."

"Very good, ma'am."

She waited until the servant had withdrawn, rose from her carved mammoth-bone chair, and just for a second allowed herself to stretch upwards and not just that: to transform to her freer form.

Humans, and in fact all animals, are powered by mitochondria in their cells, the result of symbiosis between two species of archaic bacteria, back when life on Earth was young.

Bimodal daemonids, evolutionarily speaking, result from another kind of symbiosis between ancestral species from two levels of reality. Or so Vanessa had always been taught.

She grew taller as she rotated around dimensional axes impossible for a human to perceive, pulling her daemonid aspect into the macroscopic level of reality, stretching all the way up to her full twelve feet in height, allowing her skin to darken to a shiny, healthy purple, and her talons to extend, as her expertly tailored gown fell away without tearing.

She shook her wings loose, and flapped them.

Nice.

For a minute, she enjoyed the thrill of naked freedom. In eleven-dimensional geometry, she understood herself to be a single fluid shape, but from a more human perspective she enjoyed a bimodal form, and the choice of which mode to bring into the three macroscopic spatial dimensions was governed mostly by tactics: to survive among a largely human population, she chose to look and more or less think like one of them.

Which aspect was her truer self? Neither, really. With her wings extended, she felt great power inside her; but in fact, that power held true regardless: it was always there for her to use.

Enough for now.

Vanessa drew back down to her human form, pulled the fallen dress – her exclusive Shervorne gown the exact hue of deathberries – back up around her nubile body, a form that came with pleasures of its own, and she tidied herself up.

Hedonism and ruthlessness, and knowing what you wanted: the secrets of her success.

After a moment, she picked up the platinum teapot with the inlaid mage-bone handle – she'd killed the mage and flensed his body herself, many years ago in Surinam – and poured some Javorian-blend helebore tea. The scent promised a flavour that would taste just right, which was – like every other luxury around her – exactly what she deserved.

It felt good to be her.

So very, very good.

TWENTY-NINE

"Hey, Lieutenant." It was Joel's voice. "We got back word. The scanbats deployed okay, and the streets are clear on the other side, just like you ordered. It worked."

Bellis nodded, but his gaze was focussed downwards, on the depths of Cataclysm Chasm. He stood ramrod-straight as always because they'd drilled it into him in the Mordantelle Academy: a form of discipline that could never leave him, even though he'd decided, as a novitiate, that the life of a mage was not for him.

To the other cops, most of what happened in the Chasm remained invisible, inaudible and unfelt; but Bellis possessed a mage's sensitivity and sensibilities: he was perceiving patterns of unrest that boded ill, because the beings that moved down there were evincing a significant concern with the outside world.

They weren't supposed to do that.

This was the strangest day on the strangest case he'd ever been on, and Donal Riordan, maybe the best detective he'd ever worked with, was wrapped up in the whole affair in some way that felt... weird. As if it should have been obvious, but instead remained utterly obscure.

Donal wasn't actually to blame, though. That was the one part Bellis felt sure of.

How would I feel if my family were kidnapped?

Bellis shook his head. He wasn't even sure he'd be able to function.

"Are you even alive, Donal?"

The patrols on the far side of the Chasm, using binoculars, had observed the floating composite of bloodghoul-with-Donal-inside, and declared that Donal looked alive even though he wasn't moving within the ghoul's form, but whether he remained truly aware, they had no way of telling.

No one survived absorption by a bloodghoul, according to common understanding; but Bellis had studied enough at Mordantelle to know that common understanding was riddled with blind spots.

Still, whatever was going on, it wasn't normal ghoul behaviour. Not in the slightest.

"Sir?" It was Martina, who was possibly even smarter than Joel. Bellis sometimes thought the best part of his current job was encouraging these bright young detectives and seeing their careers begin to flourish.

"What's up?" he asked her. "Anything at all about getting SOC diviners here?"

"Not a chance, according to Despatch. There's something odd going on in crawlspace. It's affecting the diviners, apparently. Half of them are with the medics, getting tranquilised or something."

Bellis let out a sigh, partly deliberate. "I suspected as much. I mean the crawlspace thing, not the diviners. I felt the effect myself, though only as a kind of distant tickle. That's the best way to describe it."

Besides their bright-eyed-and-bushy-tailed energy and attitude, the other thing that Martina and Joel had in common was their awareness of Bellis's background, specifically his time in Mordantelle. It wasn't common knowledge inside the Department.

And here was Joel, hurrying over, the nictitating membranes flicking metronomically across his otherwise standard human eyes, a sign of agitation.

"Sir? We had a call from Commander Bowman at HQ."

"Why would he be calling anyone in the ECU?"

Bowman was a perfectly decent senior officer, but he worked Robbery-Haunting and not the Esoteric Crimes Unit, which meant he wasn't in the direct chain of command.

Or maybe Bellis had spent too many of his formative years in hierarchy-conscious Mordantelle, and not enough among people with actual flexibility in their behaviour.

Joel swallowed. "Sir, he said it was for your ears only."

"What have you heard?" Because a high-priority radio signal was hardly any reason to look disturbed, at least not to the degree it had affected Joel.

"I'm not sure. I think, um… I think Commissioner Sandarov might have been murdered. Or at least wounded badly."

"*What?*"

"I might be wrong. It's just…" Nictitating-membrane blinks followed. "I overheard some kind of—"

"Never mind."

The only way to find out was to take the Death-damned call from Bowman. He started to jog towards the patrol car he'd ridden in.

What the Hades is going on?

A whole pile of odd things were happening at once, the strangest of cases occurring simultaneously. He understood the probability distributions that governed quantal hex phenomena, which included the clumping of random occurrences, so he knew for sure that there *were* such things as coincidences.

But even so...

He was gasping by the time he reached the car, and wondered whether he should have boasted about his exercise routine to Donal. Then he dismissed the thought as the uniformed driver held out the hand-microphone through the open window.

Trying not to stretch the cable too far, he thumbed the call-switch. "Bellis here."

"Lieutenant, this is Bowman. We have a situation here at HQ."

"Sir?"

"Commissioner Sandarov fell into Basilisk Trance some time ago, along with another officer. Do you know Sergeant Yorak?"

"Um, no, sir."

Basilisk Trance. The Police Commissioner was trapped in Basilisk Trance.

Bellis realised he still had the mike set to transmit. "It happened inside HQ?"

"Correct. In his office."

A click indicated Bowman was waiting for Bellis to respond, or more likely, to let the news about Commissioner Sandarov sink in.

Bellis thumbed the mike. "Is there any connection to the Riordan family kidnapping? Or the Dredgeway Avenue theft?"

There had been grievous wounding and attempted homicide, or actual homicide if you counted gargoyles – which Martina and Joel clearly did, siding with Donal in that regard – but the exploit had been geared towards stealing an artwork that was stored in the tower's supposedly secure cellar.

Bowman's voice crackled from the dashboard speaker. "I was hoping to ask you the same thing, Lieutenant. Since you're working both cases."

"Sir." Maybe if the diviners weren't able to carry out their normal duties, asking a washed-out, half-trained former novitiate mage for an opinion was all that was left. Except it wasn't technical ability he'd lacked, only motivation.

Bellis went on: "The artwork in question was an abstract sculpture of some kind. Bone and nerves, I think. Not the kind of thing I'd like to spend time with, but not actually illegal."

He let his thumb slide off the transmit switch.

It's just a sculpture. No hidden inlaid hex.

That much, he was certain of: it was a nasty piece of sculpture, but nothing more than that.

Although he made no big deal of it, his ability to parse leftover resonances was close to the level of lesser professional diviners at least, maybe higher, and his theoretical knowledge of hex manifolds and all the rest went a lot further than the practical, nuts-and-bolts expertise of normal scene-of-crime analysis.

"Okay, Lieutenant," came Bowman's voice from the radio. "Let me know if anything occurs to you. End signal."

And that was that: the transmission had finished.

The old, pre-resurrection Bowman would never have ended so abruptly; but then again, he'd never faced a situation like the present one, most likely.

Bellis reached inside the patrol car and replaced the microphone on its clip, then pulled himself back out. Slowly, he made his way towards Joel and Martina.

Joel and Martina headed towards him, so they met half-way, in the otherwise still-deserted street.

Even the air felt cold and eerie as it pressed against his face and scalp.

"I can tell you that Commissioner Sandarov and a Sergeant Yorak fell into Basilisk Trance earlier on." Bellis took in Joel and Martina's shocked expressions as he spoke. "With everything that's going on, it can't be a coincidence, but no one's found any kind of connection with" – he gestured towards the Chasm – "all this."

He didn't really mean Cataclysm Chasm, of course, but whatever was going on with Donal and the bloodghoul. They walked on towards to the edge where the road ended. Up ahead, a uniformed officer was looking intently across to the other side.

Bellis's eyesight wasn't good enough to make out details.

"Has either of you two got decent distance vision?" he asked. "Something's caught our uniformed colleague's attention, it looks like."

Martina shook her head, but Joel's nictitating membranes flicked back and forth a handful of times, rapidly, and he narrowed his eyes. "Some of our people on the far side, sir. They're looking agitated."

"That's all we need. Run to the car, will you, and crank up the radio so we can find out—"

Bellis stopped, because Martina was already jogging back to the patrol car. He was tempted to follow, but instead he turned to Joel. "Can you make out anything else?"

"Some uniforms running up and down the street on the other side. And… Looks like a Purple Harry coming this way."

Police officers weren't supposed to use the vernacular term to describe armoured vans, but Bellis was in no mood to correct Joel's diction, not today.

"What happened to keeping the streets clear?" muttered Bellis.

Joel shook his head, then flinched as a winged shape rose inside Cataclysm Chasm, almost to road level, before descending out of sight once more.

I really don't like this.

You didn't need to be a mage-novitiate – *former* novitiate – to feel how out-of-whack the world was right now.

There was a scrape of sound behind him, and Bellis felt emptiness in his stomach as he turned around, sensing Martina's disconcerted state of mind

196

even before he saw her tightened features, drained of blood. She might be young by his standards, but for the moment she looked old indeed.

And very, very worried.

"What is it?" Bellis tried to keep his voice as gentle as possible.

"It's Donal Riordan. He..." She stopped.

"Where is he? What's happened to him?"

"That's it." She swallowed. "The patrols can't find him."

Bellis closed his eyes, opened them, and tried to make sense of Martina's words. "The formation shouldn't have left any gaps. There's no direction he could move in without one of the patrols, at least one, seeing where he went."

Martina shook her head. "The teams swear they kept formation, and they sound convincing, sir."

They worked together all the time. Neither she nor Joel called him *sir* unless other officers were nearby; but today was proving different in so many peculiar ways. This was perhaps the least important.

"You're saying Donal just disappeared."

A hint of a shrug. "That's what our patrols are saying. No one saw it happen, not an actual disappearance, but he's gone all the same."

It made no sense.

But what does make sense, today?

From deep inside the Chasm, a long eerie ululation rose, followed by a sudden shriek from something that might have been human once.

The sound of agonising death.

"What are we going to do, Lieutenant?"

It was Bellis's turn to shake his head.

Totally bereft of answers.

THIRTY

The air rippled oddly, just for a few yards, enough to slow Donal down and get him worried. He walked, still following the violet trace that hung in the air, currently just inches above the roadway.

Something…

Did it split here?

He stopped, held himself still without breathing, and let his gaze play across the glimmering violet.

A tiny, slender thread seemed to fork off to the right, but it was so narrow and hard to make out that Donal couldn't follow it visually, and he certainly didn't want to wander off the main trail.

Which itself was dimmer than it had been.

This street, like all the others since crossing the Chasm, stood empty. The odd effect that rippled the air was new, but faint. Maybe it was nothing to worry about.

About two hundred yards ahead, this road terminated in a cross street. From what he knew of the area – not a great deal – the trail could go off in almost any direction after it went either left or right, because the streets beyond the T-junction forked and meandered every which way imaginable, any notion of a grid pattern totally abandoned in this part of the city.

A black park, its inky grasses unkempt, lay on the right hand side, and although low railings guarded it, two wide gates had been swung open and left that way, and something about the arrangement seemed a little off.

The feeling of oddness grew stronger as Donal followed the violet trace. He slowed his pace as the violet trace reached the park and veered into it.

"You went off road? What the Hades?"

The vehicles, by all reports, had been road trucks; but the black grassy ground appeared relatively even, enough to produce a bumpy ride but nothing worse, not enough to stop them. As Donal jogged through the open gates, he could make out tyre tracks marking the black grass. More than one truck, at least four but maybe more, and if he had time he might have been able to work it out better, but the violet trace was—

No.

—coming to an end just yards in front of him.

Not possible.

But his notions of what made sense had fallen by the wayside more than once today. Perhaps this new phenomenon was totally consistent; but it was also a disaster.

An end to the trail.

It was as if something had severed a rope: the violet trace ended with a small flat surface where it had been sheared through, causing it to fizz with white sparkles.

Donal just stood there, vaguely aware that as a redblood he would have been sweat-soaked and gasping after all the running. His muscles right now felt warmed up and ready for more, no sweating or untoward heavy breathing involved; but there was nowhere to go, so none of that mattered.

Crouching down in a rock-bottom squat, he reached out slowly, carefully, towards the end of the violet trace. He had no idea what might happen if he actually touched the thing; but if he didn't do something, then Mel and Finbar might be gone forever.

Contact.

Except that as his fingertips entered the space taken up by the severed violet trace, nothing at all changed in the way he felt. It was visible but otherwise intangible: unknowable to any of his senses save vision, and even that might arise from some kind of synaesthetic illusion.

The ground beyond, when he raised his gaze, looked different than it should: devoid of grass almost to the far end of the park, and with the soil forming an extremely shallow crater, as if something had scooped the topsoil away and thrown it into a void.

Tyre tracks continued in the grass beyond the crater, but the violet trace did not. It ended right here.

Disaster.

Another pair of gates stood open at the far end, and no doubt the trucks had driven across the far sidewalk and onto the parallel street, and from there... anywhere at all.

But without leaving the violet trail behind them.

"No," he said. "No, no, no."

His knowledge of hex barely stretched beyond the level of Academy textbooks for trainee police officers, even with all the library books he'd been reading recently; but this carried all the hallmarks of an obliteration blast, its entire purpose being to wipe out resonances left behind by hexothermic reactions and the like.

Call it the mage equivalent of wiping down a doorknob to get rid of fingerprints. Or sweeping footprints off a floor. Except the witness reports had all featured armed, dark-clad figures breaking into the gym and taking Mel and Finbar: street soldiers, not actual mages.

Perhaps the mages waited in the trucks.

Or perhaps this was something else: a mage-created device, wielded by an ordinary human street soldier.

The shallow crater looked easy enough to cross, and there was maybe some small probability of picking up a trail again on the far side; but every instinct and experience said otherwise: if Donal departed from the violet trace here, not only would it *not* resume on the parallel street, but he didn't think he'd be able to find this original trace again.

It really didn't behave like a physical thing made of ordinary matter and emitting light.

But if the trail just stops here, then coming back to it is pointless anyway.

Still, some instinct held him back from simply abandoning it.

Come on.

Intuition for zombies arises from the subconscious mind, just as in redblood days prior to resurrection; but blackblood mental architecture is normally more malleable to conscious, deliberate control.

What is it?

He couldn't identify the source of the instinct or intuition or whatever it was that was telling him not to abandon the violet trace, even though it ended right here in front of him.

"Hey!" he called out. "Any officers nearby? Assistance required!"

His voice scarcely echoed, as if the black park simply absorbed the sound. No one in sight.

Can't they see I'm not inside a bloodghoul any longer?

Well, maybe they couldn't, not if everyone was hiding. Street evacuations and shelter-in-place broadcasts had proved effective in Fortinium: no one had thought that maybe such measures could work *too* well, so that necessary help was missing exactly when someone most needed it.

He crouched there, remembering – as one of those inconsequential thoughts that arise during moments of stress for blackbloods and redbloods alike – that people in other countries, on other continents like Surinam and its neighbours, supposedly sat this way all the time, in a low squat position with no chairs involved, as a perfectly normal way of life.

But mostly, he stared at the inky grass and wondered what the Hades to do next.

Like all such insights, when it came, it left Donal wondering why exactly he'd taken so long to work it out.

How much time do Mel and Finbar have?

That time might have elapsed to zero hours ago, but that was a paralysing thought he dared not contemplate, because it left him with nothing to do. They had to be alive, and that meant he had to act.

Mel, you're the strongest fighter I know.

Wishing for reinforcements wasn't going to bring a load of officers running, and Donal didn't dare to leave the trail or simply wait where he was, so he rose to standing and carefully, carefully turned round without taking his gaze away from the violet thread.

Did it look dimmer, where it stretched back the way he came?

It does.

Just a fraction, but it was enough to tell him that he needed to keep moving or nothing at all was going to help Mel and Finbar.

He jogged back the way he'd come for about a hundred yards – the automatic portion of his mind counted a hundred and three paces – then slowed down further, knowing that he dared not miss it, that if he overshot and had to backtrack again, he might lose the trace entirely.

The glimmering looked fainter than ever.

Come on.

It was back here somewhere, he was sure of it.

Come…

And there it was.

"Gotcha."

The faintest of violet threads, even thinner and dimmer than the main trace it branched from, led off to the left.

Yes.

Directly to the front door of a dark-grey tenement house.

"Alright," he breathed. "Alright."

As he followed the thread, he reached inside his jacket and drew the Magnus, perhaps because this was entering a kind of familiar territory: kicking in a door and storming a suspect's house in the face of lethal threat.

A visiting Glian detective had told him once – with a haughty slurred voice, because he'd left sobriety behind several whiskies earlier – that the greater prevalence here of both firearms and weaponised hex contributed to a greater crime rate and a necessarily violent police response… but right now that constituted one of those fleeting irrelevant thoughts from nowhere, because Donal *was* in Tristopolis, here and now in the city he loved, and this was how you played the cards that Thanatos or the Norns or whoever else had dealt you.

The front door stood unlocked, just a fraction ajar. No kicking necessary.

I can do this.

Left-handed, crouched with his Magnus held close to his body, Donal pushed the door open. It creaked, but not too much, and he sensed no immediate threat within.

Inside stretched a long hallway, going further back than he'd anticipated. Battered paintwork on the walls; old, cracked lino on the floor.

To the right, propped at a low angle against the wall, stood an old, dark-blue motorcycle that might have been a Triumphant, a Glian import, and which looked to have been knocked over, off its stand.

Donal felt his nostrils dilate as he sniffed in a scent too faint for a redblood human to pick up.

A familiar scent, last picked up in a much posher, grander house in the borough of Keening, more like the murdered maid than the corpse of Arrhennius Hawke himself.

Another dead person, most likely an innocent homeowner or tenant, which was awful but in a tactical sense, good news. It meant Donal was still on some kind of trail that might lead somewhere significant.

He moved carefully past the motorbike – yes, the zinc Triumphant spear-and-shield decal occupied the usual position on the fuel tank – and stopped at the door to the front room, and peeked around the doorjamb, then jerked his head straight back, but in fact there was no need.

The messy, blood-streaked body on the floor would never form a threat to anyone, and maybe never had.

Donal thought the corpse might have been a twenty-year-old man just a few hours before, but now it was a dead thing, its bones soon to be fuel for the reactor piles, and its nerves perhaps, if they were healthy enough, destined to form part of a trunk line or branch exchange created by the telephone company.

Most likely, the man had not deserved to die today.

Keep on moving.

Donal crept using cross-steps past the sitting-room doorway, and onwards towards what looked like a kitchen or scullery at the rear.

Everything remained quite silent.

For whoever did this, wiping out this young man as simple collateral damage, a sudden death would form too lenient a punishment. Donal needed to rescue Mel and Finbar – *dear Thanatos, let them still be alive* – but they weren't the only victims, which meant an awful lot of retribution needed to be spread around the people responsible.

I don't know who's behind it, though.

All this, and not an inkling of who might have commanded such a strong, organised team of street soldiers. He'd probably never gone so far in an investigation without gaining at least an inkling of who might be ultimately responsible.

And he'd never known the anguish of having his own family in danger, for all the victim's families that he'd dealt with over the years. He'd thought he'd understood the depths of their suffering, those other relatives; in the event, he'd been nowhere near appreciating the agony that clutched them.

Oil and blood streaked the kitchen floor, trails left by something that might have been a motorcycle's tyres, but when Donal looked back towards the Triumphant, the hallway linoleum looked clear in its vicinity.

A second bike. It had to be.

Toppled kitchen chairs and a small table pushed up right against the sink told their own story: they were standing on grey floorboards, while the kitchen lino lay curled against the furniture, as though it had been slipped from beneath the table and chairs, rolled back and then allowed to fall in place.

Nothing in the dark yard out back. The back door remained locked and intact. If Donal had been leading a team, he'd have sent some officers upstairs to check the rest of the house; but this was all on him, and he couldn't afford to waste any time.

He reholstered the Magnus, despite the danger of doing so, and with both hands rolled back the linoleum, all the way – it squeaked during the last part, as it pulled away from floorboards it had stuck to for years, maybe even decades – revealing bare kitchen floorboards that looked old and grey.

Along with a big old hatch set right there, in the middle of the floor. The part where the lino had come up easily.

The intruder knew this was here.

Probably the dead man in the front room, most likely a tenant, would have had no clue that a cellar existed. But why would anyone hole up in a cellar, after leaving a dead body behind and with no way of putting the lino and furniture neatly back in place after closing the hatch?

With two hands Donal could yank the hatch up faster than doing it one-handed, but wouldn't be able to fire into the gap. He decided to take that risk.

He lowered himself in a straddle stance as if about to go for a heavy deadlift, hooked both hands in the iron ring of the hatch, pulled up just enough to feel the strain, then took in a breath and held it and tightened all the muscles running down the rear of his torso and legs.

Ready.

And he jerked up hard, using hip thrust to raise the hatch by two feet or more, and flipped his hands from ring to hatch edge, dipped fast, and slammed upwards and forwards with his hands, flinging the hatch open and lunging to his left because standing in place would have made him one Hades of an easy target for anyone aiming up from the cellar below.

The hatch thumped hard as it fell back, causing small clouds of dust to rise from the floorboards, but no sound save an echo rose from the darkened cellar. If anyone was down there, they knew for sure that Donal was up here and planning to descend.

All he could do was move fast and keep dodging.

As he had with the front room doorway, he popped his head forward and jerked back, and only then attempted to analyse the scene he'd glimpsed.

Shadows, a cellar floor that looked clear of obstacles directly below, a hint of ordinary debris to one side, and nothing more besides the musty smell of disturbed dust and damp wood.

So here goes.

He took one step forward into nothingness.

And dropped.

THIRTY-ONE

Anna jerked awake in the hospital bed. No disorientation: she knew straight away where she was, exactly, after dozing off while reading her book. Not only that, but the bedside table bore the remnants of hot chocolate not from the normal vending setup, but from the nurses' kitchen and made with actual dark Surinese chocolate melted in a saucepan, stirred into shadownut milk, and kept simmering for a decent length of time.

Something had awakened her, yet she felt secure, rather than worried.

Jean-Marc. I wish you'd come back.

And that life for a senior federal spellbinder was less onerous, or at least less dangerous, than it might be for the younger agents he commanded.

There was a tap on the door before it swung open, revealing the always-smart figure of Agent Dexter, first name Saul, and with luck Sister Katrina's about-to-be boyfriend.

"Senator," he said. "Are you okay in here?"

She assumed colleagues were outside in the corridor, within hearing distance, since they'd previously agreed on first-name terms when it was just the three of them alone – Saul, Katrina or Anna herself – or any two of them.

"Thank you, Agent Dexter. I'm feeling okay, almost bored."

"This is now a highly secure location, ma'am."

"I'm sure it is, and I'm smart enough to want to stay here."

Saul's mouth twitched at the corner, in a way that reminded Anna of Jean-Marc, which was a weird thought considering how few hours she and Federal Agent Jean-Marc Bouchard had actually spent in each other's company.

"I have a question," said Saul, "from Agent Bouchard."

Anna nodded, understanding from his tone that this was supposed to be all business. "Anything I can answer, I will. Of course."

"Yes, ma'am. His question was, during your dealings with Dahlberg Industries, did you have any contact, by phone or letter or in person, with

Commissioner Sandarov."

"Um… Sandarov?"

"I mean in Tristopolis, Senator."

"Ah, right. Yes, I know the name. But… No. No dealings with him at all. Commissioner Sandarov *is* a man, isn't he?"

"Yes, ma'am. Was there any Tristopolis connection that you can remember?"

"No… Give me a moment to think, please."

Saul nodded, his expression unreadable behind the standard wraparound shades.

Anna took the request seriously, but she couldn't think of anything that might help. A little frustrated, she shook her head, hair rustling against the propped-up pillows as she did so.

"I'm sure Kristof Dahlberg had offices or facilities of some sort in Tristopolis, just because the company is so big. But nothing cropped up in the matters we discussed."

"Anything law-enforcement related? A police contract, or maybe military contracts with reservists?"

"Nothing defence or police related at all, Agent Dexter."

Saul nodded. "It was worth following up, ma'am. Just in case."

He stepped further inside the room, and added: "I'm off duty this evening, but my colleagues will take good care of you. I'll be checking with one of the Night Sisters to make sure all is well."

Anna grinned, then mouthed: *You're going on a date. With Katrina.*

Saul nodded once more.

For his professional sake, Anna didn't laugh with delight, although she felt like doing so.

I want all this to be over.

Saul added aloud: "You've done a lot to help already, you know. Agent Bouchard… Jean-Marc says he's already been able to help someone on the ground in Tristopolis, before he got cut off, in a manner of speaking."

"Do you know everything that's happening, Saul?"

"Not really. I'm not sure it's even in our hands any more."

It was a spectacular confession for a federal spellbinder to make.

"But Jean-Marc's safe."

"He is. He's trying to get transport to Tristopolis, because we think something's coming to a head there. But he doesn't think he'll get there in time to do any good."

Anna shook her head. "I didn't make him for a pessimist."

"Nor should you. His, um, premonitions tend to be rather accurate, though."

"Ah."

She wondered what that signified in terms of personal relationships.

Not just any kind of relationship.

"I'll just stand here quietly until my shift ends," said Saul.

"Thank you."

If things were in fact coming to a head, and Jean-Marc didn't expect to reach the flashpoint in time, Anna wondered who might be there instead: what stranger might fall or triumph against Kristof Dahlberg's killer.

And what else might be at stake, for this was about a great deal more than a single assassination: she knew that now.

Jean-Marc...

It was the closest to a prayer she could manage.

THIRTY-TWO

It took a third of a second to drop to the cellar floor, and by the time Donal's feet struck flagstones, he already had the Magnus out and was starting to pivot, scanning some three hundred degrees of arc, discounting the area closest to the nearby brickwork wall. Nowhere there for an enemy to hide.

There was an angled shaft or tunnel leading downwards, out of the cellar.

Subtleties of air movement against his face and the echo of his footfall told Donal of the tunnel's presence even before his zombie eyes adjusted to the comparative darkness.

Phosphorescent lichen grew in streaks along the walls, with the look of once-deliberate geometric lines inlaid in stonework, long escaped to form organic patterns splashed across the shaft walls.

It sloped downwards from the cellar, and at the bottom a curved shadow lay. After another moment, Donal identified the visible portion of – almost certainly – a motorcycle tyre.

A motorbike, lying in a cross-tunnel at the bottom of the sloping shaft, on the right hand side of the opening where shaft joined horizontal tunnel, and with just a portion of rear tyre visible.

The bike explained some of the marks he'd seen earlier on the hallway floor. Whoever had killed the owner of the house overhead had also taken one of two motorcycles, and managed to manoeuvre that heavy bike down through the cellar hatch opening and wheel it down the sloping shaft to the place where it joined the deeper horizontal tunnel.

Not what Donal had expected. No catacombs lay beneath the streets round here. Not as far as he knew.

He would have reckoned the tunnel down below to be a sewer or a major drain, except that it didn't smell like either one. A cool draught played against his face, so there was ventilation of a sort down there, some link to the surface. That, or it simply stretched for miles like the catacombs, which were

208

long enough to produce something akin to subterranean weather.

But why go to all the trouble to get a motorcycle down here, then abandon it almost immediately?

If the enemy remained nearby – that was the word that came to mind: *enemy*, not suspect – then they'd have heard Donal pull and push the hatch open with a crash, even if they'd heard nothing else. That meant descending the shaft to where it met the tunnel might well mean walking into ambush.

But at least Donal could move silently from this part on, so even if the enemy was waiting, they wouldn't know whether he'd entered the shaft yet. It was the only positive aspect of the tactical geometry: it would have to be enough.

Slowly, step by careful step, he descended the sloping shaft.

Careful.

And was only three paces from the bottom when he heard the groan. It came from around the bend to the right.

"Andrei?" A desperate, accented whisper: it had to come from a badly wounded man.

Donal remembered that one of the street soldiers in the confrontation below Dredgeway Avenue, the only one who spoke directly, had possessed a Vostokian accent, as best as Donal had been able to tell.

He whispered back, doing his best to recreate the accent: "It's me."

Hoping that the fallen man wasn't expecting a reply in his own language.

"Mmm." The sound of wordless pain.

Donal paused at the end of the shaft, then crouched low and peered around the corner to the right, flicked a glance to the left just in case – the long tunnel seemed clear that way – and back towards the bulky shape near his feet and the twisted figure that lay partly beyond it.

The black motorbike had fallen and the rider had almost managed to get clear, but one leg was fully trapped along with the other foot and ankle.

No helmet. Perhaps his skull had impacted against the curved stone wall or floor.

An old mail train tunnel?

The single rail that ran along the centre looked dull, straight enough in this section but perhaps a little warped further on; and in the distance, Donal thought he could make out an actual gap.

A disused tunnel then, out of service. It might have been years since the miniature, wraith-powered trains carried letters and parcels in carriages that were little more than covered buckets on mono wheels, with side-mounted stabilisers.

You used to be able to hear such trains passing beneath the orphanage schoolyard in Lower Danklyn, if you stood near the eastern wall and put your ear to the ground at the right time. Maybe you still could.

A soft wind played against Donal's face, and there was enough phosphorescent lichen spotted around to let him see the tunnel's shape, and feel certain that the gloom remained empty save for the toppled black motorbike and its badly injured rider.

One of the men who took Mel and Finbar.

Donal crouched down near the man's head and muttered: "Hey, it's okay."

Hoping that would sound cogent no matter what language the fallen man expected to hear.

But the only answer was a coughing breath, followed by a gasp that might have been a deliberate syllable, or simply an expression of agony from a mind no longer capable of real conversation.

Donal wondered how hard the impact had been.

"And…" The rider, perhaps trying to say the name Andrei once more.

Mistaking Donal for one of his comrades? Or just calling out for someone he knew?

He sounded like a dying man, and although his head looked intact, when Donal took a breath in – his first deep inhalation since entering the tunnel – the cupric scent of blood was thick and obvious in the air.

"Amu…" Another cough, and a long wheeze.

And silence.

Four seconds passed, then a painful inhalation from the trapped man. So he wasn't dead, not yet, and if Donal ran back up to the house and out onto the street, he might be able to reach cops with a radio car or else a phone booth, and call in the paramedics who might just be able to get here in time to save the guy, if they could land their ambulance in the narrow street above.

The man's finger twitched, as if hooking the air, and when Donal's gaze followed the line of movement, he caught the faintest glimpse of amber light, either dim or hidden, beneath the toppled motorbike.

Another Triumphant, this one coated in black protective scales, but that felt quite irrelevant now, except that everyone knew these motorbikes were particularly heavy, which meant the fallen man must have struggled to get it down here from the house above.

It was no wonder he'd lost control when he tried to get it going.

"I'm going to lift the bike." Donal pitched his voice clearly, and made sure it sounded hard, because he wanted the words to sink in. "My guess is, your bones have split right through, including your femur, and cut open your femoral artery."

Too technical, especially if the guy spoke mainly Vostokian.

"You've been bleeding out," Donal went on. "But the bike is acting like a tourniquet, a little bit. When I pull it up, you've got maybe five seconds left before you're unconscious."

He paused, then: "After that, you've got twenty seconds to live, and then you're gone."

There was a limit to how much time he could wait, because if the amber glow meant what he thought it did, it was the one piece of good news he'd come across today; but its dimness concerned him, because it meant his one slim chance was diminishing fast.

"Too bad." Donal backed off, squatted down, grabbed handlebars and chassis, and prepared to launch into a pseudo-deadlift movement once again.

"Ah…" The man might have been trying to say *Andrei* or *amulet* or something else, but he was never going to get the chance to finish it.

Mel. Finbar.

Donal launched himself upwards and back, ripping the bike upright, his back muscles hot and strong with the explosive effort.

The amber token – the amulet that the rider might have been trying to talk about – was clipped to the side of the fuel tank, and it looked cracked, glowing more weakly than Donal had thought.

Gauntlets lay on the tunnel floor, grey and blackened from handling something nasty, and gave Donal his explanation for the man's presence here: he'd placed a shaped hexplosive charge precisely designed to obliterate the truck convoy's trail in the small park, and in order to do that he'd had to remain behind while his comrades drove on.

With Mel and Finbar held captive in one of those trucks.

A cough, and a long, rattling exhalation: a sound that once heard, can never be unheard or forgotten. And whose meaning cuts deep forever.

Donal stared at the fallen rider in the moment of extinction.

"You got off lucky," he said.

He swung his leg over the saddle, and steadied the bike, not minding the effort involved. Triumphants might be heavy, but they were also powerful and able to withstand punishment, a lot more than the fragile humans who rode them.

When he turned the bone key, the engine growled, and Donal patted the black scales that protected the fuel tank.

"We've got a mission," he said. "And we're going to push hard, because the navigation amulet is on its last legs."

Triumphants weren't known for their brainpower – Donal couldn't expect the bike to possess the same kind of sentience as Harald Hammersen's classic Phantasm IV – but courage and determination were hallmarks of the Glian marque: motorcycles that were anything but flashy but never, ever gave up.

"Plus we're the good guys, just you and me."

This time when he twisted the throttle, the bike roared as if answering a challenge, so Donal let out the clutch and his stomach felt as if someone slammed it against his spine, and his lips stretched back in a purely predatory way because the hunt was still on.

An amber glow stretched out a mere yard ahead of the bike. It was going to be hard to see it alter angle when they reached the junctions, but they couldn't slow down too much because the amulet had been activated too long ago.

It was surely designed to be single-use, and even if not, there would be no time to recharge the thing, even if it retained memory of its destination, which Donal reckoned unlikely: the enemy, whoever they were, hadn't put a foot wrong since this whole thing started.

On top of that, a crack disfigured the amulet, and Donal could only hope that the damage didn't alter the basic inlaid function, of finding its way back to its notional home.

Donal leaned forward over the scale-covered fuel tank, eyes narrowed against the slipstream as the Triumphant powered on, staying parallel to the disused, damaged monorail that ran along the tunnel floor and onwards into darkness, relieved by splashes of phosphorescent lichen that survived by symbiosis with bacteria that lived on inanimate chemicals in the stones and soil.

That, according to Sister Mary-Anne Styx at the orphanage school – so long ago now – made the bacteria candidates for the most enlightened form of life, since they killed no living organisms for food.

Sorry, Sister.

She might not like what Donal was about to do, although some of her fellow Sisters of Thanatos had been utterly vicious, and they might have enjoyed watching his vengeance.

Mel. Finbar.

The motorbike's vibrations pulsed back from the tunnel walls in time with Donal's mounting need for aggression, his determination to get to his family regardless of obstacles; while if the worst had already happened, he would slaughter anyone and everyone involved.

You took my wife and son.

Some fleeting memory whipped past like blurred tunnel stonework, with him telling Bellis that he and Mel weren't married except in the ways that mattered most, but he would rectify that with a legal ceremony if Mel agreed, which gave him one more reason to get there – wherever she was – before the amulet gave out.

For now, its glow pointed ahead, faint but steady, like some foreshortened ghostly lance.

He gripped the Triumphant's throttle hard, asking for more, and the motorbike responded.

Roaring as it accelerated onwards.

THIRTY-THREE

They came for her, and she fought.

Snarling, Mel used everything she knew: hook punches to the carotid at the side of the neck, straight thrusts to the laryngeal cartilage hoping to kill; and because boxing bare fist changes everything, palm heels to the side of the jaw, thumbs hooking at eyeballs whenever she could as the mêlée swarmed around the bare stone cell.

With her at the centre of the whirlwind.

Mel's fighting experience ranged further than the sparring heptagon and competition ring; but she was battling now just days after giving birth, and even though the squad of men pouring into the room were trying not to kill her, they had so many advantages: of strength and weight, of close quarter battle training of their own.

Every now and then in the whirl of action, flashes of coordinated enemy teamwork – soldiers used to fighting in twos and threes, not just solo – wore her down and made a difference.

Finally they pressed her back against one wall and even then she could snap out punches that splattered noses or bent larger men over with the shock of liver trauma; but their strategy had been sound because two of them went to the stone bed where Finbar lay swaddled, and that was all they needed.

Once they'd positioned themselves between mother and baby, their victory was inevitable.

Which didn't stop Mel from snapping out three more punches to hurt the closest men, but when one of the men near Finbar pulled out a shining silver blade she froze, not needing the command that followed: "Stop, woman."

She had to do what he said.

Had to.

Words and anger raged inside her head but there *were* no words sufficient to tell them what she thought of them, so she snarled and bottled it all inside and kept her gaze wildly scanning all around, knowing that any opening at all would have to be taken.

But not if Finbar's soft and delicate flesh was in danger from a blade: not then.

Not now.

"Sss..." She hissed between her teeth.

"We're going for a walk," said the other man close to Finbar. "You go ahead, and I'll carry the child."

Blood dripped from Mel's clenched fist, but she would not engage in conversation. This was far more primal and primeval than verbal discourse.

Ringed by wounded, angry men, she expected them to pummel her as they shuffled her towards the open door and out into the corridor, but they showed some measure of professionalism, and merely used their body mass to guide her motion.

She kept looking back, of course.

Okay...

The man who'd spoken was carrying Finbar with all the care you'd expect from someone who knew how to take care of a fragile newborn, while his comrade stayed close with the knife still unsheathed.

None of the street soldiers were women, and Mel wondered if that was somehow deliberate, since some of the people who'd stormed the gym had in fact been female. Given their trained expertise, whoever commanded them wouldn't expect female soldiers to soften their hearts just because a newborn baby was involved.

No, it was probably a matter of intimidating Mel, which hadn't worked psychologically; but still, men carried muscle more easily, while she always needed to work hard to maintain her strength, and pregnancy hadn't been the time for that, with no training at all in the last couple of weeks.

But she wasn't pregnant now, and one more strategic opening was all she needed.

"Wait here."

They stopped together, the ensemble, and it gave Mel time to count her opponents. Seventeen men, at least four of them barely able to stand – *good* – and while she might have damaged them – *they deserve worse* – the downside was that every man here knew that he dared not underestimate this particular prisoner.

One of the men went forward to a rune-decorated wall that ended the corridor. It looked more like a ship's bulkhead than a normal wall, and Mel sensed that there was some way to open it up and reveal more corridor beyond.

While the others waited, Mel glanced at the cell to her right, then back at Finbar. She stared at the man who was holding her baby.

In her peripheral vision, movement occurred. From inside the cell.

It can't help me.

Three horns arced back from the captive's forehead, and its eyes had been half-lidded and dulled compared to normal – though Mel had no idea how she knew that – when it raised its head to look out through the grilled window and see what was happening.

Alertness grew stronger in those eyes.

Chains that might have been platinum clanked and slid as the grey-skinned captive moved, but only slightly: there wasn't much play in the chains or room in the cell.

The creature was sitting or crouching – Mel hadn't been able to tell as her gaze passed across the cell door – and its wings had been partly spread but crooked, and dark purple wounds had streaked its body, which for some reason brought Hellah to mind, even though the Guardian's skin resembled fresh, glistening blood and she terrified Mel at a deep level that Mel couldn't explain, and wouldn't need to with anyone else in the world.

As far as she could tell, everyone shared that innate fear response, apart from Donal: the one person that Hellah didn't scare at all.

The bulkhead-like wall scraped open in some way that Mel didn't see because her focus was on Finbar in the soldier's arms.

Finbar was visible but only just, through a small opening in the group that surrounded her. And that opening was strategic on their part, she was almost certain: calculating that she would remain easier to control so long as Finbar was in her sight.

In sight, but out of her protection.

"Come on," said another of the men. "You don't want to keep her waiting."

"Keep *who* waiting?"

But someone jostled her shoulder from behind, and she started to walk amid her ring of guards, knowing that conversation meant nothing right now, because these weren't civilised human beings.

They were obstacles and targets, and she would put them down and rescue Finbar the instant they let their guard down.

Walls on both sides were covered with murals in which shades of blood predominated, depicting scenes that Mel thought might have turned her stomach if she stopped to examine them.

Irrelevant. She already knew this place felt awful.

Directly ahead, a rune-chased vault door of bone and steel was swinging open, to reveal an elliptical chamber on the far side of the threshold. For a second, Mel paused, not wanting to walk into this deeper trap, even though she really had no choice.

There was nothing she wouldn't do to save Finbar, including giving up her life if that was what it took.

She stepped forward, over the metallic threshold, and felt waves of coldness passing upwards along her skin, while some deep vibration caused shivers in her core.

To one side, at one of the focal points of the elliptical room, stood a framework of black and silver in which a kind of misty blue fire was playing: a shade of sapphire blue that she recognised all too well from the random moments when she and her baby boy's eyes were linked by some faintly glowing phenomenon that no one had yet explained to her.

Not even Ingrid, a trained and experienced security witch, had been able to say what was going on, although Mel hadn't been able to tell whether that was genuine lack of knowledge or a desire to hide a hard truth from a new mother.

The fate of Ingrid and her apprentice Ludka and even the schoolkids who'd been waiting to train at the gym… All of that, Mel had been trying to shove aside in her mind, because she had no idea what had happened to them, and fear and grief might weaken her when she needed to fight.

No distractions.

She couldn't allow anyone or anything to shift her away from her purpose here.

"She's injured." An imperious female voice. "I didn't want her damaged."

Was this the true enemy?

Mel turned, taking in the figure of the dark-gowned woman with coiffed hair piled high and polished fingernails of solid gold, and found herself growling.

"What do you want?" Mel's voice came out rasping and hard.

"You don't even feel the pain, do you?" Ruby lips and a half-amused, half-haughty smile. "How very… authentic. Don't worry." This, to her street soldiers. "I see she fought back. You did what you had to."

Mel felt her broken lips pull back from her teeth. "You want authentic, you simpering cow?"

The woman blinked in what looked like real surprise. Then she recovered, shook her head, and addressed the street soldiers again. "Put her in the framework, with the least damage to her possible… But put her in."

Near the doorway, just inside, the soldier bearing Finbar raised him a little, while the man next to him altered the position of his knife just enough to catch Mel's attention.

Mel shook her head.

"I won't resist," she said.

Hands guided her to the extended framework of metal and black chitin or ceramic – she couldn't tell the difference and didn't care right now – and they strapped her inside the thing while blue fire played all around their limbs, and their features might have been strained due to whatever effect the blueness had on them, but Mel felt nothing.

216

Only something deeper than hatred, as she stared at the woman, her enemy.

I will kill you.

Mel didn't know how, or when, or what it would take to create an opportunity.

Finbar…

The man still held him, her baby, as before.

"My name is Vanessa Frisch, and I'm…"

Perhaps there were other words to follow, but the oceanic washing in Mel's ears drowned them out, because she didn't need to know anything more.

Nothing beyond a name.

Vanessa Frisch.

The name of her enemy.

THIRTY-FOUR

For seven ninths of an hour, Donal rode the Triumphant hard along the old mail monorail tunnels.

Its engine roared, and the roar echoed back from the stone walls, while Donal wondered if anyone overhead might hear them. Maybe citizens in their cellars or pedestrians on sidewalks felt passing vibration beneath their feet.

Or maybe not. The city was old and solidly built, and perhaps the tunnels ran deep enough for the earth itself to absorb the sound.

Eventually – at some point – they would pass beyond the city boundary. Perhaps they had already: Donal couldn't tell.

Twice when the tunnel forked he sensed people off in the distance: workers with bone lanterns the first time, performing maintenance on one of the sections that would normally have remained in use; while on the second occasion he glimpsed a shambling group of denizens, down and out and mostly human.

They probably made their home in one of the disused sections.

He and the Triumphant roared on without stopping or even slowing, because the amulet's light was growing weaker. It was like following the violet trace all over again, with similar limitations, because if he sidetracked to summon help he might lose the trail before the end and all of this would count for nothing.

There were sections where the monorail was broken or simply missing, sometimes with fallen stones or other debris littering the tunnel floor, and navigating the worst section had nearly required Donal to dismount and carry the motorbike over a pile of broken stones and rusted junk.

He'd managed to manoeuvre around the mess, thanks to the Triumphant's determined strength. In these awkward stretches, Donal kept pushing with one foot or the other against obstacles on their left or right, helping to keep the bike upright.

Finally, they rode into an unbroken tunnel and kept going, because this section ran for many leagues and appeared to remain in use, given the polished condition of the monorail, though he couldn't hear or see a mail train in front or behind.

He did spot three trains running in different side tunnels along the way. One of the trains looked spectacularly long, although the carriages – more like crates on wheels – barely reached waist height. Just another part of Tristopolitan infrastructure that people rarely talked about.

Donal almost missed the significance as the amulet's foreshortened beam of light altered angle. He and the Triumphant were travelling fast, riskily so, when the amber light shifted a tiny fraction to the right, and a few degrees upwards.

"Slow down," he muttered into the slipstream as he throttled back and squeezed the bone grip of the brake.

We've been travelling for an hour and three minutes.

It must be almost time to climb up from the tunnel system.

Some of the exits they'd passed had comprised sloping shafts, similar to the one he'd used to enter the tunnels in the first place. Presumably most connected to maintenance stations or just raised cylindrical miniature towers at ground level, similar to the entranceways for the catacombs.

Donal had seen such things from time to time and paid them no attention.

Against his face, the air felt warmer, but that was just a subjective illusion, caused by the lessening speed of the Triumphant.

The house he'd entered the tunnel system from must have been a relatively new addition to older tenement housing, built on the site of a demolished maintenance station; but you'd expect the builders to block off the shaft when they built the house.

Exactly why the cellar maintained access to the old tunnels was a matter for Lieutenant Bellis or someone to investigate.

Slowing further, but Donal and the Triumphant hadn't reached an exit shaft here, not yet.

Cops in the Alkadian Wilderness used tracker wraiths to follow suspect's movements, although that part of the Federation was so desolate and sparsely populated that few crimes – beyond obvious domestic incidents – were ever actually solved.

Donal wondered if Bellis could come up with some way to track the Triumphant's journey along the tunnel system. Then he dismissed the notion, because random thoughts always intrude in the middle of stress and prolonged action but they never mean anything and here was the exit from the tunnel coming up now.

Time to go up.

The beam angled up and right and Donal turned the handlebars and increased the power to deal with the rising gradient as they hit the slope and began to climb. Echoes bounced oddly all around as they climbed further and further, leaving the tunnel behind and below.

It was surprising, the length of time it took to ascend the angled shaft.

Maybe the monorail tunnels had descended subtly to greater and greater depths as Donal rode the Triumphant along them; but it surely couldn't account for the whole discrepancy: not only did the tunnels run deeper here, but the ground must also rise higher.

His hands remained dry on the grips because zombies don't sweat, but something about this exit shaft was making him nervous all the same.

It looked twice as wide and high as the one he'd descended from the house cellar. It was also far longer, but when Donal and the still-strong Triumphant reached the end, it wasn't a normal opening.

Instead, a vertical iron wall confronted him.

There was a door set into that forbidding wall, definitely not leading into a house cellar.

Is this where Mel and Finbar are?

Four black, curved legs of shiny chitin snapped out of the motorbike's chassis as Donal switched the engine off. They stabilised the bike even on a slope like this, and Donal patted the black scales of the fuel tank before swinging his leg back and over the saddle.

He dismounted.

Carefully, paying attention to everything, he walked up to the iron door, feeling the floor's gradient in the way his calves stretched, the relative stillness of the air, and the absence of sound from whatever lay beyond the iron barrier.

Donal pressed his left hand against the cold, hard metal. Faint streaks of rust felt like powder, but all of this sensory information felt useless.

No obvious handle or other mechanism: there was nothing to work with.

He pushed but nothing happened, which was hardly surprising: the door looked like the kind of thing that led to a vault. Nothing that heavy would move unless it was perfectly balanced on well-oiled hinges.

These faint blooms of rust weren't consistent with constant professional maintenance.

Donal couldn't even work out whether he should be pushing or pulling, although there was little enough to grab onto and yank at, if the door was supposed to open towards him.

Supposing it only opens from the outside?

He looked back at the Triumphant, as though the stationary motorbike might offer some answer, but of course it didn't. If anything, it looked like a trusting animal waiting for Donal to tell it what to do.

"No," he muttered, keeping his voice low just in case there was someone on the other side to hear. "No, we can't stop here."

Not after everything it took to get this far. He couldn't be stymied by a simple door, even one as big and heavy as this, not when the stakes were Mel and Finbar's lives.

He went back to the Triumphant, laid one hand on the fuel tank, and stared up at the iron door and wall, looking for anything that might help, seeing nothing at all.

What the Hades do I do now?

It took longer than it should have.

He'd been looking in the wrong place. Any kind of emergency release needs to be obvious, and he found it when he was almost considering a return to the main tunnel below: he looked down the angled shaft and realised that three metal bars along one wall, bound together and running parallel to the floor, looked different from the other beams that supported the structure.

Subtle scrapes and a lack of rust indicated that the bars were supposed to move in some way.

When he descended to check, it became more obvious: the lower end, closer to the tunnel, looked like some kind of hinge or coupling, while the higher end, when Donal jerked hard enough, came free of the clips that fastened the bars to the wall.

The whole thing formed a lever. A very long one.

Donal hauled backwards, steadily, feeling it in his back, while some ratchet mechanism clacked steadily inside the wall. After a moment – he glanced over to check – the big vault door began to open inwards.

Draughts swirled in the shaft, and Donal caught the smell of fresh air with a hint of countryside.

Several metallic squeals had accompanied the big door's opening, but it would have sounded louder in here. Perhaps if there were people out there on the surface, they hadn't realised the thing had opened.

He strode to the opening, patting the bike as he passed it, keeping his voice low as he said: "Wait here while I check."

Donal wasn't sure the Triumphant understood, but he thought it might, and he wondered whether the street soldier who'd killed the Triumphant's owner and tried to steal the motorbike had lost control of it through accident and fatigue, or whether the bike itself had helped to cause the toppling that broke the man's bones and severed the artery.

Deliberately, Donal undid his suit jacket – his clothes were a little torn and definitely stained, including a splash of blood on his lower leg that had come from the dying would-be bike thief – freeing up access to his Magnus, but keeping it holstered for now.

No need to be provocative, if innocent people were standing outside.

He crouched low and peeked, drew back, and processed what he'd seen, which was nothing untoward: a grimy coal-coloured yard with broken machinery that looked abandoned, and nobody at all in sight.

No sense of anyone nearby.

I made enough noise.

It wouldn't have carried far, necessarily, but an armed team in the vicinity, if they'd been on full alert, would have had time to drop into hiding and prepare an ambush. It wasn't as if the enemy's street soldiers lacked training.

But he didn't want to waste time checking the place on foot if Mel and Finbar were still far away.

"Okay." He returned to the bike, swung his leg over the saddle and settled himself. "It looks clear."

The Triumphant growled into motion, its parking legs snapping into the chassis as it rolled up the slope and bumped its way onto the dark, uneven ground that looked like black clay and coal slag. The Triumphant's silvery headlight beam came on.

With the contrast of that beam, the navigation amulet's glow looked weaker; or perhaps it was actually dying. It curved towards the fuel tank, which Donal knew meant he had to turn in that direction, following a rough track between dilapidated buildings formed of corrugated sheets that had rusted and partly fallen or been torn away from the skeleton girders inside.

A pale face shone in the Triumphant's headlight just for a moment, and Donal rolled the bike to a halt and let the engine idle.

"Hello," he said.

"Uh, hello." The answering voice was slow and dull.

Its owner shambled into view and stood there, hands awkwardly positioned, mouth partly open, looking at a loss for words and thought.

"Do you work here?" said Donal. "Live here?"

"Uh-huh."

Marvellous.

"Is there a phone in one of these buildings?" Donal remained in the saddle, not wanting to dismount from the Triumphant without good reason.

"Uh-huh." This time a pale hand rose and pointed.

"Great. Could you dial sixes and—"

"Don't work though."

"Oh."

This was pointless.

The amber light from the amulet was definitely duller now.

"Alright." Donal sat back straighter on the saddle and raised his gaze beyond the ruined industrial buildings, to what seemed to be the tops of blackiron trees, hard to make out against the deep purple sky. "Listen, is there a place near here with lots of people?"

This had to be a disused industrial plant or depot of some kind, but located in the countryside, maybe in actual wilderness.

The pale man took a half step back, looked downwards at black mud, and gave a disjointed shrug.

"Maybe bad people," Donal went on. "People who like to hurt others."

Some drool showed at the side of the pale man's mouth as he raised his gaze and nodded.

"Could you point in the direction of their place?" Donal didn't like to press the poor man, but he needed this information. "Please."

A shaky hand pointed to the clumped darkness of forest beyond a broken corrugated building to Donal's right.

It gave Donal a direction to follow, and though it didn't match the direction that the amulet's weakened beam was trying to indicate, that was okay: the amulet sensed nearby paths without giving any indication of an overall heading or final destination.

He felt confident that the amulet was trying to lead him around the disused depot's broken roads and trails so he could travel to the place that scared this man.

"You should hide for a while, my friend," said Donal. "There might be trouble coming."

The man gave an empty nod.

Donal coaxed the growling Triumphant forward, not minding the bumpiness as the motorbike navigated uneven, slag-like ground, because he felt certain their goal was growing nearer.

There is definitely trouble coming.

He and the motorbike bumped their way among the industrial ruins, heading for whatever trail or roadway lay beyond.

I am trouble.

And his time was growing closer.

THIRTY-FIVE

Mel allowed them to bind her to the chair, because the silver blade looked so very sharp against Finbar's dear, soft skin and she had no way to reach the man who threatened Finbar, not in time, not with all his comrades in the way and ready to fight.

She knew it was bad: the near certainty, as cold metal slipped around her neck and wrists and ankles, that her chances of getting out from this were close to zero.

As locks or catches of some kind clicked into place, she felt sick in a deep, awful way; but she'd known from the moment she realised she was pregnant that her own life no longer mattered as much as the new generation.

I can't be a mother if I'm dead.

But Finbar would have died if she'd made a move. Ideally, she should have broken free when they came for her in the gym. She should have fought harder or found some way to run, but that time was gone.

"What the Hades is this?" It didn't matter, in the absolute sense, because all she had to know was that these people around her, and especially this Vanessa Frisch in charge of them, were a threat to Finbar.

They deserved to die, but she didn't care about defeating them so much as surviving whatever they threw at her, so long as survival included Finbar and only optionally herself.

"Oh, my dear." The Frisch woman's haughty, cultured voice – or maybe it was pseudo-cultured – cut through the air. "I hear you run a prizefighters' gymnasium. I doubt you would understand a technical explanation."

She moved to block Mel's view of Finbar. Her dark gown, clearly costing enough money to cover a year's mortgage payments for the gym, maybe even more, formed a kind of insult, or maybe just signalled wrong-headedness: so often people get caught up in chasing after goals that aren't, in the end, worth anything much at all.

But when someone attacks you, right there in the moment is not the time to question the enemy's life choices or childhood influences or anything else in their background. Only the immediate tactical details count for anything.

"Try me," said Mel.

Hoping that the Frisch woman might lean in close enough for something to happen. Biting range would be ideal. Any soft target would do.

Preferably the throat.

But the Frisch woman shrugged and stepped back, not closer. "Quantal entanglement of living cells is a rare thing. Most people have either never heard of it or else assume it's all powerful, a way of running myriads of concurrent conjurations to completion no matter what the hex involved, all in a fraction of a second. Simple ignorance, either way."

Finbar wasn't crying.

He should have been, and Mel couldn't understand why he wasn't, but he was so tiny and fragile and needed to be held: she didn't need a signal from her baby to tell her that all of this was wrong, that she needed to be out of here with him in her arms once more.

"But you can carry out some very specific categories of hex process," continued the Frisch woman, "with paired clumps of complex matter. I'm using the term *complex* in a somewhat technical sense, since the brain of a boxer isn't exactly the pinnacle of cultural and biological evolution."

"Maybe you should come over here, you nasty cow, and explain that in simple words so I can understand."

"Oh, my dear. You're quite delightful, in your own rough way." The Frisch woman crooked a finger, causing liquid reflections to slide along her golden fingernail. It looked like some precious metal talon. "Straighten her out, will you."

It was a command to her servants.

The chair that held Mel began to shift beneath her, sections sliding apart, caused by mechanical means, not hex.

Even though the struggle was physical and desperate strength coursed through Mel's muscles as she tried to hold them in place, fighting isometrically against the attempt to unfold the chair, the principles of leverage and simple mechanics were stacked against her.

It shifted back and extended, straightening Mel's body and tilting it backwards, until she effectively stood on a tipped-back trolley, the kind of thing that the delivery guys had used to deliver the screw-together sections for the sparring heptagon when they were equipping the gym, back when life felt simple.

Hands rotated the straightened chair, which was in fact on wheels or castors of some kind, so Mel could see the strange, enlarged framework once more: big as a cage, large enough to hold several humans or one larger creature. The frame consisted of metal and black ceramic parts, or maybe some kind of chitin rather than ceramic, with sapphire-blue light playing along the struts and hanging in the centre, softly glowing.

"I call it my interrogation framework," said the Frisch woman. "But it's rather more than that. True torture calls for surgical precision, you see, and today *surgical* is the operative word."

Mel tried to tilt her head forward, but the metal binding bit into her neck, and when she tried to turn, to see where Finbar was, she could only manage a few degrees of rotation. Street soldiers with hard faces blocked her view in any case.

There were maybe fifteen of them inside the chamber now, which still left plenty of room. A sudden insight told Mel that the tri-horned creature she'd seen in the cell outside, looking to be eleven feet tall at least – had it been standing upright instead of slumped on the floor – had occupied this chamber before her.

And not just the chamber: the glowing construct that the Frisch woman called her interrogation framework.

"No," said Mel. "No."

"Have you worked it out? How wonderful. Not just a decent-sized lump of quantally entangled organic matter, but a better quality of matter than I'd expected. It's still just a kind of structured fatty lump, you know."

"I'm going to kill you."

The Frisch woman was talking about the human brain.

"I rather doubt—"

"NO!"

Two human brains, entangled – whatever that meant – and the realisation had already exploded inside Mel before she noticed that one of the men was walking in time with the wheeled chair-turned-trolley that held her.

Finbar was in the man's arms.

NO.

Carrying Finbar to the same framework that was opening up in preparation for taking Mel inside. For carrying out surgery.

For removing organic matter from inside two human skulls, one of them still soft and not yet properly formed.

Mel struggled, fought against the bindings, felt hot slickness like sweat but most likely blood as the metal strips cut her skin but remained too tight for her to wrench free of.

"You'll unlock a new level of power for me." The Frisch woman's voice, almost lost beneath the crashing surf-like sound of overwhelming stress. "Crack the necrofusion condensing problem that will give me abilities even my cousins don't dream of trying to—"

Sense and meaning fled as they wheeled Mel forward and the struts of the framework loomed over her, some kind of quasi-living fluid moving along them and radiating a sense of awful *hunger*, while pseudo-gentle hands lay

Finbar on a metallic section of the framework and sapphire light enveloped him.

And finally, he cried. Wailed, as any newborn should.

NO!

Blueness exploded in front of Mel.

Filled her eyes, her mind.

Her world.

THIRTY-SIX

Donal rode the Triumphant into a broad clearing, roughly nine-sided, where the black grass looked naturally short, not tended like a lawn, because this was the middle of forest land. Blackiron trees reared all around, and never mind that industrial ruins that might have once formed a busy depot stood a little over a league away, four miles at most.

The motorbike growled to a halt, and snapped out its four black parking legs as Donal twisted the bone key to Standby. He wanted the bike to keep its engine ticking over, just in case.

Faint now, the amber glow from the amulet clipped to the black-scaled fuel tank.

Donal prised it free.

The clip looked roughly glued in place, which meant the would-be thief had brought both the clip and some kind of adhesive along with him, in addition to the navigation amulet itself. Another indication that he'd known in advance about the Triumphant's presence in that tenement house back in Tristopolis.

So much planning involved.

Just for Mel and Finbar?

They were his entire world, but that shouldn't matter to anybody else.

And the motivation of whoever took them didn't matter to Donal: the moment those people broke into the gym, they forfeited any rights they had to be treated as rational or sentient beings.

The saddle squeaked a little as he swung his bent left leg up and slid his right foot to the ground, and swivelled to dismount. Amulet in one hand, he pressed his other hand against the black scales of the fuel tank.

"Thank you."

Almost inaudibly, the Triumphant vibrated, somewhere between a purr and a low growl, the latter edged with a hatred targeted not at Donal, but at whoever had killed the motorbike's owner.

Donal nodded, and patted the fuel tank. "Give me a minute, and I'll see what else the amulet can tell me."

He rotated the amulet several different ways as he walked slowly across the black grass of the clearing, and the thing remained consistent: its fainter-than-ever beam, less than three inches long and continuing to fade, remained pointing down towards the ground.

It didn't shift as he walked, so it wasn't pointing to a well-defined spot. The entire clearing formed the locus it had been set to point to, which would have been alright if there'd been anything to see, but this was stupid.

A landing spot for a pteracopter?

Donal looked up at the featureless, dark purple sky. Since the only light came from the Triumphant's silver headlight beam, the world appeared dark; but back in the big city, light from windows and streetlamps invariably caused the sky to appear darker by contrast. All in all, this clearing felt like a perfectly ordinary location beneath an ordinary-looking sky.

But that couldn't be right, could it?

A pick-up for one man?

The would-be motorcycle thief, who'd laid a shaped hex charge to obliterate the trail of the vehicle convoy – including the captive Mel and Finbar – before dying in the tunnel without even getting the Triumphant started... Maybe he'd been issued with an amulet to lead him to a pickup point that was solely for him.

The enemy had proved utterly professional. They might go to extreme lengths simply to ensure that none of their number was ever left behind during an operation. And they probably thought of their work that way: as operations, not crimes that would disgust an ordinary citizen.

"Maybe he's missed the rendezvous."

In some parts of the military, failing to make a rendezvous constituted a form of suicide if the enemy were on your tail, because you didn't get a second chance, and for sure no extraction team would hang on past the deadline.

If that were the case here, then the trail dead-ended in this clearing and everything was lost.

No. That can't be right.

Donal turned around on the spot, staring into the trees that formed a perimeter for the clearing, seeing nothing but woodland, hearing nothing beyond insect life and a few rustling lizards, smelling nothing but ordinary mulch and mud and general forest scents.

This couldn't have been a pickup point for the larger group who'd gone ahead, because they'd have left tracks. So it was either a single-person rendezvous point, perhaps for a pteracopter that had never descended to ground because it didn't receive a signal in time... or something else was going on.

"I don't see it. I just don't see it."

The Triumphant's headlight flickered, as if to acknowledge his frustration.

If I were Mage Kelvin or Lamis, what would I do now?

It was an odd notion for someone incapable of shaping hex with his patterned thoughts, or whatever the Hades mages actually did.

Or a witch, like Ingrid?

He'd seen her dangle the call-amulet, the one supposed to summon Hellah in emergency, over a tangle of wires and twigs that she'd created on a small table in Donal and Mel's bedroom. It had looked like a bird's nest, and flickers of light had played over it as Ingrid took hold of the amulet by the sinew-cord looped through it, and held it close above the nest-tangle.

Like a pendulum, the amulet had swung back and forth, tracing out a nine-pointed star above the tangled twigs and wires. Ingrid had nodded and declared herself impressed at the amulet's power – that's what she'd been analysing, apparently – then she'd smiled and looked up at Donal. "You think I'm just swinging the amulet myself, don't you?"

"Maybe not consciously," Donal had told her. "But yeah, I'm kind of sure you are."

"Perhaps that's all this is," she'd said. "But you never really know, do you?" And then she'd winked.

Witches. Almost as bad as mages.

This navigation amulet wasn't strung from a cord, and Donal certainly didn't have any spare lengths of sinew to hand, but perhaps the material didn't matter. Pocketing the amulet for a moment, he undid his tie and slipped it out from his shirt collar, and opened the top button.

Like most ties, his comprised a kind of flattened tube, with the fabric folded back and sewn along the back of the tie. He took the amber amulet from his pocket, pressed it inside the tie at the big end, pushed it further in, and tied the very end of his tie in a large, ugly knot.

Mel bought me this tie.

He held the tie by the small end and let the enclosed amulet dangle.

"Come on," he said. "Show me something."

The original beam was gone now, almost invisible before he'd stuffed the amulet inside the tie, and for sure too weak to penetrate the fabric.

Nothing.

The damned thing just dangled there.

There has to be—

Something.

It was slight, a tiny raising of the makeshift pendulum, but the concealed amulet rose just a fraction of an inch, and remained there, which meant it couldn't be anything to do with movement on Donal's part, conscious or otherwise.

The whole thing was raised at a slight angle, and if he followed the line of the tie, it indicated a spot on the ground a mere nine feet away.

He walked carefully across the black grass and noted the angle of the tie was shifting, until he was at the indicated spot and the tie was pointed straight down. Slowly, he squatted down, and pressed the fingertips of his free hand against the soil, and found it: a small stone with a tiny depression on its surface.

Except the stone was part of something greater underneath, Donal felt suddenly certain. He undid the clumsy knot and shook the amulet out from the tie. He wrapped the tie around the knuckles of his left hand and formed a fist, and with his right hand he pressed the amulet down into the depression in the stone.

What am I hoping for?

He didn't know, but anything at all might count as progress.

"Please tell me this is leading somewhere."

The amulet began to pulse with amber light, strobing brightly. A good sign, or some kind of alarm?

He had warning, just a fraction of a second when translucent shapes appeared to coalesce at ground level, nine of them, an inch high amid the grass, but Donal didn't move and then it was too late as ghouls rose up from the ground.

Nine iceghouls, the kind that guarded City Hall and killed intruders and occasionally, according to rumour, snatched innocent passers-by beyond the perimeter walls of Möbius Park, where the ghouls were in theory not supposed to venture.

They rose in a ring formation, and that ring was centred on Donal.

No point in drawing the Magnus. Not even hex-piercing rounds could affect creatures like these.

In total synchrony, they drifted closer, converging on him.

This can't happen.

His flesh would dissolve as if dropped into a tank of hydrofluoric acid, and the ghouls would feed, driven by the eternal hunger that nothing and no one seemed ever to satisfy, because that was their nature and they couldn't help it.

As the ghouls closed on him, something scraped inside the ground, and off to the right, a two-yard-wide circle of grass rotated and began to rise, shedding soil, while further off the Triumphant growled and revved its engine, though its parking legs remained extruded.

Cold as ice, their touch. The ghouls were well-named, this breed known as iceghouls.

Grasping him, their ghostly pseudo-hands reaching *inside* his skin, while Donal forced himself to stand rigid and not attempt to fight or flee, knowing this was exactly the right thing to do without understanding why.

Something is different.

The ghouls stopped, all nine of them, suspended in place and billowing, just a little, though Donal felt no breeze. He did feel their grasping pseudo-hands holding him inside his own flesh, a sensation that should have disturbed him, and yet it didn't seem to matter.

The words of Federal Agent Bouchard, or rather the federal spellbinder's holomantic projection, came back to him now.

"The ghoul is inside you. Call it a role reversal. You've pretty much absorbed its body."

Donal had pressed on as if he'd never heard those words, just because he had to. But he hadn't actually forgotten.

A bloodghoul inside him, though he couldn't feel it. The notion was appalling and stupid and hard to believe, but he'd gained the ability to see the violet trace earlier, and now he was among creatures that should have killed him but hadn't.

"Something affecting your appetite?" he asked the iceghouls.

Empty hollows in their not-faces were trained on him. Whether they saw light or sensed reality in other ways, Donal couldn't tell. But they weren't acting the way ghouls were supposed to: that was certain.

From their point of view, he probably wasn't acting like a normal human either, but right now he didn't care about that.

Where the ground had risen, an open braided structure stood. A platform of mud and grass on a person-wide disk of stone formed a kind of roof, supported on helically twisted columns of what looked like fossilised bones, tortured into the desired shape.

White worms wriggled in the revealed soil, and something told Donal that they were the reason the concealed disk hadn't been obvious before: their role was to return the soil to a normal state that looked undisturbed, once the disk was lowered back into place.

It was an entrance that led downwards, and Donal guessed the iceghouls were supposed to carry intruders' remains down there as they fed.

But not today.

"You're in my way," he said.

He pushed forward and their grips slid away from him, apart from the one rearing iceghoul he was walking straight towards and *into* as if it scarcely mattered.

I can't show fear.

Like a thousand jellyfish sliding across his flesh, the iceghoul's body enveloped then slipped away from Donal as he strode right through its form and walked onwards towards the revealed underground entrance where he stopped and looked down inside.

A spiralling ramp of bone-turned-stone led downwards for what appeared to be two hundred feet, give or take. It was like some ghastly atrium, with a central hollow space drilling down – the spiralling ramp in its centre – and ringed with balconies that led to Thanatos-knew-what.

Donal had the sense of people down there, maybe dozens of them, and maybe other entities that were no more human than the iceghouls who'd failed to eat him.

Silvery headlight and a powerful growl.

Donal looked across at the Triumphant, and felt a kind of sad smile grow on his face, the kind of look that comrades exchange before entering a firefight when everything is at stake.

"You want to help some more?"

The bike growled back.

Nine iceghouls began to drift towards it, but the Triumphant wasn't their normal kind of prey, and Donal didn't feel worried at all. This was their moment, his and the motorbike's, and no Death-damned ghouls were going to get in their way.

Not now.

"Let's do it."

The parking legs snapped back into the bone chassis as the Triumphant leapt forward, straight through the pseudo-limb of a reaching ghoul and accelerating this way, towards Donal.

He crouched, ready, still with his tie wrapped around the knuckles of his left hand, the weight of the holstered Magnus beneath his left armpit, as ready for battle as he would ever be.

Slowing just a fraction, the Triumphant: enough for him to grab a handlebar and jump, twisting to land on the saddle, and pulling himself low and squeezing his legs inwards hard, relying on the strength of his muscles, holding on as the bike reached the edge of the opening while still speeding up.

Its nose and front wheel dipped down and Donal felt a moment of vertigo as if he were a redblood, and then they were onto the head of the fossilised bone ramp and beginning their hellride downwards.

Something shrieked loud enough to almost split his eardrums, but in a fraction of a second, Donal-and-Triumphant had descended past the thing, and when another one sounded below, and a third even deeper below that, he knew that these creatures acted as a kind of alarm at least, and even if they weren't going to move against him, there would be plenty of other humans and entities preparing to take a stand against intruders.

So let them.

The world spun around them, balconies and openings of corridors all around, as they spiralled headlong downwards, deeper and deeper below the ground, closer and closer to the heart of things.

"I'm coming," he said with gritted teeth.

A message to Mel, to Finbar, and to the one whose name he didn't know, not yet.

The enemy he had to kill.

THIRTY-SEVEN

Vanessa paused the instant she heard the banshee's wail split the air. Blue fire blazed inside the interrogation-come-surgery framework where her two unwilling donors, mother and baby alike, lay trapped, and the spillover effect had almost reached the critical threshold for shielding the entangled composites of brain matter, because you couldn't just scoop their blasted brains out.

Without proper shielding during the process, the neurons' quantal states would engage with the world at large and simply collapse to a myriad separate eigenspells and everything that was special about them would be lost.

The razorfluid licked at the struts of the framework, revealing its impatience, its need to cut things open with exquisite care.

Vanessa's street soldiers around her were already reaching for their weapons, while the lesser-trained servants had barely begun to gawp at the piercing sound, never mind react in anything like a practical, useful way.

Just one banshee. The ghouls will deal with it.

Except that they weren't supposed to let an intruder inside at all. She wondered who could get past them. Surely not Hellah or Klaudius?

But no... She'd have sensed if the crawlspace dimensions had quietened down. The denizens beneath Avenue of the Basilisks would remain rowdy enough to need both of Vanessa's Guardian cousins to pen them in.

Then the second banshee, stationed in the very centre of Inversion Tower, wailed as loudly as the first, and sounded even louder, because it was closer overhead.

And then the third, at the minus fifteenth level, just two storeys above this chamber, adding its ear-splitting concern, with the subtle pitch – comprehensible to Vanessa, though everyone else merely worried about their eardrums – that said the danger was approaching fast but not here yet.

Something or someone descending at speed, here in the place where she was supposed to feel most secure, defended from and invisible to the world at large. This wasn't *right*.

White Sunskril runes blazed on her golden metal fingernails as she gestured towards the framework, to lower the blue light to a lambent glow, to withdraw the razorfluid just a fraction, keeping the woman and baby in a pending state, because she couldn't allow the procedure to begin without being able to fully concentrate: the manipulation of quantally entangled matter was *hard*, as even the most skilled of mages could testify.

How dare anyone disturb her *now*, at a moment like this?

She snapped her fingers, and white light ran in streamers up the walls, a phenomenon that would repeat everywhere within the underground complex, all seventeen floors of Inversion Tower.

It was the signal to respond to threat with lethal force.

"In my own home."

This could *not* be allowed.

"Three of you stay here," she told her soldiers. "The rest of you get to the central shaft. I will follow in a moment."

"Yes, ma'am."

Her soldiers jogged out, their weapons held at port-arms, heading for the supposed danger because was what they trained for, longed for, and got paid for.

More than cannon fodder, but ultimately dispensable all the same.

A kind of whimper came from the still-bound captive, the mother. Her eyes glared, visible even with the pervasive blue glow within the framework.

"Soon," Vanessa promised her. "Very soon."

Weapons fire cracked from the far end of the corridor outside the chamber, the bottom of the central atrium. Shooting straight upwards? Surely that risked bullets and fragments of anything they hit falling straight down on the shooters.

All three banshees wailed their warning cry once more.

Enough of this.

She drew her power inside her, and her rune-inscribed golden metal fingernails glowed brighter and brighter until her arms seemed to end in spheres of blazing white light, which meant she was ready for anything.

Time to deal with these intruders herself.

THIRTY-EIGHT

A hellride like none other.

Donal's eyes vibrated with the spiralling motion as the Triumphant roared downwards, following the bone ramp into the depths, while all around the sides of the atrium people began to react, and for a moment it seemed that diving at a speed like this was all it took to get past them.

Then weapons blazed from far below and the bike reacted, tightening the spiral, travelling closer to the inner edge even as tracer rounds flew up around the outer edge of the spiral, in the gap between the helical ramp and the circular atrium's balconies.

I saw blue.

It had been just a hint, a momentary glimpse as he pulled his head out of the line of fire and the Triumphant tightened the turns, and it had been as if someone had opened a door on one of the very lowest levels and allowed blue light to spill out, just a little, into the central shaft.

A shade of sapphire blue that he'd seen before: when mages did their quantal bilocation travelling-by-portal thing... and when Mel and Finbar's eyes were joined by gentle curves of softly glowing light.

"They're down there," he told the bike. "My wife and baby. On the bottom floor, or maybe the one above."

You wouldn't have thought the Triumphant could growl any louder, but it did, hammering a path downwards along the twisting ramp, and for a moment Donal believed they were going to get all the way to the bottom in one go, without anyone managing to stop them.

Call it hubris.

If he'd had time to think it through, he might have wondered why the bone ramp seemed to descend from the surface overhead all the way to the very bottom of the atrium without interruption. As it was, it took a while for his brain to process what he saw next: sections of the ramp below snapping away from the spiral to form horizontal bridges, each radiating from the atrium centre to a different floor of the underground complex.

Where the radial bridges had snapped into place, they left gaps in the original helix shape, which meant the Triumphant could no longer follow a single clear path all the way down.

Nothing so easy.

They hit the first bridge either nine or ten levels below the surface – even Donal had lost count – and the Triumphant did the only thing it could, braking hard because of the sudden shift in angle, then taking the bridge and roaring onto the circular balcony, heading for a corridor but braking again as Donal twisted the handlebars because he could see soldiers taking up position further down the corridor and the whole thing formed a dead-end trap.

Screeching, they turned back onto the ring balcony and sped along it, heading for another radial corridor because there was nothing else they could do. Was there another route downwards besides the atrium?

If I were an architect, I'd include some fire stairs.

For full safety, you'd want a staircase at the far end of every radial corridor. Donal twisted the throttle grip, encouraging rather than controlling the bike, and it leapt along this new corridor, hurtling at a speed that could never be considered safe, not indoors.

An armed man – no, a woman with orange spikey features – stepped out of a doorway near the far end, and brought an automatic rifle swinging up to bear, but Donal had already whipped out the Magnus and fired right-handed as he rode, a fast triple tap because of the vibration and acceleration, not expecting every shot to hit, but they did.

The dead woman dropped and then they were past her.

Past seven more doorways – how big was this place, really? – with the rooms either empty inside or with people just starting to react, and then they reached the end of the corridor where just as Donal had hoped, a fire door stood ready to be opened by pressing against a horizontal bar just below waist height.

The Triumphant hit the thing at speed.

They blasted their way onto an abbreviated landing and with scarcely a change in pace began to follow a clockwise descent along the squared-off spiral of painted grey steps leading down.

Or up, if you were escaping a fire, but Donal and the Triumphant weren't trying to get away from danger.

They were bringing it.

Three storeys they managed, bumping and jolting and bouncing their way down, before they hit the first opposition in the stairwell. A group of soldiers had spilled onto the landing from the corridor – over their heads, an inscribed sign read -*XIII*, which had to indicate the minus thirteenth floor – but not fast enough to set themselves in place and open fire.

The Triumphant blasted straight into them.

Donal fired three shots into three faces and scarcely processed the awful bloody explosions as he raked hard with the Magnus's barrel along another face, punched with his wrapped left fist and struck lucky, a carotid artery at the side of a street soldier's neck, and then he was off the bike and into close-quarter fighting, elbows and hammer fists added to punches, dirty boxing at its nastiest, taking a blow to the side of the head from a swung rifle but the pain felt like nothing much, some distant kind of feedback, as he hammered his assailant to the ground.

The Triumphant was ramming into people again and again, and there were squeals and shouts and awful crunching sounds as the bike ran over the fallen, and then Donal was in the corridor and the Triumphant bumped over the last of the downed street soldiers to join him.

"Well done."

Donal swung his leg over the saddle and they were on the move again, hurtling along the corridor back towards the atrium, closer to their target than before, but still with three or four more levels to descend through.

They'd been lucky, hitting the last group of soldiers at close quarters before they could bring their weapons to bear – the things became a hindrance up close, especially if the weapon's wielder had grown psychologically dependent on it – but from a greater range neither Donal nor the Triumphant would stand a chance, not against a trained squad with time and distance on their side.

Someone started to emerge from a doorway and stumbled back as Donal and the Triumphant roared past. Donal reholstered the Magnus so he could grip the handlebars with both hands because they were now travelling very fast indeed, and in a second they were going to have to decelerate hard.

At the ring balcony they turned left, going clockwise, then skidded into the next radial corridor just as a fusillade opened up from below, but too late for the opposition as the Triumphant straightened up and accelerated strongly once more.

Donal felt his lips pull back from his teeth, but there was no joy in this, not even blood lust. This was far too serious.

A shot. Missed.

Another percussive bang and bits of plaster and chips of stone flew as a heavy round blew away a section of wall and if the person aiming the gun tried again they were bound to hit Donal directly in the spine and that would be that, the end forever, failure that could never be redeemed, but the fire door was close and the Triumphant was reaching incredible speeds and then they hit and the door flew open as if it didn't exist and another heavy round smashed into the stairwell wall but they were headed down already and out of the line of fire.

Two more floors, and perhaps with only one more to go, but on the next landing down – the penultimate floor, the minus sixteenth, with only one more floor below it – more street soldiers were spilling into place and this time they'd have several seconds in which to sight their weapons before Donal and the bike could get to them, and that was more than long enough for professionals like these.

"Some ignorant people think this word means the greatest ever." An image of Sister Mary-Anne Styx writing *Penultimate* in cursive script on the purpleboard with screeching chalk, a random memory from the orphanage days thrown up in the stress of the moment.

"In fact, it's the item before the final item, and the difference between the two alleged meanings is nine lashes of the chain-whip if you get it wrong in the exam, so I expect you all to get it right, do you hear?"

Good training for facing adversity, up to and including lethal force when outnumbered by the opposition.

The minus fifteenth floor and they were into another radial corridor heading straight for the central atrium yet again, and it wouldn't be long before the opposition sussed out the options and blocked every access to every ring balcony along with every stairwell and that would put a stop to everything.

So we need to do something different.

It seemed to Donal that he would be the primary target if the street soldiers had to choose between him and the Triumphant thundering beneath him, so he made a choice of his own, crouching low against the fuel tank and shouting to the bike: "Go straight ahead and then stop dead, just for a second, then you get clear and hide."

The motorbike snarled, reluctant but understanding, and two people reached out from a doorway but bounced off and the corridor walls flew past and then the bike's tyres howled and blue smoke rose up, the stench hard and pungent as the brakes locked on, and Donal was already vaulting upwards to place both feet on the saddle while still hanging onto the handlebars then the bike screeched to a stop and the rear wheel came up off the ground and flung him forwards like a slingshot.

He thought the bike might have turned and tipped itself sideways after that, to prop itself diagonally against a wall and try to appear harmless and abandoned, but then he could no longer think about the Triumphant because he was falling forward and down through empty space and a curved surface of bone lay beneath him and he struck, very hard.

Roll.

The command-to-self was automatic and the action was trained reflex as he hit the section of spiralling ramp and shoulder-rolled once, twice, the world travelling vertically across his vision, and then he was rolling sideways instead, down along the ramp, four complete rotations, five, and then he came to a stop with his chest against the surface like the bottom portion of a press-up so he forced himself up to standing – not a press-up, call it a burpee – and he swivelled on the tilted surface and whipped out the Magnus from the shoulder holster thinking he probably had three rounds remaining in the magazine but the number didn't matter because no amount of ammunition could stop what stood in front of him.

She had positioned herself at the far end of a radial bridge, one of those ramp sections that had snapped out to horizontal flatness to join with a balcony, and she was bathed in a column of white incandescent light that appeared to emanate from twin novas, one at each hand, and it was hard to see the woman inside the blaze but one thing was certain.

Utterly magnificent, this woman of power who surely ruled and commanded here.

My enemy.

She raised her hands and death was imminent and there was only one thing he could do and so he did.

Threw himself sideways, into space.

White lightning, sheets of it, brightening overhead. A crack as stonework and sculpted bone exploded.

What the Hades?

Falling now.

THIRTY-NINE

Shadows, in extended gloom.

Vast, the expanse of frozen shapes: statues and other sculptures and jumbled shapes Donal didn't know how to categorise. Mustiness and strange organic scents mingled on the still air. It was a place of great quiet, in shocking contrast to the chaos he'd escaped from.

His shoulder still hurt from the impact of landing. Plus his ankle, just a little.

He'd dropped hard and struck the bottom of the atrium feet first but asymmetrically, and converted the motion to a shoulder roll as he'd been trained, taking the forward diagonal to match the way he'd been off-balanced, but the impact had been awkward and it was only with luck that he'd been able to tuck his chin in far enough to avoid striking his head upon the hard, cold flagstones.

The shoulder roll and its follow up shed most of the kinetic energy before fetching him up at the base of a marble bas relief, a huge fragment that looked as if someone had chiselled it away from a Surinese temple and dropped it down here for no one to ever see again.

Some of the figures looked like plastinated corpses – he'd heard of such things as exhibits and illegal collectors' items, but never seen them – but as he crept past a flensed female figure, though her torso and limbs remained still, her pleading eyes turned to follow his progress, and all he could do was give a nod of acknowledgment and turn away before his own eyes had a chance to reveal the horror that rose up inside his guts.

This must be the lowest floor, a shadowed basement for storage of artworks and all sorts, and for a second his mind juxtaposed an image of the cellar chambers beneath the tower in Dredgeway Avenue, but this place was huge in comparison and he'd better keep his attention fastened on the here and now or he and Mel and Finbar would be done for.

He had to believe they were alive, his most precious family.

Supporting pillars maybe thirteen feet in diameter stood like tree trunks all around, giving the whole place the air of a junkyard in a desolate forest, and it seemed likely that this extended chamber spanned the entire lowest floor of the complex.

With entrances to fire stairs at the circumference? That also seemed likely.

When he looked back towards the central portion, the section that lay below the atrium shaft, only a gloomy light pierced the membranous sheet he'd dropped through. His passage had torn it open as he fell through – he was almost certain of it – but no rip showed, not now.

Self-healing, maybe.

He wondered what the woman, his enemy, was planning to do next.

Doesn't matter.

Because he was already on the move, heading towards a spot on the circular wall where he thought he might find a fire exit, although the darkness and the myriad shadows of large stored objects prevented him from seeing anything useful.

No sounds. Why hadn't soldiers poured into this place yet?

She knows there's no hurry once the stairwells are blocked.

So he had to move fast, before they trapped him down here and the only unknown would be how long he could survive before they took him.

The wall was blank where he reached it, but some thirty feet away a darker rectangle marked its surface, and that had to be a doorway to one of the sets of fire stairs, though no sign marked it. Perhaps the exit signs only came to life and glowed when authorised people came down here.

His ankle still hurt, just a little.

Irrelevant.

He reached the fire exit door and crouched down, drawing his Magnus once more, and pressing his left palm against the bone door itself, trying to sense vibration or heat or anything at all that might indicate a waiting ambush on the other side.

Nothing.

The longer I wait, the more likely an ambush becomes.

The reasoning felt inescapable. He reached for the horizontal bar and, one-handed, pressed it slowly, minimising the click that sounded as the lock disengaged and the door cracked open, away from him.

Light shone from the stairwell, but he couldn't hear any street soldiers at all, which meant with luck they'd gathered around the atrium balconies, but if that were true then it wouldn't last long so he had to make his move right now.

Creaking from the hinges but there was nothing he could do about that so he went through onto the lowest level of the stairwell and allowed the door to softly shut on its springs, controlling it until it closed almost silently and then he was ready to start his ascent.

Only one floor and then, unless the Norns were feeling exceptionally cruel today, he should be close to Mel and Finbar, because that was where the sapphire light had originated from, when he glimpsed it from the top of the atrium shaft.

This stairwell was five-sided, pentagonal if you looked straight up.

Donal went up fast but kept the motion smooth, hugging the wall, four seventy-two-degree turns and then he could see the last few steps to the landing marked -*XVI* where no one at all stood waiting.

Come on.

Seven steps, that was all.

She might be waiting on the other side.

Meaning his enemy, most beautiful and clearly wielding power of some frightening kind and strength.

But that didn't matter: he couldn't allow it to.

He went up very fast, accelerating.

Things were coming to a head.

FORTY

Mel gave up on the physical struggling, because the metal bands were digging into her neck and wrists and ankles and nothing was giving way: the Death-damned things felt way too strong.

But the warm wet blood, her blood where the metal had cut, let her turn her head just enough to see where Finbar lay, cradled on a kind of metal shelf, and he was looking at her wide-eyed and quiet once more.

Soft blue light all around, and that hungry-looking fluid rippling up and down and back and forth along the framework that surrounded them.

Finbar.

There was no breaking free from this, but she needed to remain alert, ready to move the instant it became a possibility.

I think your Daddy's here.

Willing her baby to understand the message that she couldn't even frame in spoken words, and not just due to the tightness of the band around her throat, because she didn't want the Frisch woman to hear anything at all, to pick up any clue as to who she faced.

Not that Mel could see the Frisch woman now, because the woman had rushed out of the chamber with her hands glowing white.

The cracks of gunfire from outside and the sounds of running footsteps told some kind of story, but for the moment all Mel could do was focus and stay ready.

Finbar's eyes twinkled and began to shine as if reflecting the sapphire-blue light, although Mel herself knew better: there was more than the obvious going on.

My boy.

Mother and baby stared at each other, forging a bond of strength, and they might not have the power to break free but they could fight the insidious mind-sapping effects of the framework that held them in place and threatened them.

The strange fluid retreated further, and this time it wasn't the Frisch woman's command but Mel and Finbar's strength that compelled the stuff to move. You could call it a kind of aura, the phenomenon that bound mother and son together.

Mel felt the smile growing on her face.

Yes, that's right.

And watched a baby grin grow on Finbar's dear, sweet features.

We just need to hang on.

Not much longer now.

FORTY-ONE

Donal burst through the fire door and into a corridor that was darker than any he'd seen on higher floors. To his right stood an opening from which blue-tinged light was shining, and he knew that was where he had to go.

Murals depicting scenes of sacrifice and torture, watched over by a disembodied eye, covered the corridor walls. Shades of red, maroon and brown predominated: all the hues of blood in different states, along with bone-grey figures suffering dismemberment and worse.

Irrelevant.

As he hugged the righthand wall, further along on the opposite side he could see a fastened cell door, and he caught a glimpse of a tri-horned head on the other side of the barred observation opening, and something about that non-human face stopped Donal dead.

The captive looked like an entity from the crawlspace dimensions, one whose mass had rotated into the mesoscopic dimensions that humans have evolved to experience, and Donal might know nothing about such creatures' taxonomy, or even whether they came in distinct species, but something about this one's eyes had caused him to pause in the midst of mortal urgency.

Emerald green fire formed a nine-sided polygon in each of the captive's eyes: nonagonal rather than heptagonal, and green rather than orange, but all the same, the resemblance looked overwhelming and quite unmistakable.

Can you appear human?

Something told Donal the answer was no, but it didn't banish the other feeling, the one of familiarity and even friendship, because whatever this captive creature was, it had something in common with Hellah the Guardian, who inspired total trust in Donal at the same time as igniting instant fear in everybody else she met.

He, not it.

Meaning the captive, and this was pure intuition. Donal had no idea where the notion sprang from, but he trusted his understanding.

At the far end of the corridor, white light was raging, but the nameless woman herself was out of sight, which meant Donal had at least a few moments in which to move, unless his luck ran out.

Horizontal bars blocked the creature's cell door, and great dodecahedral locks pinned them in place, which meant Donal needed to find the keys in order to free the captive.

I've got to get Mel and Finbar.

Maybe he was fooling himself, but he thought he saw a look of understanding in those green fire-irised eyes as he headed for the opening to the chamber on the right and then he was stumbling inside and everything else was forgotten.

"Mel!"

"I knew… it was… you."

Steel band or something around her throat, and there was Finbar too, on a kind of metal cradle while Mel was fastened to some kind of frame, all within a larger framework in which a familiar shade of blue light was shining but none of that mattered as Donal sprinted across the chamber, reholstering the Magnus and going straight for the fastenings that held Mel in place.

Just simple pins and rings locked them, although the metal bands themselves morphed and tried to wrap themselves around Donal's hands when he ripped the pins free and threw them aside to clatter on the flagstones.

He tugged a struggling band away and flung it across the chamber, hitting the wall.

A nasty semi-fluid substance began to flow along the framework struts towards him and he knew he had to do this very fast indeed.

He pulled the pins out from the remaining bands and hauled Mel clear of the frame and spun back to snatch Finbar from the metal cradle but not in time to avoid the semi-fluid that slashed at Donal's arms and sliced through his sleeves and drops of black blood sprayed out but not enough to matter.

Donal whirled away from the framework and pushed Finbar into Mel's arms and said: "You're okay."

The semi-fluid rose and fell in frustration but something bound it to the framework: it couldn't just leave it and chase down its chosen prey.

"Of course we are."

Mel was staggering a little because of the blood flow that had been constricted and maybe other injuries but not enough to stop them getting out of here.

"Donal…"

Two street soldiers peeled around the doorway's edge but Donal was already moving towards them because there was no time to draw the Magnus and then he was into it.

The first one had a stubby machine gun and it would have made an awful racket if he'd managed to pull the trigger but Donal denied him that chance, jamming his own thumb in the back of the trigger guard as part of grabbing the weapon, a hook punch with his free hand to the side of the throat, and then he had both hands available to wrench the weapon around like a ship's wheel, smacking the butt into the side of its owner's jawbone en route, and the first one was out of it.

The second carried no weapon but she came in very fast with a throat punch designed to kill so Donal blocked using the machine gun and lunged backwards as he brought the thing to bear and squeezed the trigger without needing to aim precisely as it chattered through the air, an uncountable number of round bursting the woman's torso apart and she was down as well with a liquid thump and another sound that took a moment to process.

Odd-shaped metal objects were hooked on her belt and had clanked as she hit the floor, and it took Donal another moment to recognise them for what they were, which was a set of intricate keys for unusual locks, and the problem was that time was collapsing because the machine gun fire had been very loud indeed and unless the real enemy was deaf, she would be here in seconds, and against her he was sure that bullets wouldn't be enough.

He yanked the keys clear of the dead woman's belt, said a rapid-fire prayer to the Thanatos he didn't literally believe in, took three steps towards the doorway and flung the keys across the corridor, aiming for the barred observation opening in the cell door on the opposite wall but not knowing if he'd managed it because white fire burst along the corridor and all he could do was stumble back into the chamber from which he'd tried to rescue Mel and Finbar.

But there was no other exit and that brought all the other possibilities crashing down to nothing because they couldn't get out and no power on Earth was going to stop this person, this enemy, from entering the chamber and then they were done for, him and Mel and Finbar alike, and all he could do was say: "I'm sorry."

"I love you," said Mel.

It was wonderful and it was awful, because of the fatalism that lay beneath the words, the realisation that they weren't getting out of this alive and the future that had beckoned them onwards as a family wasn't going to happen after all.

A white nova blaze erupted at the doorway.

"Vanessa Frisch." Mel named the enemy, and that was something.

Donal raised the machine gun and squeezed the trigger and the percussive blast was a deafening sequence in the echoing chamber and he kept the Death-damned thing pulled back until a final click sounded and the magazine was empty so he dropped the weapon to the floor and let it lie there.

Totally unharmed, the beautiful woman with twin white flares enveloping her hands, and something dark moving in the depths of her eyes, a hint of black pentagonal shadows inside them, and all he could think was: *No.*

In the captive's eyes, polygonal irises of fire had brought instant and pleased recognition, and what he saw here hinted at something familiar yet brought instant revulsion: not so much the same as Hellah but in some sense the very opposite.

He pulled out the Magnus slowly, and tightened his left fist – the tie that Mel had given him still wrapped around his knuckles, wet now and stained with blood that wasn't his – and got ready to go down fighting.

That was all he had left.

Street soldiers filed in to take up position behind Vanessa Frisch. Five – no, seven of them – all with firearms and the will to use them, forming a line behind her to block the doorway, as if there could be any chance in Hades of getting past her, this Vanessa Frisch whose power seemed to be something like Hellah's and something like that of a mage or a witch and all of it beyond Donal's ability to truly understand.

But understanding wasn't the issue here.

"I'll tell you a secret." Vanessa Frisch's voice was soft and seductive, likewise her smile, while the look in her eyes was redolent of nothing but evil and deep malevolence. "There is a way for you to thwart my plans."

At any other time, Donal would have made a wisecrack about her choice of words – *thwart your plans?* – but not when he and his family were seconds from death.

"All you need to do," continued Vanessa Frisch, "is to bash your baby's brains out on the floor. Or against the wall. Either one would do."

The hiss that came from between Mel's teeth was like no other sound that Donal had ever heard, and all he could do was agree with her.

"But just in case," added Vanessa Frisch, "I think I'll destroy your legs before you can try some stupid move."

She raised her right hand and the white blaze surrounding it began to intensify and that was the moment Donal needed as he lunged forward to close the gap at speed and smacked his left forearm against her right arm like disrupting a weapon's aim but this wasn't a simple situation.

He dropped his Magnus and grabbed both of her wrists, one clamped in each hand, holding them apart, and he tightened his grip and prepared for the worst.

"You can't even stop me physically, you worm." Her voice held the ultimate in scorn.

And then she raised both arms in what should have been a posture of mechanical disadvantage, but with an easy strength that took Donal up onto tiptoes and then, incredibly, right off the floor.

He was hanging from her upraised wrists and she was growing taller than before, and her strength was far beyond anything he'd imagined.

"I'm not here to kill you," he said.

"Of course you're not. So pathetic."

"But I have brought you death."

"What are—"

It hurt, which he hadn't expected.

There was no pain going the other way.

But then, he knew nothing of the actual mechanisms involved. All he knew was that something was tearing at his inner flesh, his organs and bones and everything else feeling as if they were being ripped apart and maybe they were but by Thanatos if that were the literal truth right now then it didn't matter because this woman had tried to kill Mel and Finbar and for that she deserved to die in agony, and if he had to perish with her to bring that death about, then so be it.

Hurts...

Inch by agonising inch, the bloodghoul pulled itself free of Donal, struggled out of his torso, his head, out through his eyeballs and everywhere else, and Vanessa Frisch's eyes were widening in fear as the ghoul reached her and Donal finally understood what had driven the entity to take up its place inside him.

"Bloodghouls have families too," he said. "And you've been killing this one's relatives."

She clenched her teeth, this Vanessa Frisch, and white incandescence flared to left and right. "And this one will join them. Now."

Her form started to expand once more and three protuberances appeared on her forehead at the same moment as a great taloned hand reached through the door and swiped the street soldiers aside.

"No," said Donal. "Not going to happen."

The tri-horned captive, free of his cell, grabbed Vanessa Frisch's shoulders from behind and she seemed to shrink back to her previous normal human form, the gown draped awkwardly now, and Donal didn't know whether the freed captive had stopped Vanessa Frisch from changing to a form like his or from rotating her body mass out of the mesoscopic dimensions entirely, as a way to escape and regroup and bring another attack to bear on Donal and the bloodghoul.

But she wasn't going to get that chance.

A liquid slurp, as the bloodghoul began to feed, but suddenly Vanessa Frisch's arteries were glowing white in some kind of final defence and the ghoul pulled away but Donal snapped his head forward to break Vanessa Frisch's nose and that was all the opportunity Mel needed.

She came from Donal's right and the hardest straight punch he'd ever seen drove into the side of Vanessa Frisch's neck with a meaty *thunk* and Frisch went down and the chances of her recovering consciousness in less than ten minutes were zero, and the bloodghoul needed only seconds to do what it had come here to do.

Like acid, an entire bath of it, as Donal had thought.

Bubbling and an acrid stench as the bloodghoul seeped into the flesh, and it fed, Donal somehow knew, with no sense of pleasure in the sense of gourmet or even gourmand taste, just the hard joy of vengeance served at last, seasoned with a hint of regret that the woman's death couldn't have been lingering and agonising while she stayed conscious and aware of the entire process, but she was far too dangerous for that.

Donal watched Vanessa Frisch die while Mel retrieved Finbar from the spot on the floor where she'd placed him, standing well back because this was a bloodghoul after all, and the tri-horned entity that scarcely fit through the doorway was shaking its wings as if to start some kind of action, though so far it – he – had acted like an ally, not a threat.

When the bloodghoul had finished, it rose up, wraith-like, from the remains and drifted a few inches above the ground as it rotated and hung there, facing Donal for what seemed like a year or a century or an aeon even as the automatic part of Donal's mind counted only nineteen seconds elapsed before the ghoul made a move.

It raised a pseudo-limb towards Donal's face, like a lover touching their beloved's cheek, then bowed its head and sank slowly but inexorably into the floor, and in just three seconds more was entirely gone.

"Oh, bleeding Thanatos," said Mel, swearing like a Tristopolitan born and bred, while hugging Finbar to her. "That wasn't creepy at all."

"Um," said Donal.

He looked up at the tri-horned creature, and the green fire burning in those nine-sided irises looked familiar enough to bring a smile to his face, and the creature's mouth widened in what might have been a genuine attempt to mirror the expression, causing Mel to take a step back, and turn a little to shield Finbar from what might happen next.

Then she stopped, looked at the creature, and said: "Thank you."

"Yeah," said Donal. "Thanks."

The creature bowed its head, turned in on itself, and rotated through impossible angles, becoming smaller and smaller, twisting out of the mesoscopic dimensions in a way that looked anything but wraith-like. Donal wondered whether Hellah and Klaudius could do the same kind of thing.

But the tri-horned creature had seemed incapable of human speech. Perhaps the similarities weren't that great, not really.

"We knew you'd come," said Mel. "We both did."

Donal could say no words as he hugged them.

Two of the street soldiers remained alive. Donal brought them back to consciousness, but not gently, and made them look at the acrid, rank remains that lay on the floor, and said: "That's what's left of Vanessa Frisch."

They slumped, psychologically as well as physically, the defeat clear in their eyes. One of them, a scar-faced woman, said, "We won't get paid now, any of us, but you're still in danger. Especially if the others don't know Mrs Frisch is dead."

"You're trying to make a deal," said Donal.

"There's a tannoy system," said the woman's comrade in a thick Larossian accent. His eyes were of stone: sniper implants. "Loudspeakers everywhere, just in case. Let me make an announcement and the others will retreat to the surface."

"And you want me to let you go in return."

"Just give us a chance. Every guard station has a phone to the outside as well as a tannoy mike."

Mel said just one word. "Donal…"

It spoke volumes, and made his priorities and responsibilities clearer than ever. They had to keep Finbar safe, and that mattered more than anything.

Donal had reholstered the Magnus but gained a fully loaded Viper pistol from a dead man's hand, along with three spare magazines ejected from his comrade's weapons. The magazines distorted and weighed down the pockets of Donal's jacket, while the Viper felt pretty good in his hand: he'd fired such things on the range at Avenue of the Basilisks, though it had been a while.

He pointed the Viper at the Larossian. "Lead the way and I'll let you go now, but no guarantees for later."

"Yeah. Understood."

Donal looked at the scarred woman, and she nodded.

If they were telling the truth then he was going to be able to call Despatch or the ordinary emergency number, and given the number of cops that had already been deployed on the streets of Tristopolis, there would be people heading this way in force soon enough.

Except that he didn't know exactly where this was. All he could do was describe the route through the tunnels and the ruined depot on the surface, and the direction he'd followed from there to here.

He could question these two further, but that might end their cooperation. Better to leave the location as another problem to solve afterwards.

"Come on, then. Stand up."

Donal backed off while the two street soldiers – more than that: genuine mercenaries – helped each other upright. Either or both might retain a concealed dagger or even a derringer, because he'd not been able to frisk them properly, but it wouldn't matter so long as he kept the Viper trained on them and retained awareness of distance and geometry on the move.

"Lead the way," he added.

"Okay."

"And after you've told your comrades that the boss is dead and it's time to scarper…"

They stared at him.

"…get out and don't look back."

Both of them nodded.

I won't break my word.

In extreme circumstances, when every sense is strained and the slightest error means the end of everything, it is said that no human being can lie to another, because of the deep unconscious signals both sent and received. Donal hoped they understood him clearly.

But I will kill you, if you break yours.

Their mouths moved, a serious expression but akin to the beginnings of a smile, as if to acknowledge those unspoken thoughts.

And together, moving slowly, they led the way out of the interrogation chamber – a place for interrogation and worse – and along the corridor to the guard station near the end.

Donal and Mel, with Finbar in her arms, followed carefully. Letting their guards down now, when the greatest individual danger had passed, could still prove fatal. It took only a single street soldier motivated by revenge for a fallen friend or simple annoyance at losing their payday to let off a well-aimed shot and the day could still end in terminal disaster.

They reached the door to the guard station, and went inside.

FORTY-TWO

Bellis had hitched a ride on one of the federal pteractopters, and Donal felt glad to see him.

They stood near the edge of the five-sided clearing and watched as armoured SWAT teams swarmed down into the underground complex they were calling Inversion Tower, which apparently was the name its occupants had known it by.

And one Hades of a gesture of trust on Mel's part: Bellis was holding Finbar in his arms and rocking him gently and making coochy-coo sounds even though Mel had only just met him, minutes earlier.

"There's a motorbike down there," Donal had told the SWAT commander. "A Triumphant. It helped me. More than once."

On the way up through the various levels of Inversion Tower – there were seventeen subterranean storeys in all – a crazed servant of some kind, not a street soldier as such, had rushed at Donal and Mel from behind, but a growling engine had sounded at the same moment, and the black-scaled motorbike had driven straight into the attacker's lower body and knocked him over the parapet to fall into the atrium shaft, and that was that.

Regular cops mostly thought of Sorcerous Weapons Assault Teams as comprising gung-ho veterans with no understanding of subtleties or ordinary civilised values, but the commander had listened to Donal's explanation, asked some clarifying questions in a calm voice, and observed him with intelligent grey eyes.

"We'll get the bike out of there unharmed," she promised.

The spiralling ramp had been damaged by gunfire and Donal and Mel had used the fire stairs all the way to the top floor. Fully fuelled, the Triumphant probably could have made it up the steps with them, but it had growled to Donal in a way he somehow understood as an invitation to look at its fuel gauge, which he had, then nodded and patted the bike's fuel tank and promised to see it soon.

"Who's a smart clever boy?"

Finbar gurgled up at Bellis.

"You're a natural," said Donal.

"He's telling me stories." Bellis's eyes twinkled. "Quite the adventure, too."

He handed Finbar back to Mel.

"Come and visit any time, Lieutenant," she said.

"If I do, my wife'll get broody." Bellis tilted his head. "Not that that's a problem."

Then he looked at Donal. "You want to tell me more about the job you were doing for the Commissioner? He's going to authorise full disclosure."

If it had anything to do with Vanessa Frisch and the events inside Inversion Tower, then full disclosure made sense. Especially since Sandarov's motivation hadn't been secrecy, just an unwillingness to use Department resources to investigate underhand political moves against him.

"You talked to him?" said Donal.

Mel had turned away from them and moved towards the blackiron trees, because it was past time to feed Finbar and they didn't need an audience.

"I talked to Commander Bowman just before the 'copter landed." Bellis glanced at the pteractopters in the next clearing over, beyond the trees. "The Commissioner was still groggy but looked to be making a full recovery."

"Say what? Recovery?"

"Oh, right," said Bellis. "You wouldn't know. He fell into Basilisk Trance, but the trance broke when Vanessa Frisch died, which apparently is a cast-iron guarantee that she was the one who induced it in the first place."

"Huh."

"Forget the *apparently*. Another thing you wouldn't know, Donal, is that I spent seven years at Mordantelle. I know for sure that's how Basilisk Trance works, at least the kind that was used on the Commissioner."

"You were a junior mage? A novice? Neophyte?"

"Novitiate. Same thing."

"Remind me to introduce you to Mage Lamis sometime. You'll either be great friends or hate each other on sight."

"I'll take you up on that. Lamis has an interesting reputation."

For a while Donal and Bellis watched the continuing SWAT operation, as servants were led up from the Inversion Tower complex in handcuffs, and led off through the trees to a waiting area: armoured prison vans were en route from the city.

"Oh," said Bellis after a while. "Before Federal Agent Bouchard arrives and takes over... I'll need a proper statement about that dead banker. Arrhennius Hawke?"

"Yeah. He was a crook, worked for Bloodfist Bank, but whoever killed him took out the housekeeper too."

Bellis shook his head. "Don't weep for her. I talked to a Sergeant Levison on the radio as well. He's taken the case, already searched the house with a diviner in tow."

"I know Lev," said Donal. "Good man. A friend."

"Well, turns out there's a basement where some bad things have happened, I mean really evil, and the housekeeper helped and actually took part. So she wasn't an innocent victim."

"Alright."

As for non-innocents, the scattered mercenaries were subject to a widening hunt with more federal pteracopters on the way, but they were professionals, those mercs, so a certain percentage was pretty much guaranteed to escape. Donal wasn't entirely sure how he felt about that.

Some shouts sounded from the lip of the opening to Inversion Tower, and for a moment it seemed a fight had broken out, but then two SWAT guys appeared, lugging a heavy black motorcycle into view.

From Donal's left, two more officers came into view, carrying jerrycans full of fuel, heading towards the Triumphant.

Which gave a blink of its silver headlight. Donal waved back.

"Guess you've got a connection there," said Bellis.

"Looks that way."

He'd already explained about the dead owner and the subterranean route that got him here. That had caused Bellis to make another trip back to the pteracopter and get on the radio once more.

"I couldn't get an SOC diviner to go there straight away," Bellis had reported on his return, "because they're still recovering from whatever was going on in crawlspace earlier. But you'll probably find the dead merc and the houseowner knew each other way back. Or maybe one of the other mercs knew about the cellar and the tunnel entrance and the bikes."

"Yeah." Donal felt glad that Bellis and others had the responsibility for writing all the reports and filling in the details. "Bound to be something like that."

Mel was heading back this way with Finbar in her arms.

"You need to get home," said Bellis. "All three of you."

There were still things to discover here, but Donal made the decision: they weren't his responsibility. Mel and Finbar were.

"I don't think we'll all fit on the Triumphant."

The SWAT guys had finished refuelling the bike, and its engine was rumbling back to life.

"And I don't think there's anywhere for a pteracopter to land near Hel Ave," said Bellis, meaning near the gym that Donal and Mel called home. "But I'll send you back in one of the vans, and let the prisoners wait a while longer."

"Appreciated."

"And I think you'd better take the motorbike, because it's going to need a new home."

Donal looked at Mel. "We'll take it in for now, but long term… I don't know, until we discuss it."

Bellis clapped Donal on the shoulder, an unusual gesture. "You're a good man, Donal Riordan."

"I do my best, that's all."

Two hours later, a purple armoured van pulled up outside the deconsecrated former temple with the *Mel's Gym* sign over the side door. Two adults with a baby climbed down from the rear, and uniformed officers, struggling, helped wheel a black-scaled motorbike down to the road surface.

And rolled it into the building when the man opened the door, and he and the woman and the baby went inside, while the officers waved goodbye and climbed back into their purple van and a minute later drove away.

Mel and Finbar and Donal were home at last.

Along with a grateful Triumphant motorcycle, curious about its new surroundings.

FORTY-THREE

They were in a commandeered interview room in the 401ˢᵗ Precinct, even though Bellis and the rest of the Esoteric Crimes Unit officially operated directly from Avenue of the Basiliks, just because the location had proved convenient.

Two coffees in beetlespume cups stood on the battered table, alongside an open cardboard takeout box of doughnuts and a wormskin bag of scones.

"Doughnuts from Fat'n'Sugar," said Donal. "This really is like the old days."

"Tempted to rejoin the Department?" Bellis was nibbling from a tarantula cream.

"I guess." Donal picked a purpleberry special, and bit into it. "This is very bad for me."

Zombies don't eat so much, and the sense of taste is rather different than in redblood days, but some things transferred pretty much intact.

Donal had already signed the official statements, and Bellis had handed them off to a sergeant before they ended up with jam and sugar and coffee stains on the vellum sheets.

"How's young Finbar getting on?" said Bellis.

It had been nine days since the events inside Inversion Tower. There had been a lot of arrests, but Bellis hadn't given the exact number, and Donal hadn't asked. Some of the mercenaries for sure were still at large, and might never be caught.

Federal Agent Bouchard had returned to Fortinium without meeting Donal.

Donal hadn't seen Commissioner Sandarov in person either, but they'd talked on the phone and Sandarov had sounded grateful, and his cheque hadn't bounced, so everything turned out okay in that regard.

"Good," said Donal. "I think he's going to be the world's greatest genius, is Finbar."

"I believe that's what all new parents think about their kid."

"True. But someone's got to be right."

Bellis laughed. "I'll grant you that. Listen, you're all done with the case and everything, but I thought I'd better let you know... That, er, professional lady who calls herself Melody de Sonance, the one you saw in Councillor Smythe's apartment? We're looking for her, so if you catch sight at any time, get on the phone, will you."

"I'm not expecting to bump into her," said Donal. "But you never know."

"The SOC diviners' evidence is enough to send her to the execution table, but we've still got questions for her."

The *Gazette* and other newspapers had written up Councillor Smythe's murder as if the police had no idea who might have done it, and if the smarter crime reporters knew better, they were playing along regardless, not to tip the suspect off.

"I saw her leave Niflhame Towers from the coffee shop across the road," said Donal. "If I'd moved faster, I might have realised she'd been up to something other than the obvious hanky-panky."

"You couldn't have known that she'd strangled him. Her real name, by the way, is Stephanie di Granno. We've found out that much. I'm sure we'll track her down eventually."

"Fair enough." Donal put down the doughnut and took a sip from the too-strong coffee. "This is definitely nostalgia for me."

"But you're still sticking with the freelance investigation work?"

"At least for now."

They'd talked about finances earlier, and the need for stability when you had a young family.

"And Levison's still working the Arrhennius Hawke case?" said Donal.

"For what it's worth. Nasty, nasty piece of work he was. Levison is doing his job, but whoever took out Hawke deserves a medal instead of hookwraiths and the execution chamber."

"That bad, what you found in the house?"

"Yeah. That bad."

Donal was glad he hadn't seen Hawke's basement.

"And Bloodfist Bank itself?"

Bellis shook his head, finished chewing his doughnut, and said: "Tricky, and it's a specialist federal case, but I don't think it's getting anywhere. Whoever made the call to get Arrhennius Hawke killed, they were getting rid of a link in the chain. Very strategic."

Donal looked at him. "You don't think it was Melody de Whatsit, do you?"

"Well, the timing is right, but she might have just phoned Vanessa Frisch, who then arranged the hit, because we're pretty sure the two women were connected, though the details still aren't clear. And the Frisch woman had some pretty professional people working for her."

A twitch tugged at the side of Donal's mouth. "That's what Mel calls her. 'The Frisch woman.' Got some other names too, but I have to cover Finbar's ears when Mel comes out with them."

"I should think so too."

They spent a minute concentrating on the coffee and doughnuts, and in Donal's case wondering just how many hours he'd spent in interview rooms like this one, usually as an interrogator instead of a witness.

He leaned back in his chair and sighed, almost in an automatic redblood fashion. Close enough.

"Arrhennius Hawke's house had decent defences," he said, suddenly remembering. "Disabled when I got there. My guess at the time was a professional team, not a single person."

"Could be," said Bellis. "I guess it fits. SOC diviners found nothing much, according to Levison, but I picked up an odd resonance when I went to check the place myself. Really odd. Not a wraith and not a ghoul, but something else. Or several things."

Donal looked at him.

"Really," he said.

"What?" said Bellis. "You've thought of something."

After a moment, Donal shook his head. "I got sucked in by a Death-damned bloodghoul, got carried along inside it for miles without getting eaten, then somehow *it* hung on inside *me* for ages afterwards until it finally popped out and did for Vanessa Frisch. Ghouls ain't exactly a neutral topic where I'm concerned."

"You private investigator types do lead interesting lives."

"Tell me about it."

"I do have one very important question, though," said Bellis.

"Which is?"

"Do you want the last tarantula cream, or are you easy?"

"I think you should have it," said Donal.

"The perfect answer."

Donal drank from his coffee, and thought.

Three hours later, he was drinking coffee again, this time sitting at a window table in Gandolfo's, the far-too-expensive coffee shop located across from the doorway to Niflhame Towers. He wasn't alone.

Karlasdóttir drank from her latte with indigoberry syrup, a concoction that Donal wouldn't have dreamed of ordering when he was a redblood, and certainly wouldn't drink now.

"You didn't bring company," said Donal.

"Can you imagine what it'd be like, walking down the street with them?"

She was talking about the three ghasts that she commanded.

"I travelled inside a bloodghoul," Donal told her, "and the cops cleared the streets for miles around."

"Right. I heard, by the way. One Hades of an adventure, Mr Riordan."

"Donal."

"Then I'm Tanya."

They'd kept things more formal earlier, when he'd called in at Dredgeway Avenue to check if the security team was still in place. Karlasdóttir – Tanya – had been working as before, and agreed to meet him when she came off shift.

This had seemed like an appropriate rendezvous location, given everything that had happened across the road.

"Do you leave them at work?" asked Donal. "Or at your home? Or somewhere else?"

"Let's just say… Out of sight, but always within calling distance."

"That's pretty handy, Tanya."

"Isn't it. Donal."

There was a lot of hubbub, but no one sitting close to them. The coffee shop felt warm and comfortable, but Donal didn't kid himself: he needed to word things carefully, given the calibre of the woman sitting across from him: someone who'd once been in the military police and more: the 666th Regiment.

Someone who could call on three ghasts to help her at any time.

"I heard there was a nasty piece of work, truly evil, got his comeuppance from a real professional. Posh part of town, too. Near Keening Broadway."

"Really." She put down her coffee.

Donal didn't think it was because she'd gone off the indigoberry syrup.

"I talked to one cop, said the person who did the job deserved a medal."

"And you?" Her grey eyes showed no expression. "What do you think?"

"I'm just wondering. The cop I know, he talked about a professional, but I'm thinking maybe the person didn't even do it for money."

The sound around them died a little, but it remained enough to submerge any individual conversation.

"On a totally unrelated note" – Donal pointed across the road – "a professional woman, that being what you might call a euphemism, strangled a crooked councillor in that very building."

"Really." Tanya's voice went very low.

"Weird timing. That woman might have dropped the florin on the evil guy near Keening Broadway. Maybe indirectly. Or maybe she knew just who to call, to take out a particularly nasty individual who really deserved to die."

"Is this the kind of thing you normally talk about on a date?"

"I've got a newborn kid at home. This isn't a date," said Donal. "I'm only shooting the breeze, you know?"

"Pity," said Tanya.

That stalled Donal, but just for a moment.

"Cops are looking for said professional woman," he said. "I'm just wondering whether they'll ever find her."

Something moved inside those grey eyes, though they remained unreadable.

She shrugged. "Say there was someone you bumped into a year ago, maybe longer, and you got them out of trouble. The kind you could handle but they couldn't, kind of thing."

Donal nodded. "Got some of my best snitches that way, back in the day."

"And say they worked out you had some kind of… issues. From the past. And they could point you at the same type of people who once caused a lot of pain to your family."

"I get that. Yes."

"But then you found out that this person, who you thought was kind of a friend, actually knew about one of the bad types for a long time but didn't tell you until it became convenient. Until getting rid of the bad person meant getting rid of a problem for the wrong kind of people."

Donal touched his coffee cup but didn't lift it. He nodded, nothing more.

"Person like that," continued Tanya, "if people were looking for her, well, seems to me, they most likely would never find her."

Not if ghasts had done for Stephanie di Grasso, aka Melody de Sonance: but that was a thought that Donal didn't want to speak aloud, even in a noisy coffee shop like this.

"On a totally unrelated note" – her tone altered as she used the same words that Donal had employed earlier – "my company got the gig at Dredgeway Avenue just because a dodgy not-friend recommended us to a family who got robbed. Said not-friend did business with one of the men in that family, if you know what I mean."

"Huh."

"Yeah. Right."

After a moment, Donal raised his coffee cup. "To unsolved mysteries."

Tanya lifted her own cup and clinked it against his.

"The best kind," she said.

"Not always."

"But sometimes, right?"

"Absolutely right," said Donal.

FORTY-FOUR

It was the biggest bouquet of flowers that Anna had ever seen, and after years of official engagements as a Federal Senator, that was quite a feat. The massive thing came through the door of her hospital room as if under its own propulsion, except that a pair of hands were just about visible.

Then Jean-Marc turned and leaned the mass of flowers against the wall, and came over to her bedside, and stopped.

And took off his wraparound shades.

I didn't imagine it.

His eyes looked as spectacular as she remembered.

"Everything worked out," he said. "Most of the important stuff happened in Tristopolis, and I think the most useful thing I did was to inform a resurrected man about... something inside him. I'll tell you everything over dinner. Or maybe after we've finished eating."

"Dinner, Federal Agent Bouchard?"

"A pretty nurse, who seems taken with one of my subordinates, told me they're likely to release you this evening. Once the doctor has visited and come to the same conclusion that the Night Sisters reached hours ago."

Anna smiled. "That seems about right."

"We've got a lot to talk about."

"I'd say so, yes."

"And not just about some case in Tristopolis. Even though you provided a solid lead right there."

She reached out her hand. "No, not just about that."

He took hold of her fingers, and that simple touch felt breathtaking.

"Maybe the most important things aren't even said in words."

"Maybe not," she said.

And some moments are perfect, even in silence.

FORTY-FIVE

The boxing gym was closed today, which was just as well, because Hellah was visiting.

She'd turned up an hour ago, knocking on the rear door and entering like a normal person, though how she'd travelled to the street outside from Avenue of the Basilisks, Donal didn't ask. Neither did anybody else.

"Oh," said Mel as Hellah drew near. "Oh. Look at that."

Hellah's red skin glowed the exact hue of fresh liquid blood, and the orange fire in her eyes burned as always, forming twin heptagons. Even the two witches, Ingrid and Ludka, withdrew to the far end of the gym, to where the altar had stood when this was a temple, when Hellah came in.

But Finbar gurgled and stared at Hellah and reached up to her.

"Um." Mel swallowed, but stood her ground. "Would you like to hold him?"

"Oh, of course I would."

And she did, taking Finbar in her arms with exquisite gentleness, and as she did so he fell fast asleep.

"You'll have to stay in exactly that position," said Donal, just teasing.

"I can do this forever." Hellah's orange eyes focussed on Mel. "Thank you for the honour."

"Er, sure."

When Hellah spoke again, it was little more than a murmur, so as not to wake Finbar. "The entanglement effect, the thing that made an evil person want to, well, you know…"

"Sure," said Mel again.

"It'll wear off soon," said Hellah. "Mostly. Nearly all, if not the full entangled state. Maybe a neuron or two left entangled."

"That's kind of what Ingrid said." Donal nodded towards the witch, who looked worried, but only for a moment.

The punch bags hung in place, waiting for use, along with the sparring heptagon and the barbells in the corner. It was a place for becoming strong and inoculated to fear, and in some ways represented the most intense trials that a human being could face; but in other regards, it seemed so much simpler than the world of witches and mages and Guardians.

"I owe you both an apology," said Hellah. "Everything that Klaudius and I were dealing with, it was all just a diversion. And it worked."

There were things that Donal remained curious about, such as the resemblances between her and Klaudius on the one hand and Vanessa Frisch on the other, but that might prove a delicate conversation and this wasn't the time.

Finbar seemed very happy in Hellah's arms, but Mel was beginning to sweat, because for all her fighter's courage, she felt the same kind of fear as everybody else in Hellah's presence.

"Here," said Hellah. "You'd better have him back."

"I... Yes."

So tiny and so trusting, Finbar let himself be transferred from one set of arms to the other, remaining totally asleep and at ease.

I can't believe it.

Donal had never realised how precious a life could be, not really.

"He probably wants to see his Auntie Ingrid and Auntie Ludka," he said.

"Probably," said Mel. "But not actually see them, because I think he's going to sleep for a while."

"Oh, I hope so," said Donal.

"You don't need to sleep," said Mel. "Ever."

"No, but you do."

"Oh."

She carried the sleeping Finbar down to the far end where Ingrid and Ludka were waiting.

"It worked out," said Hellah. "But this was a weird one for you, wasn't it?"

"You can say that again. Stuff that you might be used to dealing with, my dear, but I found utterly mad."

"Don't go trying to follow my example on how to live."

Donal smiled. "I'll try not to. You saved us all, so thank you."

Red eyelids blinked. "Saved you? What do you mean?"

"Sending the bloodghoul." Donal gestured towards the side door, meaning the outside world. "I know it had its own motives, but sending it here and making sure it wouldn't, you know, eat me... Thank you."

Orange fire whirled in twin heptagonal irises.

"I'm in a quandary," said Hellah.

"What do you mean?"

Hellah looked in Mel's direction. "I knew she was pregnant before you did, but I didn't tell you. I thought it was up to her."

"Well, yeah."

"But sometimes it's not obvious whether to share what you know or just keep quiet, my good friend."

"Bleeding Hades, Hellah. What are you on about?"

Shadows in the comforting gym. Overhead, the flamesprites were dancing, because they loved being in Hellah's presence. They liked her, and so did Donal, and that was that.

"I didn't send the bloodghoul to you, Donal."

He blinked, and the surf-sound of stress rose in his ears, as if he were a redblood, which he wasn't.

"I don't—"

"You called it yourself, my friend."

"But…"

"Yourself."

The word seemed to hang there like a heavy bag, waiting, inviting a response.

But Donal didn't have one.

ABOUT THE AUTHOR

John Meaney writes thrillers, science fiction and fantasy. He has won the IPPY Award and been a finalist for the Locus Award, and for the BSFA Award multiple times. He has several series in progress.

His contemporary cyber thriller series featuring spec-ops cyber specialist Case and his fierce partner Kat, begins with Destructor Function and continues with Strategy Pattern.

On The Brink is the first in a new series set in the 1950s and featuring schoolteacher-turned-spy Paul Reynolds.

Near-future thrillers feature Josh Cumberland, an ex-special forces cyber specialist driven by family tragedy, in a near-future Britain wracked by climate change, a legalized knife culture and political corruption.

The Donal Riordan novels feature a detective in the city of Tristopolis, where the sky is perpetually dark purple, and the bones of the dead are fuel for the reactor piles.

The seven Pilots novels include the epic Ragnarok trilogy, which begins with alien influences on humans at the dawn of the Viking era, covers the birth of the digital age at Bletchley Park, and concludes with a galaxy-spanning conflict, a million years from now.

Outside the world of writing, Meaney is a lifelong martial artist, a computer consultant with degrees from the Open University and Oxford, and a trained hypnotist.

Visit John at www.johnmeaney.com for the latest news.

Made in the USA
Coppell, TX
07 May 2022

77548672R00163